A CROWN OF ICE AND FURY

THE WINTER COURT SERIES

A CROWNS OF MAGIC UNIVERSE SERIES

ASHLEY MCLEO

MERAKI PRESS

For my found family and found families everywhere. Life is better with you.

THE NORTH SEA
THE SNOWSWEPT LANDS OF
WINTER'S REALM
MAPPED IN THE PRESENT AGE
TO THE VAMPIRE KINGDOM
WESTERNLANDS
TRALISKA
HOUSE QIREN
GULDTOWN
HOUSE LISIKA
MIDLA
GERSEMI MINE
ODELIA
HOUSE VAGLE
RIIS TOWER
REDMIST MOUNTAINS
SISAVAL
LIEKOS
VITVIK
MYRR
HOUSE BALIK
LOST KINGDOM OF DERGIA

MAJOR SETTLEMENTS
MINOR SETTLEMENTS
NOTABLE LOCATIONS
MORIAL
HOUSE
ARMENIL
VIRTORIS
ISLAND
ORTH LANDS
LEIRE
HOUSE
VIRTORIS
FARVERG
THE
SHIVERING
SEA
AVALDENN
HOR
BORG
AABERG'S
RAL SEAT
BITRA
HOUSE RIIS
EASTERN LANDS
VANTALIA
STORMY
BAY
UTHLANDS
GRINDAVIK
HOUSE
ITHAMAI
ICE TOOTH
MOUNTAIN RANGE

PROLOGUE
KING ÉREBO OF HOUSE NIKAO,
RULER OF THE SHADOW FAE

The king trudged across the snow-covered land, his destination a city of frost and malice. During the daylight hours, every step through the glittering snow and crusted ice proved laborious. But he knew it was only a matter of time before shadows stretched over the glistening landscape. Then he could move faster. Stronger.

And once night came, he'd *soar* on wings made of shadows. Wings that did not tire or succumb to the cold when darkness ruled over light. Wings that allowed him to fly far faster than wings made of blood and thin, flexible bones and tender membranes.

In those fleeting hours of the night prior, the king had relished in the freedom he hadn't felt in so very long. The freedom his mate had stolen from him. Had Sassa Falk still lived, King Érebo would hunt her down and make her pay, but as it were, he would have to settle for the next best thing.

With each step, the King of Shadows, of fae long

banished from this world, drew closer to King Magnus. Closer to revenge. Together, the Kings of Winter and Shadows would cripple Sassa's line and drive it into the frozen ground.

After his enemies drifted to the afterworld, the Shadow King would set about bringing his people home and unleashing their glorious darkness upon Isila.

Just as it should have been so very long ago.

CHAPTER 1
NEVE

I stared at the Drassil tree in Valrun's courtyard, wondering where the Shadow Fae King lurked. If he'd found King Magnus yet.

Or did the fae we'd accidentally freed have different plans?

As if it enjoyed my musings about the king who had unlocked it, my shadow magic roiled beneath my skin, unseen, but starkly felt. Dark and oily and foreign. My wings tightened, and, hoping to distract my wandering mind, I focused on the crowd.

The fae standing before us were the only soldiers we had until we reunited with the Dergian forces. In total, that amounted to two hundred fighting fae out of the three hundred and fifty rebels. Not nearly enough, if something should happen in the next few days.

"The Shadow King said he saw our base through the network of Drassil trees." Thyra spoke to the crowd of loyal fae, her face hard and tight.

The events under the mountain had been traumatizing for everyone involved, but Thyra was taking it especially hard. She'd lost two loyal rebels and friends, Ulfiel and Xillia, to ice spider barbarity.

"That's how he knew about me," Thyra said. "About all of you, too. Now he's free from that tree and prowling through the kingdom, likely on the move for Avaldenn."

"*How* did the Shadow Fae see through the trees, though? He's alive, not Faetia, right?" On delicate navy wings, a pixie rose above the rest. Small though he was, his tinny voice cut through the vast room.

"I don't know." Thyra tossed back her long black hair. "Neve?"

"I'm not sure either." My voice broke from disuse. Thyra had done most of the talking for the last half an hour, with only Prince Thordur and Princess Bavirra introducing themselves to the stunned crowd. As if learning that a Shadow Fae King had been living in our kingdom for millennia wasn't enough, the rebels were learning of the survival of the Dergia on the same day.

I cleared my throat. "But talking to him was not like speaking to the Faetia, which I have done before."

"How exactly are the trees connected?" the pixie prodded.

His question was justified. Most fae had seen a Drassil, many might have touched one, but spoken to the tree and the spirits within? Few could claim such a thing, and those who could, would likely still be lost. Mystery cloaked Drassil trees. I suspected even the Grand Staret in Avaldenn, a fae learned of the gods and the stars and all things in the great beyond and afterworld, could not comprehend our experience.

"I don't know exactly how they're connected, only that they are. Which is why neither Thyra nor I should touch the one out there." I gestured to the courtyard. "Some fae with winter magic can sense others with the same magic if they touch the tree, so us laying a finger on the bark might alert the king to our location."

"A Shadow Fae doesn't have winter magic," someone called out.

They could say the same about winter fae not having shadow magic, and they'd be wrong. Still, in this instance, I believed the speaker was right.

"You're probably correct, and I certainly can't explain how King Érebo lived in a tree for so long, let alone how he viewed the rest of the kingdom through other trees. I'm sorry to have so few answers."

"Prince Vale?" Thyra cut a sidelong glance to my mate, who stood at my other shoulder. Vale shrugged, so my twin continued.

"Perhaps we'll learn more of the mystery of the trees later. If so, we'll keep you informed, but what you need to know now is that after we gathered the injured, we flew back here and held a meeting." My twin swallowed. "A consensus was reached quickly. Valrun is no longer a safe place. Rumors and fear of the curse upon this town will not protect us. Not when the Shadow King is likely seeking King Magnus."

"You're sure about that?" a rebel asked.

"Érebo already showed King Magnus favor once—

indebted the king to him by handing over the Ice Scepter."

"So where will we go?" asked Tanziel, a fae who had been with me on my mission to find the Frør Crown. She'd suffered acid burns on her face and while her skin looked better, a scar lingered. Perhaps it always would.

Right on cue, Vale took a half-step forward. "Your recent reports indicated that rebels scouted House Balik and their soldiers moving south on the King's Road. They were within a day of Myrr, which tells me one of two things: either the Courting Festival is over, or those of the Golden House have left on their own."

We believed the latter was more likely. After all, King Magnus was preparing for war. Why would he let members of a noble house with a large army leave his territory when the kingdom was on the brink of war? No, it was far more likely that the king would force House Balik to remain in the capital and have Lord Tadgh Balik call his soldiers north.

"We believe the members of House Balik left Avaldenn for reasons that are their own," Vale continued over the murmurs that had broken out. "Hopefully reasons that will pit them against the king. So a small team will travel to Myrr and find out. If it's safe there, we will seek refuge for all of those present today."

"We've raided southern villages!" one male called out as the crowd erupted. "Do you expect the Warden of the South to let us through his golden gates after we've raided his people?"

Another female in the front row sneered. "Raids aside,

we cannot risk Thyra to a great house that did not defend her in the face of *your father!*"

Others shouted their opinions or rude remarks. Though Vale and I had won the trust of the rebels after our heists, we'd had a hunch this would happen. We needed to ease the rebels' fears that the great houses they'd been up against for many turns would harm them.

Thyra raised her hands, and slowly, the shouts stopped. "Do you think I'd do this if there wasn't a potential upside?"

Everyone in the crowd looked shocked for a moment before the heads shaking began. Fae could say what they wanted about my sister, but the rebels were very loyal to her.

"Good. Now, listen to the prince. If you have questions and concerns after, we'll discuss them civilly." My sister nodded to Vale.

"I realize the rebellion and the great houses have been at odds for many turns." My mate clasped his hands in front of him. "But I have strong ties with House Balik. My squire is their heir, and one of my dearest friends is the high lord's eldest."

Filip and Sian. Fates, I missed them. Saga, Sayyida, Marit, and the Balik sisters too.

Vale pressed a hand to his chest. "I will speak with Lord Tadgh Balik on your behalf. I'll make sure all of you are safe within the gates of Myrr, or we will not seek sanctuary there at all."

"If you can secure sanctuary for us, how long do you think it will take?" asked Ratha. The ancient whisperer faerie who once delved the depths of Vale's mind sat in the front, to the far right, her palms folded together. Unlike others, calm radiated from her.

"That we cannot say," Vale admitted. "But I *can* say that Tadgh Balik is an honorable male. Once he learns the truth of what's happened, I believe he will side with us. That he might fight for Thyra and Neve, too."

"And if he doesn't?" Ratha countered. "Say the golden Lord Balik left Avaldenn for his own reasons. What if he's done playing the game of great houses? Or what if the hatred of House Falk still flows in his veins?"

Enough gray shot through Ratha's dark hair to indicate that she was quite old enough to remember the time when my father turned into a monster. Lord Balik would also recall those days. After all, Harald Falk's actions caused all but one great house to turn against him and back the White Bear on the throne.

"Either of those things could happen," Vale allowed.

"Say he accepts us," another rebel waved a hand for attention. "How will we be told it's safe to come? You'll journey all the way back here?"

"We have gryphons and pegasi, so getting there will be faster than walking," Vale answered, "but no, we will not be returning unless we must. Aleksander is coming with us, and Arla will remain in Valrun. Once a decision has been made, she is to carry a pre-written note to Ratha. One with directives to stay. The other will give directions to march south."

"Ratha, you do not mind being left in charge?" Thyra asked.

"I will keep order," Ratha confirmed.

"Thank you." Thyra gave the elder a soft smile before

her face fell back into hardness. "Does anyone have other questions?"

No one spoke. No one raised a hand. Some of their faces still bore signs of skepticism, but they trusted Thyra enough to go along with the plan.

My sister clapped twice. "Then, as many of you are aware, we haven't slept since leaving Valrun two days ago, so we'll call this meeting to an end."

I exhaled. We'd covered much of what happened, though there was one matter we had not touched upon. One secret that needed to remain hidden from the majority.

That secret of the shadow magic inside me and Thyra. Only Brynhild, Duran, Anna, Clem, and those who had entered that spider-filled mountain with us knew of our shadow magic. We hadn't even told the fae half of our Valkyrja for good reason. As a result of the Shadow Fae's legacy of war and a lust for power, few in Isila trusted their kind. Only those we trusted the most had been told, and everyone else would learn our secret only after Thyra and I mastered our dark powers. We hoped that would make us less fearsome in the eyes of others.

The crowd broke and milled about, though no one left the dining hall. I sensed they were waiting to catch Thyra or Brynhild on their way out. Surely many wanted to know how Ulfiel and Xillia had died. Or they just wanted more information that they didn't feel comfortable asking in front of others.

"Let's go," I said to Vale.

I was dying to lie down and rest. To allow my brain to not think of what had happened over the last two days.

His hand slipped into mine, and I leaned closer to my mate. He smelled of gryphon and sweat, but beneath the scents of travel were notes of sandalwood and freshly fallen snow. Of Vale. Of home.

We hadn't gone more than ten steps when the double doors to the hall slammed open. My heart jumped, only to squeeze in recognition at the sight of the new arrivals.

CHAPTER 2
NEVE

A travel-worn, yet somehow still regal, Princess Saga stood between Lord Riis and Arie. The rebels who had traveled with Arie to retrieve his father congregated around them, plus ten others. Presumably the additional fae had been on guard around the town while the rest received a debriefing.

"What's Saga doing here?" Luccan whispered.

"Lord Leyv Riis and Princess Saga Aaberg," announced Bac, one of Thyra's most trusted advisors.

For the second time in ten minutes, the room erupted. Fae rushed the doors, and my heart rate spiked.

"Stop!" I grabbed onto someone's wrist as they joined the tide. They didn't spare me a glance before yanking free.

"Princess Neve?" Astril, the eldest of the pale, raven-haired vampire sisters and part of my Valkyrja, came to stand next to me while her sisters hovered behind.

"Shall we protect them?" Astril arched an eyebrow, the suggestion clear.

"Oh!" It hadn't occurred to me to do anything but interject. "Yes! They're friends. Don't let them come to harm."

The vampires surged forward, and thanks to the great speed of their magical order, they reached the spymaster of Winter's Realm and the princess before anyone else. They drew their swords, pointed the deadly metal at the rebels.

"The spymaster and princess are guests of Princess Neve," Astril stated. "An attack on them is as good as an attack on the Falk royal line."

Sure, I'd go with that.

"That's the *king's* spymaster!" Someone yelled, unrestrained fury in their voice. "He needs to be locked up!"

"We need to question them both!" Another voice added.

I cut a glance at Bac, a bastard son of Lord Balik's deceased brother. He looked so much like the rest of the Balik family, brown of skin, gold of eye and wing, with lustrous, golden-brown hair. He'd gone with Arie to assess the Lord of Tongues, and Lord Riis was here, so I assumed Bac hadn't found him to be untrustworthy. Why wasn't he speaking up?

Vale shoved through the crowd, pulling me along with him. It was good that the rebels had met unarmed, else we'd be in a larger predicament. As it was, the hardest part of closing the distance between us and the doors was getting people to move.

The pink-haired, petite princess smiled at me when I stopped before her. "We didn't mean to garner so much attention."

"Oh, please," I laughed dryly. "That's kind of your style."

"Enough with the joking." Thyra surged around me and Vale. "We had Arie go to collect the spymaster, but I still want Lord Riis questioned."

"Thyra!"

"He *is* the king's Lord of Tongues, Neve," my sister retorted, her tone flat and tired and hard. "Raised to a lordship by Magnus and therefore indebted, even if he does have a relationship to some fae that we trust, that is suspect."

Lord Riis was father to Thantrel, my sister's own mate, Luccan, and Arie. And though only a few fae and one half-dragon knew it, Lord Riis was also Vale's father.

"Why is the princess here, Bac?" Thyra's narrowed gaze took in my friend.

"You can ask me." Saga's hand landed on her slight hip. "I'm standing right in front of you."

Thyra snorted. "As if I could miss that hair."

"Would you like my colorist's name?" Saga asked, unbothered.

"No. As I said, I'd like to know why you're here and not relaxing up in some plush castle tower eating sweets."

"*Enough.*" Vale growled. "They'll tell us if we give them a bit of breathing space."

My sister waved her hand in a circular motion, and the rebels took a few collective paces back. The Lord of Tongues stepped forward, filling some of that space.

"I'm Lord Leyv Riis. I've journeyed here, in this time of crisis and upheaval, to be with my sons and show my true allegiance."

"And the princess?" Thyra asked.

"Her mother asked me to accompany and protect her. I promised that I would."

The capitol was getting too dangerous for Saga? My stomach churned. Nearly everyone in Winter's Realm loved Saga Aaberg, and for good reason. She was charming and warm and fun.

"If I find out that you're not being entirely truthful, or you're somehow still working for the king, I'll gut you." Thyra laid a casual hand on the dagger strapped to her thigh. "I cannot have an Aaberg loyalist in my company."

"I no longer call Magnus Aaberg my king." Lord Riis looked at me and Vale, and something made me raise my hand.

Saga gasped loudly, and while the spymaster stayed quiet, his keen gaze caught on my soulmate marked fingers. When Vale mimicked my action, Lord Riis dropped to one knee.

The High Lord of the Sacred Eight stared up at us, gaze resolute. "If you, the last surviving members of House Falk will have me, I wish to pledge my house to yours. My sword and my army as well. I will pledge to the new Queen of Winter's Realm."

I sucked in a breath as first shock, then gratitude roared through me. A High Lord was making a stand, showing the realm that he would side with Vale and his mate. Throat tightening, I pivoted to my sister and found my initial shock was reflected in her ice-blue eyes when she met my gaze.

"I trust him," I said softly. "I wish to accept, and you know as well as I that we need the army."

That same trust did not flow from my twin, but she nodded, her every line having shifted from protector to leader. A leader who understood that ruling meant she would have to accept help from others, particularly when danger knocked at her door.

"My sister and I have not yet decided who will wear the Crown of Winter's Realm at the end of this war, but our House will accept your oath." Thyra's chin lifted. "Say the ancient words then, Lord Leyv Riis."

"I'm ready when you are."

Thyra cut a glance at me. "Use the Blade to begin the ritual."

She nodded to the sword hanging at my side. Sassa's Blade, a Hallow of the realm dating back to the Unification. I'd found the legendary blade in the bowels of Frostveil Castle. The bite of its *zuprian* steel and the secrets hidden inside had saved my life on more than one occasion.

I swallowed, cleared my throat, and my sister leaned closer.

"One shoulder, then the other, and finally the head. No words from you, and he will recite the oath," Thyra whispered in my ear, correctly guessing that I didn't know what to do in this scenario. Thyra had grown up as a commoner in our homeland, and was more familiar with the rituals of the fae.

I pulled the sword, touched the flat edge to the spymaster's shoulder, then the other, and finally, pressed the metal against the crown of Lord Riis's head. I'd no sooner lowered the tip to the ground when the spymaster spoke.

"By blood and bone, by frigid wind and winter's touch, I bind my fate to those of House Falk. Let my sword sing in your name. My magic weave your victories. My kin and those sworn to me will heed your call as we would commands from the dead gods themselves. From this night until the final dawn, when the roots of the last Drassil wither and the final lürhorn is blown, I will stand as your sworn shield and spear. Your flaming arrow in the darkest of nights. Whatever you may need from me is yours. May the dead gods bear witness, and may Winter's Realm reject me should I break this oath."

A soft breath left my lips as Lord Riis stood. He faced us, awaited our word.

"House Falk accepts your allegiance, Lord Riis," Thyra said. "And we swear to protect you, to aid you, to be loyal to you in times of ease and times of trouble."

"Princesses." Lord Riis bowed, and with that motion those in his family followed.

My chest tightened as I recognized the end of the ritual and the start of something new.

CHAPTER 3
VALE

I breathed my first full breath since my sister and Lord Riis appeared.

The rebels' bodies loosened, the anxiety lessened. They might not agree with everything Thyra did or said, but I had to hand it to her, Neve's twin held incredible sway over those loyal to her.

Lord Riis clasped his hands in front of him. "Thank you for accepting my banner."

Thyra cleared her throat pointedly. "As pleased as I am to call your house loyal to mine, I do still have questions. One of which I'd like answered in front of everyone present today."

"Anything."

"What's your magic?"

"I can negate the magic of other fae."

"So if Neve or I tried to freeze you, would you warm?"

"Not exactly. I simply wouldn't freeze. That's why I took the ice spider as my sigil."

I shuddered. My father had no way of knowing that we'd recently fought more ice spiders than one usually saw in a lifetime. Many lifetimes, in fact.

"How would that power work on others?" Thyra prodded.

"I can protect others—if I'm close enough to focus my magic on them."

"Many opponents?"

"No more than three, and that's dependent on their strength."

"Hmm, that's useful."

"Indeed."

Thyra considered for a moment longer. "Are there types of magic that yours doesn't work on?"

"None that I've come across. That being said, I've tested my power on many types of magic, but not all."

Hence why my mother had practiced her whispering on him when they were young. Most would be defenseless in the face of Inga Vagle, but Leyv Riis let her manipulate his mind because he could, if needed, get out from under that magic. That and he had simply loved her that much.

Thyra turned her attention to Saga. Their eyes met, both the same shade of ice blue. "You command no armies and have no actual power other than a title. Is that right?"

My sister's chin lifted. Thyra was at least a head taller than Saga, but my sister had a way of holding herself that made her seem much larger. Pride welled in me at the sight of her standing proud and strong.

"I'll take that as a yes," Thyra said smugly. "And

despite knowing you have no real power, I still wish for you to swear to us."

"I never claimed to have no power. And I will do no such thing," Saga announced.

Whispers began washing through the crowd.

I longed to insert myself. To be the big brother and protector my sister needed in the face of so many who did not trust her. But my insertion wouldn't help her. The rebels may trust me, but they'd assume love clouded my judgment. In this, Saga needed to stand her ground and show her own power to earn the rebels trust and respect.

"I will not, *right now*," Saga corrected. "Not until we've had a good and long conversation about what you plan to do with my mother."

Just our mother. Not Rhistel, or her father—a fae who was once my father in heart and, I'd thought, blood.

"Not worried about your brother or the king?" Thyra asked, clearly thinking along the same lines.

"What would be the use in worrying?" Saga's tone was firm, though her gaze flitted to the ground for a second as she spoke. "I mean, I'd prefer that my father not die, but considering the things he's done and the present company, that is a lot to ask." She inclined her head to Thyra, a daughter of the former King of Winter's Realm.

Saga was admitting the king wasn't fit to rule in front of his enemies, but it was what my sister was not saying that caught my attention the most. Saga didn't care about Rhistel?

"However, I will promise I won't harm anyone fighting in the rebellion. And I will offer you information freely." My sister twirled a hand in the air and frost covered her fingers. "I have winter magic, and I'm a seer. The former is far stronger than the latter, which I have little control over."

"The entire realm knows that." Thyra twisted to Neve. "You trust her?"

"Saga was my first friend at court. She was kind to me and took me in when she didn't have to do so, and she's protected me many times since then." My mate looked at my sister and offered a small smile. "Now, she's also my family, so yes, I trust Saga with my life."

Thyra let out a breath, heavy with exhaustion. "Fine. We can have a conversation regarding Queen Inga later. The princess can stay in the annex with the rest of you. I'll see that a cot is brought in. The Lord of Tongues will have a room nearby because I believe that with the addition of the princess, you're at capacity?"

Thantrel was in the healing sanctuary under Rynni's supervision. His wings had been torn in the battle beneath the mountain, so for the time being, Thordur was taking his bed. Bavirra would bunk in the smallest room with Rynni—that was, if the dragon-fae ever returned to the annex. Half of the time she slept in the healers' sanctuary. My sister would have to squeeze in with Anna and Clemencia.

"We'll make it work." I didn't want my sister to stay far from Neve and me.

"Brynhild, see to it that Lord Riis has a bed." Thyra rubbed the spot between her eyes. "Now, I'm off to bed. No one wakes me unless they want their feet frozen."

Thyra left and one by one, the rebels followed, some tossing dubious glances at my sister and father, but most simply looked curious as they left. Finally, only our friends remained. I performed quick introductions, noting how Saga paled when she met the vampire assassin sisters.

Upon being introduced to Prince Thordur and Princess Bavirra, however, Saga's lips formed a surprised O. She curtsied, and they returned the gesture.

The formalities seen to, Saga beamed at them. "I'd love to hear more about Dergia! And how Vale and Neve found you. I'm sure that's a great tale as well."

"We've been awake for two days, Saga." I laughed, as though I wasn't dying to question her myself. Not now though. Best to do that in private. "And the dwarves raced from their home to save us before traveling here. Perhaps tomorrow would be better?"

Bavirra grinned. "Give me a long sleep and I'll tell you anything you want, Princess Saga."

"Maybe not *anything*," Prince Thordur corrected. "We dwarves of Dergia must keep certain secrets."

"Of course," Bavirra rolled her eyes.

"It's a date!" Saga chirped. "I suppose we should go to your—what did she call it—the annex?"

"That's where we're staying." Neve slipped her icy hand into mine. "Come on then."

Brynhild approached my father, exchanged a few words, and then the pair joined Luccan, Arie, Anna, and Clemencia, as our larger group made their way to the annex. As much as I wished to speak with Lord Riis myself, I waited. Answers on the events that brought him here will come in due time.

When we reached the castle's doors, Neve waved over the vampire sisters.

"You're ready to go?" Neve asked Astril, the oldest of the assassins. "And you have the letter to King Tholin?"

The dwarven king and his army were still waiting near Eygin for word of what we'd do next, where we'd go. A raven would deliver our letter to the abandoned coinary in Eygin, where a scout was waiting to take it back to King Tholin. From there, the army of Dergia would march to meet us in Myrr.

"I'll send the raven now," Astril confirmed. "We'll see you in the southlands."

"Travel safe." Neve waved them off as the vampires slipped out the door, setting our plan in motion.

I snorted. As if the sisters, Red Assassins, had anything to worry about on the journey. If anything, I worried over others glimpsing them and being scared half to death.

It was not ideal to separate from the vampires, but Rynni was remaining behind to care for the injured and would not be able to fly a large contingent south. That left us with only six gryphons and two pegasi to make the journey, so the vampires were heading south on foot and wing. If we calculated right, we'd arrive at nearly the same time.

Speed was one of the vampire qualities I envied. That and their need for very little sleep. Both would be quite useful in the war to come.

We were halfway to the annex when Saga detached herself from Bavirra's side and sidled up beside me.

"I have something to ask you."

"Go on then." I smiled.

"I saw you entombed in something white, and it scared

me. At the same time, you were going west on the map. The Riis brothers told you about their map, right?"

"I do. And I know what you saw." She was always curious about her visions. I supposed it was natural, considering many featured other fae, sometimes people she'd never met. Saga could never be sure if those came true or not.

"What?"

"We were trapped in ice spider silk."

"Excuse me!?"

"We fought hundreds of ice spiders," Neve cut in, and I had to chuckle. Her tone made it sound as though the battle was nothing at all. "It's a long story. One we can tell you later?"

"Seeing as you're safe and here, I guess so. But Fates alive, I can't believe all that you've been through!" Saga's teeth dug into her bottom lip.

For the rest of the walk, much of our group fell into silence. We were exhausted in each bone and needed a few hours' rest to be prepared to travel when dark fell.

We passed by a window, broken at one edge and allowing cold air into the corridor. I inhaled the frost and scent of the thick ice on the lake. Valrun had been an experience, but I was glad we were leaving. No matter how many sentinels kept watch, I'd never felt safe in this rundown castle. Never truly protected, nor sure that I could protect those I loved inside the castle's crumbling walls.

When I opened the annex door, I allowed my mate to enter first, then waited for my sister. But Saga stopped at my side and cleared her throat, allowing others to pass instead.

"I have more I want to say, Brother. And I don't want to wait."

"Of course." I nodded to Lord Riis as he and Brynhild continued on to wherever Thyra's advisor would put him up during our last day in Valrun Castle. Luccan swept by us, and I patted his shoulder. "Tell Neve I'll be a few minutes. Saga wants a word."

"Will do."

My friends and family disappeared into the annex for a well-deserved rest. I shut the door and turned to my sister.

Discomfort swept across her delicate features, and not for the first time, it struck me how much Saga looked like both our mother and her father. She had King Magnus's ice-blue eyes and naturally white hair, which she colored pink. However, Saga's cheeks, chin, and face shape were from our mother. As were her dark wings. Vagle wings, many in the realm called them. They were nearly black, a rare hue for faeries that were not Shadow Fae. Or so I'd read.

The only Shadow Fae I'd ever seen was King Érebo. We hadn't been able to see his wings properly because he'd been trapped in the tree, though I imagined they were as black as night. Just like his heart and soul.

A low breath left Saga, bringing me back to the moment. To my sister, who needed me to listen. "Lord Riis said I had to leave Avaldenn because I was in danger, but he didn't say why. Did you wonder?"

"Of course I did. Still do," I answered. "I assumed he

didn't offer the information in front of everyone for a good reason."

"An excellent reason," Saga affirmed. "I hate to tell you this, even more than I hated to live through it, but you have to know, Vale. Have to know how much he's changed . . ."

"Father?"

"No. Rhistel."

My jaw tightened. "What has he done now?"

"Mother told him who his father was. Your father too." Saga met my gaze. "Who here knows?"

"Only those sleeping in the annex," I gestured to the door, to those people I trusted with my life. "Thantrel too, obviously. He's in the healing wing. Caelo and Duran are keeping him company. They know as well."

"Right." She looked away before focusing on me once more. "Well, Rhistel didn't take the truth well. He accepted it, but he also thought of those who could take that truth and use it against him. Take what he sees as his."

"The Crown of Winter's Realm?"

"Yes. And obviously, the closest person to him that posed a threat to that future was me. The only trueborn daughter of King Magnus."

My entire body went rigid.

"He threatened my life, Vale. He said he'd get rid of me and any threat to him taking the throne. Mother felt that she had no choice but to seize control of him. Mentally, that is."

By the dead gods. Saga had not only learned that

Rhistel and I were bastards, but that our mother was a whisperer. My blood ran cold.

Kind and generous, Saga didn't have an evil bone in her body. She shone, a polished jewel, while the rest of us bore jagged edges and rough faces.

And Rhistel would have killed her. That meant my brother, the one I'd wanted so often to make excuses for and to see the best in, was well and truly gone.

"Lord Riis had been listening to the whole thing. You know, in the place where handmaidens can wait to be called. When I arrived, Mother had a hold of Rhistel and told Lord Riis to take me away. Basically to keep me far from our arsehole of a brother, and to find you."

"I'm so sorry, Saga." I folded her into my arms.

Though she'd been away from home for days, somehow she still smelled like Frostveil. Or perhaps that was my imagination producing a distraction to the shame welling up inside me. I was her older brother, the protector of the family, and at the time when my sister had needed me most, I hadn't been there. Hadn't considered what danger she might face.

"I'm sorry too." Saga pulled back and brushed away tears with the back of her hand. "It pissed me off and broke my heart. If I could spare you those emotions, I wouldn't have told you, but it also clearly shows that he's changed, Vale. Obviously, that's been happening for a while, but I don't think there's anything left of the brother we grew up with."

"I've feared that for a long time," I admitted. "He tried to harm Neve."

To kiss her too. The memory of the day he'd whispered

my mate, and how I'd nearly beat Rhistel to death afterwards made me both furious and upset.

"We're all in danger from Rhistel," Saga swallowed, "but her and Thyra, maybe more so than anyone else."

It shattered my heart to hear her words, true as they were. If Rhistel was willing to harm Saga, there was no line my twin would not cross to keep the Crown of Winter's Realm.

CHAPTER 4
NEVE

I perched on the bed, my nape still damp from my quick bath.

Vale had been speaking with Saga for longer than I'd expected, and despite having braided my long tresses to avoid them dripping everywhere, a chill was setting in. I was debating pulling a fur over me when the door opened.

My mate appeared, and though just seconds before I'd had every intention of losing myself in his body, my shoulders stiffened. His face was pale. Bloodless.

"What did Saga say?" I crossed the room and took his roughened hands in my own.

"The reason she's here."

Which I thought we'd already covered. Apparently not. "Which was?"

"Rhistel threatened her life, so she fled."

My chest stilled. I despised Vale's twin, and yet, when I looked up at my mate's face, pain cut through me. Vale and Rhistel were brothers. Twins. I knew as well as anyone who had a twin how unique that relationship could be, how intensely you felt towards one another, and I hadn't grown up with Thyra. Stars, she hadn't even liked me just a few weeks back. Still, from the moment I'd learned who she was, how we'd come into this world together and survived when the rest of our family did not, I'd had the urge to win her over. To be true sisters.

Vale, on the other hand, had grown up with Rhistel, but the passing turns had only torn them apart.

"I'm sorry, my love." I hugged him, and my hands began to rub his back comfortingly. He returned the gesture, embracing me as if I was the only thing holding him together at that moment. "That must have been diffi-cult to hear."

"I don't deny that Rhistel has murder in his heart, but Saga . . ."

"I know."

We stayed that way until Vale heaved a long sigh and pulled back.

"I thought you might already be sleeping when I came in."

Heat filled my cheeks. "Not quite."

Vale arched his eyebrows as his thumb absentmindedly rubbed the top of my hand, right below the snowflakes lining my index finger. "What did I say?"

"Well, I was planning to seduce you, so I was waiting up."

The sadness left his face to be taken over by surprise. Then he chuckled. "Seduce me? We've been awake for two days, Force."

"I nearly lost you." I savored the pet name he'd given

me, one that showed respect and love for my power, and pressed my right hand to his chest. A soft exhale parted my lips. He was still so solid, his breath coming and going, steady, just like my mate so often was.

The image of Vale inside a cocoon of spider silk, lined up against a craggy cavern wall with my friends, would never cease to haunt me. Had the dwarves and the other rebels not discovered where we were in time, Vale could have become spider food. Or worse, he might have suffocated inside the silks like poor Ulfiel.

If our journey to the village of Eygin had taught me anything, it was that time was not a given. Vale and I might live many centuries together. Or one of us might die tomorrow. The latter thought sent a visceral stab of pain through me, and my fingers pressed harder against the fabric covering his heart.

"Impending death brings out the most primal of urges." He lifted my other palm, kissed my hand. "And I won't say no to loving my mate, but first I should wash. I'm covered in filth and can still feel that silk on my skin."

"I already drew you a bath."

He left for the bathing chamber. I wrapped a fur around my shoulders, crossed to the window, and pulled back the thick curtain keeping the sunlight at bay. If I laid down, I might pass out.

Outside, the day was bright. Rebels moved in and out of view. Many were talking to others animatedly. Most of the rebels had been present during our assembly, but those few who had been absent were likely now learning what had transpired.

I wondered if Astril, Freyia, and Livia were already on the King's Road. Racing for Myrr to meet us there in time. Thank the dead gods, they had retained their fae wings after their transition to becoming vampires. Wings meant the sisters would alternate between flying and running. And according to Livia, their wings were less sensitive than they had been when they were fae, so they also could fly for longer than I would be able to.

I wasn't sure how long I stayed at the window, mulling things over, but it seemed like no time at all before the door opened again. Vale slipped inside, a towel wrapped around him, showing off his powerful Vs and plethora of tattoos.

My heart rate kicked up. No matter how many times I had him in our bed, no matter how long we were together, I doubted the sight of Vale would ever cease to affect me.

"Force, why are you not snuggled beneath the furs and quilts?"

When he reached me, I tilted my chin up, sighing as his dark brown eyes met mine. "Didn't want to fall asleep after all that talk of seducing."

"Ah." Hands gripped my hips. "There'll be no more worrying about that." He lifted me easily, and I smiled, relishing that he could do so as I wrapped my legs around his middle. "Are you ready to make me forget?"

Forget what his brother, the fae he'd shared a womb with, had done. Forget that cavern filled with spiders and an ancient king who wanted to command me. Forget all the bad that had befallen us in our short time together. If only for a little while.

"Give me a night to remember."

"As you wish." Vale settled me on the edge of the mattress, and his hands found the hem of my nightgown, teasing the fabric up until my thighs saw the light. His hands ran along the soft skin of my thighs, and heat seared at the apex of my legs.

Stars, I needed him more than I'd allowed myself to believe. Needed his pulse pounding against mine. His body finding pleasure in me. *In us.*

My mate eased my legs apart. The motion effectively tugged the nightgown up the rest of the way, exposing me. A low, masculine sound left his throat as he stared down, then dragged his gaze up to meet mine.

"Sometimes, I still find it difficult to believe that you're mine." His left hand, the hand that bore our soulmate mark, caught my chin as he dipped so that our lips hovered just above each other's.

"Every piece of me is yours," I replied, recognizing that while I'd been the one to initiate tonight, my mate wanted something different. Tonight, he desired control, and I was happy to oblige. "Now take your pleasure, love."

His lips crashed into mine, and a sense of home, of him being that place for a fae like me who had not had a true home in so very long, skittered through me, like frost forming across a window covering each surface and crevice. I whimpered as one of his hands climbed up my dress and caressed my nipple. My hands settled on his hips and eased him closer before I tore his towel clean off.

He smiled into a kiss. "In a hurry?"

"I need to feel *more*." To prove my point, I slid one

hand between us and grasped his malehood, already hard and proud.

"By all means, I'm your plaything."

I laughed, and he caught the sound on his lips again, swallowing it as though it were the most decadent dessert. Or perhaps that was just how he tasted to me. Like something I could never get enough of.

I almost lost him. At the reminder, my heart seemed to seize.

But no, I did not lose the person most precious to me. He was before me. His tongue dancing with mine. His hands dropping lower, tickling me as he went, his scent of sandalwood and fallen snow assuring me. He was here. Alive. We were *alive.* As if to drive the point home, Vale's fingers found their way to my center, and he rubbed the sensitive spot that both sent shivers up my spine and curled my toes.

"Wet for me already," he murmured.

I shuddered as he varied the pressure and speed. All the while, his lips trailed down my neck. My fantasy of seducing him had been turned on its head, but I didn't mind in the slightest. Not when he seemed to relish in my pleasure as much as his own.

Vale's lips explored my own, my face, my neck, as his clever fingers continued to rub and tease and ratchet the tension in my hips ever higher. My legs tightened around his waist.

"Ah, my queen is nearly there."

His queen. By the dead gods, this male. The topic of queenhood had been testy between Thyra and me, but to my mate, I'd always be his. And he would always be my king. The male who, when I needed a protector most, stepped up. The person who helped me grow into the force I'd become. He'd never been hesitant or jealous as I grew. As my power strengthened and changed. As I stepped into the shoes of a leader. A princess of the realm. And yes, a potential queen.

"Come for me," he whispered, his tone raspy, wanting, just as two fingers slipped inside me and the heel of his palm pressed into my core, I did just that.

My eyelids fell and stars exploded behind them as Vale wrung pleasure from my body. When I opened my eyes again, it was to find him watching me, smug as could be. I smiled, my body feeling wrung out, even if I wanted more. Vale and I were here together, but I wished to feel him within me. To carry him within me.

Perhaps to start something new this night?

The thought startled me. As a slave, I'd always known that I'd one day bear younglings. My master would have forced me to procreate, most likely with another tragically caged fae. After I'd escaped, I thought only of freedom for so long. When I began falling for Vale, it was difficult to imagine that my reality was true.

But it was. We were in love. Mated. And hopefully, we'd both survive the war to come and begin a new life. Perhaps it would involve younglings.

Not now though. No matter how much sharing that journey with Vale appealed, that day would have to wait. There was too much danger. I would never forgive myself if I became pregnant and something happened to the child. So after we slept a few hours, I'd seek the healers and get what I needed to prevent pregnancy. Later though, I'd dare to hope for a stunning future filled with younglings with dark wings and silver hair and my mate's smile.

Oblivious to the debate going on inside my head, Vale kissed me. I kissed him back, one hand on his face as the other guided his malehood to my entrance.

"I want you inside me." I shifted to pepper kisses on his strong jaw.

He eased himself inside, slowly, achingly slowly. When he was fully sheathed, Vale lifted both my legs high.

Stars! The sensation multiplied tenfold as he found a new, deeper way to connect. My head tipped back as pleasure coursed through me again and Vale thrust deeper.

He pulled my arse to the very edge of the bed and lifted my legs higher, adjusting the angle to his preference. A low moan escaped my lips, and my mate's searing gaze went feral.

"Fates. You're perfect," he said in the same moment that his soulmate mark glowed.

My heart fluttered. We'd had sex many times since the occurrence when snow and magic swirled around us, but that hadn't happened again. We didn't know how it had happened or what made it occur, but I savored the moment that our magics found as special as I did.

Vale's hands dropped from my legs to my arse, and he lifted me more, shifting his angle yet again, and intensifying the pressure building inside me once more. He was close too, his breathing shallower, his face deliciously flushed.

"I'm there. Neve, are you?"

"Yes." My voice came out husky, wanting, and I wriggled closer to Vale, not wanting even a hairsbreadth between us.

That slight movement tipped the scales. Light blasted from our soulmate marks, turning the room an icy blue. No, not just turning it blue, covering the walls, the floors, the door with a glittering film of ice! The temperature plummeted, but we barely noticed as our shared climaxes pummeled through us with the strength of a winter storm. Vale swallowed the cry of passion with a kiss as he came. Our bodies shuddered together, our hearts raced, but the magic coursing through the room vanished.

"That was something new." Vale pulled me close into his warmth.

Clinging to him, I trailed a hand over the top of his wings. He shuddered with pleasure, making me smile. "At least the bed isn't covered in ice. Would be hard to sleep that way."

He laughed and retrieved the towel I had tossed to the floor, and cleaned me first, then himself. Finally, once we were done, we lay in our bed, my back tucked into his chest, as we stared at our room.

The magic we'd expelled was gone, but much of the ice remained, a strange glimmering blue color. Not at all natural.

"I wonder why that happens?" I mused.

"Me too, though I'm not inclined to ask around."

Awkward indeed. "Few would know anyway."

Only mates, and those were precious and rare.

"I'm so glad you're still here, Vale. That we both are."

He squeezed me closer. "When I go, I feel that it will

be with you. That we'll enter the starry halls of the afterworld holding hands."

My throat tightened, and the words he'd said once rang through my mind, truer than ever. "And our souls will stay that way until the stars fall from the sky."

"Until the stars fall," he echoed.

INTERLUDE
LORD VIDAR VIRTORIS, HEIR TO
THE HOUSE OF THE SEA SERPENT

Vidar pressed his palms into the driftwood table and stared down at the map of Virtoris Island, the land on which they stood. His family home. His people. His legacy.

All safe, at least for the time being.

"It's only a matter of time before King Magnus comes for us, Mother." Exhaustion clung to his voice, his every motion, even his bones, but rest would have to wait. "We should have our defenses ready. Scouts on the Shivering Sea at all times and sailors on call, if not with their boots on the decks. Preferably I want ships waiting in this area." His brown finger drifted west and south of Leire, to a cove where fifty large vessels could easily hide and wait.

Outside the arched windows, gray, churning waters crashed upon the rocks at the base of their castle. Even four stories up, he tasted the salt of the sea in the air.

His mother nodded at his suggestion, offered no other.

The king's ships might not be as fast or as good as the vessels House Virtoris commanded, but numbers mattered. In addition to the king's own vessels, the loyal royalists of House Qiren and House Ithamai commanded fleets too. Combined, the three great houses possessed a force that could cause Fayeth Virtoris's armada great damage.

All that was not taking magical prowess into account. Vidar despised the king, but he could not deny that the White Bear was among the most powerful fae in the realm. If not *the* most powerful.

Or perhaps that is Neve now. The king seems scared of her rise . . .

Vidar didn't know who wielded the stronger magic, only that Neve had been revealed as a Falk princess and that family line had been known to be very powerful indeed. If only he could ask the lost princess himself.

The Lady of Ships broke her tense silence. "Once, House Virtoris ruled this island with an armada four times the size of the one we have now. Then, no one would have dared to come at us on the water."

To be fair, attacks were still rare. However, in the thousands of turns since House Virtoris bent the knee to Queen Sassa Falk and subsequently, King Magnus, their fleet dwindled. Ship by ship. First, they'd lost ships in the Shadow Fae War, then in other battles with other kingdoms. Most recently, the Mage Court had sent two of their ships to the depths of the sea, where only mermaids and selkies and other water creatures could roam the decks.

It was far easier to destroy a ship than to rebuild one. Particularly in the Kingdom of Winter, where trees did not grow as fast or as tall as trees in the south. High Lady

Fayeth had ruled her lands well, but she, like her predecessors, had neglected to rebuild most of their lost ships. Now she would be the one in her family to pay the price.

And the cost was high.

"The king will remain distracted by Neve for a long while. At least until he captures and kills her, but after that, you're right. We'll be a priority. A problem." The Lady of Ships locked eyes with her son and heir. "Sayyida disobeyed Magnus by disappearing from court. She made him look like a powerless fool." Though the high lady claimed to be furious with her eldest daughter, the corner of her lips curled in the slightest of smug smiles.

"If only breaking my betrothal with Saga had been enough for our families to be at peace."

It wasn't that Vidar had not loved Saga. He had loved her—as a friend—almost like a sister. Still, he'd never met someone else he'd rather be engaged to, so he'd gone along with the betrothal. To become heir to House Virtoris and husband to a princess of the realm was a great honor, after all. And with Saga's strong winter magic, it was practically guaranteed their children would have possessed a good deal of the very magic that kept the kingdom in balance.

His mother snorted. "Of course not. He tried to tie Njal to yet another inlander! The king is a lunatic, and I fear he'll stop at nothing short of ending our lives to soothe his ego. Perhaps he'll keep Amine alive. She's still young and unwell. Easier to control."

Vidar wasn't so sure. Yes, his youngest sister had been a victim of the blight and was routinely ill, but if the king killed them all save for Amine, she would not take that lying down. One day, his youngest sister would make him pay. She would be quieter about getting revenge, but Amine was much like Sayyida, with the fury and power of a tempest in her heart. The difference was that Sayyida allowed that tempest to guide her, then struck fast and true and hard with the help of the storm at her back. Amine favored patience and was far more calculating.

The door to the room slammed open, and Vidar turned to find the elder storm-born sister marching toward them.

With each pounding step, Sayyida's black curls bounced around her. Though lighter in complexion than their mother's deep brown skin, Vidar often imagined that at Sayyida's age, she and their mother would look identical. Both with the same curls, sharp cheekbones, skin that was regularly dusted with salt, and eyes that looked like the waters of the Shivering Sea.

"I got a letter from Saga." Sayyida tossed a weathered sheet of paper on the table. The page, curled from days of being contained in a tube, rocked a bit before settling.

Neither Vidar nor his mother picked it up.

"You should be on the opposite side of the island." The Lady of Ship's jaw tightened. "*Hiding.*"

Sayyida snorted. "I'm not scared of the king."

She should be. King Magnus was not the king because of his bloodline. No matter that he was illegitimate and bore the name Aaberg, not Falk like the fae who sired him, Magnus was powerful and still had many supporters.

"Read the letter, Mother," Sayyida demanded.

"How did Saga learn where you were?"

"She knows all my hideouts." Sayyida shrugged a single shoulder.

Lady Fayeth Virtoris rubbed her temple, but picked up the paper and scanned the message before setting it down with a flat, tense palm burying it into the table. Her blue-gray stare burned through her daughter. "What do you want me to do about the princess fleeing Avaldenn?"

"Saga left?" Vidar's body tensed.

"With Lord Riis at the behest of the queen," Sayyida said. "They're going south, heading for Myrr. Judging by the date, they'll be there in less than a week."

"And?" The Lady of Ships spoke as if she intuited what her daughter wanted, and she probably did. Their mother knew her children well.

"I want to go with a small fleet."

"Why?"

"They're searching for Vale and Neve and, I bet you anything, Saga intends to stand with her brother as they fight the king!" Sayyida tossed her hands in the air.

She was fire on the sea, but her words did not warm Vidar. Rather, a trench-deep cold spread through him.

"You wish to go against the king and side with a Falk in an open rebellion?" Lady Virtoris asked with a carefully measured tone.

"In case you didn't notice, I've already gone against King Magnus."

A fist slammed on the table, making both Vidar and Sayyida jump and the letter roll off the edge, to the ground. "Why do you think your brother and I are here?! We're trying to work out a way to defend the island when the king comes, because *he will* come, and he'll want revenge for my children defying him."

Sayyida's chin jutted out. "I'm proud of Njal for standing up for himself and saying he didn't want to marry that lady. It's not our way. We belong by the sea."

"Mother isn't denying that." Vidar cut in before things got ugly. "But Sayyida, we're sending ships out to protect the people of our island. And now you want to leave? They respect you and will want you at their side."

Three heartbeats passed in which his sister looked chastened, but when she met his gaze again, she nodded. "I do wish to go. And I'm aware that it's selfish, but don't you two see? This could be the start of something new! Something better!"

"The Falk princess posed as a commoner her entire time at court." Their mother pressed her lips together before continuing. "Lies were told. How can you trust her?"

"She's with Vale," Vidar said, surprising himself. "I'd trust Vale with my life." His mother didn't know, but he had already done so more than once.

"And I know Neve better than you think, Mother," his sister added.

"Isolde. Her name is *Isolde Falk*," the Lady of Ships spat out the name as if she had not just been using Neve herself. "She's the daughter of the Cold King, a ruthless ruler if there ever was one. You can't recall the end of his reign, my loves, but I do, and it was horrendous. That same blood that needlessly tormented and killed so many fae runs in her veins."

"That's the name she was born with," Sayyida said

softly but not meekly. "That's the family she was born to. But that is not who Neve—*Isolde*—whatever you want to call her is. You may not know that, but I do."

Their mother leaned back against the table. "Tell me then. Convince me to give you *my* ships and allow them to sail south when they're needed here to defend *my* land from *my* children's choices. Convince me to lend the might of our house to a princess I do not trust."

Vidar trained his attention on his sister.

"She was born here, but Neve grew up in the Vampire Kingdom. A blood slave."

"That's common knowledge now," their mother said.

"I'm not done." Sayyida scowled but continued on to spin a tale of horrors and fear at the hands of the vampires. She told them of Neve's time in the Winter Court since, and how the female was not one to abuse power. Sayyida wasn't sure she wanted power, but one thing was certain: The lost Falk princess always stood up for those who needed her to.

"From what she's told me and what I witnessed during our mutual time at court," Sayyida continued, "I consider Neve a dear friend, Mother. House Virtoris may sway with the sea, but we do not abandon our friends in its cold and deadly waters." Sayyida pinned her mother with a stare as cold as a mage's touch.

"I'll consider it," the Lady of Ships conceded. "Until you hear my decision from my own lips, do not even think about taking a ship. Now, leave, Sayyida. Your brother and I have much to discuss."

Sayyida's mouth dropped open. "Mother! I—"

"*Leave us.*" The tone was final, the tone of a high lady.

Sayyida spun and stormed from the room. Vidar watched her go, and when the door slammed shut, he exhaled.

"You don't approve?" His mother was staring at him now.

"I like Neve and love Vale like family."

"You cannot imagine what would happen if we brought our people into a battle that I'm not even sure this lost princess wants, only for Isolde Falk to take the throne and then turn out like her father."

He didn't speak. The only sound in the room was the constant crashing of waves against the rocks below the castle. But then Vidar drew in a breath as he scrubbed the back of his neck.

"You're right. I was young during the Cold King's final turns. You and Father shielded me well from that talk. Talk that younglings need not worry about. However, I agree with Sayyida. Neve is not her father. And Saga wouldn't be going south if she thought otherwise."

"You can't say exactly why Saga left the capital."

"No, but she wouldn't be going to Myrr in the hopes of finding Vale and Neve if she didn't believe in them. On that matter, Mother, I believe in them too. I trust them. And if I were the head of House Virtoris, and war erupted between Neve and Vale and King Magnus, I'd send my ships to fight for my friends."

"I made a poor decision once, Vidar." She crossed her arms over her chest as if trying to sink in on herself. "Two decades ago, backing King Magnus seemed the right thing to do. However, since then, he has not proven worthy of the throne, and I must admit, I cannot bear to make another wrong choice. Not one this important."

It wouldn't be only their families affected. The choice of House Virtoris would affect every lesser lord and lady still sworn to them. Every fisherfae. Every sailor and fighter. And every fae left on their island while their loved ones went to fight.

Considering all of that, they could never bend the knee to King Magnus again, and he did not believe Neve was anything like the stories he'd heard of the Cold King.

The heir to House Virtoris lifted his chin and went to his mother. He took her hand, weathered, like his, and squeezed.

"You may hold on to the fear of the past, but I fear a future under King Magnus's continued rule. So I ask you to trust Sayyida and me. Allow us to go south and see what they plan. We need not take the entire fleet, just a small one, just in case."

"I understand you sticking behind Vale, and Sayyida siding with Saga, but how can you be sure about Isolde?"

In truth, he didn't know, but Vidar had a feeling that this wasn't all happening by chance. That Isolde had arrived back in Winter's Realm right when she was needed most. When things needed changing the most. He would follow that nudge.

"I just am, Mother. Vale is another brother, and his wife is a friend, one I've come to care for in a short period of time. And you have always taught us to stick with those we really love, and to fight for them. For the life we all deserve."

CHAPTER 5
NEVE

The healing sanctuary of Valrun smelled like all others. A pleasant blend of herbs and potions mixed with the odors of blood and sweat. My nose wrinkled as I passed a bed occupied by a sleeping male with a festering wound. He hadn't been with us when we'd found the Shadow King. What had he tangled with to be in such a state?

I heard Rynni speaking with patients down a hallway connected to the large, rectangle-shaped sanctuary. I tried to make enough noise that she'd hear me coming, but not so much that I woke the sleeping patients.

When I was halfway across the main room, Rynni poked her head out of a private room.

"Princess? What brings you here?" She entered the hallway and came to meet me.

I hadn't set foot in this sanctuary since we'd first arrived, preferring instead to have Rynni heal my injuries brought on by combat practice inside the annex.

"I was hoping to speak with you about a couple of

things and get a tonic. The one that lasts a full moon cycle." My hand passed over my belly, telling her what I meant. There were many healing tonics with a long active cycle, and more than one way to prevent a pregnancy, should one wish to do so.

She nodded.

"I'd also like to check on Thantrel first, if possible."

"He's asleep and should remain so if he's to heal enough to fly tonight." She gestured to a room across from the one she was in. "But if you absolutely must see him, he's there."

"If he's asleep, I'll leave him be." I was not about to wake someone who had just gone through so much. "I'd still like to talk with you though."

"Right." The dragon-fae shifted, allowing me a glimpse beyond, into one of the six private rooms this sanctuary boasted. A female faerie stood there, heavily pregnant, one limp hand resting on her belly and the other pressed to her back. Her eyes were closed, and her breaths looked labored. "I'm finishing up a massage to ease her into labor. Can you give me ten minutes?"

"Of course."

Rynni shut the door, and I perched on the end of an empty bed. Only three fae in the sanctuary were unrecognizable to me, one being the male with the festering wound. How strange and wonderful that I hadn't been at Valrun for very long, but I knew most of the rebels. By face, if not name and personality. In a short amount of time, I'd gone from an outsider to someone who felt like she belonged.

"Here's that potion." Rynni appeared, a vial in her hand.

I accepted the tube, popped the cork top and drank it down. It tasted similar to one I'd had in the Vampire Kingdom.

"So, have you already found the information you're looking for?" Rynni asked.

She'd saved our arses beneath the mountain, and knew Thyra and I would devote what time we had left at Valrun to researching shadow magic.

"No, I woke up and came straight here." I refrained from asking how she was so active after flying for many hours and not sleeping as long as the rest of us. "I'm on my way there after this. What I need you to answer is research of another kind."

Rynni gave a soft laugh. "I'm a healer, not a scholar."

I looked around. "Are there wards around the beds? To deaden sounds?"

Rynni gave a wave of her hand and magic shifted all around us, activating the wards. "I keep them off during the day because when they're awake, the patients like to chat. Or eavesdrop on other's conversations." She gave me a pointed look, clearly telling me to get on with it.

"I was wondering if you've made any headway on the lindwyrm venom?"

Luccan had taken a fang from a lindwyrm guardian during our heist of the coinary of Avaldenn. He'd thought that one of our more academically inclined friends might be able to replicate the venom for use as a weapon.

"I did not. Last I heard, nor have Duran, Clemencia,

or Anna, but I haven't spoken to them much since we returned to Valrun."

I shrugged. Her answer didn't surprise me. In fact, I'd expected it. "You'll get there, I'm sure."

"Yes, well, what did you really want to ask?" Rynni arched her brows.

I'd been caught stalling. "It's about the Shadow King."

The dragon-fae let out a breath. "I cannot tell you how sorry I am that I breathed fire on him. I—"

"You've already apologized." She'd done so profusely when we first landed at Valrun. "There's no way you could have known that your fire would destroy the tree. Or that he'd live through such a blaze. *No one* would have guessed such a thing. Had I been in your place, I'd have done the same as you."

She said nothing.

"Anyway, I believe that the king being trapped in that tree might have eventually caused the blight," I continued. "That he could have slowly poisoned the Drassils, and as a result, the magic weaving through their network and the kingdom."

"The blight has been an issue for a long time, longer still in the Spring Court than here. But it hasn't affected those in Winter's Realm badly until two decades ago."

Sassa Falk trapped King Érebo over a thousand turns ago. The blight had cropped up over the centuries but not often until my family lost power.

"He might have taken some time to learn how to expand his magic within the trees' network. I'm not sure, but when we spoke to the rebels upon arrival, the Drassil in the courtyard no longer looked like it was dying." I cleared my throat. "It was getting a little better before. I think that was due to King Magnus finally having the Scepter and using it. Now, I'd say it's healed all the way."

"I recall." Rynni played with the hem of her shirt. "I don't see what this has to do with me though."

"I realize that you can't speak to the Drassils, but I want you to observe your patients. See if fewer get ill from the blight. And you have two pregnant fae, right?"

"Both days from giving birth."

"I want to know if their children are born healthy or if they show effects of being injured by the blight." The illness often targeted fae wings, horns, and sometimes ears. It also left scars that differed from those that occurred naturally.

"Of course, but two fae births don't mean much. You'll need a larger pool to study to draw any real conclusion."

Even then, I may never know. This idea might not be something one could prove. Perhaps even King Érebo could not say that he'd been causing the blight. It might have been his mere presence within that tree that threw off the magic of the realm over time, and when the Ice Scepter was lost that imbalance had been amplified.

"I'll be contacting the healers in Myrr, too. The ones in the castle should be able to speak with others within the city."

Rynni nodded. "I'll keep you informed."

"Then I'll leave you to it and get to the library."

"Good luck, Princess Neve."

"Thank you." I would need all the luck I could get.

CHAPTER 6
VALE

Dusk loomed, hours away. Soon, we would fly south with only the stars as our witnesses. If our gryphons flew at a moderate speed, we'd arrive in Myrr around the eighth morning bell. Both Sian and Filip Balik had told me a dozen times that their father insisted that the family breakfast together at that hour. Should Tadgh Balik be less inviting than I believed he'd be, we hoped to take advantage of that family togetherness and the good will of our friends sitting at that table.

"You alright?" Caelo came up alongside me, a saddle in his arms.

I poured more of the fish heads and innards into a gryphon's bowl. My nose wrinkled. By the dead gods, the smell was horrendous. "As well as can be expected. Why?"

"You've been quiet. I thought with Lord Riis back and your sister here, you'd be more excited." Caelo arched an inky brow.

My best friend understood me better than most people. I loved my sister with all my heart and even before

I'd learned of our blood tie, I'd been very fond of Lord Riis. Seen him as an uncle.

"I can't help it. I'm still thinking about Rhistel."

After everyone woke up, but before we'd set out to prepare for our journey, we'd congregated in the annex and finished sharing what needed to be shared. Others wanted to know why a princess of Winter's Realm had arrived at Valrun, so I told the story of how Rhistel had threatened Saga's life, leaving out any mention of whisperer magic, of course. Very few knew about that, most of them blood—though, considering recent events, I was sure the secret wouldn't remain in the dark for long.

That outing of my twin was a moral issue that I wrestled with. He often used his power for ill, but Rhistel hadn't asked to be born with illegal magic that would earn him a death sentence. What was more, telling the world of Rhistel's power might put Mother at risk. Losing both of them to the laws of the land might be more than I could bear.

"Throw Rhistel from your mind." Caelo nudged my shoulder with his own. "He's not worth it."

"It's difficult."

My friend gave me a stiff smile and swept a hand toward the stable door. "I can't remember when it was this warm."

He was right. One still required a cloak to work outside, but it did not need to be quite so thick. Nor pulled so tight around the shoulders. Soon fae with delicate wings, faeries like myself, might walk about with them uncovered by furs and cloaks for more than a few minutes.

"I suspect that Magnus is using the Scepter to gain favor with the people. We might soon see snow melting."

Caelo let out a long hum. "If he can give them green grass, many will forget all of his wrongs."

To hear the elder fae tell it, the kingdom had never been warm and lush like the Summer or Spring Courts in the south, but there had once been moons on end in which grass sprouted, soft rains nourished the land, and the sun warmed fae faces.

Neve and Thyra might go up against the king just when the public turned favorable eyes upon him.

"At least the warmth will make the south walk easier," I said.

"If Lord Balik agrees to house the rebels."

"He will. Eventually." I'd make him see sense.

Caelo gave a single laugh. "I'll take your word."

The closest gryphon's head lifted from his food and turned sharply to the door. We followed suit to see my father enter the stable.

I waved, and Lord Riis made his way over, his wide shoulders taking up much of the walkway between the rickety wooden pens.

"I was looking for you, Vale." Lord Riis joined us. "Might I have a word?"

As a knight used to being dismissed by other lords and ladies, Caelo left wordlessly.

"Have you seen Thantrel?" I asked. That had been my father's plan after we awoke in the late afternoon.

"I just left the sanctuary. He was asleep but looked to be in decent shape. Or as good as one can manage with such a recent wing injury. Luccan tells me you brought that healer, the half-dragon from Vitvik?"

"Rynni."

"She's quite skilled."

One corner of my lips twitched upward. "That she is. In more ways than one."

"Oh?"

"She healed Caelo, Neve, and me after we came across a band of orcs. Good healer, there's no doubt, although I'll admit, I didn't intend to invite her along with us. She used our wanted status against us and said she'd be on our side for a place in the White Tower. You know, if we win the war to come."

Lord Riis's eyes twinkled. "So she's tenacious. An admirable quality."

As a son of a wealthy merchant, Lord Riis had risen in society to become a member of the illustrious Sacred Eight. He must have used buckets of tenacity to accomplish his goals. Perhaps one day, when things were calmer, I'd hear the stories of how he managed a feat that normally took families generations.

"At any rate, I'm relieved that she helped you out. Since you left Riis Tower, I've been worried about you and Neve." He clapped my shoulder with a meaty hand and squeezed. "I'm glad the lads found you."

"True brothers." The words had barely left my lips before I winced. Lord Riis caught the motion, and his lips pressed into thin lines.

"Seeing Rhistel threaten your sister and mother." He shook his head. "It was one of the most difficult things I've experienced."

I leaned back against the wood of the pen. "I can imagine."

"Yes, well, Inga is a strong fae, but I don't think even she could have fathomed . . ." He trailed off with a sigh.

Stillness settled between us, until I broached the subject I'd wondered about. "Why didn't you two marry?"

My father's eyes, near twins to my own dark brown ones, locked on me. "It was never in the cards. Your father had learned of Inga's powers long before they wed."

"How?"

"He overheard Lord and Lady Vagle, Fates rest her departed soul, talking about them and how *they* might use Inga to secure some boon to the family." He scowled at that, clearly not liking the idea of anyone using my mother. "From that day forward, Lord Vagle kept your mother in Odelia—at least he did until Queen Revna called her to court."

"She was at Frostveil a while before wedding Magnus. And returned only for a short stay before the Rebellion, yes?"

"Yes. And during Inga's first stint at court Magnus did not spread the word of her power, which led Lord Vagle to believe that his daughter was safe. That Magnus would stay quiet. That fantasy came crashing down the day Magnus came and asked for Inga's hand." He snorted. "It wasn't like old Airen Vagle could say no."

"You two could have run off long before that." I ran a hand along the rough wood of a post, trying for nonchalance.

"She didn't want to put a target on me by association. No matter that I would have accepted it." A long breath left his lips. "And for a while after Magnus discovered her secret, we stayed away from one another."

"Not forever though."

He gave me an impish smile. "No, not forever. After she wed Magnus he went away, and I happened to be in the same city. That was before Inga went to court to serve Queen Revna for a second time, back when your mother lived in Aalborg. Inga and I spent a few nights together. During one of those nights, you and your brother were conceived."

"Our lives might have been better if you were our father."

Simpler, certainly. I suspected more full of love too.

He barked out a laugh. "Bold thing to say, considering I have many children. Most of them see me only as often as their mothers will allow, which is to say not often."

I fiddled with a piece of wood coming off a stall. "If you were with my mother, you never would have taken another lover. Destiny favored you."

My father looked down at my hand, at the soulmate mark there. "We might have been destined by some higher force, but the stars did not make us mates."

"It doesn't make your love less powerful."

"No, it doesn't." He gave me a sad smile. "I worry about Inga. Always have, but especially now."

I understood the feeling. Saga had told me that Rhistel was fighting mother's powers when they left Avaldenn. What if he'd broken free?

My stomach tightened, and I cast about for something more upbeat to consider. It was then that I caught sight of

Arie and Luccan leaving the stable. My heart warmed. I didn't have to look hard to find joy in the world.

"Then again, if you and mother got together when you were younger, I wouldn't have Luccan, Arie, or Thantrel as brothers," I continued. "So perhaps things turned out as they should, and now fate is turning in your favor. After this, you should be with my mother."

Slowly, he placed two hands on my shoulders and pulled me into an embrace. I inhaled. He smelled of the spiced tea that the rebels served in the dining hall.

"That would be my dream." The spymaster's voice was rough with emotion. "And speaking of your mother, she tasked me with delivering a message to Neve."

I broke the embrace. "Oh?"

"Not that I do not want to tell you, son, but your mate should hear it first." He took a step back.

The joy that had been on his face mere moments before dropped. Replaced by something? Unease? What could Mother need to tell Neve that would make Lord Riis, a fae well practiced at hiding his emotions, so clearly troubled?

"Do you know where she is?" my father continued.

"You look ill."

"What I must say won't go over well."

"Neve is understanding." I couldn't say the same of her sister, but my mate always tried to see the best in people. And Lord Riis had always been so helpful towards us.

"Everyone has their limit," he replied. "So, Neve?"

"In the library," I answered after a pause filled only

with the clicking of gryphon beaks and the stomping of pegasus hooves in the far back pens. "With Thyra."

CHAPTER 7
NEVE

High above me, balanced on a rickety ladder, Thyra tossed a book.

I caught the soft leather-bound tome one-handed, and took a handful of steps to place it on the table where Duran, Clemencia, and Anna scoured page after page.

"This shelf is clear. Coming down." My twin's silver wings, a shade darker than my own, fluttered gracefully as she descended.

The library at Valrun Castle wasn't large, and precious few books were on the top uppermost shelves, but we'd been checking each and every one for information on shadow magic.

"The stacks are getting high over here," Duran called out. "We would appreciate some help before adding more to the piles."

We only had a few hours until we left for Myrr. After that, I didn't trust anyone staying behind to research the Shadow Fae.

"If only there was some sort of magic to find isolated words within a text," Clemencia muttered. "That would make this far easier."

You knew it was bad when the two most studious of your friends were complaining about reading.

"How many mentions?" Thyra took the seat across from Duran. I settled in next to her and pulled a book from one stack.

"Only five worth investigating further." Duran placed his hand on the stack to his left. "Shadow Fae take up multiple paragraphs in these books. The rest only had a mention or two. Nothing that isn't common knowledge."

"You're aware that Myrr has a wonderfully enormous and supposedly lovely library, right?" Clem spoke without bothering to lift her gaze from her text. Her thin finger trailed across a line, helping her to keep her place. "They might have entire shelves dedicated to Shadow Fae or their magic."

"They might," I agreed. "They equally might not. And what if the one line Thyra and I need is here, in one of these books?"

"We can't risk it," my twin said. "We have to figure out how to use this magic safely."

We were certain that, eventually, the Shadow King would make himself known. And while he would be met with suspicion, at least *he* had mastery over his power. Mastery and a tale about Sassa Falk—his mate and our ancestor—that would throw more ire on our family line. Add to that the support of King Magnus, and I had a feeling that the Shadow King would find acceptance sooner or later.

Thyra and I did not know how to use our magic, and our father was famous not just for being a king, but an unstable one. We had to keep it together. Whichever one of us took the throne could not be seen as a Cold Queen. A dangerous queen.

Our group fell into the silence of skimming dusty texts and flipping pages. After some time, my vision blurred with the words, but I blinked heavily and soldiered on. The work might be dry and, mostly, boring, but things could be far worse. The smell of old books surrounded us. We were warm, and there wasn't a monster in sight. A significant improvement over our circumstances of two days prior.

"Here's an entire chapter!" Anna took a scrap of paper, slipped it in place, and shut the book with a snap. She handed it to Clemencia. "To the useful stack it goes."

"That author is the same person who wrote two other books with large Shadow Fae segments." Clemencia's face brightened with recognition. "If you see this name, pay extra careful attention." She flipped the book around to show everyone.

I memorized the name and began to skim once more. I was closing in on yet another end to a chapter when a motion among the freestanding shelves beyond caught my attention. Lord Riis appeared, his long red hair tangled and a pungent reek of fish coming off him.

When the Lord of Tongues reached our table, he bowed. "Princesses. Friends."

"Hello there. Where did you come from?" I asked with a teasing smile. "You smell of the docks in Avaldenn."

"I was with Vale as he fed the gryphons. Some of the fish juice may have splashed on my pant leg."

"I'm afraid there *is* a faint whiff of fish about." I chuckled, an effort to soften how my twin was glaring at the spymaster. "Is all going well out there?"

"Indeed." He swallowed and an unplaceable look flashed across his face before disappearing so quickly I questioned if I saw it. "I came here to speak with you."

"Go on then." I leaned back in the chair.

"Actually, I had hoped to talk with you and Thyra. Alone." Vale's father peered around. "Is there a more private space?"

"The library is small enough that you'd be heard no matter what corner we crammed ourselves into," Thyra answered, her tone perfunctory though it softened as she turned to those helping us search through books. "Do you three mind giving us the room?"

"I won't take long," Lord Riis assured them. "Wait next door? I can tell you when I leave."

The others grabbed the tomes they were skimming and left the room, the door shutting behind them.

"Take a seat," I said as that same look rippled across his features again. The faint pursing of the lips, the tightening of his throat alerted me that something was very off. "What's going on, Leyv?"

He let out a long exhale. "I have something to tell the two of you. Something that Inga wishes for me to divulge."

The queen. Was she going to hand over information that would make defeating her husband easier? Vale's mother and I were not close, but he loved her. As did Saga.

What was more, Queen Inga didn't love her husband. Their marriage was purely political. Between the love for her children and the dislike for her husband, I could see the whisperer queen giving us information we might use to great effect.

I placed my elbows on the table. "I'm listening."

"As am I." Thyra leaned back in her chair.

Lord Riis cleared his throat. "You're aware that the queen was a handmaiden, even a sort of friend, to your mother?"

"Yes." Emilia, the human slave I'd met in the hidden bowels of Frostveil Castle, had said as much.

Thyra nodded, too. She might not have been in the castle since we lived there, but my twin had connections, and she had gathered a lot of knowledge about the place over the turns.

"Well . . ." he trailed off and looked away.

"Can you please stop with the dramatics?" Thyra hissed.

"Thyra!" I placed a hand on her forearm. "He loves her and, well, I don't know what's going on, but clearly it's not good."

"It's not." Lord Riis swallowed. "The queen harbors great remorse over her actions of the past. I hope you both will be able to see this."

"Who knows? First you have to tell us what she did." Thyra growled, and the spymaster and my sister exchanged heated glares.

Lord Riis folded first, the fullness of his gaze landed

on me. "The kingdom at large knows that Inga is an excellent mind reader, but she is much, much more. She's the strongest whisperer this kingdom has seen since the time when those with her magic were permitted to live long, full lives." He looked at my twin. "That power—"

"I am aware of such magic," Thyra interrupted coldly.

She'd known of the queen's whispering powers since Ratha told her after interrogating Vale the first time. Ratha had known for decades, and Thyra was the first person she'd told. My twin had never brought up using this information against the queen. Perhaps because she considered King Magnus the real enemy.

"Fae with that forbidden magic can read *and* control minds," Thyra added. "They're far more dangerous."

"Right." Lord Riis spoke slowly, perhaps shocked at the depth of Thyra's knowledge. If that was the case, he didn't question it. "Inga not only has impressive control over her power, but she knows how to use it so that no one detects she's in their heads—from her studies on other whisperers, very few can do that."

"So?" Thyra asked.

"Inga had access to not only Queen Revna, but to King Harald before the White Bear's Rebellion."

My eyes widened.

"She used her magic to attack the king as Magnus commanded. Under threat of her own life, of course. Inga would never have—"

"Leyv, are you saying that . . . by the dead gods." My hands flew to my mouth as the pieces shuffled into place. The timeline crystallized.

"Inga poisoned your father's mind. Bit by bit. Day by day. She turned him into the Cold King that the realm despises." The words were rushing from him, as though if he said them fast enough, they'd hurt less. "And when she left the castle, her hold was unbreakable."

"Not even our mother could help him," my voice broke, and Thyra stiffened.

Long ago, I read a little of the queen's diary. Before she became queen, my mother had been on track to become a Master Healer. She'd believed that she could have healed her husband from his madness, if only she'd completed her training.

But no. My mother would never have succeeded in healing the king. Not with a whisperer hiding nearby, attacking his mind. Turning Harald Falk on himself. On his people. His kingdom.

"Look at me, Lord Riis," I demanded.

He lifted his gaze. Shame ran heavy along his every feature.

"How long have you known this?"

"As it was happening."

An orc might have punched me in the belly with one of their meaty hands, and it would have had less of an impact. My heart raced, and every part of me clenched, as if bracing for something worse to come. And yet somehow, I managed to tower over him.

He was a male I'd trusted for many moons now. The first one to suspect who I was at court. Vale's father. Someone I cared for.

And he'd betrayed me. He'd known what his lover was doing and allowed her to destroy *my family*. Frost formed on my fingers and began to bloom around the room. I struggled to call my power back, to gain control, and managed, though just barely.

"Why is she admitting this?" Thyra's voice rang out in the empty library, as hard as ice, whereas I felt like a flurry of snow—going in every which direction.

"Inga has regretted her actions for a very long time," Lord Riis repeated, "but she had our sons to think of. Now, she sees the way things are going and knows that Neve is important to Vale. She thought that, given their love, Neve deserved the truth. She didn't know about you, Thyra, but she'd think the same of you."

"*Leave.*" I straightened. My entire body felt so cold, as though I'd explode in a storm of ice at any moment.

"Please, Neve." Lord Riis leaned closer, his gaze beseeching. "I should have told you when I learned who you were, but I love Inga with everything that I am. I could not bear to—"

"*I said leave!* I don't want to see your face!" I spun away, my chest heaving as breath became very difficult to come by.

A chair scraped against the floor, and heavy footsteps walked toward the door. When it shut, I exhaled.

"I have to say," Thyra came to stand by me, "I imagined a lot of treachery at court during our parents' last days, but I never suspected this." A tear trailed down her cheek. "Nor did I think I'd be crying over our family now, all these turns after they died, but—"

"He wasn't insane or cruel." I took her hand and found it was as cold as mine.

"It was all a lie," she agreed.

Our father wasn't perfect. We'd heard the stories of the harem he kept before he'd met our mother, and other tales revealed him to be as flawed as any other fae. But he wasn't the monster that history would write him as either. "Magnus told his wife to make our father do those things so he might gain support among the other nobles. *And it worked.* Our family is dead because of King Magnus's plan."

It all stemmed from the male on the throne. From the king's hatred of our family—of the father who had never claimed him, our uncle, Prince Calder Falk. A memory of the skeletal prince, clinging to life in the dank and stinking eastern dungeons of Frostveil, made me scowl. If he'd shown his son the slightest bit of love, would any of this have happened?

I'd never have an answer. No one could change the past. Not even the dead gods. And if they possessed such magic, I doubted that they'd try. Those gods were long gone, dead. Or hiding among the stars like cowards. In the here and now they didn't matter.

What mattered was that Lord Riis had betrayed me, and I didn't know if I'd ever be able to forgive him. Or at the very least, see him in the same light I once had.

More chilling was my second thought. One that would very much affect my mate.

If I was not mistaken, Queen Inga had tasked Lord Riis with giving us this information because she didn't believe she could hold Rhistel in her thrall for much longer.

The heir to Winter's Realm would, eventually, break free. And when that happened, I was certain Rhistel would seek revenge on his mother. Likely, he'd take her life.

As much as I despised both Lord Riis and Queen Inga, they were my mate's parents. He loved them. And I loved Vale.

"You still trust him?" Thyra whispered, tearing through that horrible realization.

I looked away, unable to answer.

CHAPTER 8

NEVE

We dipped out of the cloud cover, and the City of Myrr revealed itself, gold and gleaming in the rising sun's light.

Arava neighed, making me smile as I ran a hand down her neck. The pegasus and I were new to each other, but she'd claimed me, and I had to admit to feeling a shocking amount of affection for the ebony mare. Affection and the occasional odd inclination that I knew what she wanted.

Thantrel and Caelo claimed that my bond with Arava would continue to grow the longer we knew one another. While I'd never speak to Arava like those with elven blood could with other animals, it would be the next best thing.

Behind me, Vale shifted in the extended saddle. Probably to get a better view.

Arava allowed him to ride behind me, just as Thyra's white pegasus, Lasvin, allowed Thantrel to ride with her. Really, Thyra had taken more convincing on that score, but we had a lot of people going south and only so many flying creatures so my twin gave in.

"Stunning, isn't it?" Vale squeezed my middle.

"So beautiful. Not that I'd expect anything less from House Balik."

"Wait until you see Ramshold up close."

The Golden House. If a name ever fit, that one suited House Balik.

The pointed tops of every tower gleamed golden in the lazy sunrise, and the stonework was a creamy pale gray—the rocks likely from the Ice Teeth range framing the city. From this distance, Ramshold seemed as large and as lovely as Frostveil Castle in Avaldenn.

"Should we send the signal?" Thyra called out from my left.

On the other side of Thyra were Prince Thordur and Princess Bavirra while Saga and Caelo soared to my right. The others trailed behind. With only eight flying creatures, Thyra and I could not bring the three fae in our Valkyrja, but if everything had gone to plan the vampires would be lurking in the woods below.

"Now is the time." I waved to Caelo and gave a nod.

The knight placed a hand on his gryphon and said something that was lost to the wind. A second later, the beast began shrieking. The others followed suit, creating a ruckus. If the vampires made it in time, they'd know what to do.

"By the dead gods, what a sound!" a voice called out from behind.

A scowl hardened my lips as I placed the voice. Lord Riis.

I'd been inclined to leave the deceitful High Lord at Valrun, but Vale implored me to see sense. It would be easier to sway House Balik to our side if we'd already secured a great house.

Leyv's inclusion was politics, plain and simple. And while I didn't like having to play the game, I would. For my family, my own safety, and a better kingdom. I may never forgive Lord Riis, but I needed his help all the same.

As for Vale, he was experiencing complicated emotions. Not only had his biological father kept such a dire secret, but his mother had been involved in killing my family.

Tears pricked my eyes, but I wiped them away before they fell. With only my mate as witness, I had cried silently as we flew. Vale had comforted me, nearly to the point of forsaking his own kin, though I'd stopped him there. As someone who had precious few family members, I couldn't allow Vale to disown those who loved him.

"The banner!" Thyra commanded.

The sounds of rapid snapping filled the air as the cloth unfurled and streamed behind us. Anna and Arie rode together, and he held a banner of peace for those at the gate to see. Not a moment too soon, either.

"Breathe," Vale whispered into my ear as we began our descent, my twin and I in the forefront. "You're tense."

"What if they don't let us into the city?"

There were many reasons the gates might be closed to us. The first being that Thyra and I were trying to lead a rebellion against a king that Lord Balik had sworn allegiance to. But we might also be denied for something as simple as having vampire fighters as part of our court.

Our court . . . It was the first time those closest to Thyra and me, those whose opinions we valued most, felt like a real court. Something more than just loved ones and friends and advisors.

"They will let us in." Vale squeezed me.

He had strong ties to House Balik, that much was certain, but I couldn't help but fear he was a little *too sure* about them joining us. We wouldn't be negotiating with Filip, Sian, or the Balik sisters, all of whom were friends, but the High Lord of the Southlands. And we were asking the family to stand against King Magnus, likely sending their people to war. Such requests were no small matter.

I put on a brave face, and when we landed in front of the towering city gate, Vale and Thantrel slid off the pegasi and extended their hands to their mates.

After shifting Sassa's Blade out of an awkward position, I took Vale's hand, shot my sister a glance. She nodded, and we dismounted. Two feet on the ground, Thyra pulled what appeared to be a plain sack from the saddle bag. Inside that bag rested the Frør Crown, a Hallow of Winter's Realm and one of two priceless items in our possession.

We approached the gate in lockstep, as a smaller door to the side of the larger, heavier gate doors opened. Through it walked a dwarf dressed in a black uniform with a golden ram's head across the chest. The soldier's cloak billowed behind him, heavy and thick despite the rising temperature.

The soldier came to a stop a few paces away. "Might I ask your names and business in visiting the Golden City?"

Myrr was the southernmost city in Winter's Realm. Fae traveled through the area, but only if they were heading to the Autumn Court and wanted to make their life difficult by not sailing. Otherwise, if fae visited this part of the kingdom, they were returning home or stopping for business or pleasure.

"We're here to speak with High Lord Balik," I said.

The gate guard cocked his head. "As you can imagine, our lord is quite busy—"

"My name is Isolde Falk." A thrill went through me at the use of my birth name. For the first time, it felt natural, right. "And this is my sister, Thyra Falk. We're the rightful rulers of Winter's Realm, accompanied by our court. So, while I agree that Lord Balik is likely very busy, he *will* make time to see us."

The soldier swallowed, and then, just as planned, Vale stepped forward.

"Tell him Prince Vale Aaberg is here with the Falk sisters. And that we come bearing a white banner of peace. We only wish to talk."

"And Lord Leyv Riis." The deep and steady voice from behind made my fists clench, but as much as I didn't want Lord Riis around me, I said nothing, just continued to stare at the gate guard.

A look of great discomfort crossed the guard's face, but he turned to go. "I'll send word to the castle."

He'd only just disappeared through the door when my shoulders loosened. It was official, Thyra and I had announced ourselves to the wider realm. Claimed our house and birthright. The rest was up to those who held power in the form of fae, gold, and acumen.

"*Isolde.*" Anna's whisper came from behind. The name sounded so odd coming from her lips. She'd known me for nearly my whole life, always as Neve, but no longer. From this day forward, I was Isolde.

I twisted to find my best friend and blinked. Three more had joined us. Astril, Freyia, and Livia stood with the others, as if they'd been there all along.

"Just slipped out of the woods," Astril said. "When the soldier's back was turned. The others too. I expect they left their posts to gossip about your arrival."

One glance at the top of the gate and the connecting wall that soldiers would usually occupy told me she was right. Not a fae in sight. The vampires had timed their arrival to perfection.

"Keep your hoods up." I motioned pulling their hood over their faces a bit. Though their eyes weren't red, indicating that they'd eaten during their journey, they would forever have the look of a vampire. Something off-putting to most fae. "Just until we're in the castle."

The Valkyrja nodded, their chins dipping downward as one until they were hidden in plain sight.

"How long will it take?" Thyra asked.

"Not long," Vale assured her. "I would bet good gold that someone is already on wing to the castle. Lord Balik won't make us wait once he hears who has come to see him."

The desire to lean into Vale, to transfer some of his confidence to me via touch, was strong, but I refrained.

When the escort arrived, I could not be seen leaning on my husband.

So I stood tall and proud as we waited. The time seemed to pass slowly, though it was likely only twenty minutes or so when the vast gate doors swung open. A smile cracked across my face when Sian and Filip strode out to greet us. The former's long honey-brown hair fluttered in a breeze and the sun glinted off his honey-brown wings and the ring in his nose. Sian, as ever, was absolutely striking, whereas Filip was much more relaxed in both attitude and stance.

"We were having family breakfast when word of your arrival came." Sian folded Vale into a hug.

"Why else do you think we planned to arrive at this ungodly hour?" Vale barked out a laugh. "As if I haven't heard you complaining about the early family breakfasts turn after turn. Always the eighth bell on the dot."

Sian released my mate. "So you do listen to me. Sometimes I wonder."

Young, shy Filip, hung back and waved, only for Vale to scoop the heir of Myrr off his feet. Sian laughed as he came to me, pulled me close.

"Father is not pleased to have Falks at the gates," he whispered. "But Filip, Baenna, Eireann, and I vouched for you."

My heart warmed. I'd known I had friends in the great house of the south, but after all that had happened, all the gossip about me, I was relieved that they still counted me as such.

"We might be the only reason he's allowing you into the city, but we will not be enough to sway him if he doesn't want you here. You and your court have a plan, right, *Isolde*?"

"We do," I whispered back.

Sian broke away and scanned the rest of our party. Bac, with his Balik features, didn't fail to garner his interest. Neither did Aleksander, who looked a lot like me. Or the dwarves bearing house colors I doubted Sian could place. For centuries, those of Winter's Realm had believed that Dergia was lost to mountain dust. But it was Saga's presence that seemed to stump him the most.

"What are you doing here?"

"It's a long story. One best told over a goblet of mulled wine later tonight." Saga winked.

"We'll make that happen." Sian's warm, gold eyes landed on Thyra. Knowing sparked there. "Princess Thyra, I presume?"

"Yes, and you're Lord Balik's heir?" Thyra asked.

"I'm a Balik, but not the next High Lord of the Southlands." Sian gestured to Filip, who was still pink-cheeked from Vale's hug and standing two paces away. "That's my brother. You can call me Sian."

"I'm Filip." The heir ran his hand through his golden-brown hair nervously.

Thyra nodded. "So, are we allowed to enter?"

Sian smirked. "Follow me."

The Balik brothers led us through the castle. With each step, I mentally ran through what could happen, hoping Thyra and I might gain another ally today, and praying that the Warden of the South wouldn't dismiss us. Or worse, toss us in a dungeon for King Magnus to collect. And yet, despite being engrossed by the '*what ifs*', I simultaneously found myself mesmerized by the castle that those of House Balik called home.

The halls were a symphony of black and gold and hunter green, colors of the ruling family. Ramshold was a shockingly bare name for a place I suspected was opulent in every nook and cranny.

"Stop here." Sian held out a hand at an intersection. "The door is just there. But I don't think you all should go in. There are simply too many of you."

"No," Thyra retorted before I could consider his words. "We all go."

Sian cast a glance at the vampires. Their heavy cloaks had been enough to disguise them from the curious fae of Myrr, but not Sian. As we walked, I'd heard him whispering to my husband about the trio.

"They're sworn to us," I said. "You can trust them."

"Sworn?"

"*As Valkyrja.*" Thyra's chin lifted as she spoke the name of the ancient order of female warriors, the likes of which had not been seen in centuries.

Sian's eyes widened, and an impressed expression came across his face, but before he could respond, Filip chimed in.

"Father will see their court as a sign of strength. Everyone should come."

Sian shrugged. "Have it your way."

We entered the grand hall, and my breath hitched at the beauty before me. The ceiling of onyx studded with diamonds reminded me of a more luxurious version of the walls in the Tower of the Living and the Dead. On each wall mountains had been rendered in gold, giving the impression that we stood in a valley beneath a cloudless sky.

Lord Tadgh Balik sat on a seat, black and dark green, with two enormous, golden horns sprouting from the top and curling back. Surely that seat had been a throne, back when the Baliks were the kings and queens of the southlands.

Lady Kilyn Balik stood beside her husband's seat, her back straight, long red hair braided back. Their many children were present too, fanning out on both sides of their father's impressive chair. Nothing about this show of unity surprised me when it came to the Baliks.

What I had not expected, however, was to find Lady Marit Armenil, and a member of Vale's cabal, Sir Qildor, standing just off to the side. And they *held hands*.

Marit caught me staring, and with her free hand, gave a small wave. As much as I wanted to know what was going on between them and why my friend was here when she should be in the midlands, I kept striding behind Sian and Filip. Lord Balik's glower told me he didn't wish to wait any longer to hear why two princesses long-thought dead had sought him out. And the contingent of twenty guards in the hall emphasized the fact that the high lord saw us as a threat.

I was suddenly very glad Thyra hadn't allowed us to be separated from the rest of our court.

"This is going a touch overboard, Father." Sian gestured to the guards.

"I'll be the judge of that." The high lord's golden eyes burned through me. Demanding answers.

During my time at Frostveil, Lord Balik had always sounded calm. Soft in the way of a male who was certain of his power and did not need to speak loudly or harshly. Today, restrained anger brimmed in his voice.

I swallowed as I took him in. With golden-brown hair a few shades lighter than Filip's, dark brown skin, and gold wings, it was easy to see that Lord Tadgh was a Balik. Heavy gold bangles in the shape of a ram's head weighed down his wrists, and the faintest dark green tattoo swirled out from the corners of his eyes to his temples. A striking man made more powerful by his central position in the room and the family motto hanging above him. The words were in Old High Fae, but I knew just enough of the language to read them.

Family. Honor. Wisdom.

"I allowed you to retrieve them," the high lord continued. "But now it is I who will speak to this so-called *court* and determine what is necessary and what is not. Fall in line, my sons."

Both Filip and Sian cast glances at us, but did as their father said.

"Isolde and Thyra Falk," Lord Balik continued. "Approach."

We did, with Vale and Thantrel at our sides. Lord Balik shook his head.

"I did not request your approach, Prince. Nor yours, Thantrel Riis."

"No one will separate us from our mates," Vale said loud and clear.

Gasps rippled through the line of Balik children, and I swore I heard Marit squeal.

"Mates . . . I see." Tadgh Balik shifted in his seat. "I expect there is nothing to be done about that."

"No, there's not," Thantrel replied, shoulders pulled back.

Lord Balik snorted. "I don't care about your status, Riis. What I care to know is why there are Falk princesses in my city. Why would they bring danger to the southlands?"

"You've already done so," I replied. "Didn't you leave court without the king's approval?"

Lord Balik's eyes narrowed, then swept behind me. I'd bet the fabled sword filled with shadows hanging at my hip that he was glaring at Lord Riis.

"Avaldenn was no longer conducive to the safety of my family." The Warden of the South lifted his chin ever so slightly. "What with the vampires hunting you, and the continued undignified matches that the king set—and expected to be fulfilled." He stared at me. "Your presence here puts my family in even greater danger. I should chain you two and send you north."

"I'll take blame where blame is due. The vampires hunting fae in Avaldenn *are* there for me, although I hope you believe me when I say I only killed their prince in self-defense."

"That does not change the issue of my family's safety."

"No, but back to the whole sending me north in chains issue."

Lord Balik was respected as a fair and thoughtful lord. One who saw sense. I only needed to edge him towards it, make him see that due to his own actions, he wasn't safe here either. It didn't matter if I was here or journeyed all the way to the Summer Kingdom. Eventually, Magnus would seek revenge on House Balik for disobeying him.

"You don't believe that King Magnus is a just and good king any longer, so why would you send me to him?"

"I crave peace."

Internally, I winced. Peace was not something I could give this male in power. Not yet, anyway.

"I recognize what you want. What it will bring to my people. Which is why I do not want you here," Lord Balik said. "But more importantly, why I must speak with Princess Saga."

At Vale's side, Saga appeared, her face bright, hopeful. How? My hope was diminishing. Perhaps turns at court had made her a better actress than I'd thought possible.

"You stand with them, Princess Saga? You betray your blood and bring the possibility of war closer to Winter's Realm?" Lord Balik asked.

Saga cleared her throat. "We're hoping that, if you join us, we might avert war entirely."

"That's unlikely, Princess. Fanciful even."

"Perhaps, but it's clear to me that my father has not been fit to rule for many turns. He harms others, his own people, and I can no longer abide by his actions."

"You're not mates with either Princess Thyra or Princess Isolde, yet you've sworn to them?"

"I have not," Saga admitted. "However, I have not ruled it out either. Just as you have seen flaws in the current king, I have too, Lord Balik. I love my father, and truly do not wish him to be harmed, but as I stated, I also cannot stand with him."

The head of House Balik turned to Vale. "And you, Warrior Bear? You're the head of your father's army. He might be a miserable fae, and done unspeakable things over the turns, but your father loves his children. I understand that you are mated to Isolde, but could you not have reached a peaceful agreement with your father rather than forsaking him?"

"For my mate, I'd do anything," Vale replied, and I didn't miss when Lord Balik looked at his wife. "And, as for forsaking my blood, I am clean of that as well."

The air in the room seemed to still. Thyra and I had spoken to Vale about this at length, and the time was here. The moment he claimed his name. Just as I had.

"What do you mean by that?" Lord Balik leaned forward in his seat.

"What I mean is that King Magnus is not my father by blood," Vale spoke so that everyone present heard. So that soon, the word would spread across the kingdom far and wide. "I am the son of Lord Leyv Riis."

INTERLUDE
KING MAGNUS AABERG, THE WHITE
BEAR, PROTECTOR OF WINTER'S REALM

The king stared at the throne room's door and envisioned the line of commonfae standing outside, all waiting to see him. To hear his judgment.

He released a long breath. Was it not enough that the snow was melting? What more could these people want?

And then arose the question that continued to plague him: Had the Shadow King and those spiders finally finished Isolde off?

"Husband?" Inga asked. "The lords and ladies do not wish to wait all day."

Nor did she, though she did not say as much; it was clear from her annoyed tone.

The king stared down at the smattering of lords and ladies in the chairs below. All witnesses of the public requests made on the day. Among them were Warden Roar Lisika, Lady of Silks Nalaea Qiren, and the Master of Coin, Lord Airen Vagle—all fae he planned to keep close after the betrayals of Houses Virtoris, Balik, and Armenil.

"The sooner you're through here, the sooner you can deal with other issues," Inga added tersely.

By the dead gods, she was in a state. The king wondered if Rhistel was giving her trouble. Not that he'd dare to ask.

"Show the next in." Magnus waved a moon-pale hand through the air.

"Presenting Ragnor of Avaldenn, Your Majesty," a Clawsguard at the door announced the next in line.

A dwarf appeared. He wore simple, well-made clothing, and his long blond beard was tied in sections with leather cords. A kept-up appearance that was ruined when the dwarf got closer and the reek of onion and garlic wafted up the king's nostrils.

"Rise," Magnus drawled after the dwarf knelt. "What can I help you with today, Ragnor?"

"My king, I come with a request for a business expansion."

"What is your business?"

"I run a cart that sells hand pies. The best in the city." Ragnor puffed his chest out.

"We know your wares." Inga broke into the first smile that the king had seen on her face in days. "I favor the wild boar flavor, myself."

"Thank you, my queen. I'll be sure to send a few up after I leave here today."

"What sort of expansion are you requesting?" Magnus asked, already bored. His wife might be taken with the dwarf's cooking, but he only wanted to get through his tasks and move on.

"I would like to take advantage of the improving

weather and build a greenhouse on the outskirts of the city. In the allotment where a few local merchants have built theirs."

"To grow what?"

"Wheat, so I don't have to import it or buy it from others in the city. Perhaps vegetables for my pies too. Would be nice to have whatever variety I wished, my king. Not to mention more of everything. I'd like to expand my business."

"Hmm." Magnus drew a slender finger down the arm of his throne.

Those private greenhouses were owned by wealthy merchants, lords, and ladies. All of whom lined the king's pockets for allowing them to build their own greenhouses and grow whatever crops they pleased. The dwarf might be well-dressed, for a commoner, but Magnus did not think the pie cart owner was in league with those merchants, lords, and ladies who could pay more coin.

"I shall have to consider this request. Leave your information with the servant outside, and I'll have a messenger send word when I make my decision."

Ragnor's shoulders fell. "Thank you, Your Majesty." He paused. "Did you know that the owner of the oldest, most decrepit greenhouses died? I could knock that one down and build anew. Beautify the area a bit."

He had to hand it to the dwarf; he had balls. "Dismissed."

The dwarf filed out, and the Clawsguards showed in the next three subjects, all of whom bored Magnus to tears. When the fourth walked in, his hood up and hiding his face, the king did not think much of it. Before entering

Frostveil, guards searched each subject for weapons, and it was not so odd for fae to hide their faces. Particularly not if one had troll, orc, or goblin blood, making them less trustworthy to most. However, when the subject pulled a severed head from the folds of his cloak and tossed it to the bottom of the dais, the witnesses below gave a collective gasp.

Magnus sat up straighter. "What is the meaning of this?"

"This is, *was*, a vampire, King. One of the assassins sent to kill Princess Isolde. I heard there was a bounty on their heads, should someone be able to kill one. I am here to collect."

Magnus stared down at the head, and his attention locked on the fangs, extended in death and ready to bite. Or they had been until this fae got the better of the assassin. The death had to have been recent if the vampire wasn't already turning to ash.

The king had announced the bounty less than a week ago, and in that time, only two other Red Assassins had been caught and killed. Both by the local Assassin's Guild, not a random fae working alone. Reluctantly impressed, Magnus nodded. "Where's the rest of him?"

"Ah, well, our fight was near the docks. I decapitated him as he leapt and only caught his head. So I expect the body is somewhere at the bottom of the Shivering Sea." There was a hint of amusement in that tone.

The king's lips curled. He may have been willing to use the vampires to get rid of Isolde Falk, but now that the harlot was far from Avaldenn, he no longer wanted a single Red Assassin in his city making trouble when he had enough to deal with. Not that they cared what he, or any other fae, wanted. The bloodsuckers had come to his kingdom to hunt down Isolde, but since their arrival, a slew of deaths had penetrated the city. Drainings. Vampires liked little more than fae blood. Hence, the need for the bounty on their heads.

"Winter's Realm thanks you for your service—what was your name again?"

In answer, hands lifted and the fae removed his hood.

The king's heart stilled as a smile he'd seen only in the face of a tree blinded him.

"Érebo."

Magnus stood.

Below, the lords and ladies followed suit, some nearly falling out of their chairs; they were so taken aback by the king's sudden movement. Magnus swallowed, realizing how odd the reaction looked. How uncontrolled and unlike him.

But by the dead gods, how was this Shadow Fae standing among them?

"Husband?" Inga asked. "What's wrong?"

"Everyone out. I'll see no one else today," Magnus bellowed.

Lord Roar's spine straightened. "Majesty, there are at least one hundred more people in line. Don't you think—"

"*Leave.*"

The merchant witnesses rushed out of the room, followed swiftly by the lords and ladies of lesser houses. When only his wife, those of the Sacred Eight, and the Clawsguards remained, Magnus pointed to the door.

"Make no mistake, I meant all of you. My Clawsguards too."

Roar glared at Érebo but left with the others of his station. The Clawsguards saw them out, and Magnus turned to Inga.

"I'd like you to go too."

"Is that so?"

"Yes."

A silent battle of wills ensued, broken only when Érebo gave a soft cough.

"My queen, perhaps you do not know this, but your husband and I have a long history. From the rebellion days. We have much to catch up on, and clearly, I've caught him off guard."

Inga's eyes softened, buying the lie because she had no way of knowing that a Shadow Fae stood before her.

That Érebo, like Inga herself, could lie.

The queen nodded, and left, giving her husband one last long look before she shut the door to the throne room behind her.

"How are you here?" Magnus asked, sweeping down the steps.

"They came. A fight ensued, and incidentally I was freed."

"By they you mean Vale and Isolde?"

"And her twin. Thyra. Both bore shadow magic, as I thought they would. I have released it."

Magnus's stomach tightened. So the twin lived. He'd believed the rebellion against him was led by some pretender, or another Falk bastard. Had it been her all along?

Then the second part hit him.

The Falks had shadow magic. Just like the dangerous fae before him.

"They will seek allies," Érebo said. "In fact, they already found some. Their allies are how they escaped my cavern."

Magnus had an idea who the Falks would turn to for help. "Then we must discuss calling our own allies. And our own alliance."

The Shadow King had already given Magnus the Scepter. He'd held up his end of the bargain—and somehow he'd even gotten free of that blasted tree. The King of Winter didn't trust Érebo yet, but he knew this fae was a force to be reckoned with, and he wanted that kind of force on his side.

CHAPTER 9
ISOLDE

"Bleeding skies!" Sian's exclamation resonated through a room so silent you could have heard a sewing needle drop. High Lady Balik shot her eldest son a warning look, which he blatantly ignored. "Another Riis! You've got to be joking."

"Afraid not," Vale replied.

The high lord stood from his seat. "How did this stay hidden?"

Vale opened his mouth to respond, but Lord Balik shook his head. "I wish to hear it from Leyv."

I stiffened as Lord Riis came to stand beside my husband.

"It's as Vale says," Lord Riis stated, loud and clear. "I'm his birth father."

Lord Balik's lips parted. "And the Crown Prince's?"

"They *are* twins, Tadgh."

"It seems one can't be too sure about much of anything these days."

A soft snort left Sian.

"How was this hidden from the kingdom?"

I'd wondered this too, at first. The vast majority of fae couldn't lie, although, as a whisperer, Queen Inga was able to utter untruths. But the answer was far simpler than that.

Lord Riis inhaled deeply. "No one questioned the circumstances of their birth, and Queen Inga didn't say otherwise. After King Magnus claimed them as his, a father by actions and his own form of love, he was their acting father. I simply never mentioned my part. Why would I?"

"Lies by omission," Lord Balik took his seat once more. "So, Prince Rhistel is not the true heir. Rather, you are, Princess Saga."

My pink-haired friend cleared her throat. "Should my father keep his crown. Which I've already stated, I do not support."

"You renounce the throne and all the privileges it affords you?" Lord Balik asked.

Yes, being a princess came with enormous privilege. She lived a life most fae, even the well-off commoners, dreamed of. But there was one matter in which being a royal princess did not suit Saga, and it was a large thing to contend with.

Saga loved Sayyida Virtoris. Normal fae, maybe even those of lesser houses, were free to wed and create a family with whomever they wished. Saga, however, was royal and needed to further their line. First, she'd been betrothed to Vidar Virtoris, then to that snake, Roar—neither engagements were her choice.

If Saga renounced her blood right to the Crown of

Winter's Realm, she could have more freedom. It might still be odd for a high lady of the Sacred Eight to wed another lady, but it was not unheard of. At least two members of great houses past youngling-bearing age, and who had lost their husbands or wives, had done so. While Saga would not have that age on her side, if her father was dethroned, he'd be in no state to tell her, or anyone else, who to wed. And Thyra and I would not do as the king had done and force matches. If we won, Saga would be free to do as she pleased. Anyone would be.

"Yes," Saga said finally. "I would give up the throne. He may not be an Aaberg by blood, but Vale is worthy of being a King Consort. And as for Ne—Isolde, well, she has shown she possesses the grace, courage, and power to rule this realm well." Saga looked to Thyra. "I don't know Thyra well enough to say the same. But I trust in Isolde and Vale's judgment."

My heart warmed even as my sister scowled. Saga had great trust in me. And while my sister and I had not settled on who would rule, my friend saying those things meant the world.

Lord Balik leaned back in his chair as his wife spoke up.

"This is quite a lot to take in, but including both Prince and Princess Aaberg in the Falk court changes things, does it not, husband?"

He looked up at Lady Balik and smiled before training his gaze on my twin and me again. "My wife speaks the truth. I need to consider all that I've learned."

"We understand," Thyra said. "However, you should

be aware that there is more you need to know before deciding."

My stomach tightened, and inside, shadow magic swirled. I swallowed, hating my new power and how different it felt from my winter magic. How wrong and unpredictable.

"And what is that, Princess Thyra?"

"My sister and I stand against King Magnus not only because of what he did to our family, but because of who he aligns himself with now."

"Lord Lisika? House Ithamai and the Qirens?" Lord Balik's lips turned down at the mention of the last house. "They're powerful. I can see why you'd fear them and come knocking at my gate."

"Not them." Thyra matched his smirk. "King Magnus has aligned himself with King Érebo of House Nikao."

The Warden of the South's eyebrows pinched. "The name sounds familiar, but there is no ruling monarch in Isila with that name."

"There wasn't," I said. "Hasn't been for millennia. Not since Queen Sassa Falk trapped King Érebo in a tree and banished the rest of the Shadow Fae."

Another stillness took over the room, this one cold and with a sense of rising fear.

Lord Balik's brown cheeks had gone somewhat ashen. "You're saying that there's a Shadow Fae, a king of that race of fae, in Isila again?"

"The same one our ancestors fought during the Shadow Fae wars," I affirmed. "He's free and out for blood. King Magnus will oblige him because, thanks to our ancestry, their interests align."

"The Shadow Fae King will try to bring his people back, too," Thyra added. "And we can all guess what will happen if that occurs. How furious they must be to have been ripped from their world and placed into another. Or at least, that's what we think happened."

"They were banished via a gateway?" Lord Balik asked, using logic to fill in what my sister had not outright said.

"That is our working theory."

Luccan had confirmed that it was possible. Incredibly difficult, but possible. We were hoping to do research here to learn more *in* the Great Library of the South.

Murmurs began to ripple through the crowd, and fear shone on faces all around. But when Lord Balik lifted a hand, the room went silent once more.

"I need the entire story."

I folded my hands in front of me. "Would you like us to tell it now?"

"Later, after I've had time to consider." He stood. "You may stay within the walls of my castle. I will provide protection and my table, but that is all that I can promise."

I shot a sidelong glance at Thyra, saw the question of the rebels' safety climbing her throat. I shook my head. Now was not the time for that question. Only after we called House Balik a banner house could we seek sanctuary for the rebels.

I just hoped I was reading the signs right, and we truly had a chance to sway him to our side.

CHAPTER 10
VALE

orn of ale in hand, I leaned back in the armchair and rolled my neck to the side to gaze out the window.

A thousand faelights illuminated the streets of Myrr, and though there was no sea nearby, the Jewel of the Southlands reminded me of Avaldenn. Always bustling, always alive.

Many hours had passed since we'd spoken to the Warden of the South. Hours in which Lord Balik's household had shown us to our rooms and fed us. Hours of peace, familiarity, and a sense of safety. For the first time since leaving Riis Tower, those I loved were truly protected, and I could relax. A little, at least.

My mate, Thyra, Lord Riis, and the Fellhelm siblings were in a meeting with Lord Balik, so I would not be completely relaxed until I saw them again. Heard what Tadgh Balik had to say.

What was more, a part of me wrestled with the idea

that claiming my parentage today had been the right thing. Once word spread, and it would spread, my mother would be in danger.

But Isolde and I had discussed that at length with Saga. My sister insisted that Mother had known she'd be in danger soon enough—that maybe she'd even anticipated this. And Lord Riis had not appeared surprised or angry at my proclamation, so I had to believe I'd done the right thing. That the truth had finally come out for the better and my words might destabilize my father and Rhistel.

"I have to ask, Vale. Is it odd to call Neve by her birth name?" Sian drawled lazily. He was on his third horn of ale, while I remained on my first. Sipping. Waiting.

"No." The fire in the hearth crackled and popped, and the scent of burning wood seemed to intensify. "She spoke the name out loud today, but I've been seeing her as Isolde, as a Falk princess, for some time now."

I'd known that my wife would come out to the world as Isolde, just as I'd come out as Vale Riis.

"I've been practicing in my head," Luccan admitted. "For when the day came."

A grin split my face, as others shared a laugh, happy and easy. Of our traveling party, only Bac, Aleksander, Anna, and Clemencia had retired for the night. The vampire assassins had split, two guarding the Hallows that had been stored in sleeping chambers, and the third waiting outside the door where the princesses and the Warden of the South met.

Saga, Marit, and the Balik sisters lounged in front of

the fire, gossiping. Though separated for little more than three weeks, they talked as if they had a lifetime to catch up on.

"You don't want to go around calling a queen the wrong name." Luccan crossed his arms over his barrel chest, not finding the matter of his practice as funny as the rest of us.

"*Queen* is assuming Isolde takes the throne. And *that's* assuming we win." Caelo said.

"It's strange that the sisters haven't settled on who will sit the throne yet, no?" Sian asked.

"They only found one another a couple of weeks ago and had a lot to work through," Thantrel spoke up. His wings remained lightly bound with gauze, though to hear Rynni tell it before we left Valrun, Than's wings should heal very well. If not perfectly.

I sipped an ale tasting faintly of mountain berries. I wondered what Thantrel thought about Thyra taking the Crown of Winter. Or what he thought about his mate in general. She still had not claimed him.

"Ha!" Caelo shouted, startling me and a few others. His finger thrust toward Qildor. "I caught you staring at her again. Time to fess up. What's going on with you and Marit?"

"You two were holding hands in the grand hall," Duran pressed. "Are you together now?"

Qildor shared a long history with House Armenil— the direwolves of the far north. Before Qildor journeyed to the capitol and took his Clawsguard vows, he lived in Morial and was best friends with Connan Armenil, heir to the House of the Direwolf.

Or perhaps their lord now. I swallowed. We'd recently learned that Lord Sten Armenil died in service to King Magnus, which meant that Connan had likely already been elevated to his new title.

"She's married but not to me." Qildor stole another glance at the lady with the long red hair. She caught him this time and smiled back in a way that had me smirking.

"Doubt she cares much, friend." Caelo let out a low whistle. "From Marit, that sort of smile is as good as an invitation to climb into her bed."

Thantrel sniggered. "He's not wrong."

"You two would know best," Qildor teased.

Out of our friend group, Caelo and Thantrel were the two with the most experience with the ladies. I had to agree, though. I'd seen a grin like that on Isolde's face, usually right before she shoved me to a bed and had her way with me.

"I'm feeling jealous of all the romance in the air." Caelo wagged his sword-sharp brows. "Been traveling and protecting for too long. Do you think Lord Balik would have his guards stop me if I went to a tavern to find a lady of my own?"

"By the dead gods, Caelo, not everything is about you." Duran waved him off. "I want to hear the details, Qildor."

"What is there to tell? She's married. To Jarl Triam."

I cringed, the name bringing forth the horrible memory of the day the king had announced that betrothal. Marit had been utterly distraught. As had her family. All of that devastation had gone according to King Magnus's desire and plan.

Another reason he should no longer rule. No one should delight in seeing others so miserable.

"That murderous jarl has gone north to fight for the king," Sian said. "He left his wife at home, and you happened to scoop her up. The bastard didn't want a highborn wife that badly after all."

"I did *not* scoop her up." Qildor muttered. "Fates, you make her sound like a damsel or a treat to be gobbled down. She was trying to escape on her own, and I helped."

"After traveling south to break her out. You're not getting out of this without looking like the hero you are, Qildor. So stop trying." Sian crossed one ankle over his knee.

I stared at the knight, unable to believe that I hadn't worked it out sooner. "You forsook your Clawsguard oath to rescue her, didn't you, Qildor?"

He swallowed. Nodded.

My stomach pitted. No one here would care, especially not after the king had whipped Qildor nearly to the afterworld for bearing witness to my wedding. But if the King of Winter ever got his hands on my friend again—if any lord or lady loyal to Magnus did—they would kill my friend. They would call such a killing justice.

"Thyra and Isolde will wipe that marriage off the slate." Thantrel waved a nonchalant hand through the air. Perhaps I was the only one thinking about the broken vow, but I doubted it. Even for Than, his carefree tone sounded forced. He was trying to change the subject. "You may as well go woo the lady. It's clear you want to, and that she wants you in return."

"We'll see." Qildor took a deep drink of his ale, and I searched for a topic that would take the heat off of him.

I did not need to do so. Not with Filip, who had not said more than two words since we entered the den, took control of the conversation.

"So, what's going to happen to Prince Rhistel?"

And just like that, I wished we'd stayed on the topic of Qildor and Marit.

"I'm not sure," I admitted.

Not that those in the Falk Court hadn't spoken about it. If my brother harmed Isolde or her sister or anyone here, I'd beat him bloody. And yet, no matter how irredeemable my twin was, I still found it difficult to condemn him to death.

"Exile maybe." I swallowed.

"Right," Filip seemed to stare right through me. He was in the small group of those who knew Rhistel was a whisperer. Though Filip had learned from experience, not my lips. I hadn't shared that information with Sian, and we'd been friends since childhood.

Both of the remaining secrets I held burned within me, hotter by the day. I wasn't sure which was worse—that my wife, the love of my life, and her twin had shadow magic or that my mother and brother were whisperers.

A rumor that the Falks kept such dark powers secret for thousands of turns would suit Magnus's purposes of sowing distrust with regard to the Falk twins. Particularly when paired with the truth that the twins possessed no control over their shadow magic

"The matter of Prince Rhistel should be better thought through," Filip added, sourness obvious in his tone. I wasn't sure he'd ever liked Rhistel, but my squire had thoroughly despised my twin since the day he'd witnessed Rhistel trying to take advantage of Isolde in Frostveil's library.

"What do you want from me, Filip?" I retorted. "That I'll say my twin should die? Well, sometimes I do want that. Other times, I feel like an ogre for saying such things. It's complicated."

"You wouldn't have to do it," Filip countered.

"Why are you pushing him so hard on this?" Sian placed his elbows on his knees as he took in his younger brother. "This is unlike you."

"Perhaps I'm growing into my role," Filip replied. "If Father allies with the Falk sisters, I may end up being Lord Balik sooner than I'd like."

By the dead gods, I was a real arse. This wasn't all about me, but about what an impending war could do to a family. To the Balik family and thousands of others.

"Don't think like that." Sian aggressively tapped a finger on the arm of his chair.

"How can I not?" Filip gestured to our group. "If the worst happens in our family, you have us *and* them, Sian. Your cabal. I have only those who share our blood, and that will not be enough."

He wanted support. Of course he did. Filip had been very vocal about wishing to be in my cabal, and I'd always told him that he was too young. Thantrel too.

Things needed to change.

"I can't make promises of what will happen in the future, Filip, but I can offer you a place among us here and now." My gaze went to Thantrel. "You too, brother.

And Arie, I know you dream of the House of Wisdom, but Duran studies there, and he stands with us."

No one in the cabal countered that they were too young. No one said anything, and the high ladies had gone suspiciously quiet by the fire.

"I'm in," Filip and Thantrel answered in unison.

"Arie? We could use another sharp mind in the bunch."

"Fates, could we," Duran muttered.

The middle Riis brother cocked his head before nodding. "To my own surprise, I'm in too."

I raised my horn. "To the expanded cabal."

Filip waved a hand in the air. "Wait. There's no ceremony? No secret handshake or password?"

Duran barked out a laugh. "You think far too much of our ragtag group, young Lord Balik."

I shrugged. "We're a simple bunch."

"You do the right thing," Filip countered. "That's not always easy or simple, and that's why I want to join. Why I've wanted to join since Sian told me about the cabal."

Pride welled in me at the truth of his words. Standing with Isolde wasn't the first time I'd gone against the king's wishes. It was the most public occurrence, but I'd done so a hundred times with my cabal brothers at my side, righting wrongs done by King Magnus or others in power.

I lifted my horn again. "Don't make me try this a third time and look like a fool, Filip. This is the ceremony you're getting."

"Savor the simplicity," Caelo added. "Things are only going to get more complicated from today forward."

"Can't argue with that." Thantrel lifted his horn to the

middle. "To the cabal adding a stunningly attractive member, a brilliant one, and . . ." giggles came from the ladies as he looked at Filip, "a faerie who loves to play by the rules!"

Filip rolled his eyes as we toasted to the cabal and drank deeply.

CHAPTER 11
VALE

Aleksander's sword struck mine as the skin-changer pressed forward.

Sweat dripped down my spinal column, but I smirked, hoping to goad my sparring opponent into doing something stupid. To test if his training was well-rounded.

"Tell me, do all fylgjarns neglect their sword training for an escape behind the eyes of their animal?"

He snarled, lurched a step forward and pushed into me again with surprising strength. The smell of his sweat washed over me. "As if I don't feel your arm's trembling, oh brawny one."

A laugh tripped off my lips. After our first confrontation back at Valrun, I'd had little chance to get to know Aleksander, the most noticeable Hawk Seed among the rebels. Perhaps the only one. Given our time together, though, I was beginning to understand that my mate's half-brother was cheekier than I'd imagined. His appearance favored Isolde, but his attitude was a bit more like Thyra's.

I spun, the foreign steel sliding up and away. Before he could bring it back down, *Skelda* was there again, metal on metal, and I shoved him to the right. Aleksander stumbled backwards and fell to the stone floor. My sword tip hovered over his neck.

"Yield."

"Fates, fine! You win. As if everyone didn't already predict that."

I held out a hand. "Nice round. You should spar with Qildor next. He could teach you a thing or two."

"I'll take your word for it." Aleksander found his feet and glanced upward, as if searching for his hawk. His face fell when he seemed to remember that she was back at Valrun, waiting for Aleksander to take her over and inform the rebels if they'd be moving south or not. Still waiting for Lord Balik's word, as we all were.

"Who are you targeting next?" Aleksander asked.

"I believe you mean who am I teaching or practicing with?"

"Whatever you say."

"Actually, I'm taking a break." I darted a glance at Isolde and Thyra, sparring not too far away. Judging by the lack of strength and control in their motions, they'd finish soon. They were merely trying to out-stubborn the other.

"Next time then."

Aleksander and I parted, and I made my way around the perimeter of the vast training room. Swords continued to whine as they cut the air and metal clanged, both sounds that made me feel in my element.

I watched each match with a keen eye. If anyone required help, or might benefit from a pointer, I stored that information away to share later. As it turned out, there were many tips to give because it wasn't just the knights and warriors who had congregated in the training room after breakfast.

Much to my surprise, Saga, Marit, and the Balik sisters had opted to join too. Saga might never be a decorated soldier, and she did not naturally take to combat practice, but it brought me relief to know that she wanted to be stronger and able to defend herself.

The only people missing had good reason to be absent. The scholars—Duran, Clemencia, Arie, and Anna—were scouring the books we'd brought from Valrun Castle. Looking for information on Shadow Fae magic. Lord Riis was making himself scarce by visiting his brothels in Myrr. And Thantrel was back in the healers' sanctuary, hoping to be cleared to train as normal.

On the very far side of the room, three blurs fought one another. The vampire sisters. My fingers flexed keenly around *Skelda's* grip. Once Sian and Thordur finished their rounds, we might form a trio to go up against the Red Assassins.

I paused my rounds and contented myself with watching Sian use his light magic to tease Princess Bavirra as they sparred. The dwarven princess never angered over the jabs of light that Sian flung at her between blows. Perhaps because she was finally living out her dream—far away from her kingdom, walking the wider realm. I recalled the first time I'd been tasked with leading an army against an orc horde. It felt like having an adventure too.

"Stars, you'd think that Thyra wouldn't be quite so vicious, seeing that she loves me now." My mate appeared at my side, sweat beading her forehead and smelling strongly of smoked vanilla. I pulled her close, savoring the feel of her, the muscle she had put on beneath the soft curves that I'd admired when we first met. I planted a kiss on the top of her head.

"What good would that do you, sister?" Thyra sang, her tone smug, only paces behind her twin. "We're training for war. Not a hair braiding competition."

Isolde snorted. "Not that I'd win that either."

"Correct."

Last night, Lord Balik had merely asked more questions, not delivered the sisters an answer to their question of an alliance. Since then, the Falks had been on edge, but sparring seemed to be a good way for Isolde and Thyra to distract themselves.

"Didn't you say you had something to do?" Isolde retorted, a fresh pink hue rising in her cheeks.

Her twin sniggered. "I'm on my way out."

She swaggered out of the room, clearly pleased with how she'd performed that day. And how she'd gotten a rise out of her twin.

"She was tiring, too," I assured my wife. "I could tell."

"Not quickly enough."

"She's been training and fighting longer than you, Force. Don't let it get you down." My fingers laced through hers. "And it seems like your sister might enjoy goading you as much as sparring with you. Don't make that easy on her either."

Isolde looked up at me from beneath those long eyelashes. Tempting me even if she did not mean to. "I'm not bad by any means—"

"Far from it. For someone who has been training only a few moons, you've learned quickly."

"*But* it seems like I should learn faster. Who knows who I'll find myself face to face with next week?" She rolled her neck out.

"Are you sore?"

"No but I am feeling off today. The magic inside me is restless and acting odd. I can't pinpoint why though." Her palm rested against her belly as if trying to calm the darkness inside her.

She didn't have to explain that she meant her shadow magic.

I pulled her closer and sealed her lips with mine. My mate tasted as sweet as ever and it took great restraint to not sweep her off her feet and return to our suite.

"Will Thyra return?" I asked when we came up for air. "I could show you a few moves to knock her off her feet."

Isolde smirked. "Not any time soon. She was going to check on the Scholars and then rest."

"Rest?"

"I guess she didn't sleep well. Last night we brought up the matter of the rebels, and Thyra is worried that even if Lord Balik allies with us, he will not accept them. I think she also worries about the Frør Crown being left alone." Isolde patted the sword at her side. The legendary Sassa's Blade. "A sword fits in better than a crown."

The Frør Crown, a Hallow of Winter's Realm, like Sassa's Blade and the Ice Scepter, had not affected me as it had my mate, and yet I still did not trust the thing. It had once shown Isolde a vision. One that combined with the fact that the Crown had heated and cooled as we walked through the mountain towards the Shadow King, made me think it was manipulative.

Isolde gestured to where many of our friends still battled. "Watching Qildor today made me realize I don't know all of my friends' powers."

"You didn't get to spar with him at Frostveil. He was too injured from the whipping."

"Yes, and I didn't know Marit wielded earth magic. Back at the castle, Sayyida only trained her with weapons." She let out a breath. "To be fair, I also forgot that Sian is such a good light wielder."

She stared in the direction of my friend, who let off a blast of light so powerful, we both looked away, Isolde scrunching up her face as she did so. "Back in Avaldenn, I had no magic, so I focused on taking in the details of swordplay."

"House Balik isn't called the Golden House just because they possess an abundance of gold. They're famous for producing many limiters. Baenna is one too."

"What about Eireann and the other Baliks?"

"Eireann has winter magic, like Filip, but not as powerful, which is why though she's older, he's the heir. Eireann wields her magic as frozen water. I'm not sure about the other four Balik children. They didn't come to court as often as those you know well."

"Yesterday I only saw two teen girls and a boy who I didn't recognize."

"One is a baby. Likely with their maid."

"*Ah*. Another large family, like in Dergia. They're blessed." A wistful look crossed her face. We'd rarely spoken of our future life beyond saying that we both wished for younglings.

"Perhaps one day, we'll have that," I said softly. "If that's what you want. And if the stars see fit to give us such blessings."

Her face swept up, and her violet gaze met mine. "More than anything, I crave family. Of course, I already have it with you, Saga, my sister, and my friends, and maybe it's greedy, but I want *more*. Do you?"

"I want as many younglings as you and the dead gods see fit to give us."

She kissed me again, her curves pressing into the harder lines of my body in a way that made me ache. Fates, would I ever get enough of my mate? It did not seem possible.

"Sorry to break up this love fest," a voice cut through our moment and when we broke apart, it was to find Aleksander, Bac, and Qildor standing a few paces away.

"Back for more?" I asked the fylgjarn.

"I wasn't the one who needed a breather," Aleksander teased back. "But not quite. We were talking about something and wondered if you'd considered it."

"Don't make us wait forever before you get on with it, brother," Isolde teased.

Aleksander's face softened as he sent a wink at my mate.

Since learning that he had not one but two sisters, Aleksander had taken every chance to get to know Isolde. To bond. She grinned, which was likely what he'd wanted, and he resumed training his attention on me. "You're the Warrior Bear, Vale."

"That's what they call me." I might no longer identify as an Aaberg, but the nickname was better than being called the Warrior Ice Spider.

"You've built a career fighting with the king's army. You must have made friends with officers. Or just loads of regular soldiers."

"Of course." As a prince, I'd never gotten too close to most of them. That would have been inappropriate. However, I had a few officers I called friends.

"How many would switch sides and fight for you, if you asked?"

Aleksander's question hit me like a blow to the chest. I'd often thought of having to fight the males and females I'd stood with in the army, but to ask them to risk their lives and turn traitor?

"You're asking that risk of the great houses and their armies," Bac pressed. "Why not those you know from battle?"

"Unlike the lords and ladies of the great houses, regular soldiers and officers do not have thick castle walls to protect them."

Should anyone who remained loyal to House Aaberg find a letter I sent by raven, its recipient would face a swift and brutal execution. Likely at the hands of the king.

"A war amongst noble houses puts them in danger anyway."

It was true. No matter which way the wind blew, those

fae were about to be thrown into a war. Perhaps it was better to give them a choice as to which side to fight for.

"It will be difficult for them to find us outside the battlefield," I murmured. "We'd have to face them and offer them sanctuary right away. No questions asked, otherwise, it's not fair to risk their lives."

"I think it's a good idea," Isolde said. "There has to be a good number of them that will switch sides. You're loved among those in the army, Vale."

"And if we can sway House Virtoris, they will bring the Nava," Qildor added. "Have you contacted Vidar?"

"Not yet. Though Saga said she wrote to Sayyida on her journey south to tell her that she'd left court."

Qildor cleared his throat, an indication that he did not approve. "A raven should be winging their way to the island right now."

We'd planned to seek the alliance of House Virtoris in person, though to do so would cost us time. Weeks, if not a full moon. Sending a raven, though not traditional, would be faster. And if I sent it to Vidar rather than the Lady of Ships, he'd be far less inclined to see it as a slight.

"How much do you think they know?" I asked.

Qildor had been a Clawsguard before deserting. He'd lived at Frostveil and was in proximity to lords and ladies and their gossip.

"At least that Isolde is standing against the king," Qildor said. "And since they've left the mainland, it's safe to say that their own family has done so as well."

"Do it, Vale," Isolde whispered. "A letter isn't the best way, but it saves time. We need all the help we can get."

I slipped my fingers through hers. "Once I'm done

here, I'll send a few ravens to army officials and trusted infantry. And to Vidar."

Isolde beamed at the others. "Good ideas, you three."

"We should get back to training," Qildor smiled at Isolde. He'd never been one to linger in praise.

I nodded. "I'll join soon."

They were about to leave when my mate spoke. "Bac?"

He turned.

"Have you talked to anyone in House Balik yet? Sian or Filip?"

He shook his head. "It's not the right time." A pause passed between us. "And I'm nervous."

"Would you like me to? Or would you like to join Thyra and me at the library? Lord Balik might not grant our other requests, but I can't see why he wouldn't let us into the Great Library of the Southlands while he makes up his mind. We planned to request leave soon."

Bac's face lit up. His mother had been a librarian at that very house of knowledge where she'd met his father, Tadgh Balik's brother. "I'd like that. Thank you."

"Anytime."

They departed and pride welled inside me. "I love how you always consider others."

She let out a soft laugh. "I don't *always*."

"More often than you think." I squeezed her tight, and when I released her, she let out a contented sigh.

"I guess I should get back in the ring. Maybe Bavirra and I—"

"Princess Isolde?"

A well-dressed servant had slipped into the facility and

was striding our way, flanked by two faerie guards. The servant was a dryad with black, bark-like skin and eyes the same color as gold autumn leaves. Most notably, he had three arms, the third sprouting from just below his right arm.

"Yes?"

"Lord Balik would like to speak with you, Princess Isolde," the servant said. I was willing to bet that he was Tadgh's personal butler. "And your sister."

"Great. I bet she's in her room."

"She's not."

Isolde's eyebrows pinched together. "You're sure?"

"I checked the rooms before coming here. No one was there, and I thought you might know where she is."

"Did you check the den near our suites? She had planned to stop by and see our friends."

"She's not there either."

Isolde let out a soft hum before the confusion left her face, and a sly grin replaced it. "I might have some idea of where to find her."

CHAPTER 12

ISOLDE

I bit back the squeal of glee when I found my sister exactly where I predicted she might have gone—to the healing sanctuary.

Thyra kept Thantrel at arm's length, but I'd caught her stealing glances. I'd watched her twist his way and saw how she tilted her head in his direction when he spoke. I'd suspected something was changing inside her.

There she was, sitting at his bedside as a healer applied fresh gauze around his wings, talking with him. Secretly talking. Some might call it *flirting*.

I was pretty sure Thantrel did. He hadn't spotted me yet, hovering outside the door to his room, but I'd rarely seen him smile so widely.

Stars, if only Vale had come with me. He'd be elated to witness such a sight.

My wish to let them continue bonding warred with my desire to speak with Lord Balik. In the end, the latter won out. I cleared my throat. "Sister."

Thyra jumped up from her chair and spun. Her cheeks, normally as pale as mine, stained pink.

"I just stopped by."

"Fifteen minutes ago," Thantrel crowed.

I couldn't help but laugh.

"You must not have spoken with the Scholars for very long, huh Thyra?"

"They found nothing." She rolled her eyes. "And then I was going to my room, as I said I would, but the sanctuary was on the way."

"A twisty sort of way, I suppose." I shrugged.

It was Thantrel's turn to laugh, and my ear detected a heaping amount of satisfaction in his joy.

"Oh hush. The both of you. What do you want, Isolde?" She was irritated at being caught, but even so, as she said my name, her face loosened. Thyra had disliked that I'd clung to a slaver's name. I understood her reasoning, felt it a bit myself, but I'd needed to move at my pace to claim my birth name.

"Lord Balik has summoned us."

"Let's go then." She stepped away from the bed.

"No kiss goodbye?" Thantrel's lips puckered, and he made kissing noises.

"You should just be happy I graced you with my presence." Thyra strode my way, tossing her words over her shoulder as she went.

"I always am, love." Another sly grin spread across his face. "Especially when you wish to be so clandestine about our meetings. I *love* a secret romance!"

"By the dead gods, I never should have saved him

from that spider," Thyra muttered as we left the sanctuary and joined our escort, a butler who, since our initial meeting in the training room, had introduced himself as Valintin.

Knowing how one's mate could scatter their thoughts, I allowed my twin a few moments to pull herself together and enjoyed taking in the sights of the castle. Before our arrival, Vale had said that Ramshold was beautiful, and he was not mistaken.

Beautiful art lined each corridor. Many of the paintings and tapestries showcased the mountainside in which Myrr rested or fae who, judging by their appearance, had to be of House Balik. We'd passed through a domed intersection of six hallways with a chandelier made of gold and dripping emeralds when Thyra broke our silence.

"What do you think he'll say?"

No need to question who 'he' was. In this instance, there was only one fae who mattered.

"I don't know." I dropped my voice. Valintin walked five paces ahead. But I didn't want him listening in. "Vale's certain Lord Balik will side with us, but I don't think he expected to have to wait so long. That makes me question things."

Less than a day, but it felt longer. Felt more dire. Life or death, which for my twin and me and so many others who were loyal to us, it was.

"What if he denies us? Do we flee?"

I swallowed. If we left Myrr, where would we go? To Lord Riis's estate in Bitra?

Not an option I wished to consider. I wasn't sure I could ever trust Lord Riis again and the city where he ruled, Bitra, posed an issue. It was too close to Avaldenn, and the Riis army, the dwarves of Dergia, and the rebels combined, would not be enough to protect Bitra if King Magnus struck with the combined force of multiple armies. Waiting and planning in the far south was preferable.

"One step at a time," I replied, to which Thyra frowned.

We climbed a winding set of stairs to a part of Ramshold I had not seen yet. At the top, the vast corridor was stunningly quiet. No servants swept through the area, busy and barely taking notice of Thyra and me. We had to be in a private wing.

My suspicion was proven correct when the escort stopped before a door with two guards posted outside and knocked.

"Enter," a voice called from inside.

One guard opened the door, and the butler entered.

"You found them, Valintin?" the Warden of the South asked from where he sat behind a desk.

"We did," Valintin replied. "Would you like me to wait here?"

"Outside."

With his topmost right arm, Valintin waved us inside, and the door shut behind us.

"Princesses, please sit." Lord Balik sat behind a vast desk, papers stacked on one side, taking up a quarter of his space. The rest of the study was neat as a sewing pin, with not a book out of place, despite the fact that hundreds of books lined three of the four walls.

We sank into hunter green chairs as one, and before I'd had time to situate myself, Thyra struck.

"So? What's your answer?"

Lord Balik let out a soft chuckle.

"You've waited twenty turns to reclaim the Throne of Winter. What are you in such a hurry for?"

"Nearly twenty-one turns," Thyra corrected him.

My lips parted. She was right. Our twenty-fourth namedays were fast approaching. From one of my mother's old writings, I'd recently learned that the exact date of my birth was the twenty-first day of the twelfth moon. Winter Solstice.

"Clearly you felt every single turn." He stared at my sister. "For Isolde, things must be going fast."

Six moons ago, I'd been a blood slave to vampires. I had known nothing about my past. Now, I fought to avenge my family, save a kingdom from a tyrant, and had friends and family members whom I loved.

"I have decided." He leaned forward and tented his brown, slender-fingered hands on the desk. "I will allow the rebels to enter Myrr. And I will ally with you against Magnus and the Shadow King."

My heart leapt.

"*With conditions,*" Lord Balik added.

I shoved down my excitement, ready to do business. After all, I'd been prepared to negotiate. After learning we'd be coming south, Thyra and I had created a list of things the Warden of the South might want and discussed what we'd be willing to give. Now we learned what motivated the honorable Tadgh Balik.

"Which are?" my sister drawled, as if the idea of negotiating bored her. A good act.

"The rebels must remain in a guarded portion of the city during their stay in Myrr."

"What?!"

"Did you expect them all to stay in my home? Hundreds of people whom I do not know?"

"No, but I didn't expect them to be treated like animals either. Caged and kept away from others."

"They won't be caged. I didn't say that, nor did I intend to insinuate such a thing," Lord Balik corrected. "They will stay in a specific neighborhood where they will have all the comforts they're used to. More actually, considering I doubt there has been a bakery in the town of Valrun for a good long while."

"We have money from trading. We can rent homes."

"Rebels have attacked my people before, Princess Thyra. They have made their lives difficult because of my loyalties to King Magnus. My people paid a price that was not theirs to pay. I won't fault the rebels for past deeds but nor will I allow rebels into my city and put my subjects in a state of fear." He stared my sister down, and she glowered back. Both fae cared deeply about those they'd made promises to. "The rebels will be contained and cared for like my people, but they will not have free rein in the city. Not until I am sure they are trustworthy. I will not budge on this. Do you understand?"

Thyra continued to glare at Lord Balik. I feared she'd deny him. Then where would we be? I couldn't risk it and as he'd said, the rebels would be safe, I didn't see a reason to.

"That's acceptable," I said. "We would, of course, like to see where they'll be living. And have those in our court be able to visit them to check on them."

"Granted."

"Those already in the castle will stay too, right? All of us?" Most of those who had come with us to Myrr were my friends. Bac and Aleksander, however, were rebels through and through.

"Yes."

"And my other advisor and our last three Valkyrja." Thyra's chin jutted out.

Lord Balik gave her a small smile. "I would not dream of separating two princesses from their advisors and guards. Are the rest of your Valkyrja vampires as well?"

Last night, after he'd gotten over the shock of seeing their kind, the vampire sisters had intrigued the Warden of the South.

"A faerie, a dwarf, and a half-orc."

"Very well, I was merely curious." He hadn't balked at the mention of a half-orc, which was more than I could say for myself. Tonna might find other fae like herself in the southernmost city of Winter's Realm.

"And on the matter of an alliance?" I wanted to move things along. "What stipulations do you have there?"

"You came with a great house and a kingdom long-thought dead already on your side. I do not know what you promised them for their part in your war efforts, but I require a betrothal."

My throat dried up. "I'm wed to Prince Vale—"

"Not from you." His attention swept over Thyra. "I recognize that you are mates with Thantrel Riis. I learned that you have chosen not to acknowledge that bond."

Lord Riis must have told him. Annoyance rose at the spymaster.

"That's true," Thyra said.

"If you still have not accepted your bond by the time the war is over, you will wed my eldest son, Sian."

I cringed.

Lord Balik caught the motion. "What is it, Isolde?"

I swallowed. This was very much not my business, but if I said nothing, I'd regret it. After all, Sian was a friend. I didn't want to put him in a bad position. Or a marriage that was not to his liking. "Ah, I'm not sure that is something Sian will . . . enjoy."

"You think I don't know my son's preferences, is that it?"

"I wasn't sure."

"I do. Nevertheless, he must do his duty to our line. Especially if we win this war. Blood ties will help rebuild the kingdom."

I looked at Thyra. This was her concession to make or not. I wouldn't be the one to force her to wed.

"I agree with your condition," my sister said boldly. "However, what happens if I accept my bond with Thantrel before the war is done?"

Had we not been in negotiations, I would have squealed. As it was, I barely contained myself.

"Then one of my grandchildren. Or my youngest boy, who is still a babe, will wed one of your children. I want my line to marry into the line of whomever sits the throne, which the pair of you should settle on soon."

"I agree," I said.

If that was all he wanted, we had gotten off easily. I could hardly imagine a better family to be connected to. The only issue would be if my children or Thyra's children didn't get along with any Balik descendants or heirs. As I had no power over that, I chose not to worry.

"As do I," Thyra said.

"My last stipulation is you do everything in your power to keep my children safe." He glanced to the side.

I followed his gaze to find a family portrait, newly done because the baby was included.

"Sian and Filip will wish to fight with you. As it's their war as much as mine, I won't stop them. Eireann, Baenna, Saoirse, and Fionn are of fighting age, too. Please, do all that you can to keep them safe."

My heart clenched. This was the heart and soul of Lord Balik. His family.

"Yes," I said seriously, feeling the request in my own heart. "I don't know Saoirse or Fionn, but I love Eireann, Baenna, Filip, and Sian and would never want to cause them heartache. I'll watch out for all of them."

"As will I," Thyra agreed.

He leaned back, as if assessing us.

"I have a stipulation of my own that I'd like to add." The words were out of my mouth before I could reconsider if this was the right time.

"You do?" The question was plain in my sister's tone. I'd not discussed this with her beforehand. Nor had I made this request of Lord Riis for his oath had come as a surprise and then I'd learned of his betrayal.

I gave a nod. "You alluded to my past as a blood slave, Lord Balik. It's common knowledge now."

"It is," the high lord replied.

"Then it should come as no surprise that under my family's rule, matters regarding the keeping of human slaves will change."

Silence hung in the air, uninterpretable, so I plowed onward. "I understand that it will take time to integrate them into fae society, but humans live alongside and with fae in Dergia and that is what I wish to accomplish in the wider Winter's Realm. I want them to be free and able to live as any fae."

Lord Balik stared at me, but Thyra's gaze dropped to her hands.

Finally, the high lord broke the silence I'd left. "I'm glad you know that such an endeavor will take time because it surely will. Not only the logistics, but to change fae hearts and minds on where humans stand in our culture." He cleared his throat. "That being said, I'm in support."

"You'll free your slaves? Once the war is done?"

Ideally freedom would come now, but I was already asking so much, and to free people when the fae who could protect them was otherwise occupied seemed like it would not work. And what would happen if we lost? King Magnus would not care to protect the humans.

"I will," Lord Balik agreed. "Not that we have many slaves here, just the odd human who wanders through a portal and finds themselves in the southlands."

I sat up taller. "You don't keep them through the generations?"

"None. Just like in the Autumn Court, where some of my ancestors hail from. Our slaves are actually paid a small fee and work in Ramshold. Only here—for their safety. However, if the kingdom can change their views, I have no problem setting them free and providing them a means with which to start their lives."

"Wonderful." I exhaled a breath that had been trapped in my chest.

He gave an approving nod. "Anything else?"

"Nothing."

"Then I expect you'll want a ceremony to make my binding to you public?"

"Yes," Thyra said.

"Tonight then." He stood.

I blinked. He'd known about the dwarves, about how they'd asked for Dergia to be independent from the rest of Winter's Realm. And yet, neither Lord Riis nor Lord Balik had asked for much.

The Warden of the South took in my reaction while rounding the desk. "You think I request too little, Princess Isolde? That I would want to be king in the south? That I should want more power?"

Stunned that he read me so easily, I blinked. "It crossed my mind."

"I have all that I want and more. My family, my city, and my people. I don't need a wider realm, and if I can find a queen who is fair and just, that's enough for me."

No wonder Vale thought highly of this lord. And that Tadgh Balik was seen as honorable and wise. I understood now.

"Speaking of your city, we have one more request. It's

regarding that library everyone talks about." Thyra latched on to an opportunity before I'd had time to let his words sink in. "Might we visit it? And bring a few of our court? We have some research to do regarding the Shadow Fae."

Lord Balik's eyes widened at the mention of that long-lost race of fae. "Indeed. I'll take you there myself."

INTERLUDE
PRINCE RHISTEL AABERG, HEIR TO WINTER'S REALM, HOUSE OF THE WHITE BEAR

Deep in the cavern of his mind, the prince waited and gathered his strength. For a moment in time. A heartbeat. An instant to break free from his mother's hold.

Since the day she'd taken control, the queen had not delved further into his thoughts. Rhistel wondered if it was because he'd threatened her so often that first day that she'd grown tired of hearing his thoughts. Or maybe his resolve to kill his sister had shaken her, and she was fearful of what else she might find. If so, she was right to fear him.

Nothing and no one would stand in his way and take the throne he'd been promised. Not even kin.

He exhaled, placid on a settee, his body docile as his mother wished while he tracked that very female across the solarium. Warmth and the scent of plants and dirt enveloped him. Not uncomfortable, but not to his taste either. In his heart, frost and snow and ice reigned.

The queen, on the other hand, adored the solarium. The prince had known it would only be a matter of time until she dragged him to the humid room, so he'd made a plan.

"Set that one just over there," the queen instructed two servants, brawny dwarves carrying a potted plant fresh off a ship from the Summer Kingdom. Rhistel wondered how soon those ships would stop arriving in the harbor of Avaldenn. If there was a war trade would surely be affected.

The dwarves did as she requested, and the queen smiled.

"That will be all for today."

Dismissed, the servants exited, leaving only the prince, the queen, and the Clawsguards at the door. Rhistel stood, and the motion caught his mother's attention.

"Do you need something?" the queen asked.

"To move. I've grown quite stiff of late."

She didn't allow him to leave her side, save for when he required a toilet or sleep. In those moments, Queen Inga tightened her grip on her son and released it only slightly in his presence. Enough for him to speak and interact with those who might address him, all the while avoiding topics the queen did not wish him to indulge in. The queen's power was a suffocating vise around his body, and at night it was worse. If he broke free, it had to be during the day, in a place where the queen was at ease.

She waved her hand. "Get some exercise, my son."

My son. How dare she use that term. As if she wasn't choking the life from him.

"A million thanks," Rhistel hissed, making his derision plain.

The queen merely shrugged. She had no remorse for

what she was doing to him, for making it clear that he, of all her children, was the least loved. The one she was willing to sacrifice.

Their forbidden magic should have bonded them but instead it had torn them apart. Had made the queen distrust her eldest. He saw it even as a youngling, and he never forgot.

No matter. He walked among the plants. *Soon, she'll no longer have power over me.*

The room stretched long and housed many plants. Hundreds. Some of them grew tall enough to reach the ceiling, and all that greenery muffled noise. This place was one of the spaces in which his mother had often brought him and Vale to teach Rhistel his magic. Hidden by tall ferns and showy flowers, Rhistel had dived into his brother's mind again and again and again. But learning whispering magic wasn't all that happened here. Occasionally, the queen would see fit to teach them about the various plants she'd imported. Neither Vale nor Rhistel cared much, but the heir absorbed knowledge easily.

Many of the plants were medicinal. Six in the room were poisonous to varying degrees. The *bláth aislinge,* a flower native to the Autumn Court with distinctive pale-blue pointed petals, was among the most poisonous. If ingested, its pollen would induce a haze and sometimes even full-blown hallucinations—of which Rhistel was familiar for he'd taken the plant recreationally many times.

He located the plant, picked a few flowers from the lush bush, and stuffed them in his pocket, wiping off some of the light blue pollen that dusted the silk of the prince's

Aaberg blue shirt. A quick glance around told him his mother was nowhere in sight, but it wouldn't do to rush back to where her wine goblet waited. She might suspect something.

So he continued to meander through the solarium, and stopped to gaze out upon the city and the Shivering Sea. In the distance, Virtoris Island jutted out of the water. Rhistel scowled. That family would soon pay for the disrespect they'd shown the throne.

Even if King Magnus's blood did not flow through his veins, Rhistel still considered him a father. The king had raised him. Had tutored him.

Lord Riis? He'd interacted with Rhistel at court, and given him a few gifts over the turns, but they had never bonded. He was no father, blood or not.

Somewhere in the solarium, his mother began to hum and the soft sounds of scissors cutting and falling leaves indicated the moment was right. Moving as quickly as he dared, he returned to the settee, and after affirming that his mother was still deep in the vegetation, Rhistel pulled out the flowers. He filled his own goblet again but tossed the contents of his mother's into a nearby pot. Then, he tapped the pollen into the carafe of wine.

Blue dust floated down into the liquid. He didn't need much pollen, but to be safe, he tainted the wine with more than he'd ever used. Once done, he swirled the decanter, mixing the pollen in well, and poured his mother a fresh glass.

Then, he sat back and waited.

Many minutes passed before the queen strolled out of

the sea of green, a soft smile on her lips that vanished when she saw him.

"How was your walk?" she asked.

"Fine. The water looks calm today." He didn't care for the plants, but that he watched the sea was believable. The heir had always liked the water.

"It has been for days," she agreed and, as he'd hoped, lifted her goblet to her lips.

The queen drank. One sip. Two. Three. Apparently, pruning plants proved strenuous work, for when she set the goblet down again, half the wine was gone.

"It's time to return to your room while I bathe," his mother said.

He rose. The pollen didn't take long to work, and he would recognize when it did because his power diminished when he took the pollen. Hence, his mother's hold over him would too.

They made it to the door when her control faltered. Not enough for him to break free, but enough to feel. The time was growing close. The Clawsguards fell into step behind them, and they continued on, mother and son spending an inordinate amount of time together lately.

Down one corridor they went, and turned into another, and his mother stumbled. She grabbed onto the wall, catching herself, while he tested the boundaries around his mind. Flexible. *Breakable.* Victory swelled inside him and no longer able to wait, he struck.

She gasped, sensing his escape, and whirled upon him, but the intoxicating pollen had taken hold, and her eyes had glazed over.

Before the guards took notice, Rhistel slipped off one of

his ice spider silk gloves and took his mother by the hand. Skin touched skin and his magic, free after so many days, sank into her. Immediately it arrested his mother's power, which felt weaker. Drugged, just like the queen herself.

"You're out of sorts, Mother," Rhistel said, deceptive care in his voice as his magic delved deeper, harder into her, twisting her own powers into a cage of his making. He had her. "Perhaps a long rest is in store?"

She blinked heavily. "Yes. I think so." Her tone had taken on that flat quality he'd heard and hated in his own. It might have taken him much longer than he wished, but his practice and planning had paid off. He'd bested his mother.

Do not leave your suite until I say that you can, he commanded.

Rhistel turned to the Clawsguards. "See the queen to her rooms."

"Of course, Your Highness," the more senior guard replied. "Would you like one of us to escort you to yours?"

Since Isolde and Thyra Falk had become a genuine threat, the Clawsguards were increasingly careful about leaving the royal family alone. Even if they requested privacy.

"No," Rhistel said. "I have other plans."

Unsurprisingly, the prince found the king in his personal library.

The small space filled with books and warmth from an

ever-burning hearth was a retreat for Rhistel's father. He allowed only his family, and a select few others inside. However, today, a male the prince didn't recognize sat across from the king.

The stranger dressed in a style of clothing common in old paintings, the attire centuries out of style. He had long black hair, nearly black eyes, and pale skin that made him appear almost vampiric, but his ears were pointed. No wings, or he had glamoured them. Perhaps they were ugly, mutilated things?

The king rose, confusion clear in his gaze. "Rhistel, I didn't think you'd be joining us."

"I expect not." He sneered. "But I'm feeling much more myself."

Understanding flashed across the king's features. "Your mother?"

King Magnus didn't love Inga, but he respected her. As an extension of his house, he protected the queen. Rhistel didn't think that would last for long.

"She's much like I was." The prince strode deeper into the room and turned his back on the stranger. "I came here to speak with you. In private."

"Very well," the king replied. "Érebo if you wouldn't mind—"

"I would mind," the other fae said.

Prince Rhistel spun on the spot. *No one* spoke to his father like that. But this fae, Érebo, only smirked at Rhistel's astonishment.

"Who are you to talk to my father that way?" Rhistel glowered before his gaze slid to the male who had raised him. "It's bad enough that Lord Roar is becoming so familiar, but I don't even know this person."

The stranger rose and acted as though the prince had not spoken. "We are allies, are we not, King Magnus? And before you arrived, Prince, your father and I were speaking of the war against the Falks. If what you have to say is so important, you will say it before me."

This stranger saw himself as the heir's equal. Rhistel's fists clenched. "You dare command me?"

The odd-looking fae did not fail to notice, and his lips curled with amusement. "You're not one to back down. I can respect that, and since we'll be working together for some time, I shall be the one to bend a little in your direction."

"Meaning?" Rhistel gritted out.

"I will give you the courtesy of a full introduction." He inclined his head. "I am not some random fae. Not a wealthy merchant, or even a great lord. No, Prince, I am King Érebo of House Nikao, ruler of the Shadow Isles."

"Shadow Isles . . . But no one has lived there for thousands of turns," Rhistel replied.

He'd studied the histories of the lost fae culture. Some would say he'd been obsessed with them. Many accounts claimed that two of the Shadow Isles themselves weren't even there any longer. That the land had disappeared, like the fae who had called them home so long ago. In their place, mountains of shadows swirled on the water, a caution to ships. "Are you saying you rule yourself? If so, I fail to see why my father would want you as an ally."

Érebo chuckled. "I rule a people long banished by Queen Sassa Falk—my duplicitous mate. I rule a people who I plan to see return to Isila, with the help of your father."

Érebo . . . the prince remembered a name long lost to history. King Érebo of House Nikao, ruler of the Shadow Isles, the name this male claimed was his own.

The hair on Rhistel's arms stood on end, and he was thankful that the sleeves of his silken shirt covered them. Something told him this fae would catch that small tell.

"How are you alive? And here?" Rhistel asked.

"I've been alive all this time, my body testing the limits of age and vitality as faekind knows it. And as for where I've been—I was in the far west of your kingdom. Trapped within a Drassil tree."

Was this a joke? Rhistel studied the male, was tempted to reach out and touch his mind, when the king spoke again.

"And as I was stuck in that tree for so long, I understand why you do not want me here, Prince Rhistel. Also, I can guess at what you wish to discuss with your father."

"I doubt it."

"You think your mother did not pray to the Faetia and the dead gods before the Drassils? That she did not beg them to keep her secret?" King Érebo's reply sent Rhistel's stomach plummeting. "The trees are all connected, and during my imprisonment, I learned how to see through them. Hence, I know her secret. *And yours.*"

A long pause drew out between the three males, a pause in which Rhistel considered killing the fae.

"Don't you think a fae who has learned many secrets would be worth teaming up with, Rhistel?" The King of

Shadows made it sound like more of a statement than a question.

"Tell me what you know first." Rhistel's studies told him that Shadow Fae, unlike fae from other cultures, could lie. It was yet another quality that made their kind feared. It was what made him so like them, for whisperers could lie too.

The Shadow King loosed a long-suffering sigh. "Would you like me to enlighten the king of your other secret? The one you share with your mother and brother?"

"No," Rhistel whispered, taken aback. So this fae did know things. How . . . infuriating.

The prince took a deep breath, trying to center himself. He wanted to seize control of the situation, as much as he could, anyway, when he felt like he was walking on the slipperiest ice. "I will tell him."

The prince turned to his father. "Mother said she was keeping me prisoner of her magic because I threatened Saga."

"Is it true?" the king asked.

Saga had always been his favorite.

"Yes, but I had a good reason. One that, while you might not agree with, you'll understand." His father had ordered his kin killed in a rebellion to seize the throne. This was not so different.

"Tell me." The king didn't look upset when he spoke. Saga was far away by now, and undoubtedly the king harbored guilt about having his heir trapped.

"Vale and I are not your sons by blood." Rhistel swallowed, and knowing he would do well to show humility, the prince went down on one knee. "But I beg of you, Father, to not disown me. I have not forsaken you."

He stared up at the king, at the red splotches of anger blooming on Magnus's face. Saw the realization come in waves as the truth hit him again and again.

"Who?" Magnus asked and answered his own question in the next breath. "It's Lord Riis, isn't it?"

So he'd always suspected. If only in the back of his mind.

"Yes," Rhistel said. "That is why I threatened Saga. She's the only trueborn Aaberg, and I couldn't stand to be put aside. Could not stand to lose the connection with you and all that I've worked so hard for in my life."

Silence rang through the library until his father grunted. "Stand."

Rhistel did, and though anger vibrated in the lines of his father's body, his eyes were different. Not so hard.

"I cannot allow you to harm Saga in the future, but we will resolve that score later. I will also not disown you as my birth father did. You are an Aaberg, Rhistel. Mine. And my heir."

The prince breathed a sigh of relief. "Thank you."

Magnus nodded. "You think you can control your mother for an extended period of time?"

"I believe so."

"Then sit." The king gestured to the chairs. "King Érebo and I were discussing how best to discredit Princess Isolde from claiming the throne."

Rhistel grinned. "I have a few ideas I'd like to share."

CHAPTER 13
ISOLDE

Fae stared as we rode by. The Myrranese might not see inside the covered sleigh, but the carriage was dark green and gold and lavish enough that they knew *someone* important rode within. Gliding in our tracks was another lavish conveyance filled with the Scholars and Livia, adding to the rumor mill.

We were on our way to the Great Library of the South, hoping to bring information about the Shadow Fae to light. To learn about their magic as well, though of course our new ally did not know about that. As far as the Warden of the South understood, we were hoping to learn about the Shadow Fae history—not untrue. Not entirely true either.

My stomach was in knots at keeping the secret from Lord Balik.

"This city is magnificent," Bac murmured, peeking out the window from the opposite velvet-covered bench. Astril and Freyia sat with him, also looking out the window, but for threats, not pleasure. "A true light of the realm."

I had to agree. Myrr was clean, the streets and build-ings well cared for, and the people seemed happy. Before leaving for the library, Thyra and I had intercepted Alek-sander. He'd already slipped behind Arla's eyes to deliver the message to the rebels that it was safe to move south. I hoped that when the rebels arrived in a few days' time, they would like Myrr too.

"My city brings out the best in fae." Lord Balik's gaze was trained on Bac. It was clear that he recognized how much Bac resembled his family line.

"You said your name is Bac?" Lord Balik asked.

Thyra's friend and advisor met the high lord's stare. "It is."

"That's the river that runs through my city. Not a common name outside of Myrr."

"Yes."

Silence stretched between them, but Bac offered no information. He wanted to know more about the Baliks, but on his terms. In his own time. I respected him for that.

"Why do you say it brings out the best in fae?" Thyra asked.

"Ah, well, many of those who were not born in the Golden City come to Myrr for the library. And those who are born here use it freely and often. My city is the most widely educated in the realm. Its scholars are second only to those in the House of Wisdom." He paused, smiled smugly. "And I can't fail to mention that we're one of the few cities that trade with the Autumn Court, which means our food is excellent. Our cuisine draws some fae to Myrr too."

I had noticed the food the Baliks' ate differed slightly

from what I'd had in Guldtown and Avaldenn. Vale told me it was because Lord Balik's grandmother was from the Autumn Court, and she'd missed her own kingdom's comforts so much she'd established trade routes through the mountains where none existed before. The Autumn Court's influence was present in the names of the Balik children too.

"Here we are," Lord Balik said as the sleigh came to a stop.

The doors opened, and the high lord exited. Thyra and I followed, and Bac and Astril emerged last. I didn't miss when Bac's eyes widened at the sight of the library, the very place where his mother had worked. Where his parents had met.

A symphony of gold and dark gray stone polished to high shine, the walls of the library reflected the light of the day. Faelight torches hung around the entire perimeter of the building, which was nearly as large as Ramshold with multiple towers coming off it. According to Lord Balik, these towers had been built to look like the Ice Teeth Mountain Range. Dozens of fae sat on the long line of steps leading to the doors, soaking up the sun and relaxing.

It was warm outside. Or warm by the Kingdom of Winter's standards. That meant it was almost warm enough to melt the snow and much too warm for my thickest furs, which I was sweating beneath. Though the rise in temperature eased so many pains, I didn't like to think about it. Any action King Magnus took that could be seen as beneficial to others would only make dethroning him more difficult. Particularly in places where fae rarely saw their king and had only others' stories to judge him by. Smaller towns and villages constituted most of the kingdom.

Those in the second sleigh joined us, and we followed Lord Balik into the library. As with the outside, the inside proved a feast for the eyes, boasting so much gold, the miners must have drained entire mountains of the metal. Unlike the outside's glittering gray, the inside of the library was a calming cream hue illuminated by warm faelights.

Once Lord Riis told me that the Royal Library and the one in the House of Wisdom were the largest such institutions in the realm. He was wrong. Or he'd simply never been to this place. By comparison, the library in Frostveil seemed small. Confined to one of the castle's towers that spun up seven stories. From the bottom, a viewer could gaze up at all of them and take in the shelves filled with knowledge. Still beautiful, yes, but far less impressive than what I was seeing.

"Lord Balik, welcome. How might I help you today?" a brownie librarian appeared, dressed in a billowing cream robe that hid any other clothing. A few other librarians or assistants flitted about behind her, all wearing the same shade, though the younger fae wore pants and a top. I took a guess that the robe, which looked to be made of a luxurious material, was for librarians only.

"I'm here with Princess Isolde and Princess Thyra, both of House Falk," Lord Balik announced.

The librarian's jaw slackened before she fell into a clumsy curtsey. "Of course. Welcome, Highnesses."

"They wish to study other wars. Those involving the

Shadow Fae, as the White Bear's Rebellion hits too close to home."

"We have an entire section on their kind." The librarian had regained her composure. "It includes much of the war won by Queen Sassa. Though much information on the queen and the war is also in another section. One dedicated to histories of the various noble families. Which sounds more like what you need?"

"We'd like to visit the section dedicated to Shadow Fae," Thyra said.

The librarian's gaze drifted to my hip, where Sassa's Blade hung. Unless one was a guard, it was odd to carry a weapon in a library. But even when the vampires watched the Hallow, I didn't like being parted from the sword for long. Thyra felt the same about the Frør Crown, currently hidden in a cross-body satchel she wore.

"Follow me, then." The librarian waved, apparently deciding not to comment on the sword.

She led us through the expansive lobby. Fae of all orders stared as we filed through, and Lord Balik acknowledged many. They seemed as happy to see him as they were curious about us.

"In here," the librarian turned into a room.

A vast space, empty save for two young males, one who had to be part troll judging by his size, who were reading at a table. They looked up and grinned at their high lord.

"I hate to do this, but could you lads clear out?" Lord Balik asked. "We have research to do and would like to keep it quiet."

The larger youngling slammed his book shut. "I need to be getting home, anyway."

His friend said nothing, but the pair filed out.

"Shall I post assistants at the door?" the librarian asked. "To turn away those who will come by to see you. Or the princesses." She shot a sidelong glance at me.

"Please. Our guards will be inside too, but it's better that your assistants intercept others."

Our guards were vampires, though it was difficult to tell when their eyes were no longer red, and they took care to blend in.

The librarian left, and Lord Balik turned to us. "This is where I leave you. I will have my sleigh return after it takes me home."

"Thank you." I inclined my head.

"It's the least I could do for my allies."

As he walked out I spotted two assistants already posted at the door. The librarian worked fast.

"Split up?" Duran asked.

He, like Clem, Anna, and Arie, appeared stunned by the beauty of this place. Livia acted as their guard, but as the most bookish of the vampire assassins, she too looked charmed by the room. Astril and Freyia, on the other hand, seemed bored.

"We'll cover more ground that way," Thyra said. "But if anyone finds a section on magic, call me over."

"Me too," I added.

Anything we learned about the Shadow Fae might be useful, but learning about their magic remained *the* priority.

We made to split up, but before I got too far,

Clemencia came to my side, a faint cloud of her signature snow lily perfume in her wake as she fidgeted with excitement.

"We're here for academic reading, but—"

"Before we leave, we'll find the section with stories," I promised her, not needing to hear the rest. My friend was a prolific reader, and I enjoyed tales of adventure and romance, too. "I'm dying for something fun and swoony to read too."

Thyra smirked. "I'll never understand what you see in those things."

"Or course you don't," Clem said dryly.

Thyra's back stiffened. "What's that supposed to mean?"

Clem's lips whitened. "You rejected your own mate. Given that choice, I don't imagine you know much about romance, Princess Thyra."

My mouth fell open. Despite her respectful tone and use of my sister's title, which Clem insisted on because she didn't know Thyra like she knew me.

Red splotches appeared on my sister's cheeks, and I rushed to diffuse the situation.

"I'll find you later, Clem." I took my sister's hand and pulled her down an aisle.

"I suppose your friends all dislike me for rejecting Thantrel?" Thyra murmured.

"To be honest, it doesn't come up much anymore."

"Anymore?"

"When Thantrel was drinking a lot and crying, people brought it up. Hard not to when we were all living in the annex and had to witness his pain."

My twin winced.

"But he hasn't been acting all wounded for a while, so no one has been saying anything."

"Still, they want me to accept him."

I rounded on Thyra, exasperated. "Of course they do! He's a good male. Kind, smart, and honorable."

She glanced away.

"Mates are destined, Thyra. The stars deemed you two an excellent match. While I understood your rejection when you didn't trust any of us, I can't any longer." I shrugged. "So yes, no one can understand why you're still spurning something that others dream of."

"As if I don't know that." Thyra's attention snapped back to me. "Also, when were you going to mention that you wished to free the slaves?"

We hadn't had a moment alone since our meeting with Lord Balik, and perhaps I should have anticipated the question, but it still took me off guard.

"I'm not sure. They're often on my mind." I paused. "Do you disagree with the bargain I made?"

"Of course not," she scoffed. "I don't hate humans, or enjoy seeing them treated poorly, but I still would have liked to speak about it with you first. To appear united."

I hadn't given her that chance.

"I'm sorry."

"Let's just look for books on Shadow Fae magic, alright?" She turned away.

Discussion closed. Stars, was this going to be how the other hard conversations we needed to have would go too? I hoped not. Thyra and I had been avoiding other serious matter of who—if we both lived through the war—would sit on the throne.

Before, I thought I'd be happy to give the throne up to Thyra, and a part of me still felt that way, but an equal part liked the idea of leading. Of getting to shape Winter's Realm in meaningful ways.

I started by examining the closest titles. Many seemed to pertain to the rulers of the Shadow Fae long before Queen Sassa Falk lived. I moved on. And on. And on again. My search, and the silence between my sister and me, stretched for an hour before Thyra let out a loud hum.

"What is it?" We'd each taken one side and moved away from one another, so I found myself at the end of an aisle, and her on the other.

"Nothing about their magic. Rather, their enemies."

"I kind of thought that was everyone else in Isila, considering they planned to start wars with each kingdom." Winter's Realm had just been the first and hardest hit, due to our proximity to the Shadow Fae Isles.

"Their enemies could live in multiple kingdoms," she agreed. "It's not a kingdom that poses the greatest risk to them, but a type of magic. Limiters—though I believe the dragons and wolvea call light wielders something else."

"Light magic. That's the antithesis to their shadows?"

"I'd never considered it before but it makes sense."

It might also explain why I'd felt so off while we trained that morning. I would bet Sassa's Blade that the shadows inside me were reacting to Sian's magic, which he had been using in abundance during combat practice.

"When we were training, did you feel off, Thyra? Particularly when Sian used his light?"

My sister's head tilted. "Actually yes. I put it down to all the rich food from breakfast, but you think it was the shadows inside us?"

"It might have been. Easy enough to test."

"We'd have to let Sian or Baenna in on that secret. Will they tell their father, because I don't think we're ready for that yet."

I swallowed. "We're friends, so I'd like to think that they'd keep it a secret until we said otherwise, but maybe it is best to wait to test out our shadow's aversion to light magic. At least until after Lord Balik makes his oath."

CHAPTER 14
ISOLDE

Two bells later, our initial success in learning about the limiters was beginning to dim when footsteps approached from behind. Anna's—I recognized the unique pattern of her foot fall mixed with the sound of her crutch hitting the floor. But someone else was alongside her too. I turned and smiled at my friends.

"We found something interesting." Anna held up a book.

"Anna found it," Duran corrected.

"About the magic?" Thyra scurried down from where she'd been scanning books and joined me.

"No, but still potentially important." Anna thrust a book at us and pointed out a section. "It's right here."

"Read it out loud." Anna had found it and was excited. I wanted her to get the credit.

My friend beamed and recited the passage. "Documentation passed down from Queen Sassa Falk's inner circle at court leads us to believe that the Shadow Fae were eradicated from Isila, not by an unforeseen force.

Nor primarily by magic performed by the queen herself. But by powerful gatemakers. One, being of the Lisika line, died five moons after the Shadow Fae War. Sources close to the family say that he wasted away."

"Holy stars," Thyra breathed.

Luccan had claimed it was possible. Was this the proof we were looking for?

"The second gatemaker was a commonborn subject of House Virtoris. A sailor sent on a boat tasked to intercept a second wave of Shadow Fae forces before they made landfall. During that interception, the gatemaker created a gateway, sending the attackers on the ship elsewhere. She knew not where. Nor had she meant to perform such a feat of magic, but had done so out of necessity. However, after the war ended, she was commanded to journey to the Shadow Fae Isles and do so again. The second feat of magic cost her life."

Anna stopped. "There's more, obviously. The most important bit is that Luccan was right! Gatemakers banished the Shadow Fae. And it stands to reason they could bring them back too."

"The problem being, of course, that we don't have any idea as to where they went," Duran added excitedly. "Or if the two gatemakers sent the Shadow Fae to the same world. Some may be in the human world, and others elsewhere." Duran looked up, as though he could see the stars in the sky, and the gods said to rest among them.

"Roar once said Sassa banished the Shadow Fae. I wonder if he really thought it was a joint effort? Or if he knew at all?" I frowned. "And, actually, Roar's father was a powerful gatemaker. So it seems that power ran in their line. Thank the stars Roar doesn't have that magic."

"You're sure?" Thyra asked.

Was I sure of anything when it came to that fae? Roar had hidden so many things from me. From everyone.

"No. Actually, I'm not."

"Gatemakers have always been kept under close watch," Duran said. "It would be natural to hide that talent. If someone possessed other powers, hiding such magic would be relatively easy."

Luccan had done that. Stars, what if Roar wasn't just a shifter?

"They're not feared like whisperers," Thyra added. "Not killed but *controlled*. Always under the Crown's thumb in case the ruling king or queen wishes to use them. Or they rent gatemakers out to a kingdom where no such power exists. If I had that power, I wouldn't tell anyone either."

"Clearly they're rare among Shadow Fae, too." I chewed thoughtfully on my lower lip. "Maybe nonexistent. Or else they would have returned on their own, right?"

"That's right." Duran nodded enthusiastically "Shadow Fae magic differs from the magic the rest of the fae control."

"As if we don't know that firsthand," Thyra snorted and gestured to herself. "If this power felt anything like our winter magic, we'd be able to sense our way through this issue."

"At least we now have confirmation that a portal can be opened only one way," I said. "By a powerful gatemaker."

"True," Anna replied. "We have to hope that the king doesn't know of one. Or *find* one."

Was Luccan powerful enough? He'd told me he was still early in his training.

"Set that book aside." I rolled out my neck. "If we can take it with us, I'd like to read more."

Anna nodded. "Will do. Any luck on finding information on the magic?"

"None. Which means we should get back to looking."

Anna and Duran left, and I turned to my sister. "Today hasn't been a total flop."

She was silent for a long moment before replying. "Have you considered using the sword?"

I blinked and patted my hip. "This sword?"

"Is there another we ever talk about?"

I wrinkled my nose. "Go on."

"If one of us gave it blood, and the shadows appeared, why don't we ask it questions? To teach us or to find a book that could actually help us. They spoke to you, right?"

They had. Not to Thyra, though. Yes, shadows emerged for her, but it had taken so much blood that she passed out. Once she lost consciousness, they'd disappeared.

"We can try." I gestured to the shelves filled with priceless tomes. "Away from the books."

We made our way to the far corner of the library. No one was in sight. There was so much information about the Shadow Fae, our friends hadn't yet needed to delve so far back, and this area was far from the door. From other fae who didn't know our secret. Careful not to make a sound, I unsheathed my sword.

"Ready?" I asked.

"I'm right here if you faint."

I drew the blade across my palm, not my first choice, but my clothing showed little exposed skin. I winced as a shadow drifted from the blade.

Sensing that Sassa's Blade needed more, I placed my bleeding palm on the *zuprian* steel. The first time I'd done this I'd been facing a horde of orcs. While this experience was still scary, at least I knew what to expect. How it would feel. There was a pull of my blood as the blade drank in more and a shadow slowly teased out of the metal to form into a person. I was beginning to feel light-headed when it bowed.

"Hi," I said. "We're shadow wielders too. Can you feel it inside me?"

The shadow nodded.

"Then, we were wondering, can you teach us how to wield our magic?"

It shook its head.

Thyra swore.

Before I could ask another question, the rush of air on my left alerted me to the fact that someone had joined.

"Bleeding skies! You two terrified me!" Thyra hissed, as both Livia and Astril appeared out of nowhere.

"We smelled Isolde's blood." Astril looked us over. "We thought someone attacked you."

"Now we see we were wrong." Livia watched the shadow with apprehension. "What are you doing?"

"We hoped it might teach us magic, but we were wrong," Thyra said.

"More," the shadow spoke, its raspy voice like jagged nails scratching rocks.

I shuddered, but if I wanted it to stick around, I had to comply. I pressed my bleeding palm into the blade again, shuddered through the pull. My vision dimmed, and powerful hands supported me from behind.

"She's weak." Astril's head tilted as she listened. "Her pulse is slowing."

"Hurry, Isolde," Thyra whispered, concern plain in her voice.

I cleared my throat. Suddenly, I was very thirsty. "If you can't teach us magic, is there a book in here that can? Can you find such a thing here?"

"I sense only one that will be of use."

"Find it. Bring it here."

The shadow looked at me.

"Do as she says. Stay out of sight, though." I didn't care if our friends saw, but there were library assistants at the door, and random fae might walk by.

The shadow soared away, and I slumped.

"A chair," Astril said.

Livia moved to get one, then lowered me into it. Only three minutes passed before the shadow was back. With black fingers, it set the book in my lap.

"That's all," I croaked.

Maybe this book would not turn out to be exactly what we needed, but I couldn't give more blood and stay awake. If we had to ask for the shadow's help again, it would be in a few days.

The shadow vanished. I sighed and made sure my hand remained far from the book. "Thyra, can you read it?"

The weight of the tome lifted from my lap, but before my sister could find a place to set it, Astril bit into her arm. "Let me put this on that cut. It will heal quickly. No questions from others."

I allowed her to cover my cut in vampire blood, and it worked its magic, sealing the wound quickly. I still felt woozy, but at least I was no longer bleeding. "Thank you."

Astril looked to her sister. "Livia, can you get something to clean her palm?"

"I'll be back."

When three remained, Thyra studied me. "Are you strong enough to continue?"

"I am."

My sister opened the book, and Astril leaned closer, her ruby lips twisted with disgust.

"That book is made of fae skin."

"What?!" Thyra's spine straightened in her chair.

"Shadow Fae skin, I believe. It's unlike anything I've smelled, but it somewhat smells like your blood."

My stomach churned. But then, something worse happened. Two tendrils of shadow appeared from the back of my hands and floated towards the book. They touched it. Caressed the paper. Paged through the tome. All three of us watched, mesmerized, not knowing what to do.

As it turned out, we didn't need to do anything. The shadows stopped in their own time and, like the figure I'd summoned, disappeared.

Thyra leaned forward again and took in the page the shadows had opened to. A grin spread across her face. "Finally, we've got something we can work with."

CHAPTER 15
VALE

I stood outside the walls of Myrr with Lord Balik, his sons, and their guard, and watched the dragon's approach.

Early yesterday, Arla had delivered the note telling those at Valrun that it was safe to journey south. Most would arrive in the coming days, but those who were injured, ill, or simply could not make such a long journey were arriving today, on dragonback.

"It's been a very long time since I've seen a dragon shifter." Lord Balik shielded his eyes as he took in the sight.

"She's half fae," I corrected him. "Prefers to be called dragon-fae."

"Whatever she likes to be called, she's a dragon where it matters."

Rynni thought differently. The fae of Vitvik hadn't accepted her, and according to the healer, the dragons of the Flame Court would have been even less welcoming because she was a small dragon with little firepower.

The dragon was a minute from the gate when I stepped forward and waved my arms in the air. A roar indicated that she'd seen me, so I moved back into place, standing with the lords and their guards.

Lighter than one would think, Rynni landed and lowered her massive body as close to the ground as possible. Two fae slid off, the only able-bodied riders to make the journey in case something happened during the flight. With Sian and Filip, I rushed forward to assist.

"Good flight, I hope?" I asked one of the fae rebels, as he urged Ratha, the ancient whisperer, down Rynni's front leg. The second rebel was assisting a young mother with a fresh babe wrapped against her chest. The other new mother and youngling were present too, her little one making faint crying noises from his swaddle.

"Uneventful, which was the best we could hope for," the rebel answered.

"And the rest of the rebels?"

"They left town a bell before us. All are on their way."

"Thank the Fates."

Ratha slid down the crux of the dragon's wing and foreleg. Her wings, black as my own and hinting at her relation to my mother, fluttered to control her speed. She winced only slightly as her feet hit the ground. The rebels helped her up and motioned for the next to follow.

"Prince," Ratha said, her voice hoarse from disuse. "How's the Jewel of the Southlands? As idyllic as they all say?"

She wasn't asking about the city, I knew, but about how Bac and Aleksander, the only rebels who had journeyed here, were being treated.

"We have safety and space." I wasn't about to report anything negative with Lord Balik behind me.

"How diplomatic." Ratha muttered, and Filip, ever the gentlefae, went to her and offered his arm.

"Might I show you to the gate office? They have chairs waiting for those who need them."

Ratha's eyebrows arched. "Hmm, perhaps my worries were for naught. Show me to a comfortable chair, lad."

The pair made their way to the small pass-through office city gate guards used.

Brynhild was next, looking weary and happy to be on land. One by one, twelve fae dismounted the dragon. Those who had been the most grievously injured and two very ill rebels looked far better than when I'd last seen them at Valrun. Rynni had been working tirelessly to care for her patients.

The dragon-fae shifted, her blackish-purple scales disappearing as her form shrank into the red-haired, pale female with faint scales framing her ears.

"Are you ready for a long rest?"

"That I am," she agreed. "The others set out just before we did."

"Good timing." Had the rebels remained at Valrun for much longer, the chances of the King of Winter finding them would have increased. I smiled and gestured toward the rulers of the south. "Rynni, I'd like to introduce you to the Lord of Myrr and two of his sons."

She joined me, and I performed the proper introductions. Each Balik treated the healer with a degree of deference that seemed to surprise her, but not me. Outside the White Tower, healers were the most revered in the rugged southlands where monsters roamed the nearby mountains and often inflicted grave injuries.

"My sons and Prince Vale, along with my guard," Lord Balik gestured back to the armed fae around us, "will show you to where you're staying. I, however, must return to the castle. I have a meeting with the Falk princesses."

The dragon-fae's eyebrows pinched together. Because we'd used Arla and prewritten notes to let them know they should come south, the rebels had not been told that they'd be staying outside the walls of Ramshold.

"We thank you for your hospitality, my lord," Rynni replied, though the look she shot at me screamed that she had questions.

Lord Balik slipped through the passage, into Myrr's bustling streets. Sian and Filip went to the rebels, gathering them and doing what they could to ease any nerves.

"Isolde asked after the new babies?" I started when I was alone with the healer. "Are they well?"

Rynni's face softened. "Perfect in every way. Their mothers are healthy too. Healing still, but healthy."

My heart lifted. It was still too soon to tell, but my mate's theory of the blight might prove true.

"So," Rynni said. "Where are we staying, then?"

"In a building with many family units, large enough to house all of the rebels. There are three such buildings we've been given, all next to each other, so it's convenient." I did my best to hide my disdain for the choice. As much as I didn't like the arrangement it was still fair. "There will be soldiers in the area. For the rebels' safety."

"And the peace of mind of those in Myrr," Rynni

muttered. I wasn't fooling her. "I assume we aren't close to the castle either?"

"Correct, but it was the best we could do. These apartments are new, and no one else is inhabiting them, which is how Lord Balik secured the buildings so easily. There are exceptions, of course, for those who need the castle healers. Are there any you'd say need more care right now?"

"Not unless they hurt themselves on the journey here."

"Brynhild and you may stay at the castle. As part of our court."

Rynni wrinkled her nose. "We'll see."

I shrugged a shoulder and waved her towards the wall. "Let's show everyone to their new home"

I led the rebels into Myrr, and in the direction of the building they'd live in. When we arrived, the owner of the first building waited outside, as Lord Balik had requested.

The landlord didn't look too pleased to be housing rebels, but softened at the sight of Sian and Filip. We showed each rebel, save for Brynhild, who opted to return to the castle with us, inside an apartment. Each small home had been furnished with simple but quality items, and the building was far nicer than where the rebels stayed at Valrun. The floors were even heated, a feature that many wanted but few possessed the coin to afford.

And yet, many of the rebels were not happy.

"Thyra won't like being far from us." Ratha lowered herself into a chair that I offered.

"She doesn't," I agreed. "But it was this or her people remained in Valrun. She made a choice to compromise."

"That won't be the last time she does so." Ratha

sighed as she leaned back. "Fates bless that dragon. Without her, I'd have had to ride a horse for days. Still, her scaly hide is not comfortable."

I laughed. "Need anything else?"

"Only that you ask Thyra to visit when she can."

"She will."

Both Thyra and Isolde had wanted to welcome the rebels today, but had also recognized they had limited time to practice shadow magic before Lord Balik swore his allegiance to them. They were presently making the most of their hours to train their new powers—which included keeping them contained.

I left Ratha and had barely shut the door to her apartment when Filip appeared at my side.

"I wish to talk to you. In private." He glanced over his shoulder, to where Sian was talking to Rynni in the room she'd claimed.

"Is everyone situated?" I checked.

"Yes. If the rebels require anything, they need only ask the guards waiting outside, and they will see that they have it."

"Right," I said, certain that the rebels would ask for no more favors.

As long as food and water was delivered, which I'd been assured they would be, the rebels would make do with as little as possible to avoid feeling like they owed too much.

"Come on then, Filip."

We exited the building, and I told Brynhild, who waited by the front, that I'd be right back. As we walked down the street, Filip glanced around before leaning in close.

"I worry about Prince Rhistel."

"Ah." My chest deflated. I'd suspected he'd eventually want to speak about my brother. "He's far away."

"Yes, but his powers can extend far." Filip swallowed. "Whisperers are dangerous, Prince Vale. There's a reason they're forbidden."

Even with all my twin and my mother had done to deserve ire from me and others, I hated to think of them as gone. Death was so final.

"Will King Magnus use your brother's magic in the war?" Filip asked.

What to say? Filip didn't know that my mother held Rhistel in her grasp.

"It's possible," I answered.

"Shouldn't we first out Prince Rhistel? Such information might turn the tides of the war before it even truly begins."

He had no idea that once we began releasing secrets, the other side would follow in kind. Then Isolde and Thyra would also be distrusted, though for very different reasons. They had to master their magic first and even the field as best they could.

"We might."

Filip's eyebrows slanted together.

I was not usually so noncommittal. "I can't say what we're going to do. This needs to be discussed with Isolde and Thyra."

"Thyra knows?"

"She does." I paused but figured now was as good a

time as any. "However, there is something else I want to talk about."

"Yes?"

"Is there someone that House Balik can hire to help my mother flee Avaldenn?"

Filip's spine straightened. "Why would she want to do that? Isn't she safe there?"

"She is, but . . ." I trailed off.

"Does she still love Lord Riis?"

"She does, and she'd rather be with him than the king." A straightforward answer. And not a lie.

"I'll ask my father."

"Please."

"And you'll put some real consideration into how to deal with your brother."

It wasn't a question. I sought out Filip, and found not my impressionable squire, but the next head of House Balik, staring back at me.

I clapped the lordling on the shoulder, proud of the fae he was becoming. "I will. Now, let's turn around and collect Brynhild and Sian so we can get back to Ramshold. My mate is waiting."

CHAPTER 16

ISOLDE

I cast a sidelong glance at my sister, savoring the moment before we walked into the grand hall, and Lord Tadgh Balik swore his allegiance to us.

To witness the event were the wealthiest merchants in Myrr and their families, the High Staretess of the city, and three lesser lords of the south, all of them banner houses to House Balik. Each pivotal voices in their community, and powerful in their own ways.

"Do you feel guilty?" I whispered to my sister, though there was no one else around to hear. Everyone, including our friends, family, and mates, were inside, waiting. "Keeping our secret?"

"Yes, and I don't even care about this family like you do."

I chuckled at the remark because it was just so Thyra. "Hopefully soon we'll make headway. Then we can tell him."

Practicing today had been mixed. After hours of work,

we'd both been able to call forth shadowy tendrils, but we had little control over what they did. One of Thyra's tendrils had floated out the window, threatening to expose us. The shadow only dissipated when my sister locked down her power.

"I hope so," Thyra agreed with a small smile. "You look nice, by the way."

"You too."

The Balik sisters had lent us dresses. Mine was an amethyst gown with a plunging neckline. I wore a sword belt with Sassa's Blade hanging off it.

Thyra's dress was black with two slits creeping up her thighs. Thyra had left the Frør Crown under Astril's watch, while Livia and Freyia attended the ceremony.

I was about to peek into the chamber again when Aleksander poked his head out the door. His gaze scanned over us both, and a proud smile graced his lips. "We're ready for you, my princesses."

"Sisters to you," I corrected him, and he beamed.

"Sisters."

Aleksander slipped back into the room. We gave him a moment to find his spot before entering, side by side.

A crowd of fifty parted down the middle, displaying Lord Balik in his high seat at the end of the aisle. His wife stood at his side, and his children watched from behind. The three banner lords waited at the foot of the dais, ready to witness their lord's oath.

Thyra and I strode together in lockstep, and I could not help but marvel at how in sync we had been lately. We still had issues to overcome, but each day, my twin and I grew closer. More like how we might have been if the White Bear's Rebellion had never happened.

If Inga had never complied with Magnus's wishes. I couldn't help but find Lord Riis in the crowd. Even among his sons, all red of hair except for Vale, Leyv stood out. He was a large faerie, in body and spirit.

The spymaster caught me looking and offered a small smile. I glanced away.

I hadn't spoken directly to Lord Riis since the day he'd told me the truth of Queen Inga's crimes against my family. If I hadn't put so much trust in the male, if he hadn't sworn to keep Vale and me safe, I might have forgiven him with greater ease. But he'd gotten me to trust him, all the while knowing the truth: My father had never been mad. That the Cruel King's actions were spurred on by a whisperer, and my family had died for nothing.

Unfortunately, the people I cherished most loved the queen and the spider—shared their blood and many memories with the pair. I could not bring myself to hurt Vale, Saga, or the Riis brothers for my own revenge.

We reached the bottom of the dais. Vale and Thantrel positioned themselves just to our sides. As mates, rejected or no, they were important witnesses to the occasion.

Lord Balik descended the steps and came to a stop in front of us. His shoulders rolled back and down as he addressed the room at large.

"I thank you for journeying to my hall today to witness the sacred oath that House Balik intends to make. A promise of fealty and friendship to a royal house many thought long dead." He inclined his head. "To Princess Isolde Falk and Princess Thyra Falk."

He fell to a knee, and everyone in the room who called Tadgh Balik their lord or their father followed suit. The motion stirred something inside me, something not even Lord Riis's solemn promise back at Valrun Castle had managed. I couldn't put a name to the feeling, only that it made my chest swell as I took Sassa's Blade in my hand. I touched the edge of the legendary sword to Lord Balik's shoulder, then the next, before removing the *zuprian* steel.

"By blood and bone, by frigid wind and winter's touch, I bind my fate to those of House Falk." Lord Balik articulated the same vow that Lord Riis had spoken. The ancient words of loyalty and devotion to the Crown of Winter's Realm. The same oath that every new ruler of House Falk had required upon their ascension to the throne.

"Whatever you may need from me is yours. May the dead gods bear witness, and may Winter's Realm reject me should I break this oath," Lord Balik finished, the moment gone so quickly.

I looked at Thyra. She gave a single nod, and I stepped forward.

"We accept House Balik as our banner house," I stated proudly.

Thyra joined me. "And should others wish to make their oaths, we will hear them now. Rise, Lord Balik."

The Warden of the South rose, but others remained kneeling. Lord Balik's banner fae, and merchants who, though they had no army, wished to state their loyalty before those present.

"Thank you, Lord Balik." A smile softened my lips. "Please sit while we accept the other oaths."

The High Lord of the Southlands took his great, horned seat, and his banner fae knelt before us, began the words.

And so it went through the room, over and over and over.

Belly and heart full, I sipped my wine at the Balik's table, content to revel in the victory. The possibilities.

After Lord Balik took his vow, three influential lesser houses in the south swore their allegiance to Thyra and me. Many wealthy and well-connected merchants in Myrr promised to support us as well.

Thyra and I had come so far from the day we'd first seen one another at the Royal Theater. The day she'd almost shot an arrow through my heart.

"Oh, to be a frostfly on the wall when King Magnus learns of what happened today." Thantrel had indulged in much wine, and red stained his cheeks.

"You'll have to settle for seeing his disbelief when we trounce him on the battlefield!" Prince Thordur's fist pounded the table, his tone loud and merry. Apparently, too much wine had been drunk all around.

"I can't wait for that. Or to see Frostveil," Princess Bavirra said from where she sat by her brother, clad in a gown of gold that she borrowed from Baenna and had altered. As royals, we were sitting around one side of the high lord's table. Thantrel had invited himself up, and Lord Balik hadn't denied him. Nor had Thyra.

From the amused expression the Warden of the South was giving Thantrel, I had to wonder if Tadgh Balik even really wanted Sian to wed my sister.

"If Father lets you near the battle for Avaldenn," Thordur corrected his sister.

The dwarven princess narrowed her eyes. "Why wouldn't he?"

The Heir Prince of Dergia scoffed. "You're not supposed to be here at all, Bav. You snuck into the army to save Nev—I mean, Isolde and her friends. He should have sent you back to Dergia."

"As if I haven't been training for such a thing for turns."

The two swept into bickering, so I turned to Vale, sitting at my side. He had a certain look about him.

I cocked my head. "What are you thinking about?"

He grinned, and the effect was as devastating as it always was, sending chills through me. Would I ever tire of looking at this male? I doubted it. Even when our skin wrinkled and his hair took on gray, I'd still find Vale as handsome as the day I'd first seen him.

"I was thinking about how proud I am of you. For today, but for all the days that I've known you. For those before I met you, too." A subtle, serious shift rippled across his face as it so often did when he was considering my past in the Blood Court, but a mischievous glint in his eyes quickly replaced the seriousness. "And then I was thinking I wish to celebrate with you." He leaned closer and whispered in my ear, *"Alone."*

My toes curled at his tone. The promise.

"Well." I took in our closest dinner companions. Everyone seemed to be happily talking with those next to them. "Now might be a perfect time to slip away. It is getting late, after all. And you had such a long day showing the rebels to their new home—you must be ready to lie down." Beneath the table, my hand landed on his upper thigh, strayed close to his malehood.

"*Isolde*," he growled. "If you plan on teasing me like that, we won't be able to leave any time soon."

I laughed and stood. I expected others to notice, and for Vale and me to pretend that we could not wait to fall asleep. What I didn't expect was for everyone at the table, with the exception of Thyra, Lord Balik, and Lady Balik, to stand.

"Oh." My tone sounded so mouse-like as others stopped their conversations to watch. "Vale and I are retiring for the evening. No need to . . . do whatever you're doing."

Thyra sniggered, but Lady Balik gave an understanding smile.

"They're showing their leader respect," the High Lady of the Southlands explained. "Only those of equal standing or your hosts remain sitting on such an occasion."

Just when I dared to think I understood royal etiquette well enough, a few oaths changed things.

"Thank you," I said. "Please, continue to enjoy dessert."

The dinner party sat, and as quickly as we could, Vale and I left the room. The moment we were alone, he loosed a low laugh.

"The look on your face. Priceless!"

I punched him. "The rebels didn't do that! Nor Lord Riis after he swore to us."

"Well, my father stood today. Things are different now."

I couldn't deny that, so I took my prince's hand, and we made our way through the castle. We entered a joining of many corridors, one in which we would go right to find our room, when Vale tugged me to the left.

My eyebrows pinched together. "Wrong way."

"I know exactly where I want to take you. And I mean that in more ways than one."

My heart fluttered. "It's private, right?"

The last thing I wanted was for anyone to stumble upon us doing the deed. Especially now that I was in such a position of power.

"Very."

"Alright then." I allowed Vale to show me through parts of Ramshold I had yet to step foot in. Like the rest of the castle, it screamed luxury, family, and honor.

"Here we are." Vale stopped. He gestured to a stretch of wall between two potted plants that rose nearly to the ceiling, their leaves arching together, as if wanting to touch.

"Ah yes, the perfect place for romance."

My prince smirked as he ran his hand along the wall before seemingly grasping at something. A whine hit my ear and suddenly, the wall was no longer a wall, but a set of double doors, one of which my mate was opening. Fresh air swept over me, still cool, cold even, but not frigid. Things were indeed warming at a shocking rate.

"After you."

I stepped over the threshold and smiled. Vale had taken me to a balcony on the fourth floor overlooking the backside of the city and the mountains beyond. Stars twinkled above and faelights below, painting a breath-taking picture.

"Stars," I sighed out, "it's so lovely here with the city and the mountain view."

"And it's unlikely anyone will come this way," Vale assured me. "A grand ballroom is further down the hall. One they only use for the largest of balls. No chance of that tonight."

"I'm guessing you found this hidden balcony during some night of revelry? Am I not the first lady you've brought out here?" My tone was teasing, but the question was sincere.

Both Vale and I had pasts—people we'd slept with and claimed to love before we met one another. I wasn't envious of those ladies, though I didn't like to think of someone else standing out here with my mate. Kissing him. Doing more.

"Sian realized this balcony had an excellent view but was hidden from windows and other balconies around the castle. He values privacy, so he put an illusion in place long ago and has maintained it. Once the door closes, no one will see it unless it's opened again. Sian uses the balcony for his own liaisons, but when I'd visit for state affairs, usually a lavish ball, he and I would come out here and *hide* from ladies." Vale came closer. "You're the first I've brought out here with the intent of taking you from behind and making you gasp my name."

Oh gods. My knees quivered with want.

"By all means, then, who am I to make you wait?"

His hands landed on my hips, and he guided me back, back, back, until my rear hit the stone railing. Slowly, those large hands traveled over my body, lingering on my curves, caressing them, until finally one landed on my throat. Vale tilted my chin back and took my lips in his.

Our tongues danced, our teeth nipped, our hands explored, sending goosebumps over our skin and heat ravaging through me. Heat I wanted doused by him. I pulled back, pushed him away slightly, and smirked as I turned and looked at him from over my shoulder.

"Is this how you were picturing tonight?"

He closed the space between us, his hands gripping my hips as he pressed into me. Fates, he was already so hard, and though I loved the tension of foreplay, I was equally ready for him.

As if he could read my mind, my mate pulled the hem of my dress up and dropped it over the top of my arse, which he playfully smacked. The cold of the stone balcony dug into my hips, but I barely noticed that or the chilled air.

"I swear if you make me wait, I'll freeze you to the ground and leave you out here," I threatened.

Vale laughed, the sound wild and free. "Might be worth it to see you get more riled up."

I glanced back at him, wagged my eyebrows, which only made him laugh harder as he tugged my undergarments off. "Red. You know what I think of every time you wear red?" he asked as the delicate lace pooled at my ankles.

A grin overtook my mouth. "The time I left you hot and bothered in a closet with a Master Healer scolding you for seducing your wife."

"Right before she pointed out the slip of red undergarments on the ground," he added, his hands landing on my rear and squeezing, only to wrap around until his fingers found my sensitive nub.

I gasped as he applied pressure, rubbing at my tender skin while easing my legs wider and sliding inside me. My eyelids fluttered closed as Vale filled me, our fit as perfect as ever.

"Isolde," Vale growled. "Look up."

I did as he asked, and the magic of the moment multiplied. Purples and greens swam across the sky. The goddess Brae was painting tonight. Putting on a show.

I twisted to catch Vale's gaze and swore I felt a wave of pure happiness wash over me.

"Not the prettiest thing I've seen tonight," he said. "Not by half." One free hand caressed my hip, and the other trailed lightly over my wing.

Stars bloomed in my vision from the touch, the caress of my wing as he continued to pump in and out, teasing that delicious tension growing inside me higher. My wings tingled from his touch, so sensitive, so receptive to him.

He changed up the tempo, and I gasped as he shifted his lower hand to apply pressure to my sensitive bundle of nerves. My climax roared out of me, and a cry of pleasure parted my lips, only to be swallowed by a gale of wind. Magical wind. Vale's.

He followed me into bliss only seconds later, my inner channels still spasming around his cock. When we were both spent, Vale drew me up against him, my back to his chest, as he kissed my jawline.

"I love you, Force. Never forget that."

I exhaled joy and stared up at the sky, still a riot of color, of life and beauty. "That's not possible."

Her heart hammered as the princess and the scoundrel slipped outside to stroll the castle grounds. She stole a glance at the male, the one the stars had chosen as her equal.

"Like what you see?" He winked.

She scoffed. Why did he have to tease her so when she had a potential political marriage to tie herself to?

Perhaps because I'm acting like a moon-eyed youngling?

Still, political marriage or no, Thyra spoke no argument when Thantrel had followed her from the dinner table, saying that she required an escort. As if Thyra wasn't as skilled at fighting as her mate, and yet, she also hadn't argued then. Nor after she gathered her fur cloak from her room, and he didn't leave her side. No, she hadn't argued at all, but rather suggested they go for a walk.

"Perhaps I've rendered you speechless?" her mate added, to which the princess laughed.

"You wish."

"I'd love it if you talked *more*." He clasped his hands behind him, as though trying to keep them off her. Occupied. "I'd like to know you better than anyone else."

And there he went again, acting like she hadn't rejected him publicly and cruelly. Even if she had been kinder since those spiders tried to tear his wings off, why did he have to do that?

The pain of that day within the mountain sliced through her, as cutting and horrible as if she was reliving that moment. From the time they left that cavern, Thyra Falk understood that it was only a matter of time before Thantrel wormed his way into her heart. She hadn't expected it to happen so quickly, but the more she got to know him, the more she realized he had a way about him. A disarming manner and a charm.

But having him in her heart and accepting him as her mate were two entirely different things. The former seemed increasingly inevitable, whereas the latter would be a choice Thyra would have to balance in the face of war.

What if she did accept Thantrel and in doing so, Lord Balik pulled back his support? Thyra didn't know the Warden of the South well, and the slightest retraction could have dire consequences. So many were loyal to her. She did not wish to let them down.

"What do you want to know?" Thyra asked, gazing up at those olive-green eyes lined with gold. A stunning combination.

"Too much for a brief walk around the castle grounds." A mischievous grin overtook his face. "What do you say we find a tavern and get drunk?"

Since their arrival in the largest city of the southlands, there'd been no time to let loose. Actually, since Thyra had become the leader of the rebellion, there'd been little time for frivolity. When was the last time she'd pretended she was a normal fae and just had *fun*?

She couldn't remember, so she pivoted to the castle gate. "I expect you know where to go?"

The ale went down smoothly, far better than the swill the rebels drank.

"You aren't a stranger to the drink, are you?" Thantrel teased, fanning out his fiery wings behind him and garnering attention from others. Thantrel was a large personality. Handsome and striking without trying to be so. Everywhere he showed his face, males and females were equally drawn to him.

"This is only my second ale." She stuck out her tongue. "But no. Ale and I are old friends. Sometimes, at Valrun, we couldn't get food. Water and ale were all that we would have available to fill our bellies for days on end. Your lot joined us when our larders were full."

He leaned close enough to her to smell his fresh, spicy scent. She swallowed down the desire welling inside her.

"Where did you grow up?"

"That's your first question?" she asked. They'd set rules on the way here. Three questions a piece. One chance each to veto a single question.

"Yes."

Thyra pressed her back into the wooden booth, tucked

in a far back corner. Thanks to her long, hooded cloak, no one had recognized that she was one of the princesses their lord had sworn to earlier that day. Or one of the fae who had gone to the library with the High Lord of the Southlands. The anonymity suited her, as it always had.

"After I fled Avaldenn with Brynhild, we moved around a lot. I don't remember that time well. Too young." She took another drink of ale. It was impossible not to think about what had been befalling Isolde during the same timeframe.

Thyra's lips pressed together. Her upbringing had not been luxurious or easy, but at least she'd always been free. Had lived in Winter's Realm, where they both belonged. And no monster had ever sipped at her blood.

"We stayed in Kethor for a few moons, but Brynhild never felt safe there. Too close to Avaldenn, and I had that Falk look about me." She pointed to her eyes, which looked much like her father's.

"King Magnus has the same color eyes," Thantrel said.

"Take that back."

"His are not half as pretty as yours, though. They have none of the warmth your eyes possess."

A small smile curved her lips. "After leaving Kethor, we moved from village to village. Staying at each place for no more than six moons. When I got old enough, Brynhild settled us in Vantalia. So I guess, if anywhere is home, that is. Mostly, I grew up everywhere in the eastern part of the kingdom."

"Never been this far south?"

"Is that number two?"

"No!" He looked alarmed at having to give up a precious question for something he'd said so offhandedly.

"It's my first time in Myrr," she replied, deciding to go easy on him. "Now, my turn."

What to ask? Thyra hoarded questions concerning Thantrel. Most of which she'd never considered voicing, but the ale was loosening her up, and he was watching her as though he wanted to share the most intimate parts of himself.

"Who's your mother?" The question left her lips before she knew that she'd settled on it.

Thantrel gave a sad smile. "Was. She's dead."

"Join the club."

He chuckled. "She was a lesser noble elf, from about as far south as their kingdom goes. Her family had little coin but an ancient name. My father had already been elevated to the title of High Lord when I was born, but he still ran his merchant empire and traveled a lot. They got together, and she became pregnant. She died after I was born, and my living elven relatives sent me here." He shrugged as if that wasn't hurtful, but she could see that it affected him. That others hadn't wanted him when he was so young and innocent.

"Their loss." She placed a hand on his arm.

His gaze strayed to where she touched him, seeming to savor the sight before he looked up again. "Have you ever been in love?"

She blinked, shocked by the question and sensing what he really wanted to ask beneath it. Had she ever been in love, and was she *still* in love?

"No," the princess replied. "There wasn't time for

that, even when we stayed in Vantalia. And to be honest, Brynhild was a strict mother figure. Males held little interest for me until I was about seventeen, but if I'd been more into dating, or Fates-forbid seriously courting, I doubt Brynhild would have let me."

She remembered when she turned seventeen, being confused by how her keeper was still so protective. By that time, Thyra defended herself well enough to take down most fae who would try something untoward. Now she understood better.

Brynhild protected Thyra from males or females who might break her heart or hurt her, but also from Thyra attaching herself to the wrong person. Even then, Brynhild saw that the princess might wish to rise and claim the throne. Brynhild understood that Thyra keeping her heart to herself until the time was right would be of the utmost importance.

"Well, if I didn't already like Brynhild, I would now," Thantrel placed his elbows on the knotty table as his face brightened. "Your turn."

She wanted to ask him what his thoughts were on Queen Inga poisoning Harald Falk's mind, and if he thought his father was right to keep the queen's secret. But Thantrel, like most others, remained in the dark about the queen being a whisperer. She respected her twin's mate enough to keep that secret a while longer.

So she turned the tables on him instead. "What about you? Have you ever been in love?"

He laughed. "I should have seen that one coming."

"Well?"

Thantrel let out a long hum. "Twice. To be honest,

I'm surprised the number isn't higher. When I was young, I fell into romance with anyone who caught my eye."

"You're still young," she stated.

Thantrel had turned twenty during their stint at Valrun, though he hadn't told her as much until she'd gone to see him in the healer's sanctuary. He hadn't wanted a celebration then, hadn't even mentioned it, because he'd been heartbroken by her rejection.

"Yes, but I spent a lot of time in brothels growing up —my brothers and I were raised by the ladies there. I learned a lot from them."

"I see . . ."

"Not in *that* way," he added. "No one laid a hand on me. But they spoke about their relationships. Since the age of twelve, love and lust have fascinated me. And when I first felt those pangs of lust, I dove into a relationship and never looked back."

She remained silent, wanting to ask their names, these fae who had stolen his heart. But she wasn't willing to use her third question on names of fae she'd likely never meet, not when she had something better planned.

"I'll give you what you want," he said, reading the conflict on her face and wanting to share more. For her to know him deeply. "My first love was a nymph. We were both fourteen, and she still lives in Avaldenn. Works at a food stall."

Thyra made a note to learn which food stall and, if they won the war, never to go there.

"The second was when I was older. Seventeen. He was a squire to a knight. Our relationship didn't last long. He went to battle an orc horde and never came back."

"I'm so sorry."

Thantrel looked down at the table. "I am too. He wasn't meant for me, but he didn't deserve the end the Fates dealt him."

Before she knew what she was doing, she laid her hand on his. Her winter magic came to life inside her, swirling like a storm in her belly.

His thumb began to rub small circles across her skin, and Thyra swallowed, disliking how her head and her instincts warred.

"My turn." He put them both out of the awkward situation and broke the connection. "I've got something I've been dying to ask."

"Have at it."

"What are you and Isolde going to do if our side wins the war? Have you decided who will sit on the throne?"

Her stomach plummeted. They had not. They avoided that discussion. And it didn't feel right speaking with Thantrel about it before Thyra and her twin worked things out.

"Pass."

"Alright then," Thantrel mused. Perhaps he'd even expected her denial. "Do you have smaller magics?"

Besides her winter and shadow magics, he meant. As he'd been there when King Érebo unlocked her shadow magic, he wasn't being coy. Just keeping a secret in a public place. She appreciated the subtlety from a male who was anything but subtle.

"I do. The powers appeared about a turn back, and I haven't developed the ability, but I'm a dreamer."

"Being a dreamer is unique."

Dreamers were like seers, but they saw visions only in their sleep. And the visions were difficult to differentiate from regular dreams. It had taken Thyra many moons to have a paltry three visions, and only after the third did she realize visions were shiny whereas normal dreams were not. Since she'd understood that distinction, she hadn't had a single vision.

She shrugged. "I can't control it. Maybe if I'd grown up in Frostveil and had the best tutors, things would be different, but none of the rebels could help."

"You should talk to Saga."

"Isolde doesn't even know yet. I'll wait until I tell her."

"Why haven't you told her?"

She smirked. "I'll give you that one for free. I'm sure this won't come as a surprise, but I despise being bad at things. Best to not mention it unless I can control it."

"Should have known."

She scoffed. "Are you quite done?"

"I await your final question." He leaned forward again, filling her nostrils with the scent that sent her heart racing, and then and there, Thyra changed her question. Perhaps changed the course of the kingdom.

"Do you want to kiss me?" she blurted out.

His torso stiffened. "Is that a joke?"

"Not the best decision, considering what Isolde and I agreed to with Lord Balik, but I don't care."

"What agreement?"

Fates she'd done it. She hadn't meant to mention the intricacies of the alliance, but tonight might be her only chance to feel something similar to what her sister had. An enviable partnership. One any fae would long for.

"Lord Balik wishes for me to marry Sian Balik. Or for someone in the next generation of Falks to wed into his line." She left out the accepting her mate part. It made things too complicated when she *should* wed a Balik. That she shouldn't pass this responsibility on to another generation when she'd been the one to make the deal.

Thantrel chuckled. "You're aware that Sian prefers males, right?"

Her lips parted. Was that what Lord Balik meant by his son having preferences? She'd thought that maybe he loved a mistress at court, and Thyra had not cared to explore the matter further.

"I did not."

"He has a pact with Sayyida Virtoris to wed her and do their duty to their houses. Once that's done, they can explore their pleasures as they wish."

"*Oh.*" Her heart fluttered. "Well, in that case, I don't feel bad about asking you my question. But I wonder, will you ever answer?"

An incredulous look passed over his face, to be replaced by a feral expression that made her mouth go dry. Thantrel slipped from his side of the booth, took up the spot by her, and tilted her chin up with those slender, strong fingers.

If she'd been standing, her knees would have buckled.

"Are you sure?" he asked.

"No, but I need to do this," she whispered back.

His lips crashed into hers, and that cold magic that always swirled inside her turned to fire. A hot, blazing fire that made her toes curl and pulled an embarrassing sound from her throat.

He deepened the kiss, maybe thinking he'd never get another, that he'd need to make this kiss last a lifetime. Thyra's tongue slipped into his mouth, swept over his, and she allowed her body to fall into him. To give herself over to the moment that had been haunting her dreams for weeks.

CHAPTER 17
VALE

My hand trailed along the skin of my mate's stomach, smooth and exposed, just like the rest of her.

"Are you teasing me?" Isolde turned in our bed, and her breasts fell heavy to one side.

"Maybe." I leaned in and kissed her.

Isolde moaned into my mouth and pressed her lush body into mine. Fates, we'd indulged in each other five times the night before, and yet, we both wanted more.

"As long as you follow through on the teasing, I don't mind," Isolde whispered. "In fact—"

Three swift knocks came at the door to our suite, making us both startle. I pulled a quilt over my mate. No one would enter without our say so, not with a vampire guarding the door, but the gesture was instinctive.

"I'm sorry to bother you so early, Princess Isolde and Prince Vale," a voice I recognized as Lord Balik's personal butler, Valintin, drifted through the door. "But Prince Vale received a raven, and, well, Lord Balik thought you might want it right away."

I rolled out of bed, pulled on a pair of pants, and went to answer the door. Next to Astril, Valintin stood, holding out a scroll smelling of raven feathers.

"Thank you." I took the small scroll. "Is there anything else?"

"Nothing. Again, my apologies for intruding so early in the morning."

I shut the door and, to my dismay, found Isolde standing there, tying a robe.

"Whose the message from?"

I looked the scroll over. Blue-gray wax, stamped with a sea serpent, sealed the message. I opened it and my heart rate kicked up.

It's from the Lady of Ships herself." I scanned the letter. "She says that Sayyida and Vidar have sided with you. That they're on their way south with a small fleet. Lady Fayeth is waiting for their raven to decide if she will give you her entire fleet, but the ships in the south are to be used at Vidar's discretion."

Isolde placed a hand on a nearby chair. "Thank the stars Saga wrote to Sayyida. Though I can't see how they'd choose to side with us from that. Saga hadn't met Thyra at that point."

"Friendship." I handed her the letter.

Isolde read it over, and her eyes misted. "Sayyida and Vidar believe in us, so they stand with us." She wiped a tear that fell down her cheeks. "I can't wait to see them."

I could not agree more.

Isolde lifted her gaze to meet mine. "Vale, if Lady

Fayeth can be swayed fully, that's three great houses on our side. We stand a chance."

Yes, the Falks remained outnumbered, but the Virtoris Armada might turn the tides of any war. Especially if we took the fight right to Avaldenn. Much of the city was open to the sea, making an armada a pivotal piece on the board.

"Now that I know we have the support of Houses Balik, Riis, and very possibly, Virtoris too, I need to write to House Armenil," Isolde said. "I hope that since my maternal grandmother was born of that house, they'll be easy to win over. If we get them, then maybe the king will see a war is futile, and many lives can be saved. Would you mind adding a note too?"

I doubted King Magnus would back down, but nothing was impossible.

"I'll write a letter to Connan and send it alongside yours." The new head of house after Sten Armenil's death. "Lady Orla and Lord Sten were mates. The high lady will not be able to deal with matters of war, but in your letter add a condolence note to her."

"Of course." Isolde kissed my cheek before strolling to the desk in our room. "You should shower. I'll get to writing."

We gathered around House Balik's black-stone war table, a great map of Winter's Realm spread before us. Over key cities loomed carved stone animals representing the great houses of the kingdom. Those with wealth and influence and armies.

A white bear, a lion, a snow leopard, a silver stag, and a burnt orange fox congregated in Avaldenn, where the king was calling armies. Not just great house armies were present either, but those of lesser houses. We left those representations off, not having enough information to correctly determine the entirety of who and what we might be up against.

The ram of House Balik sat alongside an ice spider, a white hawk that came with rebel fighters, and a polished gray stone to represent the dwarves of Dergia. A sea serpent rode in the sea to the east.

The direwolf of House Armenil remained in its home city of Morial, where Isolde's letter was already winging its way. If the winds were fair and we met with no opposition from the great house of the north, we might count them as allies as soon as next week.

"Lord Lisika's army is the largest in the realm. Add four more armies to that side and we're greatly outnumbered on land," Tadgh Balik said. "However, with the Virtoris Armada dominating the sea, that might not matter so much. If we can come at Avaldenn from two fronts, land and sea, there's potential to end this quickly."

Quickly, in war terms, was relative.

I'd fought many battles. Most of those were against orc tribes, but a few had been against mage pirates that had once tried to claim the eastern islands near Grindavik for their own. Never had I been involved in a full-blown war against other winter fae. I'd been too young during the White Bear's rebellion, and we'd had peace since.

Yet here we stood, planning to shatter that peace. To strike first in a war. I tried to take heart that Lord Balik was right in his assessment. That if we took Avaldenn, the war might end up being a single large battle, and extend only to a single city.

But through all the planning, a large part of me could not help but imagine Tyiel, the god of battle, and his father, Odan. Neither were known to favor brief battles. Above all, they loved the drawn-out fight, the blood-soaked prayers uttered to them as death lurked nearby. The matter if the gods were dead or hiding away was hotly debated in Isila. In my opinion, it might be better if those two gods were gone entirely. At least in that case they could not instigate more bloodshed.

"We can't discuss the precise contributions of House Virtoris until Vidar and Sayyida arrive," I pointed out. "And I'd like not to make a move north until we receive word from House Armenil."

"That might be too late," Lord Balik countered. "With the snow beginning to melt, we could be at Avaldenn in a short time. A week and a half at most."

"I, too, would rather move sooner." Lord Riis said. "Before Magnus has time to coordinate his forces. We ought to send another raven to the north. Tell Lord Connan to march as soon as he can."

"I already sent a raven," Isolde spoke up. "And we can't offend House Armenil in that way."

My mate had been quiet during the meeting, and for good reason. She was intelligent and caught on quickly, but Isolde had limited knowledge of fighting, and none of war. Of those at the table, only Lord Balik and Lord Riis had fought in a war before.

"It will cost precious time. Souls too," Lord Riis said.

Isolde looked to Lord Balik. "Besides, we cannot force potential allies to act. If we do, then are Thyra and I any better than King Magnus? Forcing your children into marriages? Forcing fae into his disgusting harem?"

"We wait," Thyra echoed. "Besides, we have the army of Dergia arriving soon. What would be the point of having them travel here only to leave before they arrive?"

Thyra had an excellent point. I hadn't gotten the sense that King Tholin of Dergia took offense easily, but leaving before our first allies arrived would be no small slight.

Thyra lifted the hawk representing her house from the table, turned it over in her fingers. "If we must act in the meantime, my rebels are skilled in irregular means of fighting. We can send some to the capital to cause chaos while armies are moving."

The rebel forces totaled only about three hundred and fifty fae, just over two hundred of which were not suitable for fighting. At just twenty-three, with precious few resources at her disposal, Thyra Falk had gathered a small but devoted group that had caused substantial damage in their own ways.

"Very well," Lord Balik agreed in word, though his tone was skeptical. "When will the forces from Dergia arrive then? If we know that, then we can plan for a smooth and fast exit."

"*After* they've had time to recover," Isolde added, her tone cooler than before.

Now that the Virtoris Armada was within our reach,

Lord Balik and Lord Riis were pushing hard for the Falks to take on King Magnus right away. To win quickly and minimize damage and in the case of Lord Riis, to save my mother, which I wanted too. The longer a war went on, the more likely their own people and properties would sustain damage. And while I understood their reasoning, and wished to save my mother as well, I understood that she'd known this would happen. Or at least suspected it. So, I stood with Isolde and Thyra.

Together, Prince Thordur and Princess Bavirra stood. It had taken some convincing her brother that Bavirra should join us in the war meetings, but the princess had won. She had gotten a taste for adventure, and I did not think she'd let go of that ever again.

"The tunnels under the mountains aren't combed often by scouts. Only every turn or two and not all of them are done at that time. We rotate." With his finger, Thordur traced a path that ran beneath the Ice Teeth Range, a secret series of tunnels that only his people knew. "If all is well in the passages, I assume they'll be around here." He gestured to a place on the map. "Only three or four days away."

"Besides the tunnels being obstructed, what would stop them?" Sian asked. Since the dwarves' arrival in Myrr, my friend had not stopped showing his curiosity about the Kingdom of Dergia.

"Ice spiders and other creatures that are not fae, but equally as dangerous, live in the tunnels. And then there are the orcs, ogres, even frost giants that have slipped into the lost dwarven kingdoms," Bavirra answered. "Our soldiers have fought all of them. To the death."

The dead told no secrets. They couldn't spread the word that Dergia thrived beneath the Rock, when all in Winter's Realm thought they were dead and gone.

"In the meantime, should we venture into other towns and cities?" Luccan suggested. "We might be able to rouse more support around the common people."

Uncomfortable silence settled over the table, which Isolde broke.

"We might, but they could support King Magnus," my mate mused. "He's using the Ice Scepter to melt the snow. That will gain him popularity. And outside of Avaldenn, I'm not sure how far his cruelty spread."

"Mostly, fae were angry that the winter never ended, as much as it can in this kingdom, anyway," Thyra said. "Of course, they heard rumors of the atrocities the king committed in Avaldenn and closer cities and towns, but it's easy to forget that sort of behavior when it's not directed at you. When you don't have to see it and live under its thumb, and you have other matters to deal with. And especially when your hardships are lifted."

"It's worth a try, though." Excitement sparked in Sian's eyes. "A small number can roam cities. Not Thyra or Isolde or Vale—no one so recognizable. But they can get the temperature of the common fae. Recruit if they're sure it will not be in danger."

I arched my brows at my friend. "That means you're staying here, Sian."

He frowned. Not what he wanted to hear, but when his father nodded, I knew he wouldn't have been able to go, anyway.

"I can offer services there. Many in my spy network

are still loyal to me. I'll have them put out feelers." My father's gaze shifted to the Falk twins.

It seemed to take great effort, but Isolde met his gaze and nodded.

"And have you learned anything of the Frør Crown or the Blade?" Lord Balik asked. "You focused on Shadow Fae, but your Hallows might be of use, too."

"We have learned nothing new on those fronts," Isolde said. "And you're right. We need to look into those more. They're hiding secrets."

We covered a few more matters, and the meeting adjourned. I took Isolde's hand as we left.

She exhaled, looked up at me. "That was intense. Care for a drink?"

"With you? Always." I leaned closer. "Lord Balik gets spirits sent from the Autumn Court. Ones we don't get in Avaldenn."

"Did I hear you whispering about my father's liquor collection?" Sian butted in. "If so, I'm in."

"Not that you were invited," I teased. "But please, take us to that trove."

CHAPTER 18

ISOLDE

Sian took twenty bottles of expensive liquor from Lord Balik's personal stash.

Perhaps I should have felt guilty about taking so much from my ally when, so far, I'd offered little in return, but I could find no place for such an emotion. Not when the day had wrung me out. And especially not when I was surrounded by my friends in a cozy den inside Ramshold, all of us safe and a bit tipsy. We needed a moment to just *be*.

Near the window, Vale sat with his cabal. That clandestine group preferred the bite of Dragon Fire, whereas the ladies had taken to the less intense cinnamon-flavored spirits hailing from the Autumn Court. Though if Sayyida were present, I was sure we'd have a bottle of Dragon Fire, too.

My heart clenched at the thought of my storm-spirited friend sailing our way. I hoped she would arrive soon. Not just because I wanted House Virtoris for an ally, but I missed my friends. Missed Vidar's kindness and Sayyida's boldness.

"Do you remember when you said you'd make me a dress, Isolde?" a voice brought me back to the circle of ladies sitting with me.

I smiled at Marit, sitting primly with her ankles crossed. On either side of her lounged Princess Bavirra and my sister.

"I want to make it green to match your eyes and complement your hair. It'll be so lovely."

Marit clapped her hands together. "So you're still going to make it? I'll admit, I've been envious of that amethyst one you wore ever since I first saw it."

"You're that good?" Thyra tipped her goblet until it was at a precarious angle.

"I'm skilled."

"She's one of the best seamstresses I've ever seen." Anna sat next to me, Thyra on my other side. Two sisters, one of the heart, one of blood.

"You're just as good."

"That's why I said *one* of the best." Anna winked. "I was trying to be polite."

Laughter spread around the jagged circle, loosening us up even more than the drink.

"Well, I can't wait to wear my gown. Whenever you get around to making it," Marit said when the laughter ran out.

She left off that I'd have to survive the war, which I appreciated. Tonight was for fun, not for considering what doom may come.

Movement came from where the males sat, and I

caught Qildor rising, casting a glance our way. The recipient of his gaze, Marit, didn't fail to see him.

Marit cleared her throat. "But for now, I must retire."

My lips parted, and my gaze darted around the circle, caught the mirth in Saga and the Balik sister's faces. Even Clem and Anna appeared to be holding in their laughter, but it was Bavirra's expression, one that clearly stated Marit wasn't hiding anything from anyone—not even the dwarf who barely knew her—that made my laughter bubble over.

"Retire?" I asked coyly. "But Marit, it's only the ninth bell!"

"We were going to drink all night!" Saga pressed, her face full of relish.

"I'm not feeling up for it anymore," Marit replied.

Another round of laughter brought a scowl to her lips, and I was sure that she had to force herself not to look at him as Qildor passed by and bid us good night.

When her knight slipped from the room, Bavirra pointed to the door. "He's quite handsome, isn't he?"

"It's the black hair and the violet eyes," Clem added. "What a remarkable combination."

"Oh, all of you are so horrible!" Marit grinned even as she spoke. "Fine, I want a bit of alone time with him. Is that what you want to hear?"

"Not that we needed to," Eireann said, "but it *is* quite satisfying."

"I'm begging you, though, when we ask you about you two tomorrow, please have some more salacious gossip. A good, long kiss, at the very least!" Baenna tossed up her hands.

Marit sighed. "If a kiss happens, I'll shout it from the towers. But I must go, before he comes to the conclusion that I'm not coming at all." With that, she rushed out of the room.

"They haven't kissed?" Bavirra turned back to the circle.

Saga let out a long breath. "My father forced Marit to wed Jarl Triam, an absolute mound of gryphon dung, mind you, and unfortunately, they're still married."

"Not just an arsehole, but a murderer!" Clemencia added.

"That too." Saga nodded vigorously. "Qildor is very much the honorable sort. It probably nearly killed him to abandon the Clawsguard for Marit, and I'm not sure he'll make a move until her marriage officially ends."

"I hope that's by Jarl Triam's death." Eireann's eyes glinted with suppressed malice. "Marit got the worst of the Courting Festival. Even in that short time she was under his control, he hurt her badly."

I wondered what the Balik sisters made of their forced matches. Their father had seen both pairings as a slight, but neither Baenna nor Eireann had uttered a word about them.

"Isolde and I will terminate that marriage." Thyra looked to me. "And any other unwanted union set by Magnus too."

"Of course," I added, tossing my sister a smile.

The conversation strayed from Marit and her noble knight to other matters, all of them far from the war to come. A welcome respite. My sister was more animated than I'd ever seen her and had bonded well with Princess

Bavirra. I was having a wonderful time, and it seemed the males were too, when the topic of mine and Thyra's namedays came up.

"Vale told me your namedays fell on the Winter Solstice," Saga said two bells later. "And I hope you two don't mind, but we are planning to throw a little dinner party." She gestured to Anna, Clem, and the Balik sisters.

"Planning?" I asked. "Since when?"

"Four days ago," Clem supplied. Her cheeks had turned rosy from the spirits. "It's important to celebrate milestones. This one especially. Until recently, no one knew you two were alive. Now there will be a splendid meal to celebrate with you!"

I looked at my twin, who appeared shocked at the turn of conversation, but upon catching my eyes, she smiled.

"We spent our early namedays together, but none since then," Thyra said softly. "It's a nice idea."

I'd been more worried over the question of *if* we should have such a celebration with everything going on. But if I couldn't celebrate my nameday with my twin— and the very fact that we were still alive, when everyone else in our family was dead—what were we doing this for, anyway?

"Do you need any help planning?" I asked.

Saga beamed as she shook her head. "Absolutely not! You two just show up."

"I'm going to end the night on a high note." Thyra stood from her armchair. "The rest of the rebels are due to arrive tomorrow. I don't want to be hungover when they do."

As it was getting late, we all agreed to call it a night,

and our party disbanded. I went to Vale and kissed his cheek.

"Bed calls, but you look like you're having fun, so don't feel pressured to join. I won't wait up."

"Sleep well." He kissed me on the lips.

I left with Clem and Anna, both of whom had also stayed behind to say goodnight to the males they adored. We parted when they reached their rooms, across from one another, and I continued on to mine, relieving Astril of her guard over Sassa's Blade.

I was slipping beneath the quilt when a knock came at the door. I waited for Astril to speak, but a different muffled voice met my ear.

Is that coming from Thyra's door? I sat up.

My nosiness fortified by the spirits I'd imbibed, I slipped from my bed, tiptoed to the door, and placed my ear against the wood. A masculine laugh—Thantrel's laugh—rang through the hallway before the door closest to my suite shut.

A grin spread across my face, and looking forward to teasing my sister again, I threw the door open wide.

Livia stared back at me from Thyra's door, and I did not miss Astril's lips quirk up. They were hiding something.

"Thantrel is visiting her suite?"

"I was told not to say anything," Livia answered.

A laugh tripped off my lips. "I don't need you to tell me." I marched across the hallway and, without knocking, opened my sister's door.

Neither my twin nor Thantrel were in the main room. "Thyra! Thantrel! I know you're both in here!"

That same masculine laugh erupted from the bathing chamber, and my mouth fell open as Thantrel's head poked out.

"Shouldn't you be asleep, Isolde?"

"Why are you in *my sister's bathing chamber?*"

In answer, Thantrel's head disappeared. I paused, assessing the situation like I probably should have before. He hadn't been wet, and I'd seen his shirt. He was clothed. Maybe Thantrel was giving Thyra an eyeliner tutorial?

"Now that you've barged in, are you going to join us?" Thyra called out.

Well, I supposed that I was. I crossed the main suite and poked my head inside her bathing chamber. My cheeks flamed.

"You're in the bath!" I sputtered as I took in my sister, hidden beneath mounds and mounds of bubbles, a wicked grin on her face.

Thyra threw a handful of bubbles at me. "Well spotted."

"I thought he was showing you how to do his eyeliner or something." Stars, it sounded so stupid when I said those words out loud.

Thantrel gave me the most smug, self-satisfied smile.

"You're saying that eyeliner tips made you seek me out, sister?" Thyra's tone was too sweet, too innocent. "Or did you really just want to catch me kissing this pretty male?"

I said nothing, which prompted a booming laugh from Thantrel.

Thyra grinned up at him. Both of them were having too much fun embarrassing me.

My hands landed on my hips, and Thantrel rose, apparently taking pity on me.

"As much as I love hearing that I'm pretty, I'll be going now." He took Thyra's hand from where it was draped over the edge of the copper tub and lifted it to his lips. The kiss he deposited was soft and still, I looked away from the private moment. "Goodnight, Thyra."

"Goodnight."

Thantrel winked at me before leaving the suite. I held it together for three seconds after he shut the door before scurrying over to my sister.

"I cannot believe that just happened!"

"It's not like we were doing anything. I was already buried in bubbles when I had Livia let him in. We were just talking."

The way Thyra said it made me think they had. "Wait, has something happened?"

"Well, we've kissed a few times."

My heart stopped. "How many exactly?"

"Three."

"*Three times*!" I slapped her shoulder, spraying water and bubbles on the ground in the process. "Thyra, how dare you not tell me!"

She laughed. "I didn't want you to get your hopes up, but it seems I've failed in that regard."

"Why not?"

Was she not going to accept her mate? After kissing him?

I didn't understand how that could happen. Vale and I

had barely been able to keep our hands off each other when we thought our marriage was a sham and we had no star-blessed connection at all.

"Because of the deal with Lord Balik," Thyra replied as one hand swirled the thick bubbles.

I made a wild gesture with my hands. "I realize now that I forgot to tell you this after our meeting with Lord Balik, but you need to know that Sian is gay."

"Thantrel told me, but does that really matter? Royal and noble households expect what they expect, and why would I want to pass on the responsibility of marrying into a line to someone else? Someone who didn't ask for it? We are the ones who asked for the alliance. If we live and have children, they should not pay for our choices."

She had me there. And yet, I couldn't let my sister not fulfill her mating bond if she wanted to do so. I took her hands. "I'm going to talk to Sian. Would you change your mind if he flat-out told you he didn't want to marry you?"

Her eyebrows pinched together. "That would make things easier. Though I still wouldn't feel wonderful about passing the responsibility to a youngling in the future."

"That's assuming we have any." I let out a sigh, trying to be rational, though when I thought of having younglings with Vale, my musings always turned dreamy. One day, I wanted that. But one day wasn't promised.

"The thing is, you have to live for now. We may win this war, but we also may not. And if we don't, I want you to have experienced as much as you can." I lifted my left hand, showed her the soulmate mark. "This is worth it."

Her gaze trained on the snowflakes lining my finger,

and she was quiet for a long moment before nodding. "I'll think about it."

CHAPTER 19

VALE

I reached across the bed, only to find Isolde's side of the bed was cold. Blinking my eyes open, I looked around the suite and found my mate across the bedroom, staring out the window.

"Force," I whispered. "When did you wake up?"

"Not long ago," she replied, her tone strained.

I sat up. "What's wrong?"

"The snow is completely gone. People are dancing in the streets." She turned, her face pale in the weak morning light. "Is it wrong that I feel conflicted?"

Understanding washed over me. For decades, the snow dominated our land. Surely the people would wonder if supporting a new ruler was wise when King Magnus had finally bent Winter's Realm to his will.

Most fae understood little about the Ice Scepter, and less about the other Hallows. They only knew the magic and weather of the kingdom was controlled by some intricate balance between the ruler and the Scepter. But some said there were additional forces beyond anyone's control.

Godly forces. Almost no one knew that the king had not possessed the Scepter until recently. That he'd allowed them to suffer while he'd searched for the Hallow.

"At least marching north will be easier." Isolde let out a long breath.

I kissed her as she joined me and perched on the edge of our bed. "Did you sleep well?"

"Enough." She played with the hem of the quilt, then a gasp punctuated the air and my mate faced me. "You won't believe what I saw last night. Before you came in!"

I stayed up until the second morning bell, and Isolde had been fast asleep when I returned. "What's that?"

"Thantrel was watching Thyra bathe. And they've kissed three times!"

I laughed. "Thantrel has seemed happier of late. More like his old self. That explains why."

She caught me up on what her sister had said, then what the ladies had spoken of. I did the same, sharing anything I thought would bring my mate delight. Eventually, the worry of the snow melting left her face.

"I'm ready to break my fast," she said. "Should we dress and join the family?"

"Good idea. The rebels are set to arrive today. I'll need a big meal to get them settled in."

Isolde and Thyra would continue practicing with their shadow magic, but the rest of us would make sure the vast majority of the rebels were welcomed to Myrr and given housing. Later, the twins would visit.

"Let's go," Isolde said. "I'm starving!"

❄

The rebels arrived three bells later.

"I understand we can't all stay at the castle," a rebel asked as we made our way through Myrr, "but why are we so far from it?"

Many of these fae were used to being in the same castle as Thyra at all times, some having her steps down the hallway. They hadn't enjoyed learning that they'd be separated from her, and I suspected that any distance short of across the street would not be suitable.

"These three buildings have many little homes inside," Bac replied. "They will house all of you in the same place, which is the best we could do."

"You? Not us . . . you're not staying with us, are you, Bac?"

I cringed. We'd thought that such news would be better coming from Bac. He was one of their own. Perhaps we'd been wrong.

"I'm not," Bac replied. "Nor are Brynhild or the three Valkyrja who accompanied you. They'll be advising and protecting the princesses. However, I'm here almost daily checking in. And the princesses have visited."

Once and only briefly. They wanted to come down more often, but magic and combat practice took up most of their time.

Grumblings sounded off and rippled through the throng of traveling rebels. Things weren't going well, and not just with those new to the city.

As we made our way through the snow-free streets, I couldn't help but notice many of the citizens of Myrr were watching us. Precious few with welcoming smiles on their faces. No, these looks of dislike were born from turns of rebel actions towards the Myrranese and other outlying towns. Of word spreading further and wider of exactly who was being allowed to live in the city.

I did my best to ease the anxiety choking the streets, waving and smiling at some fae, and when we reached the buildings where the rebels would stay, I breathed a sigh of relief, thinking the experience was over. That soon the rebels would be safe and the citizens of Myrr would not see them as a threat.

Things will be fine, I thought, just as the first rotten apple soared into the crowd behind me and slammed into a youngling's head. She cried out, and rebels burst from the group and towards the supposed offender. So fast. As if they'd been waiting for an attack.

"Stop!" Sian shouted as he and Filip darted toward those in this city. Fae they had influence over. "Everyone stop!"

Luccan, Bac, and I veered for the rebels, who were the only ones armed since they'd had to walk for days through the kingdom. The fae Valkyrja joined us, sandwiching themselves between my line and that of Sian and Filip.

Bac thrust his hands toward the few rebels who had surged out of the protective bounds of the Balik soldiers. "Where will you go if the high lord throws you out of Myrr?"

"They started it!" a female, the mother of the struck youngling, if the way she clutched the crying child to her was any sign. "We're trying to get to safety."

"Like you deserve it! Look at those weapons!" a citizen of Myrr shouted. "Might even be the same steel that cut into my son two turns back!"

I swallowed. That fae might be right. I had no way to be sure, and I doubted the rebel did either.

"And she looks like an orc!" A male thrust a finger at Tonna, one fifth of my mate's Valkyrja.

To Tonna's credit, her facial expression didn't change in the slightest. I suspected that outside the home she'd made with the rebels, Tonna was used to being feared and mocked.

"*Quiet!* I *demand* quiet!" Filip held up his hands, and because he was the next lord of the southlands and everyone in the city recognized him, people did, in fact, fall quiet.

"My father has pardoned these people! We're in an alliance with the Princesses Isolde and Thyra Falk, and these fae are loyal to them. You will not harm them. You will not violate them. And if you do, there will be *severe* repercussions." Filip stared into the crowd, as if daring them to say otherwise. "We are allies now, and the people of the Golden City will treat them as such!"

Grumbles came from those who called Myrr home, but no one spoke out. No one struck again.

"Now," Sian broke the tension-filled silence. "If the Myrranese could give us some space to get these people settled in, it would be appreciated."

A few bowed or curtsied to their lordlings, chastened. Notable others, however, tossed sour looks over their shoulders as they left. Only when the last subject of Myrr was gone did I relax.

"Bac, Luccan, and the Valkyrja, get the travelers settled please." They nodded at my command and shuffled people into the apartment. Once I stood alone with the Balik males, I spoke freely. "We'll need to set up a larger guard right away. I don't trust that nothing will happen if we leave the rebels alone. But I don't want them to feel as if they can't leave to do something as simple as taking a walk either."

Myrr might not be their forever home, but it was their home for now.

"Agreed," Filip exhaled. "We'll leave half the guard that came with us, and I'll speak to my father about creating a rotation."

Sian gave his younger brother an approving look. "They'll be safe. We promise. It might take the Myrranese some time, but they're a peaceful people."

Yes, but uncertain times could change people. War could too. Still, there was nothing to do but proceed with the plan, and hope that we'd made the right choice in bringing everyone to the Golden City.

CHAPTER 20

ISOLDE

My fingers trembled as tendrils of shadows spun from their tips to retrieve a goblet.

"Almost there, Isolde." Thyra leaned so far forward on the settee in my quarters that she was in danger of tipping off. "I can't believe this is happening."

After days of reading the book bound with Shadow Fae skin and practicing as often as we could, my sister and I had both managed to call tendrils of shadow magic out of our bodies. And about fifty percent of the time, those emerging shadows would listen to what we wished.

The end effect was much like when we used Sassa's Blade. However, this power came from within us and not a bloodthirsty sword that King Érebo imbued with his magic for his mate. Then again, using the dark tendrils didn't sit particularly *right* with us either.

My sister and I agreed that shadow magic felt oily and off. Nothing like our crisp and clean winter magic. Like something that had forced its way into us and was not truly a part of us. Not yet anyway.

Had Falks in the past felt that too? Had they known about this dark power hidden deep within our lineage and embraced it? I didn't think we'd ever find out. They wouldn't risk writing about such things. Not even in personal journals. The Shadow Fae had a poor reputation, and wielding their magic would not be in favor.

Will not be in favor, I reminded myself as I focused on the goblet, the rim stained with red wine. I commanded the tendrils to pick up the vessel and bring it to me.

The shadows swooped around the vessel, caressed it, and I felt the coolness of metal and glass against my own fingers, smooth and faceted. An odd sensation since I wasn't touching the materials, except through my magic. I tried not to let that strangeness distract me and instead made my request again.

Pick it up. Bring it back.

The tendrils tightened their hold and the goblet hovered in the air and floated my way. I held my breath. Thyra's excitement seemed to mount as the object of focus got closer and closer. When the shadows stopped in front of me, I reached out and took the vessel in my hand. I turned to my sister and beamed.

"Nice job." She returned my smile. "I think we've got a handle on this. At least for small tasks."

"Repetition is key," I agreed.

"How do you feel?"

"Fine. Not tired." When we'd first started practicing with shadow magic, our attempts had wiped us out within minutes, but I had built up a tolerance.

"I felt stronger too. We should try to move larger objects. Or perform more complex tasks."

In learning to use shadow magic, Thyra had progressed further than me, and she wanted to move on to something that might tip the scales in the days to come. To use the shadows in battle.

"I'm all in for lifting bigger things, but I'm not ready to spar yet."

"Maybe we should study the book more and see where we can stretch our powers next." She gestured to where it sat, pages open and waiting. Not only did it have the basics of Shadow Fae magic in it, but the tome possessed lessons on advanced magic, some of it quite wicked and gory.

I opened my mouth to reply as a knock sounded at my door. To my horror, my shadows flew at the handle. Wrapped around it.

"Wait!" I cried, but my control over them was gone. The tendrils opened the door, shot past Astril, the Valkyrja on guard, and hovered—right in front of Saga and Marit.

Marit's eyes went wide, and Saga's mouth dropped open. It would have been comical if it wasn't so bleeding horrible.

Pushing my will into the shadows, I commanded them to dissipate. To vanish. They did, but the damage had been done.

Saga made to step into my room, and Astril held out a hand to stop her.

"Let her." There was no way around this.

Saga breezed past the vampire and pulled Marit in behind her. The door shut, leaving us alone, and the princess studied me with interest. "You have some explaining to do."

"We will," I assured her.

"We? Do *both* of you have them?"

I wanted to slap myself, but there was only one thing to do. Tell the truth and beg them to stay quiet until we were ready to let others know.

"Yes," Thyra said. "We only recently found out. We were waiting to spread the word, but Isolde's shadows had something else in mind."

Saga nodded. "It would seem so. Tell me what happened."

So we did. We told Saga and Marit what only a select few knew. Once we finished, Marit breathed out a long breath.

"This might hurt your cause."

"We expect that," Thyra replied. "That's why we're trying to master the power. It's only a matter of time before the Shadow King likely outs us anyway."

"Well, I'll stay quiet," Marit said.

"As will I, but now I have something to admit," Saga said slowly.

My eyebrows flew up. "Do tell?"

"I think I've seen that magic before."

You could have heard a sewing needle drop in the suite.

"It was a long time ago, so I might be wrong," Saga filled the silence. "I was on a blessing journey."

"A what?" I asked.

"It's where royals go on ships to bless the maiden voyage," Saga explained. "It was my first journey of the sort and pirates attacked. I thought they were mages, or at least part mage. Their kind can wield darkness too, and it looked just like that. I mistook it for smoke during the fight. Only later did Sayyida call them shadows, and I agreed. The dark masses we saw looked more like that. Less hazy and more like a bending of dark light. They were the oddest thing I've seen, and very much like what you just wielded, though larger."

I cut Thyra an incredulous glance.

"I wonder if I wasn't seeing Shadow Fae?" Saga's tongue pressed against her cheek, making it bulge out. "Sayyida might remember more."

"That's all you can tell us?" Thyra pressed.

"I can tell you the entire tale, but what's important is the magic looked the same, and many of those on board looked like fae. I didn't leap to the Shadow Fae conclusion because why would I? As far as everyone knew, they were gone."

"Mages, or part mages, does make more sense," I agreed. "We'll ask Sayyida more when she arrives."

"Now, I must ask, what brought you two here?" Thyra changed the subject.

"Ah! Right!" Saga's lips formed a cunning smile. "I come with news of the Frør Crown."

Thyra stiffened. "How?"

"I'm a seer. I see visions of the future. *Possible* futures. And sometimes I've seen the past. In one such vision, I saw your mother and father talking about the Crown."

I blinked. "When did this happen?"

"Before I met you. It was one of my first visions. And to be fair, I didn't know who the fae I was watching were. I thought they were a lord and lady looking at a crown their ancestors once wore before the Unification. I haven't seen the Hallow in person, but today Clemencia showed me a painting of the Frør Crown, and I recognized it immediately. The people in my vision must have been your parents." Her tone dropped at the end, unease taking over.

I blamed Saga for *nothing* and would not have her feeling guilt over her parents' actions. She hadn't even been born when her father overthrew my family.

"What did you see?" I asked.

"It was a long time ago, so my memory is fuzzy, but . . . The Frør Crown can show you things that happened, right?"

"Yes," Thyra said. "Though it's only done so once. To Isolde when she first put it on."

Inside a vault in Avaldenn, the Crown had shown me the scene between King Érebo and Sassa Falk. However, despite trying the Hallow on multiple times since, I'd seen nothing else. Neither had Thyra, and she had tried to use it far more times than I had. The only other time the Crown showed signs of life was when it had heated—just as Sassa's Blade had—as we drew close to where King Érebo had been trapped in the tree.

"Well, your father, King Harald, mentioned that the Crown can also see the future. Even manipulate it in small ways."

I sucked in a breath. *Manipulate the future*—like by working with the Blade to draw us into a mountain where an ancient enemy waited. Vale had called the Crown scheming, for it seemed to have led us to the Shadow Fae King, the very faerie it had shown me in the vision. Maybe he had been right.

"Are you sure that's what he said?" I asked.

"It always stuck with me because how can a crown be manipulative?" Saga shrugged. "Anyway, King Harald also said that within your family, it was called the Seer's Crown. I got the sense that he was explaining it so that your mother would try to use it."

"Does that mean only seers can use it for the future?" Thyra asked.

"Mother was a healer."

"Some people have multiple talents. Perhaps she had visions and our father wanted to test the bounds of possibility." My twin paused, and I got the sense she wanted to say more but did not.

Before the Shadow King freed shadow magic within me, I had only been able to use winter magic. However, there were indeed many fae with multiple talents. Like Saga, a seer with winter magic. Or Thantrel, who could speak with animals, use air magic, and had other small magics too.

"Besides, Isolde used it, so I think that makes it clear that you don't need to be a seer. More likely the power is tied to your family name," Saga said. "Maybe the first ruler to use it had been a seer and imbibed some of that magic into a Hallow of the realm? More importantly, if you learn how to use the Crown properly, small things might be able to change."

A pebble tossed into a pond caused ripples. Small matters might well change the course of our lives. Of many lives.

"What else do you know?" Thyra demanded.

"Nothing. I was ripped from that vision of the past

and never looked for it again. Not until I saw that painting."

"Can you try to learn more?" I asked. "Maybe look for people speaking of the Crown in the past? Or see the future with clarity?"

"I doubt it," Saga said. "Some of the best seers could, but I'm far from that. I won't develop my magic all the way for turns to come."

"But could you try?" Thyra pressed.

"Of course I can *try*, but I make no promises."

I shot my sister a sidelong glance. It was a step. In which direction, I wasn't sure, but at least we had an idea of what the Crown could do in capable hands.

"Please do," I said to my friend. "We'd appreciate it."

"Of course." Saga looped her arm through Marit's. The latter still looked thunderstruck to have walked in on Thyra and me using shadow magic. "Well, I suppose we'll let you get back to practicing."

"Uh, yes. Good luck," Marit said, as though she barely believed the words coming out of her own mouth.

I laughed dryly. "Thanks. We're going to need it."

Alone again, Thyra turned to me. "There's something I must tell you. Something few people know but might be useful knowing what we now know about the Frør Crown."

"What's that?"

"I'm a dreamer."

Having grown up alongside humans, I hadn't known many fae, and some magics were more common than others. Like elemental magic.

"What is that?" I asked.

"I see visions, but only when I am asleep."

I gasped. "*A seer.*"

"Not in a very useful way, though. I bet I have weaker control over my magic than Saga."

I did not doubt that. Seer magic was unpredictable and often took many decades to learn how to manage.

"Still, this means the power could run in our family to this day. Have you worn the Crown to bed?"

She laughed. "It's uncomfortable, and why would I think to do that?" An elbow hit my side. "I'm not that full of myself."

"Debatable."

My twin stuck out her tongue. "Faetia forbid a lady like herself."

"You should try it tonight," I said, ready to get to the meat of the matter. "With what Saga told us, it makes some sense."

Thyra stared at me, and after a few seconds, nodded. "I'll give it a try."

INTERLUDE
LADY SAYYIDA VIRTORIS,
HOUSE OF THE SEA SERPENT

The eastern winds blew her curls around her eyes as Sayyida Virtoris strode through the throngs of dockworkers, gaze downcast to draw minimal attention.

Sayyida and Vidar had traveled to the small eastern port with a skeleton crew on one ship, their smallest, least adorned vessel, *Slynkr*.

She wasn't a war vessel, but a smuggler's ship, owned by the family boasting the most robust armada in Winter's Realm. And today, *Slynkr* had done her job and smuggled Sayyida and Vidar into an unfamiliar city. A city that, through a letter from Saga, Lord Riis has told them to journey to.

The rest of their fleet had continued south, to anchor among the small islands closer to Grindavik. While not an ideal scenario for the Virtoris siblings to stray so far from the fleet, among those remote islands, their ships would not draw the attention of anyone loyal to House Ithamai.

"I see the flag."

Sayyida glanced up, found it too. "Should we scout the area first?"

Even if she was certain Saga would never betray her, Sayyida held no such assurances for Lord Riis. She did not know him well enough, and he *was* a spymaster, after all. House Skuld, the lesser house that ruled Vantalia, was another issue. They remained loyal to the king.

"I think so," Vidar said.

They climbed up the final ramp, feet finding the cobbles, free of snow and packed ice. As she entered the shelter of the city's buildings and the maritime winds were dampened, she realized Winter's Realm was nearly warm enough to walk about without a cloak.

The city was on the small side, and as they walked the streets, Sayyida was not impressed by what she saw.

"Eireann wouldn't have fit in here well at all," Vidar murmured.

She laughed without humor, having forgotten that Eireann had been betrothed to some rat-faced male from House Skuld. The king knew how to make enemies by mistreating the sons and daughters of the great lords and ladies.

"Not enough luxury," Sayyida agreed.

Myrr was the Golden City, the Jewel of the Southlands, and though that shining name came about because of the vast number of light fae the Baliks produced, there was quite a lot of gold, too. Vantalia, by comparison, was drab and depressing. Every shop they passed appeared run down, the wood rotting from the salt and sea water. The fae looked little better. Such sadness ringed their eyes that Sayyida had to wonder what was going on in the city that made it such a miserable place to live.

They'd walked for about ten minutes and observed nothing of note. No one appeared to be following them. And aside from the drunken nymph who had tried to force coin from their hands before Sayyida told him off, nobody on the street was paying close attention. Above, no one eased out their windows.

"I think we should head back." Sayyida nodded back in the direction they'd come. "We can wait by the brothel for a while to be extra careful. Observe who comes and goes?"

Her brother gave a succinct nod. "I agree. Let's—"

A figure dropped out of the air before them. Short, but not as short as a dwarf, with a black hood obscuring their face.

"Actually," a raspy feminine voice purred. "I have a better plan for two sea serpents skulking around Vantalia."

Sayyida drew her blade. Vidar was only a second slower.

Where did this female come from!? Sayyida chanced a glance up. The motion gave her away.

"Yes, the rooftops." The female did not appear at all bothered by their swords. "You're not as inconspicuous as you think."

"Who are you?" Vidar demanded. "And how do you know who we are?"

"*Ooooh,* that voice!" The fae leaned one shoulder against the closest building. At her touch, blue paint chips fell to the cobbles. "You must have all the ladies dropping their garments, Lord Virtoris!"

"Don't say our names!" Sayyida hissed. More could be listening from windows.

"Any other names I might give such a handsome lord are inappropriate, so you tell me, what else am I supposed to call him? I was told that only you'd be here, *Lady Glia*."

Sayyida's spine straightened at the name. The one she was supposed to use when they entered Lord Riis's brothel. "How do you know that's who I am?"

The female pulled down her hood, and they got their first good look at her face. Thick black lashes framed startling amber eyes. Her face was heart-shaped, her lips rosebuds, both pleasing, delicate features offset by a head of copper-red curls even more wild than Sayyida's black ones.

"I'm Yrsa, daughter to Lord Riis, at your service." She swept into a deep and somewhat mocking bow.

A grin spread across Sayyida's face. "You live in Grindavik, don't you?"

Yrsa nodded. "With my sisters."

"Sváva and Geiravor?"

"So you have heard of us!"

"You're absolute legends!"

It was common knowledge that Lord Riis had dozens of children, but many of them weren't at all well-known. The Terrors of Grindavik were a notable exception.

How many times had she heard Thantrel Riis laughing because Lady Ithamai complained that Lord Leyv Riis needed to get his daughters under control? Fates, at least a dozen.

Sayyida had never met any of the Terrors, but it hadn't been for lack of desire.

Yrsa bowed again, but this time it was with a flourish, like an actress accepting a call for an encore. "We do what we must to keep life interesting in the east. And I have to say, I'm a fan of yours too, Lady Glia. Already a captain in the Nava? Not many could do that so young."

Sayyida beamed. It was true that she'd risen quickly in the Nava ranks. She doubted that she still held her title after she angered the king.

Vidar held up a hand. "As much as I'm sure you and my sister could talk for hours about stirring up trouble, I need to know why Lord Riis has one of his most notorious children following us?"

Yrsa pouted. "To business already?"

"I'd prefer it."

"Is it really true, what they say about the Virtoris heir?"

Sayyida pressed her lips together, sensing something that would throw her brother off and loving it.

Vidar didn't give them the satisfaction, but when Yrsa didn't continue, he let out a long-suffering sigh. "And what's that?"

Yrsa pushed off the wall and when she was but a pace away from Vidar, she lifted her hand and ran a finger along his collarbone. "That he's stiff as a plank." She cocked her head, and Sayyida nearly burst with glee at the way her brother's eyes widened.

"While I don't mind a bit of stiffness in the right places, I think they miscalculate you. There's something more to you, isn't there, lordling?" She batted her lashes. "Perhaps it takes the right person for you to show your more flexible side?"

Vidar took a step back. "Answer me."

"You were supposed to go to the brothel, yes?"

"That's right," Sayyida replied.

"Seeing as it's my father's establishment, it's being watched by those loyal to the king."

"Your father sold us out?" Vidar asked.

"Not at all. When Princess Saga sent you that letter, things were fine, but they turned soon after."

"When did people start watching the brothel?" Sayyida asked.

"They turned up three days ago. Right after I arrived."

"Is it just you?" Sayyida half hoped the other two Terrors would fall from the sky.

"My sisters are in Grindavik keeping an eye on those properties. There are more of them there. The city is larger."

"Right." Sayyida's brother still appeared uneasy. "Well, thank you for finding us. I presume you have a sleigh elsewhere to take us inland?"

"No sleigh."

Vidar's lips slanted downward. "Horses?"

Sayyida shuddered. They were seafaring people, and while they could, of course, ride horseback, that long of a journey would be uncomfortable.

"I have something better, but you have to swear to me that you won't say a word about it."

"Is it dangerous?" Vidar asked.

"Not at all. And it's the fastest way to join my father and the princess in Myrr. Many others too, if the rumors are to be believed."

Sayyida cut her brother a sidelong glance. "I trust her."

"Of course you do." He pressed his lips together tightly before conceding. "Fine. Show us this other means of transportation."

"Your wings work, correct?" Yrsa fanned her wings out behind her, and if there was any question that she was Lord Riis's daughter, it would have been erased from Sayyida's mind upon seeing those wings. Like Lord Riis, Luccan, Arie, and Thantrel, Yrsa had what many had dubbed 'fire wings'. Faerie wings in blended shades of reds, oranges, and yellows. The combination was rare and hard to miss.

To answer Yrsa's question, they slipped their wings through the cloak slits.

"Come along then." The Terror shot into the air.

The Virtoris siblings followed Yrsa as she landed on the rooftop of the nearest building. She proceeded to walk along the rooftops, jumping and fluttering to the next, all the way back to the harbor, where she tucked her wings in tight.

"Isn't that the ice spider banner?" Vidar pointed to the top of a flag, discernible from where they stood. The red flag and the long legs of an ice spider sprawled across it.

"This is the brothel. You said it was being monitored," Vidar accused Yrsa. "Why bring us here?"

"And it's still being watched. From *below*. Lucky for you, though, there's a secret entrance."

"Your whole family is full of secrets."

Yrsa barked out a laugh. "You don't know half of it, sea serpent. Remember that you promised not to breathe a word of what I'm about to show you. If you do, it could harm someone I love. Someone I think you are quite fond of, too."

Vidar looked like he wanted to press, but just nodded. At that, Yrsa glided to the far side of the roof, where old ale barrels and assorted junk waited.

It was an odd place for barrels. Even empty ones. Why not get them refilled? Or use the wood for fire?

She got her answer when Yrsa moved two of the barrels aside and revealed a trapdoor. The Terror of Grindavik pulled a key from her pocket and unlocked the door. It opened on a whine.

"In you go." Yrsa pointed down.

Sayyida and Vidar approached the door and peered inside. A tidy, elegantly furnished office waited below.

"My father's office."

"Why does he have a trapdoor above it?" Vidar asked.

"Father has many exits in his establishments. The king's spymaster can never be too careful."

Sayyida supposed that was true, and so she hopped into the office. Vidar joined her, and Yrsa came last. Once inside, the redhead waved her hand in the air.

At first, Sayyida was confused, but then she heard Yrsa's hand hit something. The female grabbed an invisible thing with two hands, tugged, and the trapdoor shut behind them. Softer than Sayyida would have imagined.

"Invisible rope and a barrier of air," Yrsa explained. "Keeps it from being noisy. There's one on the other side too that keeps it airtight. Took Thantrel forever to perfect how to manipulate the air like that, but he was too proud to give up."

"Right," Vidar said. "Why are we in an office?"

Yrsa went to the side wall. "Because this is in here." Yrsa pulled a dagger from a sheath beneath her cloak and poked her finger. Blood welled, only for the Terror to smear it along the wall, which then began to glow. "To Myrr."

"Fates," Sayyida breathed. "A gateway. But those are—"

"Illegal unless sanctioned by the Crown." Yrsa sucked the blood from her finger as the gateway grew wider and brighter. "Hence why you're keeping the family secret."

"Who made it?" Vidar asked.

"Luccan."

Vidar appeared stunned, and Sayyida understood. To have Luccan hide this from Vidar would be like Saga hiding something important from Sayyida.

"You'll need to go through quickly," Yrsa said. "They don't stay open for very long. I'll come through last."

"Are you staying in Myrr too?" Sayyida asked.

"No, I'll return here to tidy up." Yrsa pointed to the ceiling, where the barrels were out of place. "Then I'm going to return to Grindavik."

"Right. Well, when you come back, can you do us a favor?"

"Perhaps?"

"Tell the fae aboard the *Slynkr* that we're safe and to join the rest of the fleet."

"Consider it done."

Sayyida nodded her thanks. "Alright then. Vidar?"

Their hearts thumping wildly, the Virtoris siblings stepped through the gateway to find their friends.

CHAPTER 21

ISOLDE

L uncheon was fast becoming my favorite time of day. In those short, midday hours, I got to see my love and my friends as we collectively broke from researching, training, or other tasks. To top it all off, the Baliks had a habit of ending lunch with a delicious, gold-dusted chocolate.

Thyra and I had spent the morning first practicing with our shadow powers, then taking turns with the Frør Crown. Even with Saga's information, we had made no headway with the Hallow, which frustrated us to no end.

The shadows, though? Things were moving along there. Before lunch, Thyra had shifted my bed across the room with her shadow tendrils, and I'd gotten my tendrils to serve me a cup of tea without spilling a drop. These menial tasks we'd accomplished were likely nothing compared to what King Érebo could do, but progress was progress.

"Whatever we're having, it smells amazing," Thyra said as we entered the dining room.

"The kitchens prepared pork." Filip waved us over. Already sitting with him were Vale, Bac, Sian, Saga, and Aleksander. The spots near the head of the table, closest to Filip, remained perpetually reserved for Thyra and me.

"Wonderful." I smiled at the next Lord of Myrr. "Where's everyone else?"

"Thantrel, Caelo, and Prince Thordur are still in the training room, taking on your Valkyrja," Vale said, amusement plain in his tone. "Others wanted to watch."

Of course they did. Considering Halladora and Sigri had escorted Thyra and me to lunch, I assumed that Tonna, Astril, and Freyia were the ones sparring.

"Is Livia in on the action too?" I asked.

Livia had sworn her blade to Thyra and me until we took our thrones, but had chosen not to be a Valkyrja. After the war ended, she hoped to open a shop and live in peace, rather than wield a sword.

Filip smirked. "Four on three, against those ladies? They'd never stand a chance. They asked Livia to moderate."

"Best of luck to the males." Thyra took her seat. "They'll need it."

Vale kissed my cheek as I settled in and, one by one, we caught each other up on small matters of our day. I was discouraged to learn that there had been another tussle between the rebels and the fae of Myrr. We'd known that housing the rebels would be difficult for the Myrranese to accept, but I hadn't expected violence. How foolishly optimistic of me.

I'd devoured all my pork and most of the vegetables and was considering requesting another full plate—practicing magic of any sort gave me a hearty appetite—when sharp and heavy footsteps sounded from somewhere down the hall. The others caught the noise too because we all turned to the door.

"Sigri?" I asked the dwarf standing guard outside.

She stared down the hall, at the person coming our way. "It's Luccan, Princess Isolde. He appears to be in some state of stress."

Chairs pushed back as we rose. Vale and Aleksander were already at the doorway when Luccan rushed through, chest heaving. No one spoke as he caught his breath, but when he did, his words made my heart sink.

"Someone has passed through one of my gateways."

"From where?" Vale asked. "Can you tell?"

"If I'm paying attention. But in those occurrences, I'm waiting for someone to arrive. This time, I just felt an opening, but I believe they're here now. Proximity helps me sense sometimes."

"What if someone got through without Riis blood?" Aleksander asked. "What if they're from Avaldenn?"

"The one in my home in the capital is gone," Luccan reminded me. "I'm fairly certain the one in the Warmsnap still exists, but that would mean a gatemaker with greater power than me forced someone through. It didn't feel like that."

"Should we go find out who it is?" Thyra asked. "The brothel isn't that far, right? And if your father is there, he'll apprehend them."

Of late, Lord Riis had been scarce. I suspected his distance was due to my anger towards him.

"Down the street," Filip confirmed, and then, realizing

how he'd sounded, his cheeks flamed red. "Not that I've been there. I've only heard from visiting lords and ladies."

"Sure you have," Vale teased his squire. "I've seen you in a brothel, Filip."

"The tavern part! And I didn't realize that server was also a fae of the night!"

Vale burst out laughing. I got the sense that a story lingered there, and it wasn't the first time my mate had teased poor Filip about it.

"We won't tell Papa Balik. Don't you worry."

"Let's go." I took pity on Filip because Sian appeared seconds away from joining in on the fun. "I'm dying to figure out who it is."

We walked as fast as was appropriate for lords and ladies and princesses to move through the castle, and when we made it outside, we were met with the smiles of two friends.

"*Sayyida!*" Saga picked up her skirts, and nearly knocked Aleksander over when she sprinted for the younger Virtoris sibling. Vidar laughed, hanging back with Lord Riis and a young faerie with red hair and no small amount of mischief in her eyes.

"We wondered when you two would show up!" Vale shouted as a wide grin cracked his face in half. "Didn't expect it to be in this manner."

"Neither did we," Vidar replied.

The groups came together. Saga wept as she embraced her best friend, and Sayyida, tough as she was, looked near to tears too.

My heart squeezed. I'd always had a hunch that there was more between them, a romance they never allowed to bloom. Or perhaps they had never acknowledged those feelings. After all, what would be the point? Before her father broke the engagement, Saga had been betrothed to Vidar—who seemed none the wiser that his fiancée preferred his sister.

"You came from Grindavik?" Luccan asked as he embraced the red-haired faerie.

"Vantalia, actually. Father has me stationed there to intercept the sea serpents." The redhead met my eyes. "I'm Yrsa, Lord Riis's daughter." She curtsied, hinting she knew who I was.

"Princess Isolde," I replied with an incline of my head. "And this is my sister, Princess Thyra Falk. I presume you've met the others?"

Yrsa scanned the group. "Not those four."

Of course not. Why would she know rebels? Bac, Aleksander, Sigri, and Halladora had not been included in the wider society. Even now, they hung a few paces back, not quite part of the group.

The introductions were made. All the while, I sensed Lord Riis's gaze upon me. Wanting my thanks for bringing the Virtoris siblings here? Or did he simply desire an acknowledgment?

He'd get neither.

"So, the snow is gone here too," Yrsa commented. "Seems like the entire kingdom is free of it." She craned her neck to peer at the mountains framing Ramshold. "Well, maybe not up there yet."

She couldn't understand that this was a sore spot, so I merely nodded. "We were finishing lunch. Would you all like to join us?"

"I need to be getting back to the tavern." Lord Riis bowed shallowly. "I only wanted to make sure Sayyida and Vidar got here."

"Hmmm. Well, the rest of us should head inside," I said flatly.

Sayyida shot me a confused look. I'd been friendly with Lord Riis the last time I'd seen her.

"Yrsa, you too. Fill your belly before traveling home," Luccan put his arm around his half-sister.

"Oh, yes. Traveling via gateway is so taxing!"

"I don't get to see you often enough."

"True, and don't worry, I'm staying. It's rare that I get to eat castle fare."

"We have excellent desserts," Filip offered. "Not for lunch. We usually just have a truffle, but I could have some of the better desserts brought out."

Yrsa smiled at the young lord. "You know how to woo a girl, don't you, Lord Balik?"

Filip swallowed loudly. "I didn't mean for that to come off as——"

Luccan laughed. "Yrsa is the realm's biggest flirt, Filip. Take none of what she says seriously."

"I'm serious about some things." Yrsa winked at Vidar.

The Virtoris heir looked away, and I pressed my lips together to hold in a laugh. I'd have to ask Sayyida what that was about later.

The others bid Lord Riis goodbye, and we returned to the castle, intent on finishing our lunch. Or beginning it, in the case of the newcomers.

Along the way, the Virtoris siblings caught us up on

what had happened to them since I'd last seen them, and what was happening elsewhere in the kingdom. As they'd fled to their island home soon after the king betrothed their young brother to a lady of the midlands, it turned out they'd heard little more than us.

My shoulders were beginning to relax again when we turned the corner, and I caught sight of a figure waiting before the doors of the room that we'd been taking our lunch in. The dwarf appeared young. Nervous too.

He spotted us and darted towards the group. When he reached us, he bowed low.

"I have a message for Princess Isolde." With trembling fingers he handed me a small tube, the kind that fae tied to ravens' legs for transport.

"Thank you. Anything else?"

"No. I mean, no, Princess Isolde."

"You may go."

The youngling ran off, and I opened the message to pull out the rolled-up paper.

"That's King Tholin's seal," Vale said from where he stood at my side.

"It is." I cracked the seal, unfurled the paper, and read the short plea that made my stomach drop to my knees.

CHAPTER 22
VALE

Our horses trudged through the snowdrifts, not yet fully melted this deep in the mountain range.

Keeping a bird's-eye view of our small army, Isolde, Thyra, Lord Balik, and three of his sons soared above. As many gryphons and riders as House Balik and the rebellion could spare flew behind them.

The letter the dwarven king sent was short, but clear. His forces were trapped beneath a peak in the Ice Teeth Range. Hedged in by none other than a tribe of frost giants.

I shuddered. Normally frost giants ate animals, not fae, but King Tholin had already lost ten soldiers to this particular tribe before he called for aid. Ogres were more commonly known as cannibals, and they would be bad enough to come up against. I could think of few things worse than fae-eating giants.

"Your mate looks at ease leading." Vidar shifted in his saddle and readjusted his gray fur cloak so it did not bunch beneath his arse. Qildor and Luccan rode with us at the head of the army column.

"She does," I agreed. "And she learns more about leading every day."

"A good thing too," Luccan said. "Once we get Dergia out of this mess, the high lords will want us to move north as soon as possible."

"After a few days," Prince Thordur commented from his position right behind us. The prince of Dergia rode nestled between his sister and Sayyida, all three armed to the teeth. "My army will need time to rest. They have undertaken a long journey—part of why they're in this mess."

I couldn't argue, though I doubted that even a fresh dwarven army could take on so many frost giants without casualties. Not when they were trapped within a mountain tunnel with only one exit.

"A few days' rest," I assured Thordur. Besides wanting the best for our army, I had plans in a few days. Plans that had nothing to do with the war and everything to do with what my mate deserved.

"How close do you think we are, anyway?" Qildor asked.

A good question. As I was not so familiar with this path through the range, and we had left Myrr in a hurry with little time to debrief, I could not answer. I waved forward a soldier wearing the black, green, and gold of the southlands. Three hunter green stripes running over his shoulders from back to front marked him as a ranger. A fae who had likely done this trek before.

"How far along would you say we are?" I asked when he reached me.

"Very close," the soldier replied. "Soon, the path will taper, leading to that narrow defile that cuts through the mountains. I believe that in little more than an hour we'll be in the valley the king described."

"Can you make sure that everyone knows that information? The rebels weren't present during the initial debrief, and they haven't traveled this path."

Seeing as the rebels had only recently arrived in Myrr, not that many had joined us, but there were enough to warrant spreading the news.

"Of course, my prince." The ranger rode back, passing the word along as he went.

And so we continued, riding through woods, down uneven pathways. As the ranger said it would, the mountain road began to narrow bit by bit. I cast a glance into the trees when I caught Luccan stiffen in his seat.

"What's going on?" I asked.

His nose, sensitive even by fae standards, lifted into the air as he sniffed. "Something is . . . musty. Like——"

The neigh of a horse, followed by a guttural cry, cut him off. I twisted and swore.

"*Direwolves,*" I shouted as wolves that were half the size of my horse and with fangs the length of my smallest finger flooded the path. "At least thirty. More rushing from the trees."

Qildor swung out of his saddle, and the rest of us followed. Our horses darted into the woods, fleeing the wolves as we ran toward the pack and the havoc they were wreaking upon our small force.

"Off the horses!" Luccan swung his sword as a wolf twice my size leapt from the trees. "*Everyone, dismount!*"

Releasing the horses into the woods wasn't ideal, but they had good survival instincts and were well-trained to return. If we kept them in this cramped space, the wolves would go for them first. The soldiers of Myrr knew this too, but the rebels had been slower to dismount, not as used to direwolves. As a result, three steeds went down, their blood pooling in the snow. Two of the riders had already sustained injuries as well.

I spotted Thordur swinging his ax to protect one of the fallen rebels. His sister and Sayyida fought at his back as wolves closed in.

"Back to back!" I shouted. "Protect each other!"

Skelda took down one wolf, then another. I stopped to scan the area as a massive wolf barreled out of the nearby forest. I braced for the impact, protecting my face and neck with my arms, just as an arrow speared through the beast's skull.

"Incoming!" Thyra yelled, and Lasvin's hooves slammed into the dead wolf.

I exhaled. "Good timing."

"You think I'd let my sister's mate die?" Thyra's pegasus lifted higher into the air. Behind her, Astril and Freyia rode on gryphonback, both shooting at the wolves with vampiric speed and precision. "There are so many."

Mountain packs were far larger than those in the flatlands of Winter's Realm. But even for a mountain pack, this one was enormous. The initial thirty wolves had grown to what I estimated to be one hundred. The coordination of their attack told me they had likely been stalking us from afar.

"Not for long." At my declaration, Thyra grinned and soared away, her white cloak a banner flying behind her. The vampires stayed near the ground, leaping from their mounts and switching to using their swords.

Wolf after wolf went down. Two of them put up a fight fit for the gods but went down by my sword all the same. In the fray, I spotted my mate, flanked by Sigri and Halladora, fighting wolves back into the trees. What felt like hours later, the ground ran red with the blood of direwolves and the few wolves that lived were racing away, seeking refuge in the woods.

"How many injured?" I shouted when the threat had passed.

Eight replies came back, two of them dire. One rebel had lost a foot, and a Balik soldier had sustained such a large injury that his innards had spilled out. The light left his eyes before the healers could try to perform miraculous magic.

In total, we'd lost fifteen lives to the wolves' teeth and claws. The six who sustained only minor injuries still wanted to fight. Knowing they wouldn't be of much use, I instead gave them instructions to return to Myrr. The soldier who had lost a foot had been stabilized and would join them.

"By the dead gods," Isolde said as she and Arava landed, with Lord Balik following behind. "They were *merciless.*"

"Direwolves always are." I was so glad I hadn't needed to worry about her during the fight. Direwolves were fierce predators, but wingless. "Stealthy, cunning, and they work together like few other creatures can, making them incredibly dangerous."

"We didn't see them fast enough." Isolde sheathed Sassa's Blade, the only Hallow traveling with us. Though Thyra had initially protested leaving it behind, the Frør Crown remained at Ramshold, guarded by Livia.

"They're masters of blending into the forest." Tadgh Balik watched the healers and the injured retreat the way we'd come.

"We're lucky they didn't take more," I agreed.

Lord Balik gave his ground soldiers and the aerial unit commands to work together to find the horses. All the while, my mate stayed quiet. Listened and learned.

"How will this affect us later?" Isolde turned her gaze away from the dead to look up at me. Her violet eyes shone, wetter than normal, but she did not let the tears fall. I understood. To lead often meant putting on a brave face when you were drowning inside. Hoping to help my mate in some small way, I took her hand, squeezed it.

"Much of our plan relies on surprising the giants. That remains possible."

"But this feels like a bad omen, doesn't it?"

I exhaled, unable to deny her words as I'd been thinking the exact same thing.

CHAPTER 23
ISOLDE

My fingers trailed through the white fur of my cloak as I studied the defile cutting between two towering mountains. Fates, it was so narrow.

As the sun sank in the west, Lord Balik had signaled for those of us who were airborne to descend so that we would not be spotted before our ground forces. Those same forces who would soon have to walk two-by-two through a craggy pathway that led straight into a valley full of hostile frost giants.

"There has to be a better way," Thyra said to the crowd of royals, lords, and soldiers gathered together.

She too wore a white cloak, light armor, and fighting leathers. Though we'd had little time to prepare for the journey, Lady Balik had pulled us aside and made sure we knew how important it was to look the part of leaders in battle.

As I'd created garments for royal and noble vampires

most of my life, I knew that fact all too well. Although the vampires were often engaged in a different type of battle, the concept was the same. With Lady Balik's assistance, Thyra and I had quickly acquired new combat attire.

Thyra pointed to the defile I'd been assessing. "Trickling into a valley crawling with hostile frost giants is asking to be torn apart one by one."

King Tholin's letter claimed there were around fifty giants lying in wait. According to others, that was about as large as their tribes got, save for larger gatherings during equinox celebrations. These giants were also unique in that they had already killed several dwarves and were waiting to pick off more. To eat them, no less.

"The only other route would take the ground forces two more days to access," Lord Balik replied. "This defile is narrow but very short. Horses can run through it in a matter of minutes."

"We can't make them wait." Princess Bavirra's hands landed on her wide hips. "I won't hear of it."

"No," Prince Thordur echoed. "We have to risk trickling into the valley. We'll just have to move quickly to get the layout of the valley before the light is completely gone. And of course we're relying heavily on those in the air to prolong a distraction."

"Humor someone who has never seen a frost giant." I held up a hand. "Let alone fought one. What do we have to be on the alert for?"

Vale answered. "Their thick skin can repel magic for a long while—until something penetrates, then they're more susceptible to subsequent attacks. Sometimes attacks will even rebound off their skin. And a very rare giant will have magic of their own, but we don't have a way to tell who has powers and who doesn't."

"That's usually only older giants, and even then one in a thousand," Luccan added. "But truth be told, it's difficult to tell which are the oldest. A lot of them have white or gray hair and living in the elements makes them look weathered."

Sian cleared his throat. "Weapons like arrows or blades can hurt them, but it takes a *very* deep cut. Or repeated injuries, which we're unlikely to get unless we overrun them."

"What about arrows to sensitive areas?" Thyra asked. "Noses and eyes? Or the face in general?"

"Anywhere on the face will hurt a lot," Vale answered. "But unless you hit them *very* hard in a delicate spot or slice open a vital blood vessel, they'll live."

"And we want that?" Thantrel asked. "We'll have a sizable head start during a retreat because they can't possibly slip through that defile, but if they're alive, they can leave the valley. Dead frost giants can't chase us through the woods."

Silence shrouded our group. We knew killing giants was a possibility, but the entire tribe? I didn't think it sat right with anyone. After all, they were still fae, like us. And while they'd committed the unspeakable act of cannibalism everyone suspected they'd only done so to survive a horrific stretch of winter.

"Kill only when necessary. Otherwise, knock them out. A powerful blow to their temples will do the trick. We'll have to leave that to the fae with wings," Vale said, and the other seasoned warriors in the circle murmured their agreement. "As for the possibility of them chasing us, well, we might have to deal with that, but that seems unlikely. Giants don't like to approach cities."

A few more questions were asked and answered, until finally, we were ready to move out.

Vale caught my hand before I made it a single step. "Fly safe."

"And you watch out for yourself and our friends on the ground." I stood on tiptoe to kiss him. He had been in more battles than he could remember, but only a handful were against frost giants.

Still, my mate did not appear scared or worried, and I took his confidence to heart as I mounted Arava. The mare twisted to look at me, and a wave of reassuring warmth filled my chest.

Not far away, the healers were setting up a working camp. We'd lost a few horses in the direwolf attack and needed every mount for the soldiers. As a result, Rynni would be the only healer to join the fighters, but in her dragon form. As she had only one or two good fire blasts a day, and she wasn't a trained fighter, Rynni would attack when she could do so without risk. Her primary objective was to search for the injured and transport them back over the mountain separating us from the healers.

Halladora approached, her expression wary as she took in Arava. "Are you sure you want me to come with you?"

She had never looked so hesitant before, and I understood why. Bonded pegasi were particular about who they allowed on their backs. Even more so than gryphons, which Halladora had ridden here. But now, Luccan would fly on that gryphon, and Dora with me.

"I'll need an archer." Unlike my sister, I was not so skilled in archery, and I'd rather not use my sword against the giants. Arrows made for a far better distraction and flew at enemies from a distance.

I patted Arava's neck. "She understands that this needs to be done for our friends' survival," I repeated the words not only to calm my Valkyrja, but to remind Arava of our talk. She wasn't able to speak back, but through our ever-strengthening bond, I sensed when she understood things.

Halladora respectfully came to stand at Arava's side. The mare snorted.

I patted her ebony neck again. "She's going to watch our backs, Arava. We want to be safe and go back to Myrr."

The tension in the mare's neck loosened. Like most of us, she had been enjoying the comforts of Myrr, particularly all the treats that came with being a princess's pegasus.

"Good girl." I twisted to wave at Halladora. "Get on."

She joined me and made sure her arrows were ready.

"You have enough room to maneuver?" I asked.

"Just." The Valkyrja scooted back a touch on the elongated saddle that allowed us to ride double. "If you leaned forward over her neck as you fly, it would help."

"Got it."

"Everyone is ready?" Thyra called out.

Forty fliers affirmed they were, and a wave of nods traveled down the line of soldiers preparing to ambush the valley.

"To the skies!" my twin shouted, and the gryphons and pegasi flew for the top of the mountains blocking our army from the giants' sight.

I leaned over my mare's mane as Arava surged higher, giving Halladora as much space as possible to shoot. Flanking me, Thyra had her bow tucked beneath her arm, one hand on the reins.

"There they are," Halladora said. "Stars, they're *huge*."

The giants, most of which were gathered around massive bonfires, had to be as tall as Vale stacked six times over. The smallest among them were so large and strong looking that going up against the creature struck me as lunacy. I had to hope that the bonfires meant they'd begun settling in as night crept closer. Perhaps they would be lethargic.

"I count fifty-five," Halladora said.

I scanned the mountainside the giants huddled closest to, searching for a crack in the rock. It took a bit of searching, but I found the opening, not large at all, but big enough for dwarves to walk through in singles or pairs. A rock I estimated to be only slightly larger than the hole in the mountain was on the ground nearby. That had likely been covering the opening, but once the dwarves moved it, they'd exposed themselves.

"Break and descend," Lord Balik commanded.

We scattered. Luccan, Thantrel, my sister, and our Valkyrja flew with me and Dora. The other aerial company that would remain closest to us, watching our back as we watched theirs, comprised Lord Balik, Filip, Sian, Caelo, and Aleksander. Others paired off too, all of them Balik forces. With each steady beat of her wings, Arava brought us closer to the ground, confidence in her bunched-up muscles.

Knowing we'd have only seconds before we would have to focus wholly on the giants, I cast a glance behind. A long exhale gusted out of me.

Vale and Qildor had cleared the short defile and were already barreling down the valley. I spied Vidar and Sayyida close behind. Unlike in the city and surrounding flatlands, there was still snow at this elevation but nothing the horses weren't used to.

The rest would follow. We only needed to buy them the time.

A roar cut through the quiet, and our advantage vanished as two male giants rose from where they'd been sitting around their fire and charged. Most followed, but I was relieved to see that ten hung back. Smaller giants—possibly two younglings among them.

Fates! They were fast. Much faster than their enormous size would suggest.

Arrows flew, and though I'd been warned it would happen, I could not help the disappointment that coursed through me as most of them bounced off the giants' skin.

"Need more space!" Halladora pulled back another arrow, and I leaned flat against Arava's neck, trying to give my Valkyrja the best shot. The archer released, but another arrow was already soaring for the same target. I gasped as it landed clean in the giant's eye.

The giant fell, and I imagined the ground shuddered

upon impact. Being so high up, I couldn't feel the quake, but I certainly felt the spike of fear as the ten giants who had hung back roared in anger and joined the rest of their tribe.

"Dora, keep shooting!"

"On it!"

I instructed Arava to dive. To weave. To dodge. She took each command easily. Once, we came so close to a giant, within their reach before pulling back to safety. Then we did it again, and again, and again—enraging the giants yes, but also slowing them. Distracting them from the army on horseback that was filling the valley.

"Isolde!" Thyra screamed as she zipped by on Lasvin, the pegasus little more than a white blur at duskfall. "This way!"

I tracked my sister and gasped. One giant was holding someone—a dwarf wearing the colors of Dergia who was alive and thrashing in the creature's grip.

My stomach twisted at the implication. The bonfire. The time of day. We'd interrupted dinner.

I changed course and called my magic to unleash a hailstorm, each ball the size of my fist. The hail pummeled the giant's face and his arm dropped. His grip too.

Lasvin swept beneath in time to catch the captured dwarf. Thyra pulled the dwarf into position, making sure he was safe. It seemed like he was, but then the giant's fist came swinging.

Halladora sent an arrow at the creature's face, while I directed more winter magic at his body. The giant screamed as the arrow struck along with the hail, and the overly large fae stumbled backward.

"Thanks!" Thyra yelled as she flew by, the dwarf behind her still barely hanging on.

"Get him to safety!" I replied, but my sister was already on it, her pegasus soaring towards the mountains.

"The army is through the defile," Dora announced.

Arava pulled up, up, up, until we were out of range. I took a good long look back the way we came. Many of those on horseback were already wrapping long ropes around the giants' legs, pulling them tight, felling one large fae after another. Even as some giants tried to dodge, they also had to keep their eyes to the skies, and they couldn't do both at once. Most of the giants escaped one trap, only to become entangled in another.

A giant fell. Two. Three. Four. With each creature hitting the frozen ground, my heart soared. A whoop of victory that sounded like it came from Thantrel resonated from below. One by one, our small army fell upon the giants and knocked them out with swift and hard blows to the temples.

"Ten down. Three likely dead," Halladora said. "We should go that way."

I took in the area she pointed. Five giants had separated and ripped trees from the ground. They swept the trees in front of them, keeping away the Balik soldiers on the ground.

"Let's go." I steered Arava that way. In seconds, Lord Balik, Filip, and Caelo closed in right alongside me. I did a double take. Caelo was covered in blood, presumably from a giant, as I couldn't find an injury on him.

We converged on the frost giants, and Halladora, Filip, and Caelo took their shot. Filip's arrow struck true, hitting one's oversized pupil. The giantess fell, her great form toppling forward, threatening to crush soldiers.

"*Move!*" Lord Balik bellowed, and maybe because he was so concerned for his soldiers, he didn't see the incoming attack. No one did. Not until the tallest of the giant's trees was in the air, smacking Filip off his gryphon.

I waited for the heir to House Balik to use his wings to right himself. To fly away and out of danger. But he only continued to fall, his trajectory straight for the ground. Too fast. And from much too high up.

Tendrils ripped out of me, startling Arava as much as myself when they shot in front of us, aiming at Filip. They caught the squire seconds before he would have hit the ground. My heart thrashed in my chest as the shadows retracted, quick as a whip, only to stop right in front of me. Condemning me.

"By the stars," Halladora breathed. She was Valkyrja but hadn't been with us that day in the mountain tunnels. She knew Shadow Fae existed but not my secret, and she wasn't the only one to learn it at the most inopportune time.

Lord Balik hovered, frozen in the air, his mouth agape. Though the sun was nearly set, it was not yet dark enough to hide what I had done.

"I'll take him," someone closer said.

Sian had joined us, and he looked at me with such reproach that it broke my heart. Swallowing the pain, I commanded the shadows to ease Filip on to his brother's gryphon.

"Get him to safety," I commanded.

Sian stared at me, and a thousand questions flashed across his face before he soared off with his brother.

"It's not over." Dora looked at me cautiously.

I inhaled deeply to steady myself once more and rejoined the fight.

CHAPTER 24
VALE

igh above, the shadows disappeared, but the fear that struck my heart when Isolde had unleashed them remained. She'd done so to save Filip—right in front of Lord Balik, and although I was quite far away, I could see the Warden of the South's reaction well enough.

I wished to fly to my mate. To comfort her and then go to Lord Balik and convince him the shadows were nothing to worry about. That Isolde was learning to control them.

But the battle still raged, and fresh blood spilled across the trampled snow. I needed to focus, and focus I did, weaving my destrier between the legs of giants, slicing at their tendons. I struck true once more, and the giant fell, the ground shuddering beneath his weight.

A series of whistles pierced the air. The sound wasn't recognizable as anything our small force had devised to signal. Nor did I believe it came from a giant. Their whistles would be far louder.

Maneuvering out of the danger, I scanned the valley,

hunting for the source, only to see dwarves burst out of their mountain prison. Their stocky horses' hooves pounded the ground with vengeance as the first wave of dwarves joined the fight.

I changed course and rode to meet them, locating the king easily in the throng of dwarves, thanks to his golden-handled battle axe. When King Tholin spotted me, he held up a hand. His soldiers parted around him, around me, as we stopped to debrief.

"That darkness was Neve's?" the king asked.

I pretended to be distracted by the dwarves streaming around us.

"I was watching, Prince Vale. I only ask as a courtesy."

I cringed. "Yes."

The king exhaled but nodded. "Considering what she's doing right now, I can't complain."

I gaped. Far away from other battles, Isolde and Thyra were fighting together again, and this time both wielded shadows. Their tendrils wrapped tightly around the giant's thick neck, choking it. The creature thrashed, but the shadows remained steadfast until the giant's knees buckled, and he toppled.

"I should join her," I said.

"As will I."

"Out of the way!" I shouted as the king and I veered out of the river of dwarves in the direction of my mate.

We raced, side by side, through the melee. A handful of dwarves, knights of the Dergian royal house by the looks of them, joined. Giants approached, slowing us, but we were all trained warriors. We downed one, and began work on the second, then the third. However, when a fourth barreled our way, no one saw her until she extended her hand and the king flew off his horse, right into her waiting palm.

"She's a magic user!" I pivoted to charge the giant holding King Tholin, but the light-footed giantess was already rushing from the fray for the far end of the valley.

"Summoner?" Sayyida called out.

"I think so," I replied but didn't dare to look back to see where they were.

Not only was this giantess a rare magic-user among her kind, she was fast, far faster than the other giants, and her long legs ate up the ground. I could not lose her in all that was going on.

Qildor, Thordur, and Sayyida pulled up to race alongside me. I caught the Prince of Dergia's eyes, stony and hard.

"We'll get to him in time," I promised.

"We'd better!"

Pushing the horses to their limits, they wove through chaos until we ran alongside the female giant. Careful to keep a safe distance, I sized up the situation. The giantess was clutching the king in her fist, so I could not see him, could not make sure he was safe. We had to operate under the assumption that he was not. Ropes wouldn't work here, not when we were all traveling so fast. No, we had to attack from above.

"Qildor and I will fly," I shouted. "Sayyida, when the king falls, catch him." Once the giant fell, the king would too. "Otherwise, try not to draw her attention." The last thing we needed would be for the giantess to summon more people into her palms.

Thordur didn't need instructions. The moment his father was free from the giant's clutches, he'd go to his aid.

"Now, Qildor!" We shot out of the saddles, our wings lifting us high.

The giantess's bloodshot eyes widened as we neared her face. "*Monsters!*"

Monsters? How rich, considering her tribe was eating other fae.

She waved her free arm in our direction but we scattered like frostflies, avoiding the hand that could take our lives. Her magic pulsed past me, narrowly missing calling me into her hand. We zigged and zagged out of her reach, until finally, I spotted an opening.

I soared closer and lanced my sword straight through her temple. Qildor's sword struck her neck—both relatively delicate areas, if anything about giants could be considered delicate. He sliced at just the right angle, opening an artery.

The giant shrieked, and her hand opened as she fell. The King of Dergia tumbled from her grasp.

"Sayyida!" I bellowed.

She soared upward, arms extended, ready. I held my breath. Only released it when she caught the king. They were safe. They were—

A rock twice the size of me slammed into Sayyida. She let out a cry, and the pair dropped to the ground. Landed hard.

"Over there!" Qildor pointed, and I spotted the culprit.

One of the smaller giants, a youngling I thought, was hurling boulders at our forces. He'd taken down a good number too, but wouldn't be continuing. Isolde and Thyra had already spotted him, and their tendrils were already wrapping around his neck as Astril and Freyia sliced at his tendons, immobilizing the young giant.

Somewhere else in the valley, I caught a blast of fire that lit up the dusk. Rynni's flame for the day.

"They've got the stone-thrower. Care for the king and Sayyida." I soared to the ground.

Thordur arrived with me, his face bloodless as he took in his father, splayed on the ground with an unconscious Sayyida at his side. Red spattered the snow, and it took me only seconds to figure out why.

The king's lower leg was gone at the knee, the tear of the skin horribly uneven. Possibly done by the giant's long, jagged fingernails while she ran.

Sayyida moaned. A good sign that she was alive. I gestured to Qildor to help her and focused on the king.

"He'll bleed to death." Panic fluttered across the prince's face.

"Not if we work fast." I hoped it was true. Many times, I'd saved soldiers in battle. None, however, had been hurt this badly.

Could such a large wound be cauterized? I did not know, but I pulled off my belt and tied it above the knee. The blood flow slowed. Not enough, though. Not nearly enough.

"Hold the wound," I instructed. "Try to reduce the flow."

Thordur complied clumsily. I got the sense that his brain was no longer functioning as it should. He was in shock.

I searched for the dragon-fae, but she was so far away. I was about to take my chances and soar off to get Rynni when Isolde landed mere paces away.

"Halladora, watch our backs. I have an idea," she said as she leapt from Arava. The Valkyrja was right behind her, turning to do as her queen commanded.

I shifted, allowing my mate closer, giving her room. She pulled her sword and sliced her hand open. I blinked, confused, and then understanding dawned.

Isolde had told me once that the shadows within Sassa's Blade had asked her bidding. Presumably, they would do whatever she asked for the price of her blood.

"Save him. Seal the wound," she said.

The shadow figure that materialized glided over to the king and the body morphed, covering the injury, stopping the blood. I watched it all in amazement. In relief. And when no more blood dripped from the king's leg, I placed a hand on Thordur's shoulder.

"He'll live. Isolde will make sure of it."

"I will," my mate said, her tone off.

I turned to her and that brief flash of relief that I'd felt vanished. She held the blade to her palm, but then I recalled what happened when we'd fought the orc horde. How she'd passed out.

"Can you use your shadows?" I asked. "They don't need blood, right?"

"I can try. But mine are weaker and not as reliable yet. This kind can do much more because they're from *his* magic."

She didn't have to tell me who he was. Long ago, King Érebo's shadow powers had been placed in the sword. In exchange for blood, shadow figures did the bidding of his mate.

"We need Thyra to help." I worried at how long my wife could hold out.

"It's not taking as much as with the orcs, but it is a constant suck, and we're far from Myrr. One of the vampires would be better, I think. They're probably sticking close to Thyra."

The vampires! Of course. Their blood could ease the king's pain and injury, lessening Isolde's need to give blood to that shadow.

"I'll be right back." Not wanting to waste time getting to my horse, I rose in the air.

As I scanned for Freyia or Astril, I assessed the damage done to our side. Some had fallen, but fewer than we'd guessed. Only a handful of giants remained on their feet, most of them entangled with our soldiers. It was in one such battle that I spotted the eldest Red Assassin, working with her sister to bait a giant very near where Thyra flew.

I flew towards her. "Astril!"

Her hearing, as impeccable as ever, caught my shout. She located me, and I waved her over. A blur came my way, and a second later, the vampire was there.

"What?"

"Isolde is over there, keeping the King of Dergia alive, but barely. She needs you to give him blood."

"We do not make it a custom to share our blood."

My shoulders hardened. Isolde was no normal person, but a princess. Their princess who one day might be a queen. "I do not expect you to help the entire army, but if you do not do as she asked, I *will* rip you apart."

The vampire scowled, but gave a single nod before she disappeared, her blur of motion heading for my mate. I followed, and when I arrived, I found Astril's wrist already pressed against Isolde's lips. My stomach clenched. In what little time I'd been gone, Isolde's cheeks had paled.

Upon seeing me, Isolde released the vampire's wrist and took a long breath. "See to the king."

"Will he be fine with it?" Astril asked.

"Do it," Thordur said, his tone raspy. "Do it, please."

At the prince's plea, the vampire stalked over to the dwarf king, knelt, and assessed the damage.

"I'll have to apply blood to the wound first. Then have him drink. My blood won't heal all this damage, or even ensure the wound stops bleeding during the journey home. This damage is far too great."

"He must survive," Thordur said. "That's all I ask."

"Very well. Remove the shadow bind so I can apply blood. You'll have to reapply it afterwards to be safe, but take the rest while you can."

Isolde did as the vampire asked, and the effect on my mate was instantaneous. She sucked in air and stood straighter. I went to her side as Astril worked, dripping blood over the king's wound.

"How are you?" I asked.

"Weak," she admitted. "She's right that the injury is extensive. I wouldn't have lasted the whole way back."

I pulled her close.

"But if she can stabilize him enough and stop the bleeding, I think the bind to keep the wound from re-opening will be minimal," Isolde continued, seemingly trying to convince herself as much as me. "I'll ask Thyra to help too, when necessary. And of course the healers, though I think they'll need more supplies than we brought."

I cast a glance at the battle. Or, more accurately, the lack of fighting. Not a single giant remained standing, leaving a relative hush where their roars and bellows had been.

We'd won, but we weren't out of the dark yet.

"Burning seas, what happened?" a groggy voice came from behind.

Isolde pulled away just enough so that we could both see Sayyida rise to sit with Qildor's assistance.

"I'm almost certain the fall severely strained some muscles in your arm. Maybe even fractured or broke a bone," the knight said. "It's already heavily bruised. Take care."

"Fates," I muttered. How many more dire injuries would there be?

Isolde let out a long sigh, mirroring my inner turmoil. "You should go help the others. See if anyone else needs stitches or the like. I'll be fine here."

I kissed her forehead, knowing she spoke logically, even if I hated to let her go. "I'll flag down Rynni and send her over. Call if you need anything."

"I will."

I squeezed her hand one last time, and in the last light of day, went to assess the damage.

INTERLUDE

PRINCE RHISTEL AABERG, HEIR TO WINTER'S REALM, HOUSE OF THE WHITE BEAR

The heir of Winter's Realm wrinkled his nose as he stepped on to the dock.

"By the dead gods, what is that *smell*?" Rhistel asked no one in particular.

"Grindavik is a port city. Fae fish here," the king replied dully, as if he were sick of his son's attitude.

Rhistel bristled. Days ago, they'd left Avaldenn, and his father had been testy throughout the voyage. Likely because the king had left his capital in the hands of Lord Roar.

Or perhaps his father had noticed that, after their rough first meeting, Érebo and Rhistel actually got on quite well. Two pages of the same book, or so Rhistel thought. There was really something to be said for an ally who had seen so much. Knew so much. Rhistel could not help but respect the ancient male.

Currently, however, the Shadow Fae king's existence remained a secret known to only Rhistel, his father, Lord Roar, and others of the royal high council. Those who commanded armies. But soon, after they released the news of Isolde and Thyra wielding shadows, King Érebo would have to out himself too. When he did, how would the people of Winter's Realm take it, small-minded as so many were?

And after they'd defeated the Falks, would Érebo try to take what belonged to the King of Winter as he and his queen had done millennia ago? Like the shadowy fae though he did, the heir thought such deception very likely. Perhaps it was that which had his father in such a foul mood too.

But instead of worrying, Rhistel waited. Considered. Learned more of their new ally. And most important of all, he kept to the plan.

If his father was smart, he'd do the same. Pity that, Magnus Aaberg, for all the tales and rumors told about him, had never been known for his intelligence. He was smart enough, certainly, but Rhistel and Saga had inherited most of their intellect and their powers of the mind from their mother.

Speaking of Mother.

Rhistel took in the queen, trailing behind them, walking next to the Shadow Fae King dressed as one of their Clawsguard until they entered the Ithamai's castle and revealed his true name. The queen's face was blank, her eyes empty. Shackles wrapped around her ankles, placed there moments ago specifically so the fae of Grindavik would see them. The prince had been vigilant when it came to containing his mother.

He would never forgive his mother for what she'd done to him. How she'd made him impotent and would have stolen away his birthright. How she'd faltered and forsaken family and duty all because of guilt.

"What do you think of the smell, Mother?" he asked even as he gave her the command of how to respond.

She locked eyes with the nearest sailor, who appeared stunned that a queen was even breathing the same air as him. "Disgusting."

The sailor's face fell, but he didn't deny it. Just nodded and bowed his head. Weak, like so many that Rhistel came across were.

Beside Rhistel's mother, the Shadow King's lips twitched upward ever so slightly.

"Stop," the King of Winter muttered loud enough for Rhistel to hear.

No matter his growing annoyance, the prince did as the king commanded. If only because Lady Ithamai was approaching, and they needed the might behind her house.

Mother, Rhistel commanded. *Look repentant.*

"Lady Vaeri," the king said as they met with the Warden of the East.

"Welcome to Grindavik, Your Grace. Your Highness." She curtsied to the king and her prince, but Rhistel did not miss when the high lady's eyes narrowed upon the queen. Lady Ithamai still did not know that Queen Inga was a whisperer, but thanks to Vale's proclamation of their parentage, she had heard of the queen's infidelity with Lord Riis. When Lady Ithamai asked, the king had confirmed the betrayal, though not addressed it publicly. Soon that would have to happen, but not until Rhistel's plan was completed.

"You did not have to meet us at the docks at this early hour." The sun was only just rising at their backs.

"It was the least I could do, Your Grace," Lady Ithamai said. "After all, you allowed me to return home to see that my daughters were safe. My sleigh awaits us."

"Many thanks," King Magnus replied.

Not bothering to listen to the chatter that began as they walked to the sleigh, Rhistel wondered if the brothel that he'd visited last time was still open. Should their visit here go on longer than expected, he might patron the establishment again. See if that nymph was still around.

He began dreaming of slipping between that lovely fae's legs when a shout from a nearby crowd drew his attention. Two males, a faerie and a dryad fought with their fists. A crowd gathered nearby and took bets. Rhistel snorted at the debauchery taking place when most had barely broken their fast, but his amusement faded as one fae drew his attention. A petite red-haired female lingered off to the side, watching the fight. She must have felt him staring, for the female looked over and caught the prince's eye. She grinned and there was something so wild and untamable in the smile that Rhistel's cock twitched.

Maybe not a whore tonight. The prince waved over the closest legitimate Clawsguard.

"My prince?" the knight asked.

"See that fae over there? By the fight with the copper curls?"

"I do."

"Learn who she is. And where I can find her, if I need to. Then meet us at the castle."

The knight nodded and went to do as his prince commanded.

"Clawsguards are not meant to make it easier to wet your cock," King Magnus grumbled lowly.

"They seem to do that for you." Like his father was one to talk with his ever-growing harem.

The king did not respond, and all the better. They had reached the sleigh.

One Clawsguard and the false one took up standing positions on the back of the sleigh. The others were commanded to walk to the castle. Once the nobles were situated on the dark purple velvet, the king began speaking of his plans for the armed forces the Warden of the East had left in Avaldenn. Rhistel half listened. When they still had said nothing of note by the time the sleigh arrived at the castle, Rhistel put on a charming smile and leaned closer to the Warden of the East.

"You have cleared an appropriate cell for her, no?" he asked.

"Right after I got your raven," she replied. "It did not take long, mind you. Our cells have all the regular enchantments upon them. We added a few for her magic, though it's the ice spider silk in the walls that makes the real difference."

"So I've been told. A good thing too. She's as powerful as ever."

"The shackles are keeping her docile?" Lady Ithamai mused.

"The shame too. She thought she'd never be caught." Rhistel had to agree. When you could lie like he and his mother could, the world was ripe for the picking. Or *his* picking, at least.

"Let's show her to her room first," Rhistel said. "Just in case."

The High Lady of the East needed no convincing. "This way."

Their party followed Lady Ithamai through her castle sparsely adorned with splashes of purple and stone lions, and down, down, down, down into the deepest, most impenetrable dungeons. Ones no prisoner had ever escaped from.

"Will this do?" Lady Ithamai stopped before a small, dank hole in the wall far from the other occupied cells.

"It's perfect," the king replied, and the Clawsguard and the Shadow Fae shuffled the queen into her new home.

"She's already quite secure but as you asked for the best, I will send the warder down to activate their protections. Now, shall we move on to business?"

"On to business." The king gestured for the Warden of the East to lead and, as a pair, they left the dungeons. The true Clawsguard followed.

But the Shadow King and Rhistel stayed and stood before his queen's cell.

"Burn this moment into your mind," King Érebo murmured. "Even the strongest among us fall at times. Make sure she cannot get back up."

"I intend to," Rhistel replied, and lifted his hold ever so slightly.

She gasped and gripped the bars. The prince sensed a pulse of magic that was not his, but felt similar. The queen was trying to access her magic, but none struck him. None would either.

"Soon, we'll send forth the rumors," Rhistel whispered.

"What rumors?" the queen asked. Her tone was hazy, for she was still not herself. Nor would she be ever again if he had his way.

"Of where you are, Mother." Rhistel sneered. "Why would we waste time searching for the vermin destroying our kingdom when we can get them to come to us?"

CHAPTER 25

ISOLDE

With my sister at my side, I stood outside the gates of Myrr, my body and heart weary from travel and blood loss.

Though Astril's ministrations helped, King Tholin's injury had been so dire that Thyra and I had required the constant use of Sassa's Blade to keep the wound shut as we traversed the mountains. We'd both given much of ourselves and were feeling the repercussions two whole days later.

Not far away, Bavirra and Thordur assisted the injured soldiers of Dergia on Rynni's back. There was no denying that these dwarves were among the few with injuries so severe that they'd never fight again. Much like their king, their lives had been forever changed by the battle with the frost giants.

The dead? They were going too. Wrapped in soft, white linen, they had been placed in a large wooden box that the dragon would carry through the clouds.

We hadn't even faced off with King Magnus yet and already my first allies had experienced great losses. And that wasn't the only alliance that had been affected.

Lord Balik had yet to utter a single word to me or Thyra. Right after the battle, he'd made it clear that he was flying ahead of the armies—getting a severely concussed Filip back home. No one questioned that the lord had wanted to help his heir, though I suspected that wasn't the only reason the high lord had left Sian in charge.

My stomach soured at the memory. Had our failure to trust Lord Balik with the truth cost us everything?

Vale assured me it had not. After all, Lord Balik had not kicked us out of his city, and the Warden of the South couldn't deny that our magic had turned the tides. No, the stoic Lord Balik was simply ignoring us.

The final injured dwarf mounted the dragon and Bavirra and Thordur fell back to stand with my twin and me. Together we watched as the dragon and the gryphon riders rose in the air and banked east, back to Dergia.

Bavirra sighed. "May the winds take them swiftly home."

"Indeed." Her brother's eyes were red, as they had been so often these last days.

My throat tightened. I'd apologized to the prince and princess many times for their losses. They'd expressed pain for the deaths of their people, but also acknowledged that casualties were expected. They'd agreed to war.

It was Bavirra who spoke the most haunting words. That in the end, we'd all lose someone we loved.

Thinking in that vein brought up another question. One I'd smothered time and time again, but it continued to flare to life whenever something went wrong. Back before I'd known who I was, back when a vampire prince hunted me, I'd bargained for Anna's life.

What was that price for her life? Had I already paid it?

The past moons had been difficult. Sometimes heart-wrenching. But something told me that the answer was no. My debt remained and when I did have to pay, it would be awful indeed.

"Let's go back." Thyra's hand brushed mine.

I glanced to the dwarves. They did not look inclined to leave. More like they wanted a moment to themselves.

"We'll see you two at the castle," I spoke softly.

"See you there," Bavirra replied, her gaze still firmly on the dragon and the gryphon riders escorting her in the distance.

My twin and I turned to leave, and in doing so had to pass through a crowd of Dergians. Most were watching their friends leave, but some stared at us, anger on their faces. My stomach hardened. In the days since the battle, I'd overheard a few conversations.

Some from Dergia were already questioning if they should have left the safety of their rock. No such talk had come from Thordur or Bavirra, but I couldn't help but wonder what the king thought.

"We need to go to the healing sanctuary," I said once we passed through the city gates and our Valkyrja formed a circle around us.

"Why?" Thyra's eyebrows pinched.

"The King of Dergia awoke this morning, and we

need to speak with him. To make sure he's not having second thoughts."

"Don't you think approaching Lord Balik would be more prudent?"

"When he's ready to talk, he'll let us know."

"Not like you saved his heir or anything," Thyra muttered.

True though her words were, I understood Lord Balik's anger. Understood the frustration of anyone we'd kept secrets from.

Halladora had wanted an apology, which I thought brave of her, considering that she was under my command, but she wasn't the only one. Sian, too, had demanded answers. Had questions. Of course I'd given them both whatever information I could.

And finally there was Thordur, who had watched me place a shadow wrap on his father's leg. After his father had been placed in the healers' sanctuary, he'd sought me out too. Bavirra at his side.

Others who'd seen had not approached me, but instead spoke to Sian or Vale, two trusted warriors. They had been sworn to secrecy for the time being, and Vale assured me that it wasn't many fae. Our forces had been separated from the larger battle, and life-threatening situations had a way of keeping fae focused on the fight in front of their faces.

When we reached the castle sanctuary it was quiet. Peaceful. Thank the stars for that. After returning to Myrr, the place had been a madhouse, the healers frantically seeing to the injured, others helping wherever they could.

I scanned the front room, the less private portion of

the sanctuary where healers brewed potions and performed other tasks related to their work. On the right side of the vast space was a large wooden carving of the eight-spoked wheel and four stars, the symbol of the healing goddess. No healers were readily available.

"Hello?" I called out, not wishing to go wandering and earn a healer's ire.

"A moment!" someone replied from a private office reserved for the more senior healers. A short time later, none other than a Master Healer appeared.

She blinked when she saw us and hurried over, only to fall into a deep curtsey. Her white chain necklace, complete with the healers' wheel, swung in the air. I'd learned from Rynni that a Master Healer needed only to wear the white chains, but they often added the wheel and stars to their attire to please their dead god.

"Princesses, I apologize for keeping you waiting." The Master Healer was far younger than the one I'd met previously. With dark raven-wing hair and a youthful vigor about her, I doubted that she was even a century old.

"No apologies are necessary." My cheeks warmed.

No longer was I unused to being called a princess, or others showing me deference, but when someone like this, someone who had worked tirelessly for turns to achieve a great title and to whom I owed quite a lot, and would likely keep owing with a war on the horizon, paid me the courtesy of my title, it always felt a bit silly.

"Has Rynni flown off already?" the healer asked.

"She has. Everyone is safely aboard her back," I assured her. This healer had been one of the fae to patch the dwarves up enough so they would survive the flight.

"She was such a help to us. Astounding mind, that one."

"We were hoping to speak to the King of Dergia," Thyra cut in. "Is he awake?"

The healer smiled, and I sensed a fondness for the king that I could relate to. "I'll show you to his room."

We followed her to the far back of the expansive sanctuary, to a private room, as befit a king. She stopped at his door and knocked.

"Yes?" King Tholin's voice came through the wood.

The Master Healer poked her head inside the room. "Princess Isolde and Princess Thyra are here to speak with you." She cast a glance at our Valkyrja. "Possibly others too?"

"Just us," Thyra said. "Our guard will wait outside."

"Let them in."

The Master Healer opened the door and waved us through. Thyra went first, but I paused and leaned closer to the healer.

"Is Filip well?" I hadn't dared ask to see the heir to the southlands. Not when his father was still so furious with us.

"He was moved to his own quarters this morning. Two healers are by his door, but I doubt he'll call for them. The lad is feeling fine and has never been one to have others pander to him."

"Thank you." I made a split decision to ask another question. One that had been weighing on me since we'd inadvertently freed King Érebo. "Do you see many babies born in the castle?"

The healer blinked at the odd question. "A few. Three

were born in the last two weeks, a set of twins and a single youngling, all to servants."

I had a hunch that the Shadow King had been helping to strengthen the blight by pushing his darkness into the network of Drassil trees—a great source of magic. When my family had fallen from power, the blight had gotten worse, maybe because Magnus had not known of the darkness woven into our realm. Maybe because King Magnus hadn't had the proper tools to protect the kingdom. Or perhaps he was simply too weak or not favored by the Faetia to keep the magic balanced.

"Those babes were born without issue?" I asked, not wishing to get too deep into my theories with a healer I didn't know.

"Yes."

"And in the wider city?" I hesitated to ask one more question, but I needed to know. "Have babes been born healthy? Younglings remained so?"

"As a matter of fact, yes," the Master Healer answered slowly. "We've had quite a run of healthy births. Fewer illness too. I haven't seen anything like it in many turns." She tilted her head in a manner that made me think she was considering what else to say, but what she said next, I never would have guessed.

"Did you know I worked at Frostveil Castle?"

"How long ago?"

"Ten turns back I came here, but before that I worked in the capital."

"You knew my family then."

"Your mother in particular. She studied at the White Tower at the same time I did. We weren't in the same classes, but seeing as she was from a prominent noble house, I knew her. Everyone did."

I cast a glance at Thyra, who was listening.

"When I began working at the castle, your father had been king for some time. I didn't know him well, but well enough to see some of them both in you. To compare you to the current king, as well." She inhaled deeply. "I wasn't sure, you see, because of how King Harald ended, but these questions and your care for others helps to relieve my fears that if you win the war, more will be hurt in that castle. In that kingdom too."

"You mean hurt in the way my father did?" Stars, more than anything I wanted to tell her the truth, but I held my tongue.

"And King Magnus. I was charged with patching up many more of his victims than the late King Harald. The fae in the royal harem, mostly." She shuddered. "In the early days of Magnus's reign, those poor females were horribly used and abused."

I swallowed, remembering the time I'd been to the harem. How awful it had been to bear witness. Even Roar had thought so, and though he'd twisted a lot of truths, I did not think he'd been pretending that night. "I've seen it. And I hope to free those fae. End that practice."

"That's very good to hear."

"Sister?" Thyra interjected. I'd taken too long.

"Thank you," I said to the healer as I entered the king's quarters.

The door *snicked* shut behind me, and I found the King of Dergia sitting up, a tired smile on his face. He appeared cleaned up and groomed, his blond hair brushed back and tied with a leather strap.

"I'm afraid I can't welcome you properly, but please, take a seat." He gestured to two of the four chairs that surrounded his bed.

I settled into one next to Thyra and smiled at my ally. "How are you?"

"Alive, and thankful for it."

My throat tightened. He wouldn't have been injured if we weren't allies. If he hadn't yoked his fate to mine.

"I'm so sorry." I glanced briefly at his leg, lost at the knee. It felt impolite to look, even if it was raised to avoid swelling.

"For saving my life?"

I blinked.

The king laughed. "You think I don't know exactly what you did, Isolde? How your shadows held me together, and your vampire helped? I know and, despite my state, I do not regret my actions. Nor what you did to save me."

Thyra's lips pursed. "You'll never fight again, King. Might not do a lot of things you relished. I can't understand not regretting that, at least a little."

King Tholin's eyes crinkled at the corners, and I was reminded once again how easy he was to like. To want to be friends with. "You're young and have much life left."

"You do too," I said. Fae could live for centuries upon centuries, and while there was gray in his beard, he was nowhere close to ancient.

"I recognize that my life will not be as it once was. Truth be told, the moment I allied with you, I hoped it would not be. To lose something so small for a new life, a new world—for my people to walk beneath the sky whenever they wish—it's worth this small price." He gestured to his leg.

"So you will still call us allies?"

The king's lips parted, but he recomposed his features quickly. "You thought I'd change my mind?"

"You lost so many, and the war hasn't begun."

"Yes it has," Thyra countered. "Just because we haven't met Magnus on a field of battle doesn't mean we're not already at war, sister. The wheel has begun to turn. There's no going back."

"She's right," the king said. "And I knew, as every soldier who joined me in the tunnels knew, that we'd lose some among us. Despite that sad fact, no Isolde, I do not regret my choice. I'm a dwarf, as steadfast and loyal as the rock I have lived beneath for all my life."

He'd said something to that effect before, back when things had been easier. When the losses had been less. I'd believed him then, but since then, I'd wavered. I'd questioned.

But the king in the bed had not.

Looking upon the king's face and seeing Thyra study me, I realized I had only one choice. To move forward.

"Thank you." I reached out, took the king's hand. "Thank you so very much."

He nodded and squeezed my hand. "Why don't you fill me in on these shadow powers you have acquired? I'd like the whole story."

"Thordur was the one to tell you?" I asked.

"I would not believe that vampire blood alone saved

me. I forced the prince. Don't blame him if he wasn't supposed to."

I shrugged. Blaming Thordur was the farthest thing from my mind.

"It started in the cavern where you saved us," Thyra said, and I leaned back, content to let my sister tell the tale.

CHAPTER 26
ISOLDE

Thyra let out an exhale. "I'm glad we're finally doing this."

"Me too." I gestured to the carriage following us. "I hope they like the food."

Lord Balik had seen to it that the rebels were getting food, but we were supplying the rebels with a different kind of nourishment. Joy. Sweets, baked goods, savory cheeses, and fresh fruits weighed down the second carriage. All of it sourced by castle servants and purchased by us from the bakeries and markets closest to Ramshold.

"I'm sure they will. These kinds of treats were hard to come by at Valrun," Thyra smiled, and the pure happiness there lifted my heart too. We were both enjoying the few hours of levity after days of stress and intense magical practice. "I can't wait to see the younglings' faces when we pull out the cakes."

I grinned and looked out the window. As ever the streets of Myrr were busy with fae simply going about their lives. Shopping. Eating. A group of faun younglings played a game, and their parents watched them from under an awning. I noted that many now went without cloaks. Certainly, no one wore furs.

My gaze caught on a young male satyr laughing with a small gang of pixies. The hooved fae was probably a turn or two younger than me. He would be one of the fae called to fight for Lord Balik, one of many able-bodied males and females. My stomach hardened. How many of the families that we passed by would lose someone they loved for my family? For our cause?

For a better realm too, I reminded myself, but in no way could I know that everyone called to fight would agree. I simply had to do my best to deliver a kingdom I could be proud of.

In no time at all, the carriage slowed to a stop and, as we'd requested, the driver tapped on the wall. We didn't want our names to be called out in the middle of the city. In fact, we wanted as little notice as possible, and had gone as far as to borrow the most plain carriages the Balik family owned. No dark green and gold here, only black.

The door opened and our Valkyrja, two of whom had been riding with the driver and the other duo in the other carriage, appeared. They formed a semi-circle as Thyra and I emerged, our thin woolen cloaks over our heads.

The heat of the early afternoon sun warmed my face. In other kingdoms, they'd still say it was cold, but those of winter blood were not used to such heat.

Thyra nodded to Sigri. "Lead the way."

I studied the first apartment building. The other two lined the road further down. We'd visited before but not gone in all three. To hear the Balik males and Vale tell it, the rebels had taken up nearly every single family unit inside the housing structures.

"What happened to you?" asked the stocky guard standing at the door to the first building. A wry grin crossed his face as he took in Sigri like he knew her. Likely they'd met the day the majority of the rebels arrived in Myrr.

"Oh you mean this little thing?" Sigri pointed to her black eye, which in truth was anything but little. "Battled a frost giant."

"Fates, remind me not to piss you off."

"Too right." Sigri's voice took on a slightly flirtatious tone.

I glanced sidelong at Thyra. Did Sigri have a crush on the stocky soldier?

"What's the visit for?" the other, reedier, guard asked.

Sigri took a step to the side, revealing Thyra and me. "Princesses Thyra and Isolde are here. They've come bearing gifts."

The soldiers began to bend the knee, but Thyra held out a hand to stop them. "We're trying to keep a low profile. Hence the very small group accompanying us."

"As you wish, Highnesses." The stocky one inclined his head. "Do you require assistance?"

"We've got it handled." Thyra approached the building's door. "Sigri, show me where Ratha is staying."

In the absence of Thyra, Brynhild, and Bac, the ancient whisperer was the de facto leader of those who stayed here. She would be able to round rebels up quickly.

The dwarf did as commanded, and feeling compelled

to say something, I walked up beside her. She arched an eyebrow. "Yes, Princess Isolde?"

"I never asked you if your eye was feeling better—after the battle, I mean."

Sigri laughed. "Aye, it really is fine. This isn't the first shiner I've gotten. More like the tenth."

I cringed, which only made her laugh harder.

"I grew up with three brothers, you see. All males who fancied themselves wee warriors. Well, I wanted to be like them, so anytime they fought, I did too. We gave each other many of these." She gestured to the bruise.

"I see. Are your brothers in the rebellion?" If so, I had not put two and two together.

Her face fell slightly. "Not a one of them is walking this realm any longer. They died in the king's service."

"Oh, I'm so sorry. Fighting orcs or in other battles?"

"Two yes. The third was in the king's harem. He was beaten for not giving some lord what he wanted."

My mouth went dry.

"Don't apologize again. You had nothing to do with it." Anger blazed in Sigri's voice. "But now you know that though I love Thyra and have come to respect you greatly as well, most of us aren't only fighting for your family. We're fighting injustices of our own."

"I understand," I whispered, and we continued on, each lost to our own thoughts, which I suspected were of three dwarven males gone too soon.

We found Ratha in her apartment, knitting a sweater made of bright pink yarn.

"Who is that for?" Thyra asked apprehensively.

"Not you, so don't worry your little royal head about

that. I learned my lesson there long ago." Ratha set her work down.

"Thank the stars."

The whisperer laughed dryly. "One of the younglings needed a new one. At least *they* appreciate my work."

"Well, we have something else they might need." Thyra's grin was so infectious it beat back some of the sorrow I felt for Sigri and her family. "There's a carriage filled with goodies out there. Can you round everyone up while we begin unloading? Start with the younglings."

The whisperer cracked a smile. "You didn't need to do that, you know. We heard about the giants, and the deaths and such. No one was expecting either of you to come running back here to see us."

"We wanted to," I said. "Needed to get out of the castle."

Stars, if that wasn't the truth. I'd felt better after speaking with King Thordur, but the fact that Lord Balik was still ignoring us remained. It was nice to leave his castle, to breathe fresh air, and help others.

"I'll get them outside," Ratha said.

With our Valkyrja in tow we rushed back outside. We'd only just pulled the largest cakes from the carriage when a rush of younglings burst from the apartment buildings.

"We heard you have surprises!" A brownie squealed when she saw the cake. "Can I have that one?!"

Thyra laughed. "You'll have to share it, or you'll make yourself ill."

"I will," the girl promised and held out her hands. "Promise."

The cake was so large I had doubts that the dainty brownie could carry it, but she managed. One by one the younglings lined up for a treat, and they were soon joined by rebels of all ages.

Person by person, cake by tart by wheel of cheese given, my mood lifted. Scents of chocolate, vanilla, cinnamon, and other spices filled the air, and I became so engrossed in chatting with a new mother who had nearly died from happiness when she got an apple pie, that I didn't notice others had joined.

"We want some," said a male with the distinct accent of the southlands.

I turned to find a group of thirty fae, none of whom I recognized.

"These are for us, not your lot," shouted a male rebel with a bulbous nose. "So stop being nosy and sticking yourself where you don't belong!"

"You're in our city now," the faerie leader of the group spoke testily. "And our lord is letting you stay. For free, I think. The least you can do is give us a little cake."

"How dare you demand that of our princesses," the new mother growled.

The faerie looked at our Valkyrja and then me and Thyra. It was clear that he hadn't known who we were, and why would he? My twin and I had mostly stayed at the castle, and we'd made it a point to underdress so as not to draw attention.

"Apologies, Princesses." The leader placed a hand to his heart. "I didn't know it was you. I—"

"You bow to them." The large nosed rebel's face had taken on a violent shade of red "That's what you do or are you so uncultured that you don't—" the rebel gasped, and his hand flew to his throat.

"Choke him out!" one of the Myrranese shouted so aggressively he showered those standing in front of him with spittle. "Teach the scum a lesson!"

Fates, this was not happening, I thought as a rebel leapt from the crowd, threw a punch at a local, and violence exploded in the street.

CHAPTER 27
ISOLDE

Where moments before there had been laughter and the scent of sugar in the air, now the metallic tang of blood pierced the street.

"Stop them!" I shouted to the guards as the Valkyrja closed in around us, weapons up and ready. Unnecessary as it seemed like my twin and I had been forgotten.

The fae of Myrr probably didn't care who sat on a throne so far in the north. Not now. Not ever. But they certainly cared that rebels who had once stolen or fought them lived in their city.

"He's passed out!" a female cried.

I pivoted to find the rebel with the bulbous nose splayed out on the ground. The local faerie was still squeezing the air from his lungs.

The temperature around me plummeted as I targeted the attacker's arms, extended towards the rebel. The frost covered the elemental's hands first and ran up his forearms to his shoulders. With another push, it turned to ice.

The male screamed, and as I was attacking him, I felt the moment he released his air magic. The rebel on the ground gasped and began to suck down air.

"Stay away from him!" Thyra screamed. "If you even think about harming him again, we'll freeze you from the inside out."

The thug's eyes were filled with tears from the pain. "Yes, Highnesses. I-I didn't mean to take it so far."

It had to be true, or he wouldn't have been able to say such a thing, and though that was no excuse, in a way, I understood. My magic had gotten away from me more than once.

The air elemental ran off, leaving his victim on the ground and a giant mess in his wake.

"Halladora, Sigri, and Tonna, help separate the locals and rebels," I commanded.

Astril positioned herself between us and the bulk of those fighting as our other three sworn shields rushed into the fray, which in a shockingly short amount of time had attracted at least twenty more locals, apparently just stewing for a fight. I scanned for another use of violent magic, but I saw only punches being thrown. As bad as that was, it was better than so many fae using magic against one another.

"They don't seem to be letting up," Thyra muttered after a minute or so.

Tonna, Sigri, and Halladora were imposing and doing their best to quell the violence, as were the buildings' guards, but there were simply too many rebels. Too many locals who wanted them gone. Too much pent-up aggression and distrust.

"Should we . . ." I called my power, filled the air with a sparkle of frost that fell to the cobbles when I released.

"I'm not sure," Thyra said. "I don't want the locals to despise us but—" The next word died on her lips, and my twin paled.

"What?" I asked but got no answer. Got nothing but a massive shock when a shadow burst out of Thyra. "Fates!"

My sister jumped too, but when the shadow, distinctly in the shape of a faerie, stared at her, she nodded, as if innately understanding. "Save the kid. Stay hidden by the ground."

The shadow soared away, leaving me with my mouth wide open. I followed its inky form and found what Thyra had already spotted. The brownie youngling we'd given cake to had been caught in the middle of the fighting. She was so small she'd been easy to overlook in the crush and was laying on the ground, passed out, the cake smashed next to her.

The shadow wove through the violence, morphing from faerie-form to a ribbon that glided along the ground like a snake. When it reached the brownie, the shadow figure wrapped around the youngling, still unnoticed by those fighting around her, and came back the way it went, along the ground, all the way to us.

"Let it pass," Thyra said to Astril who looked as astonished as I felt. She knew we wielded shadow magic —had been there the day it was set free—but this, *this* was new.

We fell to our knees as the shadow joined us, unwrapped itself from the youngling and formed a body again.

"Leave." Thyra gathered the brownie in her arms, and the shadow figure dissipated. "She's breathing."

"How did you know how to do that?" I asked.

We'd both created tendrils of shadows and were slowly gaining control over that form of magic. Still, we'd never made something so lifelike. So like how Sassa's Blade produced shadows. How, now that I thought about it, King Érebo likely used his shadows.

"I'm not sure," Thyra admitted, "but I called that magic to be useful and that's what happened. Not sure I could do it again."

"Do you think anyone saw?" I asked.

"Look at them." Thyra nodded at the violence before us. "No one is even watching us. I'm fine."

She was right. Had anyone seen a shadow figure, or even a stray tendril, they'd say something. At the very least, they'd be terrified, as most fae were scared of shadow magic. But nearly every fae in the area was still fighting, and those who were not had either sustained injuries or stood on the sidelines and shouted insults or encouragement. No one was paying us any attention.

The youngling opened her eyes, and that was our cue to stop talking. After making sure the girl was fine, we told her to sit safely in our carriage.

I shut the door behind the brownie and turned to my sister. "The soldiers and Valkyrja are not having the desired effect." There were simply too many rebels and locals and too few soldiers to keep them contained when they were riled. We needed to help.

The temperature dipped as together we called our powers and sent a wave of magic over those fighting. We didn't freeze the fae solid, but stopped just short of that, essentially making it impossible for them to move quickly.

The soldiers took advantage of the break in movement and pushed themselves between the two groups. Finally, when distance was established, Thyra and I moved to stand between the locals and rebels.

We released our hold, and a collective sigh rang up from those who had felt our magic.

"Terrifying." A local glared at us.

"You know what's terrifying?" I countered. "That you can do this to a fellow fae. That you so easily spill blood on your city streets when these people just want to survive." I gestured to the rebels before shifting my arm to the other side. "And these people want assurances that their home is still their own. That they're safe here."

"You're two sides of the same coin," Thyra interjected. "And neither of you are enemies to the other."

"One of them stole from my family greenhouse!" a local shouted. "My aunt and uncle went hungry for moons!"

"I'm not saying what the rebels always did was right." Thyra held up her hands. "They, and I include myself among them, did what was necessary to survive, which I think most of you can relate to. And we all had to go to such lengths because we share a common enemy, a king who has made all of us suffer for more than twenty turns and never admitting that he was at fault. Never saying he did not have the Ice Scepter and that was why winter became so harsh."

"That's what Lord Balik said, but winter has been lifted," someone in the crowd said, "at the king's hand."

"Yes," I admitted. "But can you trust someone who kept something so important from you? All because he didn't want to appear weak?"

"Are you saying that when you lead," a local female close by stepped forward, "whichever one of you sits on the throne, you'll be open and honest with the people? I find that hard to believe."

"I would like to. I think it would bring our kingdom closer, which, we can all see from what happened here, is needed."

I recognized the hypocrisy of what I said, even as I firmly believed that what we were doing was right. Eventually, the people would know of our magic. In the future, we could and would be more open. Just not now.

"They're good people." A female rebel held up her hand. She had a baby strapped to her chest and stood safely off to the side. "Princess Isolde even made sure my babe and I were well after the birth. Had the healer look after me, she did. I doubt the king has ever done that for anyone besides maybe a few nobles."

My cheeks warmed. Of course that was true, though not entirely for the reason the female believed. I'd been wondering about the blight.

"Lord Balik cares for us like that," said a local whose face was spattered with blood. "Would be nice for a king to do the same. Or a queen." He eyed me, then Thyra, and nodded.

"We will. We *do*," Thyra said. "Our father didn't have a good reputation when he went to the afterworld, but Isolde and I—we've led different lives than other nobles. We were raised more like you."

Well, she had been. I'd grown up in entirely different circumstances, but I wasn't going to stop her when she was on a roll.

"We want to make sure that this kingdom is a place where everyone can prosper." Thyra waved her hand in the air to encompass the two sides standing on opposite sides of an invisible line. "Will you join us in making Winter's Realm a better place? A kingdom we can all be safe and loved in?"

The applause said yes, but the looks tossed across the invisible line told me that it would still take some work for these groups to accept one another.

CHAPTER 28

ISOLDE

Thyra and I had been back at the castle for hours. In that time, I'd tried to create a shadow form like the one she had made. All my attempts failed. That, combined with Lord Balik's absence and the fight we'd witnessed in the streets, had only served to drive my mood downward. So when a knock came at the door, I was not at all upset to be interrupted while practicing magic.

"Yes?" Thyra asked.

"Princess Saga and Lady Marit are here," Freyia called from the hallway.

"Let them in," Thyra replied.

Freyia opened the door wide, and I caught sight of her sister, Astril, standing guard alongside her.

"Hi!" Saga chirped as she swept into the room.

True to form, however, Saga had already hired a seamstress in the city to create gowns, and a few fighting ensembles. A brief glance told me that the seamstress did impeccable work. Another more thorough look made me smile. Hanging in Saga's pocket was the outline of a small book. The princess was a prolific writer and kept all the court secrets in a notebook she called the Book of Fae. I wondered what she was writing about the southern city and my fledgling court.

I held back from asking, but made a note to have Saga invite her seamstress to Ramshold so that I might be measured, too. The Balik sisters were generous with their wardrobes, but I hadn't spoken to them since the frost giant battle. I was sure their absence was because their father forbade it, and not because they wanted to stay away.

My friendship with the Baliks aside, sooner or later, I'd need an array of my own garments, anyway. Thyra would too. If we were to rule, we would need every weapon and shred of wisdom at our disposal. I, for one, counted clothing as a very effective weapon.

"Good afternoon," Marit said more softly than the princess. "I brought a few snacks for moral support." She held out a bag. "Chocolates. Not those gold dusted ones, but from a shop in town. Qildor took me and, believe me, they're exquisite."

"What a sweetheart that knight is!" I winked at Marit.

"Let me stop you there. Nothing has happened." She let out a long-suffering sigh. "Until I'm no longer married, I think things will stay that way."

"Fates, is he for real?" Thyra muttered.

"He's too noble." Saga perched on the edge of Thyra's bed, earning her a slight frown from my twin. For once, though, Thyra held her tongue about outside clothing on the bed.

"Agreed." Marit lifted the bag. "Anyways, do you have a platter?"

Thyra laughed. "No. We can eat them out of the box."

Marit looked appalled.

Saga gestured to the Crown, sitting on Thyra's bedside table. "Any luck?"

"I haven't made much time," I admitted.

"And I haven't had a breakthrough, despite sleeping with it every night." Thyra rubbed the back of her head. "Which, you can imagine, is about as comfortable as it sounds."

"Well, you did return from a frost giant battle just days ago," Saga said graciously. "And you quelled that squabble just earlier today."

"Barely," Thyra said. "They stopped throwing punches, but I could tell the locals weren't fully convinced that the rebels were trustworthy."

"You won't change everyone's mind in a day. But you probably planted a seed, and those can grow into the most beautiful things." Marit reached into the bag and pulled out the box of chocolates. She set the blue box on the table between the chairs and took off the lid. The sweet smell filled the room. "As for the Crown, there's no time like the present to have another go."

Not at all in a hurry to use the Hallow, I smiled at my twin. "You first?"

Thyra took the Frør Crown in both hands and set it on

her head. It struck me as lovely how well the Crown suited my sister. She was the picture of regal.

Thyra was stronger than me, with well-muscled arms and legs, and the scar that bisected her left eye gave her an air of grit. Add in that she was far more skilled with a bow and, like me, possessed powerful winter magic, and Thyra looked every bit a warrior queen.

My twin closed her eyes. By the measured way that she breathed, I could tell she was concentrating, trying to connect with the Crown.

I waited, hoping something would happen, but when Thyra's jaw clenched, I feared we had reached another dead end.

She removed the Hallow from atop her head. "Nothing. Still nothing!"

Before she hurled it across the room, I took the Crown from her. "Perhaps it's . . . still warming up?"

Thyra pursed her lips. "There's nothing we can do to instigate visions, Saga?"

"Well, there *is* a potion," the princess looked uneasy saying the words, "but it's meant for experienced seers. I haven't even tried it because it's so potent. Dangerous for those unused to visions, and maybe you don't know this, but visions can be dangerous in themselves."

"Right." Thyra let out a huff. "Give me a damned chocolate."

Marit thrust a box at my sister, and Thyra devoured three chocolates before I got up the courage to raise the Crown to my head. The metal settled over my hair, braided today in an intricate style of overlapping braids. I released the cold metal and exhaled. Waited.

"Anything?" Saga asked, gaze alight.

I gave it a few more seconds before lifting the metal circlet from my head and tossing it on the bed. "Nothing."

Thyra let out a sigh so full of relief that my irritation, so close to the surface after recent events, flared to life.

"I don't think I'll try again."

"What?" Saga's voice rose. "Why?"

"In case you haven't noticed, my sister doesn't want the Crown to work for me again." The pent-up frustration I'd been feeling laced my tone. Even though I didn't like the Hallow I knew it was of great value. "Fates forbid it helps us through me."

Thyra tossed her hands up in the air. "Am I so wrong for wanting something from our family to be mine and mine alone? The Crown has given you a vision, but not me, and I'm the one who should be most inclined to use it! The Blade chose you too."

"You can use the Blade," I countered.

And apparently make shadow forms, I did not add.

"Not as well as you."

Something in me snapped. Although I'd been sure my sister had felt this way, we'd avoided the topic. Many topics, actually. Those issues, combined with the stress of recent events, made my stomach clench.

I marched towards the door and swung it open. Freyia and Astril stood before me, as still as stone.

"What's wrong?" Astril asked lowly.

"I need space. Don't follow me."

"Isolde!" Thyra shouted. "Wait!"

I slammed the door shut and ran. Ran for distance, for air because with each second it seemed to come less freely.

I rounded one corner, then another, ignoring the questioning looks from the servants as I dashed by. Thankfully, none of my friends roamed the corridors. No one tried to make me stop. No one seemed to register the tears that had fallen.

That luck held until I swung around my third blind corner and ran right into someone. Slipped.

A hand reached out to steady me, but the moment I was on my feet, it released me, as if I were poisonous. When I pulled my gaze up, I swallowed.

"Lord Balik." My voice was raspy, my breathing irregular. "I apologize."

The Warden of the South stared down at me, golden eyes hard, though I detected a bit of concern there. But when he nodded and swerved around me, leaving me there without a word, I thought I probably imagined that concern.

Fates, he hated me. Hated what was inside me.

My chest tightened, and my already shallow breathing worsened. I couldn't get a lungful, couldn't think straight. Only once had I experienced anything close to this—when Prince Gervais of the Blood Court had arrived in Frostveil with Anna at his side.

Hide. You've shown too much weakness as it is. A small, rational part of my mind spoke through all the garbled thoughts.

I had to look strong. Had to pull myself together.

I shoved open the nearest door and slammed it shut behind me. Hand to my chest, I went to a bed that was stripped of blankets. Nothing else in the room either. I'd stumbled upon one of the spare bedrooms. Doing my best to regulate my erratic breathing, I perched on the edge, pressed my palms into the feather mattress, and tilted my chin to the ceiling, only for the door to swing inward on a groan.

My head snapped up. "I don't want to talk about it."

However, it wasn't Thyra who stood in the doorway, but Lord Riis.

"I—won't press," he blurted. "But I wanted to make sure you weren't injured. I saw you run into Lord Balik, then rush into this room. You appeared distressed."

Clearly, because I hadn't even seen Lord Riis, and he wasn't exactly a pixie.

"I'm fi—fi—" a sob ripped up my chest.

Lord Riis inhaled. "You're having a panic attack, Isolde. Like that one night."

Ah yes. Who other than the Lord of Tongues had seen me run from Prince Gervais and into the kitchen the night of the ball? Lord Riis was always there. Always watching. But unlike that night, I'd not have him touching me or comforting me.

"Leave," I muttered. "Please, just leave."

He nodded. "I'll find Vale."

Lord Riis shut the door behind him. It was closed for no more than ten seconds before the hinges groaned, and Thyra entered. She took me in and poked her head out the door.

"I have it from here, Riis. Don't send Vale."

"I don't want to talk about it," I said on the backend of a ragged breath.

"And I'm not going to make you," she replied, shocking me to my core. "I'm sorry. I've been quite jealous at times and have taken it out on you." She crossed the room and took a seat beside me before I registered her words. "Please, forgive me."

At those words, words that I'd not expected to hear, my shadows settled. My breathing too. Finally, I let out a long exhale.

"I forgive you." And it wasn't even hard to do so. I didn't want tension between us.

She nodded slowly. "The stress of figuring out the Crown and our shadows is a lot."

"Yes, but I was actually being serious when I said I didn't want to use it any more. Not just reactionary."

"What? Why?"

"If I'm being honest, I don't think I can control the Crown. And there's a chance that no matter how hard I try, I'll never be able to." The Hallow had never made me feel right, and something in me understood that was a sign.

"Perhaps not," Thyra mused. "And maybe we don't need it to reach our goals."

Who could say? I'd taken it from a Falk vault, but had the Fates helped me find it? Or sheer luck? Or had the Frør Crown itself manipulated me so I'd take it out into the world?

"There's something I wanted to propose to you, sister," Thyra said, her tone even. Deliberately so.

I sniffled and straightened my spine. "Sounds important."

"It is." Thyra took my other hand in hers. "We haven't spoken of the throne in many days, and understandably so. A lot has been going on, and neither of us wants another fight. Or to cause the other discomfort. Seeing as we're already in the thick of both, this might be an ideal time to pull the stitches from the wound."

Stars, the throne. That was truly the last thing I wanted to speak about. I opened my mouth to say as much, but Thyra shook her head.

"Please."

A pregnant pause filled the room, broken by my clearing of my throat. "Fine."

"Well, I was thinking, why should we allow the throne to come between us? We've both been through so much, seen many sides to this kingdom and others. We have compatible strengths and experiences, so why not use those to build a better kingdom? Together."

"We were always going to work together."

"Yes, but what I mean is . . . right now there's only one throne, but we can make it otherwise. Who's going to tell us no?"

My lips parted. "You want to—co-rule?"

"If you'll allow it." She swallowed. "I understand if you don't want to. I know your magic is a little stronger than mine."

"Perhaps, but you've made a shadow figure, and I haven't, so it seems your shadow magic is more powerful."

"That happened *once*. I couldn't replicate it when we were trying earlier, and I certainly can't control the shadows much at all." My sister let out a breath. "Anyway, I know that you procured us the most powerful allies, but I thought it was a decent idea. Admittedly not one I wanted before, but what's the difference between that and a king and queen ruling equally? I can't find one, though, if you ca—"

"Yes." I didn't need to hear any more. "I love you. From the moment I knew I'd once had a sister, I wished I could have known you. And then when I learned that you were alive, I desperately wanted *more*. To be a *family*. The throne is important, of course, but I don't want it to come between us."

I didn't care if, by the regular laws of inheritance, I would rule alone. Fates, two moons ago, I had never possessed an ambition to rule. Had seriously considered letting Thyra have everything she wanted.

But this idea . . . This sharing that monumental responsibility to bring greatness to our homeland, it did not sound like a bad thing. It might make the kingdom better than it ever had been before.

My sister stared back at me.

"And if we win this war," I continued, needing to fill the silence, "together we'll make Winter's Realm—no, all of Isila—a better place."

Finally, she opened her arms. "I haven't always been kind to you, nor did I show it, but after I learned who you were, some very small part of me hoped that we'd be together again. That maybe, I have family in this world." My throat tightened, and I leaned into her hug. "I love you too, sister. I'm sorry that I fought it, fought you, for so long."

An exhale parted my lips. I'd said those three words without expecting her to return them, but my body had craved them. Wanted her love back.

"I've heard that fighting is what sisters do—second

best only to loving one another," the words were strained coming out of me, but this time with happiness.

"I've heard that too. I suppose we're living proof."

A laugh burst from me, and I gripped her tighter.

"Then it's settled," Thyra added softly but with that same steadfast confidence in her tone that I'd grown to admire. "Soon Winter's Realm will have two queens."

INTERLUDE

PRINCESS THYRA FALK,
HOUSE OF THE WHITE HAWK

The day had been a long one, full of highs and lows.

Thyra and Isolde had worked for hours, and after dinner Thyra worked some more. Alone in her suite, she tried to create another shadow figure. And *finally* she had succeeded. Twice! On the second attempt, she'd been calm enough to sense a tether to the shadow figure, something she had not really noticed before. Once she could put into words how she'd done it, she would help Isolde.

But that was a matter for another day.

Exhaustion penetrated so deep into Thyra's bones that she considered not sleeping with the Frør Crown on her head, as she'd done every night since Saga told them of the Crown's powers.

But no, she couldn't. Dreamer magic was unpredictable. Double that with the unpredictability of the Hallow, and Thyra would never forgive herself if this turned out to be the one night when her magic chose to be accessible and she wasn't wearing the Hallow. She could not let her sister down. Nor herself.

Sighing, she changed into her sleeping dress and slipped the band of amethyst, diamond, and silver atop her head. Adjusting her pillow to make the circlet more bearable to wear, Thyra burrowed into bed. Even with the discomfort of the headdress, her tired body relaxed, and Thyra knew it wouldn't be long until sleep claimed her.

And it did, like a shooting star in the night sky, sleep came, plunging the raven-haired princess into a world to which she once belonged.

Thyra stood right inside the doorway and stared at her mother and father, recognizable from the portrait locket Brynhild had taken from the castle two decades ago. The queen rested on her knees before the king, laying on a settee by a window, a muscle fluttering in his strong jawline.

The princess scanned the rest of the room and concluded they had to be in the queen's bedchambers. Everything was so luxurious and feminine. She twisted and found a sitting area outside the bedroom, likely where the queen would take visitors. Most importantly, everything in the suite possessed a telltale shimmer.

This was a vision. A dream. The Frør Crown was working.

Two other male faeries lingered in the bedchamber. Both had short black hair and silvery-blue wings. One boasted a muscular frame, while the other was taller and slimmer.

"Aksel," her mother spoke softly to one of the males. "Go to my workshop and retrieve the brown bottle labeled Aconia tonic."

"Yes, Mother," the taller, reedier male replied and approached Thyra. She inhaled his scent of something herbaceous and metal as

he walked by her, pushing her to the side as he did so and sweeping from the room. Thyra's throat tightened.

Aksel Falk—her eldest brother. She wanted to follow him and see more of the male she'd never meet again, but when she tried, the Crown rooted the princess in place. What she was meant to see would be in this room.

"I don't need a tonic. What I need is more bleeding swords!" The king grumbled. "Kalan, debrief me on the mage attack."

Kalan, the second oldest Falk male. Brynhild had called him a great warrior. He'd been an adult when he died in the Rebellion—a turn or two older than Vale was now. Around thirty.

"You're too scattered to deal with that," Queen Revna hissed. "You're pushing yourself too hard, Harald."

"Why is Kalan here if not to tell me how my forces are faring?"

"He's worried about his father." The queen stroked the king's long, silver hair. "We all worry for you, my love."

"You should take him to the White Tower." Kalan's tone was so deep, much like the king's voice.

"I have, darling," Thyra's mother replied. "No one knows what's happening."

"I do!" the princess shouted from the doorway she was trapped in. "It's a whisperer messing with his head! Inga Aaberg!"

Of course, they didn't hear her. No one had paid her appearance any mind because she wasn't actually there. Frustration surged within Thyra, but she pushed the annoyance aside and reached into the recesses of her memory. The mages had been a nuisance preceding the White Bear's Rebellion. Did that nuisance extend into the Rebellion?

She tried to remember as Aksel returned, and her mother convinced her father to drink the tonic. All the while, Kalan spoke of the battles with the mages, but when a knock came at the suite door, everyone in the room stopped what they were doing.

"Inga? Is that you?" Revna called out loudly.

"It is. And young Lady Polia with the tea."

"Enter."

Though Thyra was not physically present in the vision of the past, somehow every part of her burned hot as Inga, the current Queen of Winter's Realm, entered and smiled at her parents.

"My queen," Lady Inga demanded such a presence that Thyra barely noticed the younger lady-in-waiting moving to the table carrying a tea set, presumably ordered by the queen. Odd that a lady-in-waiting carried the tray and not a servant, but maybe that was what Queen Revna had preferred? "Sten Armenil and Lady Orla have arrived. The High Lady of the Northlands wishes to see you."

The queen pressed two fingers to her right temple and rubbed the tender area. "I forgot they were due today along with those of House Qiren. I—"

The king shot up from where he lay. "I must take care of the Qirens! Kill their lord. The heir too."

A clatter arose as Lady Polia dropped the tea set and the glass shattered. The princes' faces paled, and the queen spun to face her husband, her hand outstretched as though to slap it over his mouth. Little did she know, the outburst originated from one of the two ladies. The one pretending to be appalled.

Finally, Thyra understood why a lady-in-waiting had been carrying the tea. House Polia was a lesser house, one deeply tied to House Qiren. Inga had orchestrated this. Perhaps Lady Polia was under her powers too, and Inga coerced Lady Polia into coming here to see the king's outburst.

"I apologize." The queen settled for rubbing her husband's shoulder as he fumed over some perceived slight by House Qiren. "He has a fever and is hallucinating."

"I do not," the king shouted. "Kalan, take me to the docks. I wish to slaughter mages."

Thyra's stomach sank to her knees. If scenes like this one had happened in public, it was no wonder that Magnus Aaberg had not had issue with organizing a rebellion.

"I need to find someone to clean this up." Lady Polia gestured to the shattered glass and spilled tea before rushing from the room.

Inga, however, remained, concern etched on her face. "Have you tried Helska's Milk, my queen?"

Even Thyra, with her limited healing knowledge, recognized that name. Helska's Milk was a tonic that would cause a person to sleep as if they'd been sent to the afterworld.

"Bah!" the king growled. "All of you, out of my way."

Queen Revna tried to stop him, as did her sons, but while King Harald was not strong in his own mind, he remained very strong in body. He shoved those he loved aside and stormed through Thyra, out of the queen's rooms.

Thyra watched her father go, sure that he was about to enter a public part of the castle and embarrass himself. Or worse, create more enemies who would soon join the rebellion to take him down.

The princess's fists clenched, and once again, she tried to pull her feet from the ground, tried to make it to Inga. What she would do had the vision allowed her to move, she wasn't sure.

As it were, she did nothing because the vision suddenly lifted and Thyra awoke. In her room, in Ramshold, once more.

Her cheeks were wet. Her body trembled. Thyra swallowed, and with shaking hands removed the Crown and tossed it to the foot of the bed.

They'd known what Inga had done but seeing it was different. Hearing her father's madness made her ache.

She rose from the bed, slid her feet into slippers, and pulled on a robe. Before Thyra knew what she was doing, she was at her door.

Astril awaited outside. The vampires needed little to no sleep, making them ideal night guards.

"Is all well?" the vampire asked.

"I need to speak with my sister."

Astril's eyebrows shot up. Never had Thyra gone to Isolde so late.

"I want to share something with her." She felt like a small child, explaining herself in this way, but the need to tell Isolde what she'd seen overpowered any shame that might bring.

"They're asleep," Freyia said from where she stood before Isolde's door. "I can knock. See if they wake?"

"Please."

Freyia gave a single nod, and her fist fell on the door across the hall three times. Her eyes widened. "Someone is coming."

Thyra held her breath and exhaled it only when Isolde opened the door. Loud snores came from beyond. "I need to talk to you."

"Oh," Isolde said, clearly surprised. "Did something bad happen? Shall I get a sword? And Vale?"

"Nothing like that. I want to talk."

Her twin's face softened, and Thyra cursed all the times she'd been cruel and cold to her twin. Thank the dead gods they were mending their past, becoming closer every day.

"Let me get slippers and my robe." Isolde darted into

the room and was back again in seconds. "Tell Vale if he wakes."

"Judging by the snoring, he won't," Freyia said with a smirk.

"Fates alive, tell me about it," Isolde joked and shut the door softly behind her. "To your room?"

Thyra returned to her suite, holding the door open for her sister. Isolde's gaze landed on the Crown, still sitting where Thyra had tossed it at the foot of the bed.

"I saw our parents, our eldest brothers too." Thyra swallowed through the tightness in her throat. "The vision made our father look like a monster, but I wanted to tell you about it. I couldn't stop myself from coming to you, even if it is late and—"

Isolde slipped her hand into Thyra's. "Don't apologize. I want to listen."

Upon returning to my room, I found Vale snoring soundly. I lay down in bed, and bells passed as my thoughts alternated between Thyra's vision and worrying about whether Lord Balik was still an ally. Finally, the sun spread across Myrr and we rose.

Looking at the bigger picture, I should have been happy. Thyra and I were close—loved one another as sisters should. We would not fight over a throne but *share*. Side by side, we would bring Winter's Realm back to peace and fruitfulness.

None of that will happen if we do not win, I told myself as I tightened my sword belt around my waist. *We have to win to share a throne. And for that, we will need the Baliks. Likely the Armenils too.*

"Vale," I said. "Has a raven come from Morial yet?"

He'd been pulling on his boots, but at my question, he looked up, his lips a straight line. "Not yet, but it's a long flight. And I expect Connan will have to confer with advisors."

Vale didn't mention Lady Orla Armenil, who had recently lost her mate and, from what I'd heard, would be unwell for moons to come. I believed it too. Just the thought of losing Vale was unbearable. To go through that —I shuddered.

"I see," I said.

"Don't worry, Force. Things are coming together."

"And unraveling at the same time," I muttered.

Vale pulled on his other boot and crossed the vast room to stand at my side. "Lord Balik will honor his vow. He needs time to understand what he saw."

Vale had grown up at court. He was used to the games of high lords and ladies and how long things took.

"I hope so," I said. "You're training today?"

"Eireann and Baenna approached me yesterday. They wish to spar with us." Vale arched an eyebrow. "A good sign."

I hadn't seen my friends since I returned from the battle, but if they went to Vale . . . maybe he was right. Was there hope that Lord Balik had made a choice and not yet told me?

"We're practicing shadow magic after breaking our fast," I said. "But save me a sparring session. If I don't get back into it soon, my muscles will shrivel to nothing."

Vale laughed and pulled me into him so that my backside pressed against his front. I twisted, offering my lips, and he took them in his. Fire rushed through me, potent and hot.

My hand snaked up, tangling in his long black locks. The shaved side was freshly trimmed and scratchy, but the longer part was as silky and touchable as ever. I tugged at his roots, knowing how much he liked it, and a low growl traveled up his throat as he gripped my hips and ground into me.

Stars, losing myself in a morning with Vale would be such a sweet distraction, but Thyra would be at my room soon.

As if on command, three rushed knocks came at our door. Vale groaned.

"Your sister has the worst timing."

I kissed his jaw. "But waiting will make it hotter later, right?"

"You'll be waiting until quite late. I have something planned."

"Oh?"

"Of course. With your nameday dinner party tomorrow, I need my own time to celebrate with you."

My nameday dinner party. In all that had happened, I'd nearly forgotten that Saga had planned it for tomorrow.

"Helloooo!" Annoyance settled into Thyra's every syllable. "Isolde, I'm not here for practice. There's something important, so if you're not *too busy*, stop making me wait!"

"I'm coming!"

"Not soon enough," Vale murmured, his mind still on what might have been.

I rushed to the door and opened it. Thyra took me in, shared a pointed glance with Livia, who had taken over the morning guard, and smirked. Tonna was nearby, having relieved Astril at dawn, and behind them all hovered Valintin, Lord Balik's butler.

"Oh hush." I waved a hand at her even as my heart pounded at the sight of the dryad. Was this a good or a bad sign?

"About what?" Thyra teased. "That your hair looks like you were about to be ravaged?"

Valintin looked away, his cheeks reddening.

One hand shot up, and I found that, indeed, my plaited hair was not as neat as ten minutes prior. "What's so important?"

"Lord Balik has summoned us," she spoke in an oh so holy tone that didn't suit her, and judging by the way her lips twitched with amusement, she knew it. "Hence why Valintin is still standing here, dying of embarrassment."

"Why didn't you say so right away! Let's go!"

She grabbed my wrist. "Skies, I'm serious when I say your hair is a mess. Fix it first. Make a good impression and all that."

I rushed to the mirror. Vale was standing by the window, his face lined with mirth.

"Did you hear her?"

"I have ears," he said as I set to tucking wayward strands of silvery-white back where they belonged. "Do you want me to come?"

"Only us." Thyra leaned against the doorframe. "That's what the warden said."

"You know where to find me if you need to talk afterwards." Vale crossed the room and slipped out. Fixing the last strand of my hair, I followed a minute later, heart racing.

My sister and I didn't speak as we made our way

through the castle to a quieter wing of Ramshold. Unlike the first time, I recognized it as Lord Balik's personal wing.

Valintin led us to the Warden of the South's study. The guards at the door moved aside, allowing the dryad to knock, and when Lord Balik acknowledged the interruption, the butler poked his head inside.

"The Falk princesses, my lord."

"Let them in."

It was all I could do not to run inside and beg the High Lord of the Southlands not to leave us. Somehow, I exhibited restraint, as did Thyra, and together we glided into the study. This time, instead of sitting behind his vast desk, Tadgh Balik sat in one of the four chairs before his roaring fire.

"How are you not sweating?" Thyra asked, probably trying to lighten a moment that felt as heavy as an avalanche rolling over my shoulders.

"I've been chilled from within for days," the lord replied. "But if you'd rather I snuff out the flames—"

"No," I said. "It's not like we're wearing furs. We're fine."

I was a little warm, but in no way did I want to make Lord Balik more uncomfortable than he already appeared.

My twin and I sat opposite the lord. He offered us wine. Usually, I'd say it was a bit early in the morning for such libations, but today I accepted for the sake of my nerves. After he poured three goblets, he leaned back in his chair, and a gusty sigh left his lips.

"We're so sorry," I blurted, unable to hold my words in any longer.

Thyra shot me an incredulous look, but I didn't care.

For days, I'd been dying to speak with Lord Balik. To apologize.

"We should have told you," I continued, "but we were terrified of what we might be able to do and how others would perceive us."

"I cannot blame you. Especially given my reaction after you saved my son's life."

My throat tightened. "How is Filip?"

"Well. And furious at me." Lord Balik's face softened when he spoke of his heir. "The moment he woke, he wanted me to find you two. To assure you I was still loyal, but I forbade it. I could not stop seeing those shadows. Could not stop wondering."

His gaze drifted to the fire, and he sipped once more.

"Wondering what?" Thyra asked bluntly. "We will answer what we can. This relationship is important to us, and we don't want to lose it."

"You have not," Lord Balik replied, and I swore my heart stopped from relief. "I considered it, of course, but I made a vow, and I intend to see it through." He shook his head as though remembering something baffling. "Also, Filip threatened to reject his role as heir if I broke our alliance. Unnecessary, but the steadfastness in the lad lit a fire under my arse."

Bless Filip. Loyal, noble, sweet Filip.

"Thank you for saving him," the high lord added.

"Of course," I replied. "Filip is dear to me. Not saving him was never an option—not even before we made our promise to you to watch over your children."

"However, your saving of my son doesn't mean that I don't have questions," the high lord added, his honeyed gaze turned to steel. "I have many. And I expect them to be answered openly and honestly."

Thyra replied first. "You know our darkest secret, and we won't hide anything else."

"Have you always had this magic?"

I exhaled. "No. Let me explain."

And explain I did. I took Lord Balik through that day in the mountain tunnels, the day of discovery and darkness I wished had never happened. Any time I glossed over something or forgot a detail, Thyra supplied the information. Together we worked to paint a vivid portrait of King Érebo and how he had violated us, how the magic felt being broken open and how it roiled within us. By the time we finished, the Warden of the Southlands had paled.

He set down his drink with a trembling hand. "That day we went to the library, you wished to learn more about him and his kind. *And* your magic, I assume?"

"That's right," Thyra said.

"When did you practice?"

"Any time we were not in public spaces or sparring," Thyra replied. "We were either trying to practice—for a while the shadows didn't come on demand—or studying."

"Do they come on demand now?"

I cringed, and the motion did not go unnoticed.

"I'll take that as a no?"

"Better than before, but saving Filip, while I am happy it happened, wasn't exactly planned." I pressed my lips together before continuing. "If I could have used any other power to do so, I would have, but that day the shadows acted so fast. On instinct."

"However, I did create shadow figures," Thyra said. "During the scuffle in the city."

Lord Balik frowned. "I heard about that."

"We're hoping it was a turning point," I said and meant it. Violence had bloomed yesterday, but hope had too. It only needed to be nourished, just as Marit said.

"Are the figures like those in your sword?" Lord Balik asked.

"Yes, although I'd say those are both more reliable but also riskier to use."

Thyra nodded. "We might not want this power, but it has been useful a handful of times."

Lord Balik blinked. "You don't want the magic?"

"No," my twin and I answered in unison.

"We've grown somewhat used to it," I added, "but we didn't want such a thing then, and we still don't want it now."

"Even if that magic is the only way to defeat the Shadow King? And perhaps by extension King Magnus?"

That gave me pause.

"You might be right there," I allowed.

"We could win the war first, then rid ourselves of the shadow magic. You know, if we had a choice," Thyra said sarcastically.

"You might."

I sat up straighter. "Pardon me?"

Lord Balik leaned closer, as if he were about to share a mighty secret. "My grandmother hailed from the Autumn Court. They do things differently there. Long ago, when the fae in the south committed an unspeakable crime, the punishment would be to rip their magic from them."

Thyra sucked in a breath. "Barbaric."

"It brought shame to those it happened to and their families. Eventually, the Crown of Autumn put an end to that particular punishment. Nowadays, if the crime is bad enough, the fae is killed, as is customary in other kingdoms."

Like Rhistel and Queen Inga would be killed if others learned of their magic. Or at least, that was the current law. In no way would I put it past the king to end a long-standing practice to save Rhistel.

"Do you think we could rip the shadows from us and leave the winter magic?" Thyra asked.

"We cannot rule without winter magic." Not only that but I would die before I let someone take my winter magic. I'd been magic-less once. Incomplete. Never again. "Kings and queens of this kingdom might wield varying degrees of power and smaller magics, but they *always* have the magic tied to the land. Enough to use the Ice Scepter and temper the worst of winter."

These past decades showed what happened if the ruler didn't possess the Scepter. I did not like to imagine what would happen if a winter king or queen didn't have a drop of winter magic in their veins.

"I don't know." Lord Balik set down his empty goblet. "If you wish, I'll send a raven to my kin in the south. See if they have knowledge of the matter."

"Is it too much to ask that your grandmother or anyone in her generation still lives?" Thyra asked.

"Not my grandmother, but others with the knowledge might."

Fae lived a very long time, but eventually, they

perished. Whether by violence, illness, or by their own choice.

"If we ask, they will want to know why," Thyra mused.

"Certainly. But I need not tell them about the shadow magic. I can say this is for another power. Whispering, or something similar."

"Thank you," I replied. "We appreciate it."

Lord Balik gave a single nod. "I think that, given what you've shared, our alliance is strong once more. Do you two agree?"

"Yes," Thyra said, and I echoed that sentiment.

Our ally placed his hands on his knees and stood up. "Then if you'll excuse me, I have a raven to send on a very long journey."

CHAPTER 30
VALE

"You're really not going to tell me where we're going?" my mate asked, her eyes hidden behind a silken sash.

"Would it be an early nameday surprise if I did?" I eyed her appreciatively.

Isolde favored amethyst, but for tonight I'd requested that she wear a deeper purple gown that I picked out. In the right light, the material shimmered like oil on water, and the gown hugged my wife's curves to perfection.

It was an exercise in restraint not to rip the dress off of her then and there, so I gave my hands another job. One slithered behind her back, and I bent my knees to ready the other behind her legs. "I'm going to lift you."

She squealed as I swept her off her feet. I tossed a glance back at Halladora, giving her a nod so she'd know it was time.

The faerie grinned back, pleased to be chosen for such an endeavor. I'd known Isolde would want one of her Valkyrja at our door, guarding Sassa's Blade, and at least one with us. I'd taken care of both aspects of the evening, just as Thantrel had done for Thyra. I hoped only that my brother's plans were going as smoothly as mine.

After tucking her skirt against me so that nothing but her calves would show, my wings unfurled. One beat, two, and we took to the air.

"*Stars*! You didn't tell me we'd be flying." Isolde gripped tighter around my neck. "We're leaving Ramshold?"

"We are."

"Are you sure that's a good idea?"

"I've planned it all. Where we're going there will be no crowds, and Halladora is behind us. We'll be safe."

Though there had been no sightings of Red Assassins or word of any fae sent to kill my mate, we could never be too careful when she or Thyra left the castle.

We soared over the Golden City, and I was half-tempted to remove Isolde's silken sash so she could see the glittering lights and the fae walking along the streets. Perhaps those walking in pairs were also enjoying an evening for lovers. Though our alone time was only the beginning of my surprises.

The wind gusted against me, stealing my breath in spite of its warmth. Isolde inhaled deeply, taking in the scents of the nearby mountain pines.

"Descending," I announced minutes later. "Hold tight."

We lowered into a neighborhood alive with fae. Many of them held hands or stole kisses. Sian hadn't steered me wrong in pointing out this part of the city. Not that I'd ever doubted him. He, like Thantrel, had always been well-versed in romance.

Upon landing, I set Isolde down and placed my hands on her shoulders before turning her into position.

I removed the blindfold. "Behold The Frosted Rose. It's known as the most exclusive restaurant in Myrr. Popular among young fae who are courting."

Isolde caught my eye. "No one seems to be dining. Are they not open yet?"

"They are. Just for us."

Her lips parted. "How romantic!"

"I never took you out in Avaldenn. If I had, I would have made sure our date was private."

"Always?" she asked.

"Not always. But at first, yes. I wouldn't have wanted others to watch me fall in love with you."

Her face broke into a luminous smile. "We had Ragnor's cart."

"And now we'll have this." I wove my fingers through hers. "Come. Halladora will watch the front. Astril is already at the back." Inside The Frosted Rose, workers had begun gathering near the door and window. "Don't keep your people waiting, my queen."

She blushed, and my heart gave a hard thud. I was married and mated to the most beautiful fae I'd ever known. Inside and out, Isolde was my perfect match. I didn't think I'd ever stop thanking the stars for tying our fates together.

We entered the restaurant, and the warm, savory aroma of the place made my stomach rumble. Whatever they were cooking was sure to be as delicious as Sian had assured me it would be. Beyond the food, the restaurant was also a feast for the eyes.

Candles covered every surface, basking the room in an ethereal glow. A staghorn chandelier hung in the center of the circular room, further illuminating the space. And while there was no longer snow outside, some talented fae had enchanted crystal snowflakes to hang, suspended in the air.

"So lovely," Isolde said as a server showed us to a lone table in the middle of the room. I pulled out her chair, and she settled in, taking in the tabletop and glancing up at the server. "The flowers smell wonderful. I don't know what they are, but your establishment has good taste."

The server gestured to me. "Not us, Princess Isolde. Prince Vale picked those out."

My mate beamed. "He has good taste then."

"Impeccable."

Once we were both seated, the server informed us they'd be bringing out courses—pre-selected by me—and she hoped we enjoyed the entertainment. She left us, and Isolde barely had a chance to ask what the server meant by entertainment, when the three-fae band emerged from the adjoining room. The singer stood in front and crooned a haunting song.

Isolde melted in her seat. "Her voice is magic!"

I'd noted many things regarding my mate. That night the rebels broke into the Royal Theater—the very same evening Thyra almost killed her sister without knowing Isolde existed—had started off magical too. A ride to the theater in a reindeer-pulled sleigh with a beautiful female at my side, commanding the attention of those in the room, though she did not notice it. And Avalina Truso, a rebel sympathizer and undeniably talented singer, had enchanted my mate that night.

Guilt rose inside me. Truso had been among those taken to the dungeon of Frostveil the day before the king murdered her and many other performers. I'd spoken to her and suggested she deserved what she got. I pushed my guilt down. There would be time to examine it later, but not tonight. This night was for the love of my life.

"I requested the best singer in Myrr."

Isolde let out a long hum and sipped from a glass of wine that had been brought to the table. "You miss little."

I raised my glass. "Happy early nameday, my love."

"To many more with you." She toasted me.

The servers swept in with a salad, the produce grown in the many greenhouses in Myrr. At the first bite, I made a mental note to thank Sian, and my gratitude only grew as the night progressed. With each course, each song, each smile my love bestowed on me, I could not help but feel as though I were the luckiest damned fae to ever live.

And the night was only getting started.

"I can barely move!" Isolde stretched as the carriage I'd arranged to pick us up at The Frosted Rose pulled through the gates of Ramshold Castle. "I can't wait to kick up my feet in front of the fire. Do you think Thyra will still be up?"

"It's before the eighth bell," I replied. "As your sister isn't an infant, I think it's likely she'll be awake."

Isolde slapped me on my shoulder. "We've been busy! Maybe she's tired."

If that was the case, that was too bad because I was not the only one with a surprise for the Falk twins. While Isolde and I ate at The Frosted Rose, Thantrel had taken Thyra to another luxurious part of Myrr. They should be arriving back at the castle in minutes, which meant I needed to get Isolde into position.

"Thantrel planned something for her tonight since we have your dinner with our court and the lords and ladies tomorrow," I said. "I know where they are. Shall we find them?"

"Yes, we should."

The carriage came to a stop, and I took her hand and led her into the castle. As usual, the corridors of Ramshold were alive with fae, though tonight there were a few more than was usual at this hour, which Isolde could not fail to notice.

"Is a lord visiting Lord Balik?" Isolde asked, eyebrows pinching together. "Should I have been at a diplomatic dinner?"

Yesterday, the Warden of the South had forgiven her, but I got the sense that she was still on edge. Likely because we'd soon march north.

"Everyone knew I was whisking you away, and that you needed time to relax."

"I can't deny that. But diplomacy is important."

I laughed. "Right you are, love. You didn't miss anything."

She didn't look convinced, and only became more curious as we neared our destination, so far from our wing. I listened only to hear dead silence. Had someone put a barrier of air up against the door?

We'll soon find out. My hand landed on the handle. I opened the door to find that the lights were out. Normally, faelights remained lit late into the night until servants put them out. In some parts of the castle, they stayed on all night. To walk into a room so dark was an anomaly.

"We'll have to find candles," Isolde said.

"Seems so." I strained to hear the bell outside, and when it chimed, the faintest squeal of a hinge on the other side of the room followed. *Perfect timing.*

Faelights illuminated the room. Isolde let out a squeal of shock and grabbed my arm as dozens of fae appeared and yelled, "Surprise!" in unison.

"Stars! I almost wet myself!" my mate shouted and then punched me in the arm. "Oh! Thyra is here too! This is your doing, isn't it, Vale!?"

Across the room used for middling feasts, Thyra had entered by a second door. Immediately she lifted her fists, always prepared to fight. Her balled up hands lowered as she looked around, blinking hard.

"It was a group effort," I replied. "Anna was the one to first bring up a party for just our friends. Something more casual than dinner tomorrow."

"But Vale wanted it to be a surprise!" Anna shouted, a wide grin on her face as she leaned into Arie's side. "Exciting, isn't it!?"

My mate smiled back. "Very!" She turned her face

back up to me and stood on tiptoe, bestowing me with a long kiss. "Thank you."

"You deserve it." My fingers entwined with hers. "Let's party, shall we?"

CHAPTER 31
ISOLDE

The night spun, wilder and brighter. My heart felt like it might burst with happiness.

Our friends had transformed a small dining hall into a glittering and beautiful space. A small band stood to the side of the dance floor, on which I'd spent the last two hours.

I fanned myself as I sipped water, taking a break from a Summer Isle wine smelling of plums and cherries. Clem and Luccan remained on the dance floor. They'd been inseparable all night, and as I watched them, I felt almost indecent, as though I was spying on two people falling deeper and deeper in love.

Not too far away, Sayyida and Saga danced wildly. The former leapt through the air, her head tossed back and a smile on her face, though she was careful to keep her healing arm close to her side. She'd not broken a large bone during the battle with the giants, but fractured her small finger, acquired a good many bruises, and strained a few muscles.

Even Filip danced shyly amongst the cabal—most of them having a riotous good time.

In a corner far from the dancing, Anna sat on Arie's lap, whispering and laughing. My heart clenched seeing my oldest friend so happy and falling in love.

"Having fun?" Bavirra appeared at my side, her umber cheeks shining from her time on the dance floor. She smelled of amber and cinnamon, warm and indulgent, just like my friend.

"I am." Never had I received such a wonderful gift and had so many people I loved to celebrate my nameday with. "I can't believe everyone kept this from us!"

Bavirra chuckled. "It wasn't hard the way you and Thyra hole up together to practice magic. By the way, Father sends his well wishes. He would have loved to come tonight, and is going to make an effort to come to your dinner tomorrow, if he can handle being moved."

"Truly?" My eyebrows rose. Lord Balik had poked his head in, and quickly left, stating that such wild affairs were for the young. Lord Riis had not come, smartly so, and I had not considered that King Thordur would wish to join us.

"Father *loves* a party. He's quite envious that we're here while he must stay abed."

"I wish he was here too," I said. "Perhaps next turn."

Bavirra cast me a sidelong look, her eyebrows arched and lips pursed to the side. I interpreted the look as, '*if we're all still alive*'.

"I need to relieve myself before getting back to the celebrations." I set down my glass of water.

"I'll make sure no one follows you," Bavirra replied.

Normally, I'd find such a matter preposterous, but I had barely had three minutes to myself since the party began. It had been much the same for Thyra, though I didn't see her in the room now.

She better not have retired for the night.

The bells had not yet rung in the hour of the aura owl, but there was only so much socializing Thyra could take. Seeing as there were about fifty people present and everyone had, at the very least, wanted to send us well wishes, she might very well have hit her limit.

I made my way to the door as Bavirra deftly intercepted Bac and Aleksander. Grinning, I slipped out of the room and turned left, knowing where the nearest common toilet was in this wing. When I reached the restroom, I pulled the handle, but it didn't open. Hand raised, I was about to knock when the sound of laughter caught my ear inside.

Laughter I *recognized*. I leaned closer to the door, pressed my ear against it, and caught whispers. One voice belonged to my sister, and the other to Thantrel. The last I'd seen of them, Thantrel was on the dance floor and Thyra had been chatting away with Bac and Vidar. They hadn't even been close to one another! But when had that been?

I couldn't remember. There had been so much happening. Not that it mattered. I was going to tease them regardless because that was what sisters did, wasn't it?

Heart racing, I pulled back and knocked hard. "It's Isolde! I need to use the facilities, and I know you're both in there."

"What are you talking about?" Thyra shot back, her tone a touch too innocent. "I'm relieving myself!"

"That's one way to put it."

Thantrel burst out laughing, and when I laughed too, Thyra groaned, knowing that, once again, their cover was well and truly blown. The door swung open.

My sister faced me. She looked lovely in her silver-blue gown. However, her perfectly curled raven hair was slightly mussed, her lips swollen.

"We have got to stop meeting in restrooms," I teased and then promptly, closed my eyes.

"What in all the nine kingdoms are you doing?" Thyra asked.

"Sealing this moment in my memory. I'm determined to remember what you look like, after all that talk about how you did not accept him *and yet*."

Thyra scoffed. "I haven't accepted him as my mate. But that doesn't mean I can't have a bit of fun."

She didn't sound convinced, and when I opened my eyes to see Thantrel watching her, amused and not at all offended, my heart lifted. Clearly Than was confident that one day they'd be together. So confident that he continued to put up with my sister's public denial.

"Fun indeed," Thantrel said. "We would have had more fun if a certain princess hadn't come knocking."

Thyra whirled. "No, we were kissing. Nothing more."

Sex meant the bond could snap into place.

"More time together," Thantrel said as he came up behind her and pressed a hand into the small of her back. "But I can see that our stolen minutes are up." He winked as he strolled by me, a self-satisfied smirk on his face and red marks blooming on his strong jaw. "Don't keep her too long, Isolde. She offered me a dance, and if I don't get it, I'll have to seek her out in her room."

"I'll tell Astril not to let you in," Thyra said but there was no venom to her tone.

"I can be very persuasive, love. You know that."

I rolled my eyes. "Stars, I don't want to keep you here at all. Truly, I only need to empty my bladder."

Thyra smirked and strode past me as if she were the queen of all the nine kingdoms, not a fae who had been caught making out in a toilet.

The chamber was smaller than private bathing chambers, but just as extravagant as the rest of Ramshold. So much gold in a room that was a third the size of the suite I shared with Vale. Large enough that I imagined my sister and Thantrel were far from the only fae to have stolen into the room to lose themselves in one another.

I did my business and allowed myself a few extra minutes of alone time before exiting the room. I'd expected that Thyra and Thantrel returned to the party, but found my sister leaning against the opposite wall.

"I didn't think you'd still be out here," I said.

She pushed off the wall. "I wanted to ask that you not say anything about what you saw."

"Of course not."

"Not even to Clemencia or Anna."

"They were included in that statement." I paused. "But what of Vale? He knows you two kissed. I couldn't help but tell him when I first saw it."

Thyra let out a soft chuckle. "You can tell him, I suppose. He's as invested in Thantrel and me as you are."

"Your names roll off your tongue so easily together." We fell into step. "I have to know, have you changed your mind and just not told him? You did let him take you out, after all."

"Everyone else had plans—now I realize they were setting things up, but I felt left out. What else was I supposed to do? Sit around the castle?" She cast a sidelong glance at me. "Plus, I wanted to see more of the city."

I'd already heard of their date. Thantrel took her to dinner at a playhouse. My sister, like me, enjoyed the theater, and also like me, she'd had little chance to go over the turns.

"You can just say that you wanted to go out with him."

She swallowed. "I did, but . . . and I realize how ridiculous this sounds given what you told me about Sian —I'm still conflicted."

About the marriage between House Balik and our own.

"Sian would be relieved to have freedom."

"Perhaps." She let out a long hum, and we fell silent until we were about a dozen paces from the room where the party was still in full swing. "Isolde?"

"Yes?"

"If Thantrel and I disappear later, will you cover for us?"

My heart soared. "Happily."

The moment we returned to the party, our friends fell upon us.

"We've been wanting to dance with you! A ladies' dance!" Clem took my hand and nodded over to where Anna was twirling beside Saga and Sayyida.

Happiness swelled inside me. My oldest friend's crutch was nowhere in sight. The past week or so I'd noticed that she'd been using it less and less. Thanks to a healthy diet and exercise Anna had been able to gain weight and put on much needed muscle. Just as I had. Life wasn't perfect, or even safe, but it was better in so many ways.

"How could I resist such charming partners?" Before Clem could pull me to the dance floor, I slid my palm into Thyra's. "You're coming too."

"Are you sure?" Thyra asked, though she didn't pull away. And to Clemencia's credit, she didn't balk at including my twin, even though they didn't see eye to eye on many matters.

"The party is for us after all. We deserve a dance!"

Thyra's cheeks took on a slight pink hue, a rare show of pleasure from my icier sister, as we joined Saga, Sayyida, and Anna. Before I could so much as throw my hands in the air, Marit arrived. The Balik sisters came last, allowed to socialize with me once again. I shimmied up to Baenna, a smile on my face, so happy to have them both back in my life.

We spun and swung our hips to the beat of the music, dancing far more freely than I'd done at court. More like when I'd lived in Sangrael, though back then I'd never worn such fine clothing, or had such a full belly. In less than six moons my life had changed, and yet, as I joked with my new friends, I felt the old ones tugging at me. Begging me not to forget them.

I won't. I made that silent promise, chin tilted to the ceiling, allowing others to think I was absorbing the revelry.

"Oh, no you don't! This is ladies only!" Anna's sharp tone rang out over the music.

I laughed. Vale, Thantrel, Caelo, and Qildor had dared to return to the dance floor to join us.

Vale held up his hands. "You can't blame a male for wanting to dance with his mate. I mean, *look* at her."

"Seconded." Thantrel danced in place, seemingly unbothered by the denial and with exceptional rhythm. Thantrel was all sensual and smooth movements, which I suspected no formal instructor taught him.

Thyra noticed too. Her gaze was locked on the youngest Riis brother.

"I'll find you later," I promised Vale. "I want to dance with the ladies."

Vale winked. "As you wish."

The males drifted to the side, content to enjoy the company of their brotherhood.

Thyra's arm looped through mine, and she pulled me close to whisper in my ear. "I'm glad we found one another."

I faced my sister, took both her hands, then spun fast enough the faces of our friends blurred into the night that I'd never forget.

CHAPTER 32

VALE

The scents of bacon and toasted bread welcomed Isolde and me into the Balik family breakfast hall.

The daily family ritual was one I'd always envied hearing Sian speak of. My mother and the king rarely saw one another outside of social or diplomatic events. The Baliks were different from my family in so many ways. More like how I wanted my future family to be.

"There she is!" Lord Balik boomed with a smile. "Happy nameday, Isolde!"

A chorus of voices followed as others wished my wife well on her actual nameday.

My mate beamed. "Many thanks."

"Truth be told, I was wondering how many of you would make it today," Lord Balik teased. "Sian is still sleeping off the ale, I think."

"Considering how many he drank, he might be abed for a few bells more." I caught Filip's twinkling eye.

Unlike his brother, the heir had turned in early. In fact,

the only other nobles who weren't present were Lord Riis and the Fellhelm siblings. The latter were likely visiting their father in the healer's sanctuary.

"Sian began a game of cards with Caelo, Duran, and Vidar after the party disbanded." I came to a stop behind my usual chair. "Who knows how long they stayed up."

Cabal game nights were legendary affairs that lasted for hours and involved copious amounts of ale, wine, and harder spirits. Though last night's game was less well attended than most. I had been busy pleasuring my mate, and I knew that none of the Riis brothers attended either, all three busy with their own love lives.

"We played for two more bells." Vidar held up a pair of fingers. "And yet, I'm here."

"Not Caelo or Duran."

"Neither of them grew up around sailors, and it shows," Sayyida said with a wave of her good arm. The table broke into soft laughter that transformed into many disparate conversations.

I pulled out Isolde's chair. She settled beside Thantrel, seated by Thyra at Lord Balik's direct right. Across the table were Lady Balik, Filip, and my sister, all in places of honor among the Warden of the Southlands. The other Riis brothers were further down the long table with their ladies, Anna and Clemencia.

After my mate wished her twin a happy nameday, she leaned closer. "No mark on Thyra."

"Too bad," I whispered back.

"*Indeed,*" Thantrel muttered.

I had to hold back my snort of laughter. My poor brother would wait until his dying day for Thyra. I only hoped she wouldn't allow that and one day, they'd both be as happy as Isolde and me.

Servants swept in with food and tea, and breakfast began. Light conversation peppered the room as we ate. This early, no one liked to fixate on the war or other somber matters and especially not on a day as special as this one. Breakfast was for connection and joy, and we took advantage of the time.

Perhaps because of the drink or the dancing or the hours I'd kept Isolde awake after the party, but my appetite was larger than normal. I inhaled one of every item brought out and was considering going in for seconds as I listened to Lord Balik regale the table with a story. He was nearing the climax, obvious from the rising tone of his usually subtle voice when Sigri entered—seemingly much to the annoyance of the Balik guards at the door. Beside the dwarf was a youngling around Filip's age, her fists clenched tight at her side.

"Is something happening?" Thyra asked.

"I'm not sure, Princess Thyra," Sigri said. "This messenger came from the aviary. She has a note for Prince Vale."

The youngling approached the table, curtsied clumsily. All the while her wide eyes bounced between Thyra and Isolde, giving me the sense that she didn't know how to act in their presence.

"I'll take that," I said.

"Of-of-of course, Prince Vale!" the messenger lost all composure as she scurried over, hand outstretched, knuckles white from clutching the small tube. "I would have had a servant leave it in your suite, but it's colored red on the outside. That means—"

"It's urgent," I finished. "Thank you for delivering it."

She handed it over and ran from the room. Sigri plodded out after the youngling, shutting the door behind them.

"The Armenils?" Isolde asked and didn't bother to lower her voice. Everyone at the table was watching and listening.

"There's no seal of the direwolf," Marit said from a few seats down. Many times, she'd expressed frustration that her family had not written back yet.

"They'll reply." I examined the battered tube. "This tube has been used more than once."

Not unusual. Most tubes were reused time and time again, though not the ones the noble houses sent out. They created new ones for each message and gave the old tubes to commonfae or institutions like the House of Wisdom.

I had a hunch who this message might be from, and upon opening the tube and unfurling the small scroll inside, I saw I was right.

"From a friend. A captain in the Royal Army named Gorm. I wrote to him to see if I could not get a few captains to defect and maybe bring other soldiers with them." A smile spread across my face. "Gorm has agreed. As have two of my other friends—Asmund and Helga, all of whom I've been on many missions with. They were with one another outside the walls of Avaldenn when the messages were received and thought it smarter to only send one back."

"A good idea. Too many ravens leaving an army camp draws attention," Lord Balik agreed. "They're in Avaldenn, you say?"

"Gorm says that the armies have been amassing there for weeks, but soon, they plan to march south. My friends will be working to convince others to join them as they march. When we meet, however, they will switch sides." I scanned the scroll further.

Gorm had taken a great risk in writing to me and giving me as much information as he could.

"They're under Roar's command. Close to twenty-five thousand fae." I swallowed the staggering number. At fourteen thousand fae between three armies, our numbers were far less.

"Lord Roar?" Tadgh Balik's nose wrinkled. "Why not someone more capable?"

Isolde laughed, but I understood. It wasn't that Roar could not lead fae. He had many times. He was strong in combat, or he had been before he lost his leg. And as much as I hated to admit it, Roar was unbeatable with a bow and arrow.

However, there were *many* fae better suited to the role of leading such a large army: at least a dozen knights, and the same number of captains who had fought under me. Even King Magnus himself would prove more effective at leading a large force, and the king hadn't been in the field for many, many turns. So why would the king leave his forces in the hands of Roar, a fae who he did not like much at all and trusted less? Or at least, that had been the case before I left Avaldenn.

"I don't know," I admitted.

"Does he say anything about the Shadow King?" Thyra leaned forward. "Has King Magnus introduced his ally to the rest of the kingdom?"

"No mention of a Shadow Fae."

"Is it time *we* released that information to the wider kingdom?" Lord Balik asked.

I wasn't sure that was wise. There had been instances we'd been able to hush up and nothing dire had occurred. Still, the moment we introduced Shadow Fae to the public, the existence of Isolde's and Thyra's shadow magic would be made public. In retaliation, the whisperers in my family would be revealed. It would be a vicious cycle, and I didn't think we were ready for the onslaught of public opinion amidst a war.

"We'll talk about it," my mate said. "For now—"

"Let me in!" a voice I recognized roared outside the door. "I don't need to be announced!"

Lord Riis burst through the doors. His eyes, usually placid and excellent at hiding secrets, bulged. He looked so wild I barely noticed the figure entering behind him until she spoke.

"Apologies for interrupting your meal," Yrsa said. "We have terrible news, and it can not wait."

"We should already be there," Lord Riis growled. "I should have gone ahead."

"That would have been foolish, and you know it!" Yrsa tossed up her hands. "You wouldn't make it into the castle without help, and here is the help!"

I stood again. "Calm down, Father."

My proclamation seemed to center him somewhat, but the wild anger on my father's face remained, like an unquenchable fire threatening to burn all those around him.

"What news, Yrsa?" Luccan asked, also standing, also with trepidation lining his face.

But instead of Yrsa answering, Lord Riis did.

"Inga is being held in a dungeon in Grindavik. She has been there for three days. We must *get her out!*"

My entire body went stiff, and I couldn't find any words. Had my proclamation instigated this? Or Rhistel breaking free and then delivering the news?

Either way, it's likely he's free now.

"Leyv, let us catch up," Lord Balik's voice rang out loud and clear in the otherwise silent room. "Perhaps your daughter should tell us?"

"I'd be happy to, my lord." Yrsa stepped in front of her father. "The king's ship arrived days ago. King Magnus, Prince Rhistel, the queen, and others disembarked right away and went up to the castle. Some of the crew stayed on board, but most went into the city. In the taverns, my sisters and I learned they planned to head to the mage court to recruit allies."

My stomach dropped. The mages and fae had a tenuous relationship at best, but the High King of the Mages Tyra Odarin *had* hated King Harald with a passion. He'd been pleased when the Falk line died. Would the mages ally with Magnus to spite Isolde and Thyra?

I feared the answer was a resounding yes.

"It was late last night when rumors swirled in the city that the queen sat in a cell in the Ithamai's castle. I presume because of her affair with my father, which the masses of Grindavik only recently learned about." Yrsa swallowed. "That gossip aside, are you familiar with their cells?"

"Oh yes," Lord Balik said softly. "Lady Ithamai is strict about the law and likes to see punishment done properly. Her dungeons are warded well."

A strange sound came from Lord Riis. One I'd never heard before but conveyed distress.

Yrsa cleared her throat. "True, and hearing that the queen is in a cell is big news. It took a while to track down a source that my sisters and I trust, but they confirmed it."

"I'll kill them," my father growled.

I turned to my mate and Thyra, the fae with the most power in the room. "I know you do not trust her, but I beg you, allow me to save my mother."

What Mother had done was horrible. And yet, she was still my blood, the one mother I had and a female who had loved me unconditionally. If Isolde and Thyra spearheaded this mission, I wouldn't save my mother from their fury, but at least she wouldn't rot in the Ithamai's dungeon —a pawn of King Magnus and my brother.

Maybe King Érebo too?

Yrsa had not mentioned him, but he might have gone south with his allies.

The pieces shifted. Moves and countermoves. We might not have left the safety of Ramshold yet, but this was a battle strike. Since I'd already proclaimed that I was no son of his, the king wanted the other high lords and ladies to learn about his wife's affair. To see the consequences of betrayal, on Magnus's terms and timeframe.

Or perhaps the king still wanted to use the queen in other ways, and if Rhistel couldn't control our mother for all hours of the day, he'd need a strong cell in proximity in which to hold her. Hence, a stop in Grindavik.

That struck me as true. They must have some plan to use my mother—likely at the mage court.

Thyra cleared her throat. "You're right that we don't trust her, Vale, but I believe that your mother owes my sister and me a conversation."

She desired an apology, but as my mother's whispering magic was still secret, Thyra took care with her words.

"So, I say yes. We find Queen Inga and bring her here."

My gaze slid to my mate, but she was watching Lord Riis, red-faced and tense. Somehow, my father kept it together. Barely.

"Force?" I whispered. "What say you?"

She dragged her gaze up to meet mine, and her features softened. "We will save Queen Inga, but I am doing it for Vale and Saga. No other reason."

Isolde pushed her chair back and stood. Others followed. "The sooner we put together a plan, the sooner we can go to Grindavik."

INTERLUDE

LORD ROAR LISIKA, WARDEN OF THE WEST, HOUSE OF THE SNOW LEOPARD

Atop a knoll overlooking the forested land outside of Avaldenn, the Warden of the West could not help but wonder how his plan regarding a certain lost princess had gone so far astray.

Twenty-five thousand fae had gathered outside the capital, and they were on the brink of war.

House Balik, House Riis, and House Virtoris all claimed loyalty to the Falk princesses. With that recent revelation, Roar questioned things. Mostly, the true motives of Magnus's newest ally.

Before he sailed south, the king had called Roar to his study, to join him and the prince, seemingly finally himself after many days of acting oddly. There Roar had met King Érebo and heard the tale of Isolde and her twin, Thyra, freeing him. Denying him.

The darkness in the Shadow Fae's eyes burned with black fire as he recounted the events beneath that mountain. And yet, despite also hating Isolde and Vale, throughout the tale, Roar got the sense the Shadow Fae king was hiding something. Not telling the entire story.

Roar was quite glad that King Érebo was sailing to Grindavik with his other allies, playing out some plan devised by Prince Rhistel. A plan in which Roar suspected he knew the bare minimum about and, truth be told, he was fine with that. At least for the time being. As the lord currently presiding over Avaldenn and the gathering armies, he had quite enough on his plate.

"Lord Lisika?" a voice came from behind, and the warden turned to find a soldier. He'd spoken to her before, many times, but she had the sort of forgettable face that meant her name vanished as quickly as the wind.

"Yes?"

The fae shifted in the mud that the melted snow had left behind. "The captains are in the central square."

Roar's lips curled upwards in his first smile in days. "Very good."

He left the knoll and with enhanced speed and agility thanks to his brand-new metal leg, Roar made his way into the field of soldiers from all around the kingdom.

The scents and sounds of camp came at him from all angles. Crackling embers, unwashed bodies, and dirty canvases. None of the scents were pleasant. Just another thing that made Roar wish he was at the castle. Relaxing in comfort—or better yet, having already seen his long-held plan to fruition and calling Frostveil his own.

Many of the soldiers hailed from the west, and they bowed to him, but many others were not. Those fae stared at Roar with a sort of curious wonder, equally studying his new leg and the lord himself—how he moved through the world in a manner that they never could. Most soldiers were used to lords from lesser noble houses; not a high lord of the Sacred Eight. Some may never have seen someone of his status until arriving in Avaldenn.

Here, however, each soldier fought not only for their own lord or lady, but for the Warden of the West. For Prince Rhistel. For King Magnus. And unbeknownst to them, a shadowy abomination too.

The Warden of the West neared the heart of the camp. The path between tents opened into the square, and as Roar had predicted, a crowd surrounded the captains he'd called for.

Roar, ever the showman, smiled and swaggered up to the captains, waiting in a line, their hands and feet shackled to posts.

Traitors. In the king's own army.

Never would Roar find such traitors among his own soldiers. Never would they write to the Warrior Bear and proclaim their loyalty like these idiots. Maybe the captains thought he wasn't watching the ravens coming and going, but since he'd been tossed into lordship as a youngling, Roar watched everything.

"You did not get far," Roar spoke just loud enough that those closest could hear him. Loud enough for people to lean in. For everyone in the square and beyond to understand without a shadow of a doubt who was in control.

Two males and one female were tied up. Not one of them answered, although the female, the one with the most ice in her spine, spat on the ground in front of her.

"Imagine if you channeled that righteous anger correctly. Fates, you'd be unstoppable."

"Prince Vale fights for the fae of Winter's Realm. For what's right," the female growled. "He always has."

"You think so?"

"I do."

The high lord paced in front of the poles. "Then why is he with a Falk? Have you not heard the stories of the Cruel King?"

"Of course we have," a male said, and recognition sparked within the Warden of the West.

"Captain Gorm, is it? Originally from the easternlands?"

"I've lived in Avaldenn for ten turns and reported to Prince Vale's command for five of them." The captain was decorated, though he'd left all those decorations behind after Vale's letter had been found and he'd fled into the woods.

"And so you sought to abandon your fellows and fight with the prince who has joined up with the Cruel King's daughters? Those females have as much murderous ice in their veins as their father."

Not that he knew anything of Thyra, but he did know Isolde. That was enough to pass judgment on the twin sister.

"I'm with Vale," Gorm replied stoutly.

"As am I." Asmund pulled against the metal that bound him.

"As we all should be!" Helga shouted.

The crowd took a collective step back, as though the idea might spread like the blight. Roar's jaw flexed.

Though his wings had been mangled for so long, he still hated being reminded of what had been stolen from him. That he'd never fly again.

While that had been devastating in that same turn, his mother, father, and older brother had all been killed during an effort to better his house. Roar could not help but put partial blame on the power and allure of the Ice Scepter.

The same Scepter the Shadow King had gotten his hands on, though he'd been evasive when Roar asked how that occurred. Another reason Roar didn't trust the shadow wielder.

"Your loyalty is admirable," Roar said after a pause that was long enough for the crowd to be focused on him once again. "But ultimately misplaced. The king is who you swore to. The House of Aaberg. Vale the traitor is no longer a part of that house."

Roar had learned of the queen's infidelity, right before word came that deep in the south of Winter's Realm, Vale had publicly proclaimed himself a Riis.

"The spare heir renounced his blood and stayed true to the Falk whore!"

"Say the Falk lady *is* better though." Asmund scanned the crowd, as if to sway them. "What do we know of her? Not much. But was she not engaged to you, Lord Roar? She couldn't have been all that bad, right?"

Roar snarled. "Isolde Falk betrayed me, and I have entertained you for far too long."

He called his power, the shifting magic that outshone his winter magic. The power that had saved his life.

Without it, he would never have been able to fly from that deep, dark pit.

Whispers rippled through the crowd as his magic strengthened, changing his body, growing it. Fur sprouted. He fell to all fours. The pain of shifting used to be far worse, but Roar had grown used to it. And when compared to the agony he'd been in when the blight ravaged his body, this rearrangement of bones, sprouting of fur, and growing of new appendages was nothing.

The snow leopard grew so large it dwarfed Roar's largest sleigh. A size the cats would never reach in the wild, but over his turns of practice, Roar had adapted his form to this for a specific reason. Awe. Shock. He'd always loved his shifter forms for the effect they had on others, and now he loved them even more. When he shifted he was finally whole again. His back leg returned, and in his frostfly form his wings were functional.

His claws gripped the ground, free of snow. They flexed and released, flexed and released, as a low rumble carried from his chest up his windpipe.

"Dead gods save us," Gorm prayed.

Roar took his time prowling closer to the traitors, teeth bared. Let them quiver before the creature that would end their lives.

He closed in, sensing their spiking fear. His heart rate sped up, the predator alive at the prospect of a chase. And though there would be no hunt today, Roar knew how to dull that need.

His claws ripped into flesh. Innards spilled, the tang of metal filled the air—the scent of justice and a warning to any who contemplated betrayal.

CHAPTER 33
VALE

I stared out the brothel's window, itching to take to the moonlit streets and storm the castle but forced to remain. To wait as the *tafl* pieces shifted into place.

Hours had passed since my father and Yrsa burst into the Balik's breakfast room. Hours we'd spent planning, studying the city of Grindavik, debating who should go on the mission to retrieve my mother. Who should stay behind and be in charge of signaling. Or potentially distracting soldiers that may come after us. A map with circled safe locations around Grindavik hung heavy in my pocket. We each had one. Fates willing we would not have to use them.

Hours in which the guild I'd done my best to suppress these last days had multiplied. I did not know if my claiming of the Riis name had put Mother in danger or if Rhistel had broken free first.

In the end, we'd decided two companies of five would sneak into the castle. The problem lied in the fact that three in our group looked too vampiric, and the rest of us were too well-known throughout the kingdom. Even Yrsa and her sisters, Geiravor and Sváva, three of the least-famous fae going on the mission, were very recognizable in their home city. Known as the Terrors of Grindavik, each was red-haired, fiery-winged, and tall and curvy. Caelo's glamours were the answer to our issue, and though they delayed us further, I had to admit, he'd outdone himself. I didn't even recognize myself, let alone any of the others.

A light flashed ten rooftops away, and I held up a hand. "Sváva signaled."

"Vidar did too." Thyra lingered near a window on the other side of the office.

Shortly after Sayyida and Livia, the final two lookouts, gave their signals. The city guard was on the move, rotating.

Only Lord Riis was staying behind in his brothel office. We simply couldn't afford to take a male riding such a wave of rage.

Thyra pulled her hood up, covering her newly glam-oured violet hair. "See you by the dungeons, North Star."

"Be safe, South Star," Isolde replied, her attention grazing over Caelo, Freyia, Thantrel, Geiravor, and landing longest on her twin.

"You too," Thyra smiled, and one by one the members of South Star left the office.

Our company waited five minutes before entering the streets of Grindavik. Yrsa took up position in front of me and Isolde. Astril and Qildor lagged a dozen paces behind. No one from the other company was anywhere in sight, having already blended into the crowds.

It took no time at all to see that Grindavik thrived on the darkness. Fae of every order walked the streets. So close to the docks, this part of the city smelled of salt and fish. Stallkeeps hawked wares, and the scents of many restaurants filled the air in crevices left by the perfumes worn by fae of the night.

If Avaldenn had a good number of brothels, it was nothing to what Grindavik boasted. No matter how their high lady felt about such establishments, sailors were known to love a brothel or two. Not only did the sheer number of sex workers surprise me, the varied and extravagant themes of the brothels did as well. Yrsa and Geiravor had warned us that we'd see oddities, and they were right. The fae of the night costumed as wolves, dragons, or vampires were shocking, indeed.

"The vampires in Sangrael would be furious if they saw this," Isolde whispered as we passed one such brothel where the prostitutes stood outside, dressed in scandalous attire, blood dripping down their faces. "The vampires in the capitol would never wear such things. Not in public anyway."

My eyes crinkled at the corners, but my heart didn't fall into the lightness she attempted to create. I couldn't afford to. Not when we—some of the most wanted fae in Winter's Realm—were about to infiltrate a castle and extract a fae who was sure to be under heavy guard.

Smooth as the silk the fae of the night wore, we wove through the streets, drawing ever closer to the castle. As the towers grew, the figures walking the wall came into sharper focus. Just when I thought it would be a straight shot down one road, Yrsa banked right. We followed, pivoting into an alley. Our leader paused halfway down.

"We'll continue that way." Yrsa gestured to the mouth of the alley. "The other team will have gone left. But before we get too close, I have to let you know, there are many more guards on duty than I've ever seen."

"We predicted that," I said. "The king would demand a heavy guard. Mother can be very persuasive."

She could command anyone to do whatever she wished, and if there was the slightest chance, she would free herself. So the king would put as many obstacles as possible in place to stop her from going far.

"Not one or two more," Yrsa retorted. "Dozens. It feels like a trap."

It was as though ice swept over us; everyone became so still. Stiff.

Qildor cleared his throat. "King Magnus *is* fond of playing games."

Yes, he was. How I had not thought of it before was beyond comprehension. Worry for my mother and those on the mission had blinded me.

"It might be," I allowed, "but the plan is in motion, South Star is likely closing in at the gates." They would arrive ahead of us, but had a longer way to travel on the castle grounds. If all worked as planned, we'd converge upon the dungeons at around the same time. "We can't let them down."

"Agreed," Isolde said. "Remain alert. And Astril, if necessary, be prepared to perform more compulsion than we planned for."

Compulsion had never sat right with me. Likely

because Rhistel and Mother's magics were so similar to a vampire's compulsion. I had spent many turns as Rhistel's practice subject and despised each occurrence, all the while understanding why it had to be me. No one outside our family could have known, or I'd lose my twin. Little did I know, I would lose him anyway. That life and our views would tear us apart.

And while I may not like the idea of fae being compelled by vampires, in this instance, I'd allow it. Fates, I might end up wishing that Astril could hold sway over the hundreds of fae we might come across. But no vampire was so powerful. Like whisperers had a limit to the number of people they controlled, so too did vampires.

The castle continued to grow more imposing, and I watched the walls, noting the large faelights and a series of mirrors running along the top. They wouldn't be used to shine upon the street, but into the sky, and immediately, I understood why. It was far warmer than it had been in many turns, so fae flew more freely. That meant the airspace around the castle was also being monitored more heavily. Finally, we reached the portion of the castle wall that was covered in silver ivy.

Yrsa, Geiravor, and Sváva had spent half their lives discovering the secrets of the city, using the knowledge to their benefit. According to Yrsa, they had known about this weakness in the castle wall since they were thirteen but never had a reason to use it. Until tonight.

"Make yourselves as inconspicuous as possible. Vale, muffle the sound." Yrsa pulled two thin metal rods with flat ends from her black woolen cloak and, after pulsing her magic into the ivy to negate its effects, she plunged the rods into the vegetation.

I created a barrier of air around us and the wall, hoping to muffle any sound that could give us away. Then we leaned back into the wall to wait and keep on the lookout.

This side of the castle was less trafficked, thanks to a tanner's shop located on the street. The smell of tanning elixirs was too much for sensitive fae noses to tolerate, and that included guards on the wall. Between the undesirable effects of silver ivy and the stench, it seemed the Ithamais believed no one would try to enter their grounds this way. They were probably right, and yet, there was no guarantee that no one would walk this way and sound the alarm.

Yrsa grinned when she found the lock hidden deep within the ivy. The sound of metal hitting metal filled the night before a soft click hit my ears.

"Two more." Yrsa smirked. "Give me thirty seconds."

She managed to break open the lock in fifteen.

"Your mother taught you well," Qildor muttered.

I got the sense that my honorable friend was struggling not to be impressed.

"Better than soaring over the wall and attracting attention." Yrsa pulled the hidden gate open.

The door opened just enough for us to push the ivy to the side and slip through, but before we did so, Yrsa shoved another wave of her power outward.

Few plants possessed true magic of their own like silver ivy. To touch it caused severe pain and itching rashes that only healers could calm, which had to be part of the reason no one had ripped it out by the root. No one in their right mind would touch silver ivy unless they had to, but Yrsa's magic was identical to her father's and disabled other powers. Fae, animals, and, though I'd never known this of Lord Riis's magic, plants too. For a short while, the ivy would be inert, allowing us easy passage onto the grounds.

"Safe," Yrsa whispered.

I eased forward to take the front position, with Astril right behind. Working together, we set to beating back the silver ivy and passed through the ancient gate. When I reached the other side, I remained tucked within the ivy and scanned the area. One soldier to the left, about twenty paces away. Another to the right, thirty paces.

"You go right." I caught Astril's eyes, knowing she'd cover that ground before I'd made it halfway to my target. "Qildor and I have the left."

"Let me check."

I moved to the side. As the vampire used her superior vision and scent, Qildor moved into position next to me.

It took the Valkyrja only a moment, and she nodded. "I can't scent anyone else in the area. Let's go."

She rushed out first, blurring for the guard as I sent my magic at the other to seal him within a barrier of air. At my power's touch, he shouted, but it was too late. Not a whisper of sound emerged from the tomb of air I'd placed him in. If I was feeling violent, I could eliminate all threats and rip the air from his lungs.

But killing wasn't the aim. Silencing was. And we'd come prepared.

Qildor and I rushed over. I gave the signal, and Qildor

raised an arm. As the air barrier vanished, my friend's fist came down, knocking the guard out.

I pulled a small vial, supplied by the Balik's healers, from my cloak pocket and pressed it to his lips. "Bottoms up."

The liquid vanished down the guard's throat, ensuring hours of silence. I grabbed the soldier's hands, and Qildor took his feet. Together, we shoved him lengthwise into the shadow of the wall, just as Astril had with the other guard.

Could we possibly have found a better spot? Perhaps, but this area seemed quiet and dark, and we had to work quickly. The goal was to be in and out of the castle by the time the next guard rotation occurred.

Isolde and Yrsa appeared on my side, and Yrsa gave a nod. "Follow me."

We rushed across the castle grounds as vast as those surrounding Frostveil. Perhaps larger. And like in my former home, pockets of gardens covered the grounds.

At Frostveil, the gardens had been planted and many of them painstakingly cultivated at Saga's pleasure. Was it Lady Vaeri Ithamai that we had to thank for the occasional cover? If so, she'd be hearing no thanks from me.

We were making our way through a garden with towering hedges when we came upon a brownie, taller than most of her kind, and twice as hairy. Her body went rigid as she took us in. The darkness helped cloak us, but we weren't in the deep purple tunic trimmed with white that servants wore. Nor were we in guard clothing, but nondescript black cloaks. We did not fit in.

"Who are you?" the brownie asked, her voice high and tight.

Astril's nostrils widened as she breathed in. "She's terrified."

"Not a soldier. Do not harm," I whispered back, not so sure that Astril and I shared the same moral code.

"Still a threat," the vampire hissed back.

"If you don't stop whispering over there and answer me, I'll yell. The guard is on high alert with the king in residence."

Taking control in a way I wished she would not, Isolde held up her hands and stepped forward. "We're sorry that we startled you. We're visitors."

"*Armed* visitors? That's odd, considering my high lady requires her guests to be unarmed in her home. She takes very few exceptions."

Lady Ithamai was not just a stickler for the law; she was paranoid.

"Enough of this." Astril blurred forward and stopped before the brownie. "Go back to work. Say nothing of this."

"After we enter the castle though," Yrsa added. "We don't need her walking into the servant quarters with us."

"Wait twenty minutes before you return inside," Astril amended her command before turning to us. "We should move."

And we did. Through two more pocket gardens, all the way to the entrance that Yrsa claimed was close to both the servants' sleeping quarters and the castle's laundry facility. We were met with a locked door.

"These are harder to pick open." Yrsa knocked loudly at the door. "If no one answers, I'll try it, but as a last resort."

"I forgot my key!" she shouted, switching up her accent so that it was thicker, more similar to that of the Grindavik dockhands and not a female who, despite all the troubles she'd caused her mother, had attended the best schools in the city on Lord Riis's coin.

It took only a minute of knocking before I caught the sound of footsteps, heavy and weary, coming our way.

"Is that you, Strel?"

Yrsa giggled as though the male caught her doing something embarrassing, allowing him to fill in his own blanks. "Sorry if I woke you!"

"Twice in as many weeks, girl. We're going to tie that key to your wrist." A chuckle came, and the lock inside clicked out of place. A male dwarf opened the door and had enough time to see that Yrsa was not, in fact, Strel, before Astril grabbed him by the shirt and yanked him up until they were eye to eye.

"You didn't see us. You saw Strel. Return to your room and remain there until morning," Astril said.

"Right," the dwarf replied, his tone a touch looser. "Night then." He turned and returned the way he had come, leaving the corridor wide open.

One by one, we crossed the threshold into the enemy castle.

CHAPTER 34
ISOLDE

Suspended faelights illuminated a hallway that stretched on endlessly. To my left, the scent of soap wafted into the corridor. Weak food smells—meats, roasted vegetables, and bread teased my nose from further away.

"In here." Yrsa opened the first door on the left.

We slipped inside, found a vast room crowded with empty vats and baskets overflowing with fabrics of all types. The castle's laundry.

"The servants that have the most leeway with where they go in the castle wear dark purple tunics with a white lion on their breasts and black pants. Find something that works. And make sure there are wing slits because we might need to use them."

It didn't take long for most of us to find appropriate clothing. Vale, however, was the exception. He easily found pants that worked, even if they were a little tight, but like Luccan and Arie, Vale had inherited Lord Riis's wide and strong chest. He was also very tall and more muscular than most fae. Certainly more so than the average servant.

"What about this?" Astril pulled something from the depths of a basket and held up a deep purple tunic large enough to fit three of me. It might suit a troll, but it was too long for Vale. "Tuck it in and then pull it out a bit to the right length?"

Yrsa assessed the item. "That might be our best bet. Try it, Vale."

My mate stripped off his shirt, giving everyone a peek at his tattooed chest and the daggers hanging off each hip. Swords would have been too obvious, so we'd left *Skelda* and Sassa's Blade in Myrr.

Vale pulled the tunic on, and it billowed around him comically before he tucked the ends into his waistband. Going to him, I eased the tunic out, flattening the material best I could while leaving the ends tucked in to make it look like it was the appropriate length.

"I'm sorry that we're missing your official dinner, Force."

"This is far more important."

He kissed me on the forehead.

"Good enough. Isolde, grab that basket of clean clothing." Yrsa pointed to a basket filled with laundry folded inside as she hefted one of her own. "Stuff the cloaks at the bottom of these baskets so we have them nearby if we need them later. If you haven't already, now is the time to slip the daggers into your boot sheaths."

I did as Yrsa commanded and hefted a basket filled with linens. The fresh scent stuffed its way up my nose as I crossed to the door. We hid the cloaks beneath the clean laundry, and positioned our weapons before slipping back into the corridor.

"You're sure you know the way?" My stomach felt like it was full of frostflies, despite making it this far and having acquired the proper disguises. All that was left was to find the queen and leave, hopefully as quietly as we'd arrived.

My optimistic heart told me it was possible. Experience disagreed.

"I used to date a nymph who lived here. A sleigh driver," Yrsa said. "He showed me around the servants' quarters and above, when the high lady was not around, of course. Once, I saw a deranged criminal being brought in. You could hear him kicking and screaming through the halls. Later, I asked what they did with him and when I learned he'd been taken to solitary, I wanted to see the dungeons. My boyfriend thought I was crazy, but you never know when being familiar with the innards of a castle would come in handy."

Stars, did I know. The night we'd fled Avaldenn, my knowledge of the hidden parts of Frostveil had been the only thing to save me, and probably Vale too, from a vampire's fangs.

Yrsa's continued confidence eased my nerves, and we fell in line behind her down the corridor, pausing only when Qildor spied a partially open closet and extracted a broom, another prop. Reaching the T at the end without incident, Yrsa peeked around the corner and gave the all-clear signal, and we continued down a shorter hallway that ended in a stairwell. She paused there, turned.

"We won't be too far from the grand hall."

Where Lady Ithamai was said to be hosting a gathering to honor the king and prince. She'd invited many of the lesser nobles and wealthy merchants in the city. Or so Geiravor's connections around Grindavik had claimed.

"Don't look about while we walk." Yrsa inhaled deeply, as if to prepare herself for putting on a show. "You work here. This is normal."

"Ah yes, we rescue queens from dungeons daily," Qildor muttered.

Up the steps we went, and upon exiting on the next floor. We allowed a few paces between each of us, as though we were five servants going the same way, but not together. As we walked, I performed a casual sweep of the area, trying to get my bearings. Even if I hadn't already known whose castle I was in, I'd have guessed the ladies of House Ithamai lived here.

Seated lions carrying scales of justice on their backs line the hallways. Compared to other castles I'd been in, there were few paintings and tapestries. Lady Ithamai appeared to be a minimalist, and when I thought back to the few times that I'd seen the Warden of the East, she'd always dressed in her house colors, with perhaps a lion to honor her house, but few other embellishments.

I turned a corner and scowled as Hadia and Adila Ithamai, the two blonde heiresses to the great house, came into view, strutting our way, dressed in gowns of deep purple.

Adila's face was pinched with annoyance. "Why do you think I don't have a chance with Prince Rhistel?"

"Because I'm trying to woo him!" Hadia replied as though that were all too obvious. "Mother is well in the king's good graces. This is the perfect time to plant the idea of uniting our houses."

"You're engaged to Luccan Riis." Adila spat out my friend's name like it was a bad word.

"The king won't make me wed him any longer. His father is a traitor, and our house is loyal to the Crown of Winter." Hadia gave a dismissive wave of her hand.

Yrsa had passed the sisters. Qildor was next, then me. Although my instinct told me to look down, I found myself captivated by their conversation. They'd always been horrible to me, going as far as to chase and threaten me one night, but in that moment they merely sounded like sisters. Or perhaps I was just shocked that someone would even want to marry Rhistel.

"And besides," Hadia continued, "everyone knows the prince likes his females with more meat on their bones." As if to drive the point home, she did a little shimmy and her large breasts jiggled.

"Oh?" Adila did not seem amused. "Does he plan to eat you and all that meat?"

"I should hope so. Imagine having a husband who did not like to *feast*?!"

Caught off guard, I nearly snorted in laughter. I stopped myself just in time, but not all the way and the oddest sound came out. Like a sneeze mixed with a yawn. The sisters, three paces away, shifted their gazes to lock on me.

Adila narrowed her eyes. "What's so funny?"

"I could not help but overhear." I did my best to modulate my voice and bowed as best I could with the heavy basket in hand. The act felt all wrong. I was no longer scared of these two, and I desperately wanted to show them who I was and how strong I'd become. But now was not the time. "Apologies, my ladies."

"You shouldn't be listening in on your betters' conversations."

Did they not expect others to hear them when they spoke so plainly in the open? Of course I didn't say that, just ducked my head and shifted the weight of the laundry basket.

"Away with you," Hadia commanded.

I scurried by and, as soon as they could no longer see me, released an incredulous snort. Yrsa led us down another long corridor, this one narrow and with no other high fae in the area.

She stopped and waited for us to catch up. The moment we did, she nodded down the hall. "There are steps twenty paces further on the right. They lead to the dungeons, so this is where we stash the props and prepare."

"Will the other team use this entry?" Vale asked, and I was certain his mind was whirring with strategy. Possibilities. Issues that may arise.

"No. The dungeons are vast. There are two other entrances known to most castle workers and one that is a secret."

"How do you know about it then?"

"The same boyfriend. The one the public doesn't know about travels below the castle by waterway. It's closest to the section of the dungeon where they'll keep the queen, and guaranteed to be clear of guards, but I'd rather avoid it if we can. Dangerous creatures live in there."

"You know all this from courting someone in the castle?" I asked.

"I can be *very* persuasive," Yrsa grinned, and in that moment, she looked so like Thantrel that I did not doubt her powers of persuasion for a second.

We stashed our props into two nearby rooms that were mercifully empty. At the door leading to the stairwell, Yrsa performed her magic with her lock picks, and the door squealed open.

Down the pitch-black stone stairwell we went. The faelights in my pocket called to me, but I refrained from pulling one out. Darkness was our ally, and it took only about ten seconds for my vision to adjust enough that the darkness did not feel quite so oppressive.

A full minute passed before I caught new sounds. Snores first. Then soft moans. I swallowed. How many prisoners were awake? And if they saw us, would they say anything?

"I will silence any threat," Astril said, as if she'd been reading my mind.

"If the queen is where I think she is, we won't have to pass by too many inhabited cells," Yrsa said. "But guards are down here too, and it only takes one to sound an alarm."

We descended further, and I was about to ask when the steps would end and how far below the main levels of the castle we were, when a light from below caught my eye. A damp, disgusting scent followed. That of waste and mold.

"Closing in," Vale whispered. "Prepare your weapons."

Daggers appeared from boots. As we took the last few steps downward, I held my breath. Waiting. Listening.

The bottommost portion of the first two cells materialized, as did a rotund guard. He lumbered our way, muttering to himself, not having heard or seen us yet. He seemed to be returning to his post, a rickety stool propped by the steps, after disciplining a prisoner. Or that was what I gathered by the blood dripping off the bludgeon he carried.

"I have this," Qildor and Vale whispered in unison, but not before Astril shot forward, so fast the guard didn't see her coming until she was right in front of him.

A strike to the head, and he slumped. Astril caught him and thank the stars the prisoners in the first two cells were asleep. The cover of darkness was one reason we'd delayed our mission for hours, but another reason was that fewer prisoners would be awake to witness us extracting the queen.

Astril dragged him back to the stool and positioned the guard so that he was leaning against the wall, appearing to have fallen asleep on the job.

"Potion?" Qildor asked. We possessed many more vials of the brew than we'd used outside. The concoction would keep someone asleep for hours.

"Yes," Vale said, and Qildor pulled a vial from his pocket to administer the potion. "As much as I'd like to think we'll be in and out quickly, I'm not counting on it."

"What about keys?" I asked.

"Here." Yrsa held up a keyring. I hadn't even seen her lift it from the guard.

"Lead the way." My husband flourished a hand in the direction of the darkness.

Yrsa took the right fork, barreling down the dank passage lit by faelights that flickered as though they might go out at any second. The idea struck me as cruel. No natural light made its way down here, and to lose even one faelight would plunge the closest cells into darkness. How terrifying that would be.

We hit a sharp left turn at the edge of the dungeon, I presumed.

Yrsa twisted. "We're going to pass a few more cells, then duck into the isolation wing. I think she'll be there."

We careened through the passageway, rushing by cells filled with sleeping fae until a hiss sent a shiver down my spine. I whirled towards the sound and found, of all fae races, a leprechaun. Dirty-faced, disheveled, and wide awake, the fae stared at us.

"You shouldn't be here." His voice grated against my ear, raspy from disuse.

"And why are you?" Vale asked. "I've never seen an imprisoned leprechaun."

"The high lady locked me up. But I bet she'd let me out if I called the guards. My debts, my misdeeds, are *nothing* to what you plan to do." He arched knowing eyebrows.

He didn't know who we were; the glamours were too good for that. But we were heading in the direction of the queen's cell, so it didn't take a genius to guess our motives.

"Or you can hold your tongue, and we'll let you live." Yrsa dangled the keys.

"Get me out and to safety, and I won't squeal."

"Deal, but we get what we came for first."

There was the possibility that once any cell door opened, a guard above would be alerted. We could not waste that chance on this leprechaun.

He nodded, hinting what we had guessed might very well be true. I wondered how many fae tried to escape this place and how far they got before they were captured to give a random prisoner this idea.

"We'll mark you." Yrsa turned to Vale. "Pull that faelight here?"

With a flick of his wrist, my mate called air, and one of the suspended faelights drifted our way. As it was one of the only ones nearby, it would be an obvious marker.

"Any tips on how to get her out?" I asked.

The leprechaun snorted. "I'd expect your task to be difficult."

"Thanks for nothing," Astril muttered, and we continued on until we turned into the corridor that housed the isolation area.

This section of the dungeon was even more poorly lit, with only one faelight every fifty or so paces. As we walked, I listened, desperate to hear those of South Star approach. Were they close? Or in trouble?

That question left my mind as, about thirty empty cells deep into the isolation corridor, we came across Queen Inga, staring out of the darkness.

CHAPTER 35
VALE

"*Mother.*" I approached the bars, vibrating with magic.

She was thinner, her skin had taken on a gray pallor, and the light in her eyes was dimmed.

"Are you yourself?" I asked as the female who had brought me into this world and protected the secret of my parentage for so long shuffled closer. "Or is he still controlling you?"

Astril cocked her head, and I pretended I didn't notice her reaction, but inwardly cursed my stupidity. We had not yet revealed that Mother or Rhistel were whisperers, but slip ups like that would have people guessing.

My mother came towards me, her steps unsteady. Tried to discern why she seemed aged and injured when there were no marks on her body. Only dirt.

"Vale? Is that you?" Her voice broke, gaze scanning my glamoured face.

She'd only been in here for a few days, but the isolation wing was empty and dark. The air hung around us, still and musty. Choking. A slab of stone, not even another cell with another being to make eye contact with. Perhaps the cell itself had magic upon it to amplify a sense of loneliness too. I would not put it past Lady Ithamai. She was ruthless with anyone who broke her laws, no matter how small.

"It's me, Mother."

She eyed me distrustfully. "Tell me the first thing I said to you after learning that you'd wed."

A test. She was uncertain that I was real, that any of this was.

The memory of my mother in the hallway outside my Frostveil suite, watching me with desperation and ill-concealed anger, came rushing back. Had she suspected Isolde's identity even then? Had the presence of a possible Falk reminded my mother of her past and what she'd done to keep her secret? I didn't know, but I recalled her words as if she'd spoken them only yesterday.

"You said, tell me it isn't true. You did not wed her." As I spoke, I took Isolde's hand in mine and squeezed, assuring her. "For the record, Mother, my choice is one I will never regret."

Mother released a long, rancid breath, and it took all I had inside me not to rear back in disgust. What in the name of the dead gods were they feeding her?

"You shouldn't have come. Rhistel wanted to lure you." Cold rushed through me at her words, the confirmation that this was a trap. Mother's gaze slid to Isolde. "And you. Did Lord Riis—"

"I know what you did." My wife's chin lifted. "I'm not

here for you but for my mate. That being said, we need to get you out before someone comes."

"*Mate?*" Mother whispered, but her words drowned against the sound of oncoming footsteps.

I tried to discern how many, but the leprechaun began shouting. Caelo's voice yelled back, and the creature shut up, but I feared the damage had likely been done. That fear came true when, seconds later, those of South Star appeared through the darkness and just as an alarm blared to life.

Yrsa fumbled with the keys. "Qildor and Geiravor, examine the wards."

The warders, two of the only ones in our trusted group of friends and allies, began studying the magic. Testing it with pokes of their own. I wasn't familiar with the intricacies of Geiravor's powers, but she worked quickly, prodding the bars. Trying new tactics. Testing and eliminating.

Qildor worked more methodically than his counterpart. He wasn't the best warder in the kingdom, but he was excellent. That protective magic combined with other smaller magics that he'd honed and great skill with a sword had made him an ideal Clawsguard.

"Mother, do you recall anything about the magic placed on this cell when they brought you here?" Any clue could help the warders.

My mother blinked as if weights hung from her eyelids, as if still in Rhistel's thrall. "Three warders created one protection each, likely so the others could not speak to the other two warders magic. Blood is the fourth layer of protection. The key is last."

"Blood?" Geiravor asked.

"To the locks—they applied Rhistel's blood."

"Let's hope that means his family can free her. Or perhaps the Blood of Winter," Qildor said. "That's a problem for after we break the magic, though. Wards. Then blood. Then the key."

"Anything else?" I asked.

"I—I wasn't aware the entire time." Mother blinked heavily.

Fates, my brother and the king were swines. We'd have to try my blood and hope that it worked as well as Rhistel's.

"Got one!" Pride laced Geiravor's voice as the bars glowed blue before returning to normal. "Where are you, Qildor?"

"No closer to figuring this ward out."

"I'll work on the last. Keep going."

A bead of sweat dripped from the knight's nose. Next to him, Yrsa waited with the keys. There were at least ten on the ring.

"What if the isolation wing's keys aren't on that ring?" I dared to ask.

After all, these fae were the worst of the worst. It was possible Lady Ithamai would hold those keys herself. Or that the king and Rhistel had wanted to keep the key to my mother's cell on their persons.

"We'll have to improvise," Thyra said.

Since South Star arrived, and the warders began working, the rest of her company watched the end of the corridor. Waiting for castle guards to arrive.

"With no wards on the cell, Thyra and I might be able to shatter the lock," Isolde offered.

If anyone could, it would be them. Isolde had the most powerful raw winter magic I'd ever seen. Her twin was nearly her equal.

"Hopefully, the key will work. We'll see as soon as the wards are gone." Yrsa swallowed.

"Vale?" Mother's voice sounded fainter than before. Sweat beaded her forehead, and were her hands trembling?

"What is it?" I asked, straining my ears to tune out the many prisoners shouting about us, and who they suspected we were here for, in an effort to hear oncoming footsteps.

"I think I—" She stumbled over to the side of the cell and braced herself with one arm right before her eyes fluttered closed, and she fell to the ground in a faint.

"What in all the nine kingdoms?" Qildor's magic halted for a moment, but Geiravor nudged him.

"Keep going! I think I'm close."

My friend continued but shot me a look of concern. Of questions.

But I had no answers. Just worries.

"I hear footsteps," Freyia said. "They're coming."

Geiravor let out a frustrated hiss. "Come on, Qildor!"

"*I'm trying.*"

"Weapons out." I turned to face those coming for us just as they came into view.

Row after row of soldiers, marching four across, came at us. Armed to the teeth, there were at least fifty opponents, though the dimness made it difficult to count.

"Hands up," a soldier barked. "We have you cornered."

"They don't," Yrsa whispered. "The underground passageway, we can still use it."

I stepped forward, daggers in both hands. Astril and Freyia slipped into place beside me, and Caelo and Thantrel posted up behind with Isolde and Thyra.

"We'll take our chances." With one dagger, I pointed to the front line, feeling far more like a villain than the Warrior Bear of Winter's Realm. "Valkyrja."

The vampires shot forward. The oncoming soldiers balked, and sounds of shock rang out as two of their own from each side of the front line fell. Then the middle ones. Before the second line lashed out, the vampires darted back, out of the way.

The soldiers exchanged wary glances. Debating whether to come at us or not.

"Stay there," I commanded. "Not another pace forward and we won't harm you. I pro—"

A low, cunning laugh came from somewhere in the lines of soldiers, sending the fire of rage simmering in my belly.

CHAPTER 36

VALE

The soldiers parted to reveal the king and my twin. The former stared us down, his face as cold as the ice and frost already forming on his fingertips. Rhistel, on the other hand, was the picture of calculated control with his cutting smile. Far more concerning was the fact that his ice spider silk gloves were off.

I scanned the soldiers, looking for glazed eyes or any sign that they might be under my twin's power. Nothing stuck out, but I wasn't sure that meant they were in their right minds. Mother could hide her whispering, and clearly Rhistel had been practicing more often than I knew if he could control her.

"Glamour or no, you cannot hide from me." Rhistel's gaze dragged down my body, ensuring I knew who he spoke with. "That stance. That arrogance you exhibit when you're doing the only thing you're good at. I know who you are. Knew you'd come."

"Traitor," the king spat. "Which one is your wife?"

I thanked the stars for Caelo's glamours. My brother and the king might be familiar with my posturing, but not that of the others.

Unlike Magnus, though, Rhistel did not seem too concerned with Isolde. Instead, his attention drifted to the vampires. "Bloodsuckers. Now *that* is interesting."

"We prefer Red Assassins." Astril twirled a dagger in her hand.

I took devilish pleasure in how Rhistel's throat tightened despite the fact that he recovered almost immediately.

"Even more villainous." Rhistel sounded delighted. "Hired killers. Who would have thought the noble Warrior Bear capable of working with them?"

The nickname rippled through the soldiers they'd brought with them. The whispers stopped, however, when a flash of light behind me lit up the corridor.

"Ha!" Rhistel barked. "Was that the first ward or the second?"

"It doesn't matter when we're going to break all three," I growled. "Stand down, Rhistel. We don't want to shed blood."

At least, not the blood of those behind my twin. After seeing the state of our mother, I would not balk at spilling a little of his.

"We do not have the same predilections." The king lifted a hand, and the stagnant air in the tunnel shifted. Move *towards* us.

Seconds later, I caught a whiff of bitter almonds in the air. Then the vampires' knees buckled, and ice flew through my veins.

"Come back!" I commanded the Valkyrja, and we rushed back together, out of reach.

The magic I felt didn't belong to the king, whose signature I was very familiar with. Rather, he had someone in that crowd moving poisoned air. Figuring they'd want the Falk sisters alive, the poison would likely put us to sleep.

"It burns the skin and eyes." Freyia blinked rapidly to clear the poison.

I stared down the hall at the small force opposing us. None of them seemed affected.

"There must be an antidote that they took in preparation." I called my own air magic and retaliated by pushing the poisonous air back.

Rhistel scowled. "Harder."

The force of air coming our way pressed against my own powers. I concentrated and this time detected a few unique signatures. At least five fae were shoving their magic against mine. Together they were powerful enough that, in time, they could overpower me.

"Warders, hurry!" I twisted to see how close they were.

"I'm close!" Geiravor wheezed, the effort she was spending clear. "One more—*got it!*"

The light flashed.

"*Vale, we need your blood,*" Yrsa said.

The others cleared the way, and straining to keep my magic fighting against the press of poisoned air, I used a dagger to prick my finger, drawing blood. With one touch of red to the metal, the lock clicked. Before I moved out of the way, Yrsa was there with the keyring.

She tried one key. Two. Three. With steady hands, she

moved through each one until she got to the last. The metal entered the lock. Yrsa twisted.

It didn't work.

Magnus laughed.

My jaw tightened. He wasn't even willing to come forward and fight. He was allowing others to do his dirty work, and would sweep in to take the credit afterwards. Then, the reason struck me.

He was frightened. Not of me, for the king knew how I fought, and with magic, he was very strong. No, the fae I'd once called father would never admit it, but I would bet *Skelda* that he feared the Falk twins. They were unknowns—particularly their shadow magic. He would not take a step closer until we were unconscious.

"Move." Thyra and my mate pushed me aside. "We have the lock."

I resumed my place in front and motioned for Thantrel and Caelo to join. Than had small air magic. Caelo did not, but he was a knight. They would help buy us time.

Another wave of air magic swept from me, battling with the poisoned gusts. I'd successfully gained us a note-worthy buffer when a bone-deep cold rippled from behind me. I didn't need to turn around to know that Isolde and Thyra were using their combined powers to freeze and then shatter the lock.

"The whore and her sister!" Magnus's face took on a startling shade of red, and he plowed three paces forward. "What do you say we end this now, Isolde? Thyra? If you two face me like real fae, no one else will die for this war!"

Thyra let out a condescending bark of laughter. "Like

you did against our father? We know what you did, Maggy." The king's eyes narrowed. "Without *her*, you'd never have won against my family."

Thyra didn't say who, but the king didn't need a name. His expression turned feral.

"You endangered your mother by bringing them here."

I shoved a windstorm their way, furious that he would lay such blame on my shoulders. "That was *you*. Your wounded ego. *Your pride*."

The king snarled, but that expression faltered when the lock's metal cracked and shattered. The pieces fell to the ground.

Thyra laughed, and I looked over my shoulder to find her staring straight at the king, a lazy smirk on her face. "That's all that you have to keep your greatest weapon in your control? And to think I was worried."

Yrsa and Isolde were already pulling my mother from her cell. Helping her to move, to stand, but my mother remained limp. Walking, but barely. My stomach pitted.

I locked eyes with my mate. "Go. We'll buy you time."

"I'll stay with you." Qildor stepped forward, a loyal brother.

Isolde's lips parted. "I'm not leaving you."

I felt her surge of magic, power capable of doing significant damage, but would invite the king to do the same. Once the two began, where would it end? How many others would die? And if Thyra got involved, it could be even worse.

"*Don't*," I warned. I gestured to Caelo, Qildor, and Thantrel, their weapons drawn.

"The cabal can hold them off," I assured her. "The rest must go. Get my mother to safety."

An unfair request. Isolde despised my mother, but everyone could see something was wrong with the queen, and Isolde wouldn't let an ill fae suffer.

"As soon as you can, follow," my wife said, all the command of a queen in her tone.

"I'll make sure they can," Geiravor said. "The other warder will sense my power. Right?"

Qildor nodded but kept his gaze trained on the soldiers standing with the king and prince. Ever the knight, the protector.

Thyra slid her shoulder under my mother's, and my mate loosed an exhale filled with conflict.

"Until the stars fall," she whispered, taking my mother's other side.

"Until the stars fall." I went to her and kissed her forehead.

"That one!" Magnus bellowed. "I want her alive!"

I spun to face him. "I'd like to see you try to lay a hand on her." Through the pounding of blood in my ears, I heard the three pairs of sisters running down the corridor to the hidden exit.

"Forward!" the king roared.

The soldiers ran at us, their swords bearing down. I palmed my daggers and diverted some of the air away from us, protecting us from the encroaching poison to the closest adversary. The air slammed into his chest, lifting him off his feet, up, up, and up. His back collided with the stone ceiling above, and the soldier's eyes shuttered closed. I allowed the air to drop him gently, but teased a single current from the stream and dragged the fallen's sword to me.

Before the metal met my palm, the second line of soldiers intercepted us, four already down, so many more to go. I ducked as the next came for me, spinning out of reach and landing on one knee. A slice from one of my daggers cut through the tendon above his heel. He fell, groaned, and I grinned as Thantrel darted over, relieving the male of his sword and hitting him over the head with his own hilt. Just in time, I dropped one dagger into my boot and caught the sword I'd eased my way.

Good weight. Shorter than I like, but usable.

The onslaught continued, but not a single soldier felled us, nor made it past our line. We maneuvered and struck and brought down each opponent.

And then, the arrow came, arching above the stream of air and sticking in Caelo's thigh. My friend roared and fell.

"Warder." I was careful not to use Qildor's name, to give the king that knowledge. "Get him out of here!"

Caelo could still move using his wings, but to unfurl them and stay here would only make him a larger target. And once the arrows began, they continued to come.

But from where? I used one of the downed soldiers as a shield and stood to search. The oncoming forces had thinned, giving me a clear vantage all the way down the tunnel.

In the far back, a bedraggled soldier stood in a perfect archer's stance. Practiced though she was in shooting, the archer couldn't hide that she was breathing so heavily. As if she'd just run here.

Fates. More are coming.

"Fall back," I said. "Warder and injured lead. We'll hold them off."

Losing Qildor hindered us greatly as it left us with no shield, but the warder would need his own magic to protect both him and Caelo. Thantrel and I could remain armed, and I was able to make a rudimentary barrier of air to protect us as we fled. Therefore, we were the ones to stay. To thin the onslaught, and to give Qildor time to follow Geiravor's trail.

"I'll wait at the door." Qildor helped Caelo to his feet, stabilizing our friend until he could use his wings. A ward materialized around them, and then they were off. I continued dodging arrows and fighting, casting glances behind me. Soon, they were out of sight.

Just a few more seconds. A minute tops and—another arrow whizzed by me. I pivoted out of the way and slammed my shoulder into the stone wall. Pain radiated.

Two more soldiers came at us. Both fell in rapid succession, and I took the opportunity to look beyond, to find the archer, our biggest opponent when we made a break for it. Her bow lowered.

Out of arrows.

Good, because I, too, was faltering. Not physically, but magically. Throughout the fight, I'd continued casting back the poison. Now I would have to pivot, to use my magic as a barrier that allowed us to run. Did I have enough left in me?

"Than, now." I twisted as I gave the command and rerouted my magic, condensing the air into a defense.

The temperature in the dungeons plummeted. Cries

of fae far beyond the isolation corridor rang out. The king would do anything to capture us.

"*Run!*" I shouted to Thantrel, but it was too late.

Icicles as long as stiletto daggers raced at us, their points deadly. They ripped through the barrier of air I'd created as though it were mere parchment.

"Down!" I fell to my hands and knees as Thantrel screamed in agony, right before a shard of ice slammed into my shoulder. The size and weight of it knocked me on my back. The sword I'd taken skittered away.

I tried to get up, only for something hard to strike my temple. The world darkened.

"Vale! Get up!" Thantrel shouted only to scream again. Ice shattered to the ground. Another onslaught. Had he been hit again?

I attempted to focus my vision, but everything remained blurry.

Focus. To be safe, I pushed air back, trying to keep the poison away. Through my efforts, I felt someone moving our way, barreling towards us.

I inhaled. Did my best to force my blurred vision to clear, and it did, barely. Enough to catch motion, to squint and find Rhistel, five paces away, his ungloved hand outstretched.

CHAPTER 37

ISOLDE

"Here it is." Yrsa reached the dead end of the isolation corridor. "I need to find the rock that opens the door."

I drew in a long breath. My muscles labored under Queen Inga's weight, and my ears strained to hear what was happening down the passageway. Vale, Caelo, Qildor, and Thantrel were far behind us, possibly still fighting. I prayed they'd defeated their opponents and were rushing to join us with not a single fae in pursuit.

Yrsa ran her moon-pale hands over the rocks, searching. The vampires watched the way we'd come, ready to defend at any moment. Thyra stood on the other side of the queen. Some might say she appeared calm, though the throbbing vein in her neck told me that was far from the truth.

"Aha!" Yrsa's voice rose, the sound mingling with a thud as a hidden door unlatched. Yrsa gripped the edge and pulled; the hinges groaned. "Hasn't moved in a while. Needs oil."

"I'll remember to send Lady Ithamai a letter with that suggestion," Thyra said.

Yrsa snorted. "I'd love to see the look on her face when she gets that!"

The image was satisfying, but wiped clear from my mind as the door opened all the way and stale, sulfuric air rose to meet us. My nose wrinkled. "Why does it reek?"

"A couple of the channels down here feed into luminescent hot springs inside the castle, but eventually, the streams mix. Some sort of creature makes the shimmer. The smell is from the minerals they eat."

"Gods, hot springs sound divine right about now." Thyra shifted the queen's weight.

Yrsa peered into the darkness, looking for threats. "Can't see anything threatening from here, and I can't hear anything but water. Or smell much more than sulfur. Let's go. Careful on the way down."

We entered the passage, Yrsa first, then my twin, me, Inga, and the vampires. Geiravor marked the passage with magic I could not see, but she insisted Qildor would be able to feel when the males made it our way. That done, she shut the door behind us, and descended into the dark, toward the glittering water. It would be beautiful if I didn't have a hunch that the channel would bring some horrible deadly creature.

"Astril and Freyia, can you see further down the water channel?" I asked, taking the steps more slowly than usual.

"No," Astril replied. "It appears to take a turn, blocking my view."

"Besides the bats, do you have any idea what creatures are down here?" Thyra asked Yrsa as the stairs leveled out. We'd reached the bottom and were close enough to the underground stream to see the outline of the five boats upon the shimmering water.

Yrsa shook her head. "I only know about the bats because a few got loose and fae saw them exit by the sea. A couple got bit too. Of course they had no idea where they'd come from, but I put two and two together. And it's not like I can talk to others about it. Only a few servants know of this place. The ones who have to stock emergency supplies."

"Should we take any of that?" I gestured to the cages off to the side that were filled with supplies.

"I don't want to waste time breaking it open. Not when we know who could be coming after us."

"Yrsa's right," Geiravor said. "The Ithamais might make a secret escape, but soldiers outside the castle will soon learn that we're fleeing—if they don't already know. We can't risk it or slow down."

I turned my attention to the boats. They fit four each and bobbed in the stream, about thirty paces wide. With Freyia's help, I passed Inga to Thyra. My sister eased the queen down, and propped Inga against one end of the boat. I hopped in after them. Astril joined the Riis sisters in another boat, and Geiravor took up the oars.

"I'm on watch." I caught a glimmer of amusement in Freyia's eyes as she gestured to the oars. "Better vision and faster reflexes than the two of you."

I was strong and could fight, but my sister was better at combat. Not by much after all my training, but any advantage counted in this scenario. Understanding my place in all of this, I took up the oars, Thyra untied the boat, and we were off, drifting on a current that was stronger than I'd expected, making my work more that of steering than propelling.

The shimmering channel of water below lit the way enough to keep complete panic at bay. But that didn't mean my heart wasn't racing with each paddle of the oars.

I couldn't release the image of Vale standing against the king's forces with only his cabal by his side. The urge to leap from the boat and fly back overpowered me. I could help. My winter magic was powerful. And then there were the shadows . . .

I forced my heart to hear the word as strongly as my head.

We'd come here on a mission, and we'd completed it. Vale had told me to go as much for my safety as his mother's. He needed to know that no one would torment Inga any longer. I could deliver that. I would not fail him, and he would not fail me. He never had before.

They're probably right behind us, was my last thought before I noticed the water to the side of the boat below begin to ripple.

Stomach tightening, I peered into the black water speckled by blue and white lights. The water was still moving in an eerie way.

"Look to the side," I whispered.

As if my words had cast a spell on the channel, the waters swirled. Slowly at first but gaining speed by the second.

"Something is rising." Freyia's back was taut, her weapons at the ready. She stood poised at the bow of the small boat.

Inga hadn't stirred, and a sheen of sweat now covered her brow. Had they starved her? Or was she ill? Worry rose in my chest, only to drown with a splash to my right.

Thyra stiffened and leaned over the side. "What in the nine kingdoms is—"

A webbed hand, grotesquely wrinkled and bone-white, shot out of the water.

My sister stumbled back, and Freyia caught her with one hand and flung a dagger at the water, spearing the creature through the palm.

An ear-shattering shriek filled the cavern, and to my horror, other strangled, garbled voices joined in. The question of what things made such sounds was answered when four heads rose from the water.

Their faces were as wrinkled as their hands, their eyes fully black. Fins bobbed above the surface, hinting that these things might look like the merpeople, but hideous, rather than lovely and ethereal. Nose-less and with voids for mouths, these creatures would feature in future nightmares.

If I was still alive to have them.

Freyia reached over the side of the boat for her dagger, still embedded in the hand. We didn't know how many more of these creatures existed or what else might be in the passage. Every weapon counted.

The vampire managed to rip the dagger from the thing's flesh just before the creature lunged up to hiss at her. With enviable speed and dexterity, the vampire sliced the thing across the neck. Astril had gained a sword in the earlier skirmish, and she used that weapon to fend off two creatures that swam closer.

Perhaps they had never seen steel or perhaps they were just hungry, but despite the danger, two of the water monsters leapt out of the water, allowing Freyia to dispose of them. Blood plumed in the water as their bodies fell.

The last, however, disappeared beneath the water.

I chanced a glance overboard. Found nothing. Looking up, I caught Astril's eye. She shook her head, but the way she held herself told me she was still waiting.

The creature leapt out of the water, mouth opened wider than before to reveal multiple rows of small sharp teeth. It landed on top of Inga.

"Away with you!" I batted the creature with my oar again and again. It reared at me, body coiled to launch, but Freyia's dagger lodged itself in the creature's heart.

I exhaled. "Are there more?"

"None that I can hear or smell," Astril replied as she shoved the thing in the water. "But that's not saying much. I can't sense below the water."

"What are they?" Yrsa asked.

"I've never seen anything like them," Freyia said. "I wonder if they were merpeople once."

I shuddered. The similarities were there, but I did not like to think about how merpeople could become *that*. Or why they'd be down here and not in the sea where they belonged.

"Keep an eye out for more of them," Geiravor broke the horrified silence that had befallen us. "Or worse."

The vampires simply turned and stared into the darkness. Watching. Waiting.

I pulled a faelight from my pocket, ignited it, and let the ball free. It hovered above my boat, floating along with us.

The channel grew wider. Every four strokes, we gained at least half a body length at the edges. Not only that, but rowing became easier, as if we were going downhill. Faster. The strange sensation was explained when the channel opened into a cavern. Though the faelight did not illuminate the entire area, it did enough to reveal a faint, red glimmering above.

"Are the rocks shimmering? Reflecting the water?" The same luminescence as before filled the pool, but how did the light get so high?

"Where's the exit?" Thyra asked.

"No, wait. Isolde has a point. What are those?" Yrsa craned her neck, studied above. Thanks to the extra space, the other boat had moved to float right beside ours. "Row faster."

"You can row," Geiravor grumbled. "I'd be happy to give up my spot."

"Those are the bats," Yrsa hissed, spiking my heart rate.

Carnivorous bats were native to the Autumn Court but had adapted to live in many parts of Isila. Specifically in areas of natural heat, like hot spring water. They would attack, even unprovoked. That not a single one had flown down yet meant they were sleeping.

My oar slipped in and out of the water at a faster rate,

matching Geiravor's pace as we skirted the outside of the cavern, looking for an exit.

"There!" Astril whispered. "I found the exit. Keep going straight, and we'll come right across it."

I spotted it too and pushed harder. We were only a few paddles away when Queen Inga let out a loud moan.

The sound echoed in the cavern. Wings rustled.

"Go, go, go!" Thyra pleaded, and by the stars, I did.

"Geiravor!" Yrsa said. "Move over. I'll row, you ward!"

Her sister hopped up and began working her magic, just as a waterfall of bats detached from the ceiling and dove. Fangs bared, they closed in. One came from behind and latched onto Yrsa's shoulder. She screamed, and ripped it off her, breaking its neck, but the damage was done. More bats awoke. More rustling wings and strange pitchy chirps sent skitters down my spine.

A hundred more made it down by the time Geiravor cast a full ward above us, but not before dozens swooped inside. One took a chunk out of my arm, and before I could stop them, a shadow released, wrapped around the bat, and squeezed.

The creature fell into the water, and though effective, I opted to use winter magic to do away with the rest. My power blasted upward and into the air, freezing the flying bats. They fell into the water, no longer a threat.

"Can you make it a shield over the exit when we pass through?" I continued to row. "And how long will it last?"

"Longer than we need it to," Geiravor replied with confidence, even as she wiped sweat from her face.

My boat entered the exit first, and as we passed into the smaller tunnel, a shudder rang through the air. The ward. Geiravor had already set it up for us to pass through, but no others. Bats tried to follow, flinging their hungry bodies up against the ward and falling back.

"Those were awful," Freyia muttered.

"We'll have to get the bites looked at by the healers in Myrr," Thyra added.

We'd all acquired at least one bite, but as I looked at Inga, I gasped. Four vicious bites marred her exposed skin. Dislike her or not, I didn't want to think of bats eating my mate's mother's face.

We floated through the darkness, my faelight and the sparkling water our only guiding lights. The water picked up speed again, and this time the current was so strong I stopped rowing and instead used my paddles to steer us down the channel.

"We're nearing the harbor," Yrsa said. "Right at the entrance, there's a gate that's locked."

"Have you picked it?" I asked.

"Only examined it from the other side. I thought maybe one day I'd row upstream and see what there was to see." Yrsa shuddered. "That's no longer in my plans."

The other boat got into the front position. Right in time too, for a pinprick of light appeared in the distance. Moonlight. Or maybe faelights and torches from the docks? I hoped we would not exit too close to the docks. Sailors were up at all hours of the night, and the fewer witnesses the better, for a guard would have certainly been alerted by now. Soldiers would likely be swarming Grindavik.

"We need to disguise the queen." Salt laced my tongue. The pinprick in the distance had grown into a disc. Originally, the queen was going to use a cloak, but those remained in the castle, never to be seen again. Thank the stars it wasn't cold enough to necessitate such attire, or that would be another reason we'd stick out.

"We have nothing," Yrsa said. "Flop her head over and make her hair hide her face."

"Her clothing is too grand," Freyia pointed out.

"Would you rather we paraded her naked through the streets?" Thyra snapped. "If we find something we can improvise on the way, we take it. If not, we hope the night cloaks us."

The grate came closer and closer until the other boat slammed against the metal. I breathed in, the fresh air was welcoming after so long in the confined space.

And then the gate lit up like a faelight, and the alarm sounded, the keening echoing in the cavern.

Thyra loosed a filthy stream of swear words.

"It's not so loud that many would hear it. I bet you that alarm goes up to the castle," Freyia said.

"I'm sure it does. And there are *two* locks here." Yrsa examined the grate, unbothered by the alarm. To keep my sanity in place, I took that as a sign she'd done lock picking under extreme pressure. "Geiravor, come work the other. We need a fast getaway."

The sisters crammed together. On the other side of the metal, the waters from the channel mixed with seawater, the effect providing a swirling halo of light around the area. It would be pretty if it didn't feel so much like a target.

"These are bleeding difficult," Geiravor said.

"They'd keep out any lock-picking lowlife," Yrsa

agreed. "Only the best could get in here. And still fewer would survive what they meet."

Had we come with one less person, we might not have made it. That realization did not make me any less worried about Vale and our friends.

They're capable, I told myself. What other choice did I have?

"Ah!" Yrsa exclaimed, her hand retracting quickly. "The thing shocked me!"

Geiravor leapt back. "Me too!"

"And now you've lost the feel of the lock," Astril growled. "Get back in there and don't lose it again. You'll have to endure."

"Dammit," Yrsa groused, even as she gritted her teeth and carried on.

The shocks came faster and harder, and the sisters took each one, their bodies jolting, their faces contorting, but the Riis sisters had the same spines of steel that I'd found in their brothers.

One click sounded, and Geiravor leaned back as the shocks stopped. Her hands trembled from the aftereffects. "Got this one. Are you close?"

"I think so." Yrsa's jaw tightened. "Just . . . there!" Her lock clicked too.

Astril took over at the front of the boat and eased the rusted grating open. The sound might have garnered attention if it wasn't for the alarm echoing through the night.

I braced myself to fight, but when our boat drifted into the harbor, it was to empty water and air. No soldiers. No fae in the area at all.

"They might still come," Thyra said.

We rowed to the nearby beach. The boats ran aground, and we hopped out, then eased the queen between Thyra and me.

The Riis sisters took the front position, the vampires the rear, and no one looked back as we ran for our lives.

CHAPTER 38

ISOLDE

Sweat poured down my back as we raced through the streets of Grindavik, and bells—*alarms*—began to sound.

I stumbled, and a stream of curses flew from my lips as I caught the queen before dropping her. A group of pixies fluttering in a doorway nearby watched us with interest.

"Unbelievable!" Geiravor hissed. "That's the alarm that tells us to get to our homes. Anyone still on the street in a few minutes' time will be a target."

We picked up the pace as Yrsa and Geiravor led us around the harbor. The channel exit had been clear on the other side of the harbor, as far away from the brothel as it could have been while still being near the water.

Within a few more blocks, it became clear how effective the alarm was. The crowds, which had been dense despite the late hour, had halved.

"You seven! The females!" a voice called out.

Seemed pretty unlikely that whoever that person was, they were talking to a different group of seven females.

"Stop right there!" the voice commanded when we kept going. "In the name of House Ithamai, I demand that you *stop*!"

I located the person shouting. Three faerie soldiers staring right at us from down the street, one pointed, as if his fellows could fail to see our group rushing along the streets. If the size of our group hadn't raised a red flag, Inga's attire likely had. Her clothes were dirty, but still of fine quality. Queen's clothing.

"Turn here!" At Yrsa's command we pivoted down a street, away from the soldiers. Yrsa sent up a blaze of light that exploded high in the sky. Startled screams rang out, followed by sighs of pleasure and admiration. Yrsa flung another beam of light into the sky, and it transformed into a dragon that opened its mouth in a silent roar just as the trio of soldiers appeared above us. They'd taken wing and caught up easily.

"I said *stop*!" the same voice bellowed, but we had no intention of doing so.

Scattered on city rooftops waited Vidar, Sayyida, Livia, and the third Riis sister, Sváva. We'd just told them our location, and that we needed help.

Above, fire erupted and shifted into a whip. The flame began to move and slither snake-like through the sky. Sváva was a fire wielder, and the flames she tossed about were as vibrant as they were deadly. A rope of flame snatched one of the three soldiers who had taken to the skies and almost caught up with us. He screamed and disappeared.

But there were two more, and one was gaining. About

to attack with his magic. He'd likely strike my sister and me to get three for the price of one.

Swallowing, I made an insane choice and called my shadow magic. The dark power rose and swept out of me, but this time, no tendrils emerged. Instead, a figure with the body of a fae stared back at me with black eyes.

I nearly tripped from the shock. An equally startled Astril swiped a blade at the shadow, but it remained. Unbothered. Simply moving at our speed but doing nothing else.

"It's like the sword. Waiting for a command," Thyra hissed. "*Give it one.*"

Right. I knew that. It had just taken me by surprise that I'd finally succeeded in making a true shadow person.

"Take down the soldiers behind us. And any others that come." I drew in a breath. "Otherwise keep out of sight and disappear when you feel my glamour break."

It soared away, and I felt a tether that connected to the shadow stretch and stretch and stretch. Behind us, a scream rang through the street. Thyra let out a breathy whoop.

"No time to celebrate yet." Geiravor's words came out fast with her breaths. "And you'd better believe we're going to want an explanation as to what that thing was, but for now, save your breath and run!"

And we did. We ran as if we were being chased by a pack of direwolves, muscles burning hotter with each step.

It took great control not to look back at the vast threads of fire swooping and looping and slashing and twisting through the sky. There would be no way to determine their origins, and I imagined Sváva's fire threads snatching soldiers from the sky.

On other rooftops, the Virtoris siblings were supposed to be creating spectacles of their own, hoping to catch the castle guards' attention. And last of all, Livia flew above. Cloaked in the darkness of the night, the third vampire was tasked with looking out for those who were providing us a distraction. She was the goddess of death to any who might get too close to those on our side.

My arms and back ached from carrying Inga, and a tightness filled my chest as a result of my tether to the shadow form, but my legs never stopped, and my senses remained on high alert as Yrsa wove us through the streets and alleys. We burst onto another street, this one busier. Recognizable. I cast a wild glance about and spotted a Nava-themed brothel I'd found amusing when we'd left Lord Riis's establishment.

"Ready?" Yrsa asked.

My wings threaded through the tunic, into position. The Riis sisters leapt into the air first, catching the sea wind. Thyra and I followed, and the vampires took up the rear, always watching our backs, ready to drain an enemy dry. A few fae watched us rise through their windows, but when a new blast of fire rose from somewhere behind us, the combination of the alarm and the flames proved effective on more than one score.

Yrsa landed on a rooftop five away from the brothel, and taking more care, we leapt from roof to roof, back where we needed to be.

The trapdoor was open when we arrived, Lord Riis peeking out. Thank the gods Sváva's fire was keeping most of the winged fae out of the sky. If other fae soared this way, they would not fail to see his red hair glinting in the moonlight.

"Down, Father!" Yrsa hissed. "We need to get the gateway up!"

"What happened to her? What happened to Inga?" he didn't move.

"We're not sure," Geiravor answered. "Perhaps they haven't been feeding her. She's weak and was passed out for much of the time."

Lord Riis swallowed. I could tell it took great self-control for him to turn away from his love. We dropped into the office, and our glamours broke one by one. It was the oddest sensation, especially when paired with the thread of connection with my shadow form. I shuddered, glad to be rid of the shadow form.

Lord Riis shut the trapdoor, swept over, took Inga in his arms. Tears streaked his face.

"Take her to Ramshold," Yrsa said. "Geiravor, help him."

The Riis sister eased her father toward the gateway, moving tenderly and slowly. Before she got there, however, the trapdoor lifted again. Vidar dropped inside, followed by Sayyida and Livia. Sváva would not come. She would divert until she could no longer do so.

"Thantrel, Caelo, Qildor, and Vale had to stay behind. Did you see them on the streets?" I asked no one in particular.

"No, but we need to move out." Sayyida swallowed. "Most fae have gone into their homes and soldiers are swarming the streets. Hundreds of them."

Knocking came at the office door, and my stomach dropped to my knees. Upon our arrival, Lord Riis had made an appearance downstairs because Yrsa and her sisters had entered the brothel through the front door. A father coming to speak with his daughters bothered no one, but the high lord had made it clear that he was not to be interrupted. Also that no one in the city was to know he was present in Grindavik. No one loyal to him would defy an order like that unless they had to.

Or unless they wanted to warn us.

"Who is it?" Geiravor asked.

"Minthe."

"I'll get it." Yrsa pivoted towards the door, for Lord Riis was still staring at Inga, his face pale, as if in a trance. "Everyone, stay out of sight."

I squinted. Did the queen look grayer than before, or was that the dim lighting in the office? I didn't have time to decide before Thyra pulled me out of sight.

Yrsa answered the caller, and Geiravor moved that way too, the pair of them doing their best to block our side of the room from sight. "Yes?"

"Miss Yrsa, I know your father wishes not to be disturbed, or for anyone to know he's here, but there are soldiers here. From House Ithamai. They want to search the establishment." She inhaled. "We told them that was inappropriate, and our clients deserve privacy, but they're insisting. I owe Lord Riis a lot, but I don't wish to be jailed."

"Of course not." Yrsa exhaled long and low. "I will come to speak with them."

"And the brothel?"

"Give our clients a fair warning, and then let the guards search."

"They wish to see his office too."

"Stall as long as you can."

"Very well." The brothel worker shifted, as if to leave.

"Thank you." Yrsa shut the door. "You must leave."

She rushed to the spot in the wall where Luccan had hidden a gateway. With a poke of a dagger to her finger, blood welled. Yrsa applied the blood, and the gateway opened, the light flooding the dark office. "Go, Father. They cannot find you or the queen here."

Lord Riis strode to the gateway, Inga hanging from his arms. One step through, and he disappeared.

Geiravor followed the spymaster. Then the Virtoris siblings and Livia. But Thyra and I stayed put, staring at the trapdoor in the ceiling, willing our mates and friends to join us.

Where were they? Sváva was causing a ruckus out there, and they'd understand what it meant. Maybe they were holed up somewhere until it was safe to come here?

"You have to *go*," Yrsa said to me and Thyra.

My heart squeezed. "Can you find them? Hide them?"

"I'll do my best."

I looked to Thyra, then the Valkyrja waiting for us to make the call.

"We can't be caught," Thyra said. "And they're smart and strong enough to get themselves out of binds. Have done so a hundred times."

She was trying to convince herself.

Outside the door, heavy footsteps sounded. Yrsa

waved for us to move. "Go! I need to close the gateway after you!"

Torn between seeing my mate and friends and not wanting to harm Yrsa, I made a choice that didn't sit right with me, and tugged on Thyra's hand, leading her through the gateway. Light blinded me before I stepped out of the portal and into Lord Riis's office in Myrr. Astril and Freyia followed, and the gateway closed. I swallowed, hoping that Yrsa would find the others.

"Nooooo!" A howl shattered my own worries and sent a shot of fire through me. Had someone followed us?

"Inga! Come back to me! Inga, please!" Lord Riis's voice sounded little like him. Too desperate. Too agonized.

"What's going on?" I asked Geiravor. She stood over her father, her stance stiff.

A cry of despair that would haunt me to my dying day rang out from Lord Riis as he clutched the queen to his chest, rocked her.

"What's going on?" I asked again.

Geiravor raised her gaze to mine. "The queen stopped breathing."

INTERLUDE
PRINCE RHISTEL AABERG, HEIR TO WINTER'S REALM, HOUSE OF THE WHITE BEAR

The uneven steps creaked as, guided by a single faelight, the heir descended into the ship's stowage. The glow caught first on the bastardborn's red hair. His half-brother, thanks to the harlot who had opened her legs for a merchant.

Rhistel's face twisted into a smirk thinking of his mother.

Not long after they placed Inga in the dungeons, they'd began dosing her with a potion that nullified her magic and stripped away her life, only to give the queen the antidote just in time to keep her alive. She'd missed the most recent antidote.

Those who had taken Inga would be wise to take her death as a sign—*an omen*—that any resistance, any fight they put up was futile. Especially now that Rhistel had the strongest and most respected warrior in the kingdom in his grasp. Any worries those in the army might have had would vanish once they witnessed Vale fight for House Aaberg once again.

His feet struck the bottom of the stairs, and Rhistel directed the faelight to the back, where he found them waiting asleep, bound, and propped up against barrels of water for the long journey.

"Wake up," he demanded.

His twin twitched awake. The Riis bastard was slower, his head lifting slowly, his gaze fixing on the prince. Glazed eyes, the both of them. He'd have to fix that.

Rhistel reached out with his magic, twisting and tweaking the control he had over their minds. With slight adjustments, the glazed appearance vanished. The pair looked like normal traitors now.

"Stand up, Vale. Put your left hand on that barrel."

The irons around his ankles clanked as Vale did as the heir commanded. Just like he had all those turns ago, when Rhistel had tested his emerging powers on Vale. Back then, Rhistel had practiced with their mother watching, though he'd taken liberties at other times. Times when she wasn't looking. It was after one of those unsanctioned practice sessions that Vale realized what was happening. The brothers had never been the same since.

Well, they were about as close as two could be now. Albeit in a different manner.

"Thantrel, get up. I want you to see this."

The redhead got to his feet, and with the motion, the scent of burnt skin wafted up. Most races of fae were sensitive to iron, and whoever put on Thantrel's shackles had not been careful. The exposed red skin welled and wept and as Thantrel swayed with the ship. the bastard nearly fell.

"I couldn't help but notice something about you has

changed, Brother." Rhistel pulled a freshly sharpened dagger from a sheath strapped to his thigh. The weapon felt odd in the heir's hand. He was more used to wielding a quill, knowledge, and secrets.

But sometimes steel was the only thing that would do the job.

He pressed the tip of the dagger to the finger bearing Vale's soulmate mark. Snowflakes. The sight of them filled Rhistel with a quiet rage, and not because of the bond Vale had with the Falk whore. Snowflakes brought to mind Winter's Realm—*his kingdom.*

Were the stars mocking Rhistel by painting them on his brother's skin? On *her* skin?

If so, he'd delight in taking them from her too. Right before he took other things. Her body. Her mind. When he grew tired of it all, her life.

Once he and his father were done with the Falk whore and her sister, they would rue the day they dreamed of stealing the Crown of Winter.

"When did this happen?" Rhistel asked.

"Weeks ago."

"Where?"

"In a cavern in the Red Mist Mountain Range."

Rhistel cocked his head, feeling the connection he had with Vale. His brother, unlike most fae, had developed a few feeble mental protections over the turns. Not any strong enough to keep their mother or Rhistel out, but to resist in small ways. There was something Vale didn't want Rhistel to see, and he could guess what. For a soulmate mark to appear, fae had to be intimate with one another in heart, body, and soul. No doubt the

Warrior Bear was trying to conceal his erotic memories of Isolde.

Let him keep those, Rhistel thought. *I'll have my own soon enough.*

"Father and I were not pleased to see the mark."

"He's not our father."

There it was—the fight he was used to. Slim but present.

"He's my father in every way that matters. Unlike that commoner you've become attached to." Rhistel teased the cold metal down Vale's finger, drawing up a faint red line. "Not a smart choice, but then again, no one is surprised by that."

Vale scowled. "He's a good male."

"We'll have none of that." He pushed his magic to feed his brother new lines. More appropriate lines.

"Lord Riis is a dirty commoner incapable of keeping his cock in his pants."

"That's better."

Thantrel stood idly by. Not offended. Not a single unprompted thought in his pretty little head.

"We're heading to the Mage Court," Rhistel said. "When we get there, the two of you will speak on behalf of King Magnus. You will support him, and our ally, the Shadow King."

That dark fae was on the ship with them. Had been in Grindavik too, though few took note of him because they didn't know who he was. Only Lady Ithamai and her daughters were allowed proper introductions, as was the plan. When the time came to reveal their alliance to the realm, they would need the support of powerful people.

"You will tell High King Tyra that Isolde Falk released the Shadow King, but he recognized a great darkness within her," Rhistel added as he pressed the blade into his brother's knuckle. Blood welled, dark in the dim light and tainting the salty air with copper. "You will say that she is a threat to the Crown of Winter. She plans to come for the throne of every court in retribution for them not aiding her father. And of course you will rebuke her. Say that she manipulated you into marrying her."

True or not, the prince did not care. When he was in control of them, Rhistel's whispering magic allowed him to force others to lie, and lie he would to keep the crown.

His eyes slid to Thantrel. "You will back him up."

"My mate," Thantrel said when Rhistel loosened control enough to get a response.

"The sister is your mate. We know."

"Just as we know of your brother. The gatemaker." A voice came from behind, startling Rhistel, though he didn't let it show.

The heir turned. Somehow, the Shadow King had let himself in and descended the stairs with no one hearing. Rhistel could not help but be impressed, even as annoyed as he was.

"Apologies for intruding, Prince Rhistel." King Érebo smiled, and it was a dangerous thing. "I did not want to miss the show. Now, what is the gatemaker's name again?"

"Luccan," Thantrel said confusedly.

"That's the one," King Érebo grinned. "Unless we find someone more powerful, I have a use for him."

Rhistel arched his eyebrows, and the Shadow King's grin widened. Numerous times he'd approached Rhistel.

The prince got the sense that the Shadow Fae wanted an alliance with him, as much as he desired one with the King of Winter.

Perhaps after I'm done here, we will find a quiet place and discuss such matters . . .

Rhistel turned back to the pair under his control. "So, do you understand what you will do?"

Thantrel nodded.

"Vale?"

A low breath left his twin. "I'll do what you say, won't I?"

Rhistel's laughter was a low, dangerous thing. Vale had no idea. This was merely phase one of his plan. Soon, he would stretch his magic, and they'd accomplish great and brutal things together.

"Speaking of doing what I say." Rhistel offered his brother the hilt of the blade as he tightened his control over Vale once more. "Cut off the finger with the snowflakes. Use the weapon for nothing else."

Rhistel took a few steps back and crossed his arms over his chest as Vale's screams filled the underbelly of the ship.

CHAPTER 39
ISOLDE

I stared at the spot on the wall where the gateway had closed.

Where was Vale? Our friends?

Hiding at one of the meeting points the Riis sisters had arranged throughout Grindavik?

A guttural sob rang through the office. Lord Riis was lying on the ground, next to Inga's cold body, exactly where he'd been since her last breath. Geiravor stood behind him, pity in every line of her body, but she didn't comfort her father. His grief prevented him from noticing anyone else in the room.

For the first time since Lord Riis told me of his lover's actions two decades ago, something other than anger and betrayal warred inside me. It was impossible to despise him as he was, when he looked so pitiful. So broken.

Would I look the same way soon?

I halted that thought before it spiraled me into a dark place. Vale wasn't dead. We were mates, and if death severed the bond, I'd feel it inside me. What afflicted me was not the greatest despair of losing a mate but an odd void. As if something muffled the invisible string connecting us. Perhaps distance? This was the farthest apart we'd been since the bond had formed. Though I'd had my doubts about such a power before, I found myself wishing that we were one of those mated pairs with a telepathic bond. At least then I'd know what was happening.

"It's got to be safe to check now." Thyra sat next to me. "It's been hours."

"It's not safe," Geiravor said tightly. "If it were, my sisters would make contact. Sváva hasn't returned to the brothel because it's under watch. And as far as I know, those soldiers may have harmed Yrsa."

"She has eyewitnesses that she arrived at the brothel, and as she was glamoured when we started the mission, no one can say that she ever left," Thyra said. "Yrsa is fine."

"Trust me. Stay put a while longer." Geiravor's tone brooked no argument. "And no shadows."

We'd shared that news with her, and she'd taken it rather well. Seeing our shadows as something that could be very useful.

"It seems like we have no choice in the matter." Thyra scowled.

Unlike other portals Luccan had made, my blood did not open this one. Only Riis blood did that. Lord Riis was beyond reach, and Geiravor refused.

"Would you like to force the matter, if you wish, Princesses?" Astril asked. The pair had remained to guard us, but Sayyida and Vidar were back at Ramshold, informing the others of what had occurred. Of the queen's death.

"No." I'd permitted compulsion to see the mission through, but to take an ally's blood was not something I'd allow. "We'll give it another hour."

Thyra crossed her arms over her chest as she leaned back in her chair.

The clock in the office ticked on and on and on. I glanced at it every few minutes, my resolve withering. Thyra caught me, arched an eyebrow.

"Second thoughts?"

I shook my head. Thyra snorted, not believing me at all.

Another agonizing half hour had just passed when the gateway shimmered. I sat straight up, watching the space on the wall. All others in the room, save for Lord Riis, were staring at the portal too.

The gateway opened, and Yrsa and Sváva walked through, followed closely by Caelo and Qildor, the former leaning on the latter's shoulder. I waited. The gateway closed, and a strangled sound left my throat.

"Isolde?" Caelo said. "Vale and Thantrel aren't here, are they?"

"No." My breath tightened in my chest. "Why are they not with you?"

Caelo gestured to the bloodied bandage over his leg. "I took an arrow to the thigh. Vale commanded Qildor to get me out. We went through the exit—barely made it."

Qildor maneuvered Caelo into a chair and sat him down with a soft groan. "Those water creatures are horrible. I'll be having nightmares about them for moons to come."

Unbidden, an image of the mermaid-like thing arose in my mind. I cringed. So, there had been more.

"When we finally got out of that channel, I heard the city bells and knew the brothel wasn't safe," Qildor continued. "I diverted to the closest meeting point and waited for Sváva. She and Yrsa only just collected us."

"The entire city is still positively crawling with soldiers," Sváva said. "It took us ages to get to the brothel, and I had them wait there as I went and looked for the prince and Thantrel. They weren't at any of the other rendezvous points."

My stomach sank to my knees.

"And no word of them in the underground of Grindavik?" Geiravor asked.

"Nothing, which means they're likely hiding because the glamours had to have worn off, and if the king or Lady Ithamai caught them, there would be news." Sváva swallowed. "I can go back and check again. However, it will take some time. Like we said, so many soldiers are patrolling the streets, looking for the Falk twins."

Hiding. My breathing eased a touch. Yes, they had to be in hiding. Maybe in an abandoned building or home. Vale inspired loyalty in many—particularly soldiers. Perhaps someone had seen them and helped?

"I have a better idea. One that ensures no one is caught, and it will be faster." Thyra nodded at where the gateway had been. "Can animals go through a gateway?"

"Of course. As long as they follow someone with Riis blood," Sváva replied.

Thyra lifted her face to Freyia's. "Find Aleksander and bring him and Arla here. We'll send the hawk around the city, see if they can't find the pair or hear anything about them."

The moment the door closed behind the vampire, Thyra took my hand and squeezed. "Aleksander and Arla will find them. His hawk may take some time to search, but she has never failed the rebellion. She won't fail us either."

My brother sent his hawk through the portal and then disappeared behind his hawk's eyes. Not too long after that, Rynni arrived to care for Caelo's injury.

Though we were taking action, I'd never felt so useless. So done with waiting.

I was still staring at Aleksander, willing him to come back to us with good news, when my finger began to ache. Absentmindedly, I closed my fist, thinking pressure might help, but with the motion, pain exploded through me. I doubled over in my chair and gripped my left hand with my right as agony coursed through me. White spots filled my vision, blanking out large portions of the room.

"Isolde? What's going on?" Panic rippled in Thyra's voice as she came closer.

"My hand!" I whisper-screamed. "A sharp pain in my finger!"

"Let me." Thyra tried to pry my right hand off my left, but the motion made me scream. She let go.

"Rynni!" my sister commanded. "Help her."

"Give me your hand." The dragon-fae was there in an

instant, and although it felt as though my bone was being cut with a dull knife, I offered her my shaking left hand.

I focused on the healer, and despite my vision going in and out, the confusion on her face was plain.

"Nothing is wrong other than it's red from where you gripped it tightly. Did you bang it on something?"

"This is not from a bang. Something is wrong. *Inside.*"

Everyone circled around me. Expressions of worry and puzzlement lined each of their faces.

Rynni exhaled a breath, noting how I trembled, how it made no sense. "Maybe you should go to the Master Healer?"

"Don't be an idiot, Rynni." Thyra spoke harshly, an indication of the panic that likely bubbled inside her. "We can all see that nothing is wrong with her hand. Something else is . . . what in the nine kingdoms?"

I gripped the chair with my good hand as another wave of fire, the worst yet, washed through me. I gritted my teeth, riding it out.

"Did you all see that?" Thyra asked, a note of fear in her voice.

No, I hadn't. In fact, my vision had just gone white. I blinked, trying to see again.

Breathe in. Breath out, I thought, lowering my heart rate one breath at a time. The old trick worked, and second by second, my vision returned. Bits and pieces of Thyra's face, as pale as the moon, came into focus.

"What?" I asked. "Tell me."

My sister's chin wobbled ever so slightly before she composed herself once again. "Your soulmate marks. They flickered."

I glanced down at my finger, still throbbing, but the pain had lessened. The marks did appear somewhat duller than before.

I gasped as the most horrible reason why that might happen struck me. "Does this mean Vale is dead?"

"No," a raspy voice spoke. Lord Riis's voice. Sometime during my pain, he'd woken from his stupor and sat up. He stared at me with red, grief-filled eyes, his face haggard as if he'd aged 100 turns in just hours. "If he died, the mark would disappear, and you would be on the floor from the agony in your heart."

Much like him. Fates.

"Then what?" I spoke the first words I'd willingly spoken to him since his betrayal came to light.

"You might sense his pain. Like some mates can speak mind to mind, and others can sense emotions, some can feel when another is injured. I can't be certain that's what's happening, but that is my best guess."

Cold seized me, a sensation a million times worse than whatever I'd experienced. If that was what was happening, why was Vale hurt?

I twisted to find Aleksander but his eyes were still shut.

"Let him work," Thyra said. "He'll find something. I promise."

"Vale could be *dying*!" I hissed. "And you expect me to sit here?"

"No." She placed both hands on my shoulders, as if trying to ground me. "If your hand is fine, I expect you to wait here with me. To be my rock, as I will be yours. To know that we're taking the smartest path to find the males we care for."

"*Care for*? I love him with everything that I am." The words choked up my throat. "If he dies, Thyra—I don't think I can keep going."

A world without Vale would lose all color. All meaning. I didn't want to consider such a horrible place.

"I think I can understand that," she whispered, and her inflection struck me as so sincere that I fell quiet.

Aleksander opened his eyes and turned to us, calm and ignorant to what had been happening in the room he sat in. "I have news."

"What is it?" Thyra asked.

"Did you find them?" I added.

"No, but sailors on the dock were talking about how the royal ship left over an hour ago. Bound for the mage court. Vale and Thantrel boarded along with the king and Prince Rhistel. The news was notable because Vale and Thantrel didn't arrive in Grindavik with them. Everyone was confused about when the Warrior Bear showed up. The last they heard he was a traitor and with Isolde."

"The Shadow King?" Thyra asked.

"No one saw him," Aleksander replied.

"That doesn't mean he's not there," Yrsa countered. "He could have easily boarded in disguise."

My shadows stirred. Whether excited to see the one that had released them or to battle Érebo, I couldn't tell. Nor did I care. Only getting Vale and Thantrel back mattered.

I stood. "So we go find a ship and follow."

Everyone in the office stared at me as though I'd grown another head.

"What?"

"Sorry, but that's an insane plan. Particularly after what just happened." Yrsa held up her hands. "And I don't blame you for losing your head, but you can't waltz into Grindavik and steal a boat large enough to cross the sea to the Mage Kingdom. And you cannot stroll into *that* court and expect to get Vale and Thantrel back."

"We can take more people," I retorted. "It worked to get Inga."

Astril cleared her throat. "That, my princess, was a trap. They let us take her to seize a larger prize. Two, actually."

"The queen is dead," Freyia added. "What makes you think they won't use the same poison and antidote on your mates? Repeatedly hurt them only to bring them back to life when all hope is nearly lost?"

My throat tightened. After Inga died, the vampires had examined her more closely. Both had received extensive poisoning training in their guild, but Freyia had been the one to catch the telltale notes of a poison on her breath. The assassin then needed to ingest only a droplet of the queen's blood to identify exactly what sort of contaminant they had given the queen. She'd claimed there was a trace of the antidote too, which hinted at repeated poisonings. The idea of Vale and Thantrel having to endure the same made me clench my fists.

"We can't charge into this," Thyra said. "I want to as well, sister, but we can't. We have to plan better. Be smarter."

"If we take too long?" I countered.

Another question arose. One I asked whenever something horrible happened, which was often as of late. Was this the price I'd pay for saving Anna's life? My mate's life for hers?

Thyra shook her head. "Vale is too valuable to kill. Thantrel too—especially if they learned that we're mates. They will keep them alive as lures. And of course we're going to get them, but we have to plan and anticipate any and every trap this time."

I gripped the closest chair, needing to steady myself.

"When we go for them, we have to be ready because that could be our best shot to end all of this." Thyra lifted her chin. "Can you wait? Are you with me?"

Though it shattered my heart to think of Vale at the mercy of those who would harm him, my sister was right. This could be our only chance to save our mates *and* win the throne in one blow. To minimize the death war would bring. We could not barrel forth recklessly yet again.

I took a centering inhale and nodded. "I'm with you."

CHAPTER 40
VALE

The shackles fell from my ankles, allowing me my first free breath in two days. Through the material of my pants, I'd endured the iron's insistent burn during the journey to Kuro. And although the burn was dimming now, and would soon be completely gone, I still felt trapped.

Rhistel continued to bear down on my mind, seeking to keep me harmless and weak and demoralized. As if losing my soulmate mark hadn't already done that. For many turns, I'd longed to see a mark on my skin that bound me to another.

Now that reminder of my love for Isolde and our connection was gone, just when I feared I would need it most.

Rhistel dragged an ungloved finger over my bare forearm, reinforcing his magic which was wholly unnecessary. He was in control, and because we were blood and I'd been his test subject many times, once his connection took root he did not need to touch me to give commands.

Perhaps that was the case with everyone he used his whispering powers on now. I only knew for certain that he'd grown stronger since the last time I'd been a practice subject.

And yet, I did my best to resist my twin.

Like when he'd forced me to tell him about when my mate and I got our marks. I'd kept the secret of Dergia, a place most believed did not exist. If Rhistel had learned that secret, he would have interrogated me. Would have demanded to know more about the lost kingdom. That would have put them in danger.

"When you reach the deck, you'll say you two were healing down there." Rhistel freed Thantrel from his shackles and gripped Thantrel's forearm. Thantrel shuddered, and I knew Rhistel was reinforcing his hold over my half-brother. "You were injured during the attack on House Ithamai's castle."

"Your crew will believe that rubbish?" I asked.

Rhistel laughed. "They take to heart what we tell them."

Had he warped their minds too? How many people could Rhistel hold in his thrall at once? Or maybe the crew simply feared him and would listen to save their own skin.

My brother led us up top. Fresh air heavy with salt filled my nostrils as I emerged into the light and blinked in the midday sun.

Kuro rose behind the docks. Pelted with rain, the capital of the Mage Kingdom looked as bleak as ever. Not that I had been here often. I had only stepped foot on this eastern island twice. Once in Kuro, and once in the north—that time without the knowledge of the Mage King.

"Walk with me, Vale," Rhistel whispered as we disembarked. Magnus and the Shadow Fae, dressed in an inconspicuous black robe, waited a ways down the dock. "We must appear brotherly."

He turned to sneer at Thantrel. "You remain three paces behind. And put those wings away. They draw too much attention."

Thantrel glamoured his fire wings to be invisible and fell in line. Not for the first time since our capture, a fresh wave of worry crashed over me. Than was not practiced at being at a whisperer's mercy, and hadn't developed protections, no matter how small. Rhistel could, if he were so inclined, severely damage Thantrel's mind. Mine too, for that matter, though I doubted that would happen.

The king and Rhistel wanted to show others that the Warrior Bear returned to fight with House Aaberg. They wanted me to command an army to fight my mate's forces. Hence, I needed to be recognizable as *me*, and not some mindless creature.

"Father," Rhistel said when we approached the king. "Érebo."

"They're ready?" the king asked.

Answer him. Call him your father.

"We're ready, Father," I said, my voice flat.

"You need to work on his tone." The king turned his back on me. Together, he and the robed Shadow Fae walked to a waiting carriage.

We followed, two paces behind, and Rhistel turned to me again. "Does your hand still hurt?"

My jaw tightened. "Not physically."

Rhistel cocked his head. "I wonder if she felt it too? If she still does?"

He asked with such bald curiosity. He didn't care in the slightest if Isolde experienced every bit of my pain. The idea made me ache. What was Isolde thinking?

"Will she come for you, like you did our mother?" Rhistel asked as we stopped at the carriage.

That would be my mate's first inclination. As it would be mine to find her, if she'd disappeared. But I hoped that Isolde and Thyra and those with them would stop and strategize. They could not make the same mistake twice.

"She has no plans to make anything easy for you." I entered the carriage after my brother, with Thantrel joining us last.

"Who said any of this was easy?" Rhistel tapped the sill of the window. "But I believe you're right. She's not stupid enough. What of the sister?"

A sharp smile filled my face. "Thyra is as cunning as Isolde, and you have her mate."

"She hasn't accepted him." He smirked at Thantrel.

"It doesn't matter. You should fear when they come for you."

"You welcome it."

The fae I'd once called Father glared at me. I turned away and stared out the window as Kuro rolled by.

The city was gray, made of stone the mages imbued with magic of various uses. Protection being the most common. The effect was oppressive and drab and made all the more miserable by the sheets of rain coming down.

"I hope you're regretting your choices, Vale," King Magnus said.

The address took me by surprise. I faced him and found his eyes were cold and hard. How long had he been wanting to say those words?

"Not at all," I replied when Rhistel didn't supply a script or force me to remain quiet. It seemed that he wanted to hear an honest answer. "I love her and will choose her every time."

King Magnus's eyes narrowed. "We'll see."

None of the anger on Magnus's face lined Érebo's sleek features as he leaned closer, as if he wanted to tell me a secret. "I was once like you. Trusting in my mate even when our peoples warred against one another. That trust landed me in a tree."

"Isolde would never hurt me."

"I thought the same of Sassa." His face tightened as he twisted to gaze out his rain-spattered window.

CHAPTER 41
VALE

The carriage shuddered to a stop at the castle doors.

Rhistel nudged my shoulder. "Get out and say nothing until I release you."

The moment my feet touched the sodden ground of Kuro, glances came my way. Whispers followed. Winter's Realm and the Mage Kingdom had not been at war for many turns, but the rulers of both kingdoms kept tabs on the important figures. Many recognized us on sight.

"Prince Vale." A mage dressed in the black and gold of the Royal House of Odarin exited the castle and approached. Two females waited behind him, their mouths sewn shut with shimmering golden thread.

My own lips tightened at the sight of the female mages. I'd heard of the golden thread. Heavily enchanted, the thread disappeared during mealtimes and reappeared the moment the last bite was gone but even during that brief reprieve, the punished could not speak. What had these two done to lose their voices?

"My lords." The servant bowed in acknowledgment of Thantrel and Érebo. At present, neither looked much like lords, but the servant was being cautious, and for good reason.

King Tyra's reputation for brutality and scheming was not unlike that of Magnus, though the mage's extremism extended to his own bloodline. He'd never declared an heir, and claimed he would not, all the while knowing that his future death would throw the kingdom into war. To know that, and delight in the upheaval his death would bring, well, I would be cautious around such a creature too.

"We received the royal raven not long before your arrival," the servant continued. "Will you be requiring rooms at the castle?"

I remained as mute as the servants with threads of gold binding their lips.

"Should we have to stay." The King of Winter emerged from the carriage on the heels of Rhistel. "We will sleep on my ship. After all, your king has made it quite clear that fae are not truly welcome here. Why would he make an exception?"

Above, a screech rang through the air. I looked up to find a hawk circling. My head tilted, and I squinted. Was the bird white or gray?

I swept away that line of questioning before Rhistel could sense it. Even if the bird was Arla, I didn't wish to think of that hawk or the fylgjarn connected to her. Best not to think of the rebels at all right now.

The servant bowed. "I will inform the king of your arrival. Vauti will show you inside."

The first servant left, and Vauti, one of the mage females, slid closer. She inclined her head.

"Take us to your king," Magnus said.

We followed Vauti's slender figure into the castle, made of strong black stone with few of the embellishments that fae loved. Just a painting or a statue here or there, all of them of King Tyra. Had there once been art regaling his ancestors and their accomplishments, it seemed the current ruler had disposed of such works. Or hidden them.

"I despise this place," Rhistel muttered as two passing mages inclined their heads at us and kept going.

The mages showed us the bare minimum of respect that would be due to a noble. Rhistel took offense to it, as did Magnus, though he was better at hiding it. Better at playing the game. I only recognized his growing irritation by the stiff set of his shoulders, how they seemed to harden with the minutes.

Vauti stopped before a doorway flanked by two other mages, both robed and holding knotted staffs. Soldiers in the highest military order in this kingdom.

"The king will be with you shortly," one soldier said stonily.

"Good," Magnus replied with equal ice in his tone.

We entered the small room, a den decorated with chairs scattered around a hearth that flickered with a weak fire, and a single gray table dominating the opposite side of the room. No finery. Not even a pitcher of water to offer guests.

Rhistel scoffed. "This is where he receives the King of Winter and his heir?"

"Do not let King Tyra's games get to your head, son," Magnus replied, and I didn't miss the emphasis he put on his last word as he cut me a sharp glance.

Rhistel was his son. I was not. As if I cared any longer.

"We are here for soldiers, and will endure small slights to get them," Magnus continued.

He'd never rolled over and accepted insults before, but then again, he hadn't needed to ally with a High King of Mages before, just other lords within our own kingdom. Fae who understood our ways and shared our culture. King Tyra was a different matter.

Rhistel poked his head out the door. "Have someone fetch wine."

That demand made, Magnus and my brother sank into armchairs near the fire, and the king motioned for Érebo to take the seat across from him. Once they settled, Rhistel caught my eye.

"Stand behind me, watchdog. Thantrel, you're behind our shadowy friend."

The hierarchy would be on display without anyone having to say a word to the Mage High King. The arrangement told me something else too. They planned to tell King Tyra who Érebo was. Otherwise, he'd be standing as well.

The fire crackled and popped, flushing the room with heat that the stone walls seemed to absorb right away. This damp place was not as cold as Winter's Realm, though it wasn't for lack of trying. My gaze drifted to the stark table, large enough for twenty males my size to stand around.

"Bland thing, isn't it?" Rhistel drawled and tilted his head back to look at me. "This king has no style."

I did not answer. Could not.

A satisfied smile curled Rhistel's lips. "This quiet suits someone with so few original thoughts in their head."

"He very well may need to talk about strategy." Magnus did not bother to look at me. "Tyra will likely want the Warrior Bear's thoughts on the war—how we plan to win it."

"I will release him and guide him when the time is right," Rhistel muttered.

Minutes passed. The wine and five goblets arrived, only for Rhistel to pointedly send back two. The fire continued to blaze, the wood barely burning down, hinting at its enchanted nature. With each second the king did not appear, Rhistel's jaw tightened a touch more.

If nothing else gave me pleasure, that did.

Rhistel's fingers had curled around the arms of his chair and whitened when the door finally opened. Of all the magical orders in Isila, mages looked the most like humans. Though one look at the Mage King, and you would know that he wasn't human at all.

With hair as black as a raven's wing and unlined, pale skin, one would think him a young male. A new king. But High King Tyra had to be at least two hundred turns old, and he'd ruled since his twenty-first nameday. A long time to be in the sunlight. A long time for so few to try to take what was his. Not that I blamed the mages for not challenging the king. The few who had tried were no longer walking the realm. Their deaths were said to have been as legendary as they were horrific.

"King Tyra." Magnus rose and inclined his head. "I thank you for seeing us today."

The High King of Mages hovered on the threshold of the room. He gave an equal nod to the King of Winter and looked to Rhistel. My brother bowed, and a voice in my head instructed me to do the same. Against my will, my spine bent.

"What brings you to my land, King Magnus?" The mage entered the room alone, and the door slammed shut behind him, but not before he sent a pulse of magic through the room. A warning. He was not defenseless, no matter if he kept his soldiers outside. King Tyra sat in the chair next to the one Érebo had claimed.

Rise, Rhistel commanded. *Stand at attention.*

I did as he said and cast a glance at Thantrel as he rose too. My half-brother's eyes were not clouded over, but I had a feeling he wasn't as aware as me. He simply seemed so relaxed. *Too* relaxed.

"A rebellion is rising in Winter's Realm," Magnus answered. "Two Falk princesses are back from the dead."

King Tyra's eyebrows arched. "I might have heard something of it."

From a mage living in a noble household, no doubt. The practice of keeping representatives from other magical orders living and working in royal or noble households was not so common in Winter's Realm. However, some ancient houses clung to the old ways when it came to mages. After all, their magical order was useful, unlike vampires, who were usually only admitted for diplomacy reasons.

Magnus nodded, as if he'd assumed as much. "They're powerful females. As strong as their father."

The High Mage King leaned back in his chair. "And why are you here telling me this?"

"You hated the Cruel King as much as I," Magnus replied. "And I am requesting your assistance in wiping his bloodline from the face of Isila."

"Are you not of the same blood?" Tyra asked.

Magnus hid the anger he surely felt at the jab. "I am Prince Calder's son by blood but not in my heart. He never acknowledged me."

"Why would you require such an acknowledgment?"

"We're from different lands, Tyra," the King of Winter replied. "And you have gotten me very off-topic. I seek an ally and want to know what you'd like in return should the mages come to my aid."

"How many great houses are with these Falk females?"

"Three," Rhistel answered. "One is unclaimed."

"Which?"

"House Armenil."

I hated that he'd pried that information from my head.

King Tyra's gaze drifted up to me. "The Warrior Bear was besotted with a Falk. Princess Isolde, wasn't it?"

Tell him she enchanted you. She has a darkness inside her that Isila will not survive, and you've come back to the light.

My body tightened at Rhistel's command, but while I might filter my thoughts or hide small things from him, I could not deny him entirely.

"She enchanted me," I repeated. "Isolde has a darkness inside her that Isila won't survive, but I made it out. Back to the light."

The words sounded hollow to me, but King Tyra

didn't seem to question it. He didn't know me well enough to do so.

"And who are the others?" he asked. "I assume they're important, as they're here."

"I'm Thantrel Riis. Son of the disgraced Lord of Tongues."

"And this," Magnus leaned forward and gestured to Érebo, "is someone who has experience with Isolde and her sister. Someone who could, if you work with us, change the face of Isila. A fae who would ally with you in return once we win."

King Érebo stood and removed his robe. Black, smoky wings fanned out, revealing what race of fae he belonged to.

The mage shot to his feet, and magic hummed in the air. An attack imminent.

"I wouldn't do that if I were you," Rhistel drawled. No doubt they'd all planned and expected this. "You might be the strongest of your kind, but between Érebo, my father, Vale, and myself, we can take you down in an instant."

"I allowed you into my home, and you brought this *abomination*?" The mage sneered.

"I prefer to be called King Érebo of the Shadow Fae."

King Tyra's eyes sparked with instant recognition. "You shouldn't be alive."

"It's true," Érebo replied.

"You're the same king who sought to take over my kingdom. *All* of them." He glared at Magnus. "You're a fool for working with him."

"I did all of that at the wish of my queen," King Érebo replied. "Surely you understand appeasing your wife? From what I hear, you've had enough of them to have learned a thing or two."

Three. Tyra took the fourth only earlier this turn.

The mage's magic thrummed in the air, a threat. "I'm to believe that you did not wish for more land? More power? That you started a war and intended to start more to please a female?"

Érebo shrugged. "I'm fae. So I'll admit, the power influenced me too, but it all started with my queen. And I'm sure you can imagine that many turns trapped in a tree have changed me." The Mage King's eyes widened at that, but the Shadow Fae didn't give him time to question what he meant. "My imprisonment altered my priorities. I would settle for revenge against the Falks. That and finding a means to return my race to Isila. To the isles we once called home." King Érebo's gaze drifted to the single window in the room, as if he were looking for those people.

"We intend for this alliance to continue after the present war," Rhistel added. "King Érebo will not harm the winter fae again, and the mages could be included in that bargain. And anyone who might threaten us would have to deal with the might of three kingdoms."

I wanted to laugh. To call my brother and King Magnus a fool for believing such things, but I was shackled to silence. Instead, I observed the mage. How he studied Érebo. How he weighed my twin's words.

"My story is one of legend," the Shadow Fae continued. "Shall I tell it to you, and what I hope for Isila—after we win this war?"

And there it was; a shift to building trust. As much as one could with a Shadow Fae.

"I will hear you out." The mage's magic in the room dwindled somewhat. "But first, let me call for more wine."

Hours slipped by in that dank room. Hours during which the kings and the prince spoke and Thantrel and I stood by, listening. Pretending to guard.

My calves ached from remaining in one spot. My muscles thrummed with the plans the rulers shared. Their dreams of a newly shaped realm. All of them involved the death of my mate.

If the High King of Mages considered it odd that Thantrel and I barely moved and never spoke, he said nothing. Perhaps silence would be expected of someone like me, a spare heir and a warrior. I was not a real power unless I was backed by those loyal to me. And those fae were very far away.

"Shall we make an oath then?" King Magnus asked when the conversation came to a lull.

"I must admit, the idea of an alliance is enticing. My kingdom has not had one in so very long," the mage spoke as if that wasn't his own damned fault. "However, I sense you have not told me everything that I should know."

The words landed heavily, and the other rulers tensed. For so long, the discussion had trended in a productive direction.

"Meaning?" Magnus asked.

"You see, mages, unlike fae, can develop new magical talents well into adulthood, and I am no exception. In recent turns, I have been learning how to sense magics. It gives me an advantage in many scenarios. Such as this one." He smirked. "The Shadow Fae has come as a surprise, I'll admit. And I know nothing of Thantrel Riis, but I'm well aware of what magics you, Prince Rhistel, and Prince Vale wield. However, there's an odd thread of magic connecting you, Rhistel, to Vale and Thantrel."

"Oh?" Rhistel tried to keep his tone neutral and failed.

"It's a magic I've not singled out before," the mage slowly rolled out his neck. "Powerful. Perhaps a *secret*?"

Rhistel stared at the mage. "You seem to have an inclination. Why don't you just ask? My kind cannot lie."

The king snorted as he gestured to the Shadow King. "His entire race can. Others have forgotten, but not me. So tell me, Prince Rhistel, what power are you hiding? What magic have you turned on these two?" He gestured to me, then Thantrel. "If you wish for my backing, you will tell me *now*."

Hope ripped through me. Rhistel's whispering magic was his most closely guarded secret. If he had planned to reveal it, he would have wanted to do so on his terms.

"Tell him, son." Magnus cleared his throat. "It will get out soon anyhow with that whore knowing."

"I want a promise of protection first," Rhistel said to the mage. "A guard of your kind because fae will not like what I am. Attacks might come my way, but most fae are not used to fighting off mages."

"That can be arranged. I have many powerful children

who would come, thinking they can sway me into naming them as heir." King Tyra spoke as if his children were idiots.

Rhistel gave a single nod, and if I didn't know him so well, I'd think he was calm and collected. Confident. But the telltale signs to the contrary were there. The tension in his hands. The tightness of his neck.

"I'm a whisperer. I have my brother and Thantrel under my control. Many in the armies are loyal to Vale, and he is Isolde's mate. Thantrel is Thyra's mate."

The mage smirked. "I thought that might be your power. And now I have one more stipulation."

Rhistel blinked, clearly shocked by the lack of emotion the mage showed. But then again, why would he? All mages could lie. The king had only wanted to put all the nuchi cards on the table.

"Which is?" Rhistel asked.

"You will take one of my daughters as your queen, and you will do so before you leave my land. Marriage between our kingdoms is the only way I can trust you." The mage turned his gaze to the Shadow King. "The same goes for your line."

"I know not if anyone in my line lives on," King Érebo said. "But if they do, you have my word."

"That will have to do. Magnus?" the mage went over Rhistel's head, right to the king, who nodded.

"My son will wed a mage daughter."

Rhistel's mouth fell open. "Do I not have a say?"

"Not if you want to win this war," Magnus said.

"I will give you your pick of princesses." Tyra

shrugged one shoulder. "I have many daughters around your age. Older and younger too. Whatever you prefer."

"I prefer not to be forced," Rhistel muttered, and not for the first time, I got the sense that he had someone. Maybe not someone he loved, but someone he cared enough for that he did not wish to wed another.

"You will do your duty." Magnus stood. "Now, let's see to getting my son wed so the oaths can be formally taken."

CHAPTER 42
ISOLDE

A knock came at my door.

"Y-yes?" I called out, the word sticking like syrup in my mouth. When was the last time I'd had anything to drink? I looked down at my hands to find my skin white and dry. My soulmate mark was duller than it should have been too.

Astril opened the door. Beside her stood Aleksander, black circles under his eyes, shoulders stooped. Since Vale and Thantrel had been taken, the fylgjarn had been joined with his hawk. He did not dare to rest in case he lost track of the pair.

"Aleksander." I stood from the chair. "What's going on?"

"They arrived in Kuro, the capital of the Mage Kingdom. Vale and Thantrel were taken to the castle with King Magnus, Prince Rhistel, and a cloaked figure. I can't get Arla too close, and definitely not inside. I worry about the Shadow Fae recognizing her after that day in the mountain tunnels."

"I understand." Arla was a part of Aleksander, and the hawk had saved our lives that day. "But you think the cloaked figure is King Érebo."

"I do."

"And they're meeting the Mage King. Asking for an alliance." A ball of ice settled in my belly. "Who knows how long that will take?"

"I'm not someone who would have any idea."

That made two of us.

"Isolde?" Aleksander's tone had gone softer in mere seconds, alerting me.

"What else?" I asked.

"Vale and Thantrel walked into that castle on their own *with* King Magnus, Prince Rhistel, and the Shadow Fae. They weren't shackled or forced."

Oh. *Oh.*

Aleksander studied me. Waited for an explanation.

"Rhistel is a whisperer." When Aleksander did not appear surprised in the least, I continued, "he must have Vale and Thantrel in his grips."

"I had a feeling it had to be something like that," my brother admitted. "They looked much too willing."

"Have you told Thyra yet?"

"When I passed her in the yard."

"What was she doing?" Like me, my sister had been taciturn since the mission in Grindavik.

"Watching the soldiers arrive and train in small groups." Aleksander's lips tightened. "She's watching from a window though, standing by that statue of three rams."

Those of fighting age pledged to House Balik were assembling. At first I hadn't understood why it would take two days, but then I learned of the vast numbers of fae and how many had to travel to the city. That was to say nothing of packing supplies for so many and placing them in the appropriate groups.

With the snow melted, no one was sure how long the march north would take, but the distance was not small. We guessed at least a week.

Not fast enough.

"You both should be out there," Aleksander continued. "Being seen. Heard. Those at the castle know you well enough, but to others, you're still a mystery."

"You're right. I'll go now." Remaining in this room and thinking of Vale in Rhistel's mental grasp seemed unbearable. I went to the door. Aleksander followed and made to come with me, but I shook my head. "Rest. We can guess what they're doing in Kuro, and I don't think they'll be leaving soon. As long as Arla stays there and can follow them, you should be able to get some sleep."

"If anything happens, send someone to wake me."

"I will."

The hallways of Ramshold were alive with fae, everyone rushing back and forth, completing various tasks. Assembling an army impacted not only the fighters, but anyone related to them. Anyone who provided a service that would keep the soldiers fed, comfortable, and alive. Kitchen staff. Healers. Maids, seamstresses, and those who worked in the laundry; all so busy that few noticed me as I passed.

I found Thyra where Aleksander said she'd be, standing by the three rams, gazing out the large arched window.

"Sister."

She gave me a sad smile. "Was wondering when you'd emerge."

"Aleksander reminded me it was good to be seen."

"I'm hoping this is enough. I don't have the energy to perform right now."

"Me neither." I joined her at the window.

Beyond the glass, hundreds of soldiers stood in lines, acquiring weapons. Some received lessons. To my great relief, no one looked too young or too old to fight. Lord Balik, and those lords and ladies loyal to the warden, had called in their best.

After a few minutes of assessing, I broached the subject I'd considered on and off since I awoke. "I think we should speak with Luccan about using a gateway one more time. But not to Avaldenn."

The Riis family believed one of their gateways in Avaldenn was still functional. The one at the Warmsnap Tavern. However, as the establishment belonged to Lord Riis, it was very likely the tavern was being watched. No one dared try to enter the place to find out, lest they be caught. To funnel an army through a tavern would be ludicrous.

Thyra turned. "Where then?"

"Bitra. Lord Riis's army is coming from there, anyway. Maybe the entire Balik army can enter the castle and be safe while we regather. Then, we march."

"Bitra is a three-day walk from Avaldenn," she mused. "We'd lose the effect of flanking their forces, but it could work. That is, if Luccan can keep the gateway open that long."

She'd targeted the main reason I'd hesitated. Once, Luccan had opened a temporary gateway. The effort had nearly claimed his life.

"Yes. We should speak with Luccan about it." I turned only to see the Virtoris siblings coming our way.

"We have news," Vidar said. "Is this a good time?"

"As good as any," Thyra replied.

"We sent a raven to our mother," Vidar took the lead, "detailing where the king and prince are and the route they'll likely take home. I told her where to have ships in place, and she'll see it through."

"So maybe she can intercept them?" I asked.

"It's possible but not probable," Sayyida said. "It's also possible that if they gain new allies, a larger fleet will join them in coming north. In that case, the other ships would protect the king's vessel, and depending on how many vessels the mages send, that could be too much for our armada."

Vidar cleared his throat. "We still need to send an army to Avaldenn."

"That was never in question," Thyra replied. To win the war, we'd need the capital.

"Our mother will protect the mouth of the Shivering Sea as best she can," Sayyida paused. "But she'll need all the help she can get. Vidar and I should join her."

The pair could enter the city via a gateway that led into Sváva's home, and they already had vessels hidden among the islands closest to that city. If they left now, it would be possible to make to their island before the king's ship.

"Let's discuss this with Lord Riis and Lord Balik." The

choice was not one my heart wanted. On the water, I wouldn't know if they were safe. But tactically, it made sense.

"I agree with my sister," Thyra said. "We were on our way to find Luccan. Can you gather the lords in Tadgh Balik's den, and we'll meet you there?"

"Luccan? He's in the library with the Scholars," Vidar said.

Surprise rippled through me. "Then we should go find him. See you soon."

Locating the Scholars in the vast library was easy. The trio always sat at the same table.

"Hi." I clasped a hand on Anna's shoulder. She covered it with her own palm, always knowing when I needed comfort. "Do you know where Luccan is?"

"I do," Anna replied. "I'll show you."

Her familiar uneven footsteps echoed in the silent library within Ramshold.

"Is Arie in the yard?" I asked, trying to sound normal and not like my insides were shredded.

"He is. We're meeting for lunch though." Anna gave me a sad smile. "We don't have to talk about him. Or any men—sorry, males. Not when you're hurting, Isolde."

"No matter my situation, I'm happy for you." I saw how Arie looked at her. Had seen them kiss. My oldest friend had more than she ever dreamed of, and she deserved it all. "Arie is a good male."

Warmth glowed in her brown angular eyes. "Thank you."

When we came across Luccan, he was so deep into his reading that he didn't notice us until we stood right in front of him.

"Sorry." He placed a marker in the book before shutting it. "Is there something or someone who needs me?"

I could not help but notice the bags under his eyes. Luccan, like Aleksander, like so many of my friends, had been running himself ragged to prepare for the march. That only made what I had to ask him more difficult.

"We're the ones who need you," I said softly. "Do you mind?"

"That my princesses require me? Not at all." His face split into a smile that went a long way in making him appear less tired. Anna excused herself and once we were alone, Luccan nodded to my sister and me. "What's going on?"

I told Luccan my thoughts about using a gateway to Bitra, adding that I'd understand if he didn't want to do so. Gatemaking was a highly regulated magic in Winter's Realm, and only a few close friends and family knew about Luccan. Most of them out of necessity.

Once done, I added, "This could help us get to Avaldenn faster. But again, it's up to you. We won't force you."

Luccan swallowed. "I was researching gateways when you arrived because I had the same idea. About going to Bitra and then marching to Avaldenn."

"Exactly what do you mean by researching? A gateway already exists in the brothel down the road."

"How to keep it open for that long without . . ." He trailed off.

"You dying." My stomach pitted. "Yes, you expending so much energy was one of our concerns. I can't put you through what I did back at Riis Tower."

"Gateways only like to stay open for a short period." He let out a long breath. "Minutes. Not long enough to get an army through unless the gatemaker practices manipulating the portal. And once the gateway closes after being open against its will, well, it won't open again for some time."

He spoke about gateways as if they were living, breathing, sentient things. The idea reinforced how little I understood about Luccan's magic. How little he had experience with too.

"And yet, beating Magnus to Avaldenn would be the easiest way to win this war before it gets underway," Luccan said. "It could save many lives."

"I don't want you to try so hard that the effort costs *your* life."

"This is a good time to admit that getting to Bitra with an army in tow wasn't all I was researching. I've been thinking about the Shadow Fae." He tapped another book off to the side, and I recognized it as the one we'd borrowed from the Great Library. "How someone—a Lisika, and another unnamed fae, if what I've read is right—sent them elsewhere. Making a gateway within a realm like Isila is difficult. Making one between worlds, like the ones we have to the human world, is the most a gatemaker can hope to achieve. And to make two between worlds that are large enough for an entire race of fae to disappear through? Before last moon I would have said it was impossible."

He leaned back and when he spoke again, he did so with deliberation. "No one except Arie and Clemencia knows this, but I've been practicing the more advanced facets of my magical specialty. I felt like I had to because there's a powerful gatemaker in Avaldenn. One favored by King Magnus. If she's forced to try and locate the Shadow Fae, and she succeeds, we'll have more enemies. I figured that if I could banish them right back to where they came, that would be a help."

My skin felt icy.

"You're saying that you've been trying to make portals to other worlds?" Thyra spoke slowly.

"A few times."

My mouth fell open. To attempt such a thing secret with just a few people watching and protecting you? Insanity.

"You should have told us this sooner," Thyra said.

"I haven't had success yet."

"But you're close, aren't you? You were talking about getting stronger. Can you . . . feel another world?" Stars, what would that even be like? Suddenly, my magics, both strong and bold, seemed so very small in comparison.

"I think so."

My stomach twisted at the revelation. Luccan had gone through all of this, put his life on the line in the most extreme way, and I hadn't a clue.

"Luccan," I exhaled his name. "I appreciate the effort, but perhaps focus on widening existing gates and keeping them open for longer? The other matter—well, the

Shadow King has not yet succeeded in bringing anyone over. Perhaps that will never happen."

The eldest Riis brother's stare lingered on me before he gave a single nod. "As you wish."

I gave him a weak smile, still reeling. "Then we should be going. We have a meeting and will be telling the lords we're going to use the gateways to move north."

"I should resume practicing." Luccan stood.

My twin and I left the library. Though the information we'd acquired had been largely positive, the sense of unease in my belly persisted.

INTERLUDE
PRINCE RHISTEL AABERG, HEIR TO WINTER'S REALM, HOUSE OF THE WHITE BEAR

King Tyra and Rhistel's father spoke the oaths, binding two kingdoms with a dozen witnesses present.

An hour earlier, Tyra had presented Rhistel with a lineup of over twenty females born to House Odarin. Some had been far too young for his taste. Two were forty turns. He'd nearly chosen one of them for her beauty, but then he'd spotted the ink smudges on Noni of House Odarin's hands. He'd asked her what they were from, and she'd replied that she was writing a book.

If anyone were to suit him, it would be another intellectual. At the very least, if there was never love between them, he hoped they might have something to talk about. They could find love and lust elsewhere, but to be wed to a stupid female was abhorrent.

He supposed he simply should have been pleased that Noni, born to King Tyra's third wife, wasn't one of the fae high ladies his father had been mulling over. None had stirred anything more than superficial lust in him. No one ever had, save for one female, and he could never have her as his wife, anyway.

So he pushed away thoughts of auburn red hair smelling of ink and mint, and smiled at his raven-haired wife.

Dutifully but not wholeheartedly, Noni returned Rhistel's smile. She, like Rhistel, was under no delusion that this arrangement was anything other than political. Like many other marriages between royals or nobles within Isila. "We're sailing soon then?"

"Tonight," he answered lowly as the oaths continued. "We must return to Avaldenn swiftly. The army awaits us there."

"Father is sending mages he uses on long journeys. They can funnel wind into the sails. I suspect we'll arrive much faster than you anticipate."

Fae such as Rhistel could possess air magic, but to help guide a ship for that long? Rhistel did not know any fae who could do such a thing.

The benefit of being able to use enchantments and spells in addition to natural magic, he thought.

The oaths ended, and magic sealed the promises of two kings. The sailors who had been brought in as fae witnesses left, and the mage lords followed suit, until finally only the kings, the princes of Winter's Realm, Noni, and Thantrel remained.

"Much to be done," King Magnus said. "We should get back to the ship and prepare."

"I wanted to speak to your son first." King Tyra turned his dark gaze onto Rhistel. "Your magic is powerful, and I've decided I wish to see it."

Rhistel shrugged a shoulder in the direction of Vale and Thantrel, standing docile on the other side of the room. Since they had arrived in Kuro, he'd kept them dangling on taut strings.

"You've seen the reaches of my power." Rhistel waved a hand in Thantrel's direction. "The red-haired one has not been so quiet for even a day in his life, and he's said nothing but what I've permitted since stepping into your home."

King Tyra chuckled. "I was hoping for something a bit more dramatic. A show of your brother's strength? Convince me that you'll be able to use the Warrior Bear to our required ends."

There was already a plan of how to use Vale. When the Warrior Bear reached the shores of Avaldenn and they positioned him before an army, he would be completely convincing.

"I was going to begin a transition of my brother's mind on the ship, but if you insist on an earlier showing."

"Make me believe it."

Rhistel heard the words the High King was not saying. He wanted to witness total domination.

Who was Rhistel to say no?

The heir looked around the empty room, more opulent than the den they'd first been shown to. "Might you have an enemy lingering in your castle?"

"What king doesn't have a quiet enemy or two?" King Tyra strode to the door and opened it to speak with the soldiers outside. When he joined them again, it was with a smug smile on his handsome face. "Lord Tyrili is a champion of the people, and they're getting too many ideas for my liking."

"How annoying," Rhistel said, as if he weren't about to witness this lord's murder at the hand of his twin.

In no time at all, the guards had returned and shoved a mage into the room. The male fell to the ground, his hands catching him before his nose scraped the floor.

"My king! What is the meaning of this!" The lord rose from the ground, his face red with outrage.

"I told you to stop giving people ideas. As of this morning, I learned you did not listen." The High King of the Mages smirked. "So I will warn you no more. Prince Rhistel?"

Magic spiked in the room, only to be joined by King Tyra's own power and a visible whip of magic binding the lord.

"You're sending *a fae* to teach me a lesson? Pathetic!" Lord Tyrili spat.

"There are no more lessons." The king chuckled. "Proceed, whisperer."

The lord's eyes went round. Rhistel thought he expected his mind to go blank. For a fae to infiltrate it.

Instead, Rhistel spoke into Vale's mind, loud and clear and powerful.

Behead him. Make sure everyone knows you're doing it for me.

A faint press of defiance came from Vale. Rhistel's neck tightened. He'd allowed his brother to keep a few secrets, allowed him also to believe that Rhistel was not in total control. The time had come to shatter that illusion.

His mental fist tightened, and the pushback ceased.

Vale strode over to the bound mage, his meaty hand on the hilt, the sword emerging from the scabbard.

When Vale was but two paces from the mage, he spoke as his brother commanded. "I take your life in the name of my brother, Prince Rhistel."

The sword swung, blood sprayed, droplets spattering Rhistel's face. His nose wrinkled.

"*Ugh*," Noni muttered. "My gown is ruined."

Rhistel's eyebrows arched. He expected any daughter of King Tyra to be cold, but that—*that* was positively glacial.

King Tyra stepped through the blood continuing to pool on the rug. "To the ships then?"

Rhistel lingered on the upper deck. Below, sailors scurried about, preparing to hoist the anchor. Something about them reminded the prince of rats, and he thanked the stars that he didn't have to sail often.

"Where is your new wife?" Érebo appeared and leaned over the railing, the wood groaning beneath his weight.

The heir scanned the king, seemingly in good health. Vital and vibrant even. How had the fae maintained his muscle mass when he had not been able to move for so long? Had the Drassil sustained him?

There was so much Rhistel wanted to ask the Shadow Fae, but he held his tongue. Too much curiosity could be taken advantage of.

"In a cabin," Rhistel answered. "Settling in, I expect."

"And you're not eager to get to her? She's a beauty."

The prince shrugged. He could have many beauties, could take what he wanted, however he wanted, but he only ever truly wanted one fae.

"I have work to do on Vale and Thantrel. My new wife and I will not be sharing a room until we're back in Avaldenn."

"Political marriages can turn to love. Mine became one of respect, not love, but some do."

"You loved Sassa Falk?" The question was off the prince's tongue before he could stop it.

"For a while. We were mates and that sort of bond can be infatuating indeed." Érebo smirked. "Come to think of it, you shouldn't be taking advice from me on the matter of love. I had a stunning wife. One I started wars for because we both loved power—if not each other. And then I had a mate who I loved until she showed her true colors. I'm not the best at picking females."

Rhistel snorted. "We're similar in that regard."

"Who is she, then?"

"Someone out of my reach." He'd always been determined never to take away her dreams. Now that he was wed, what would be the point?

"At least you'll never want for distractions. Princes and kings have them in great supply."

"Did you have a harem?" Rhistel asked, allowing himself another question. A glimpse into the world of the Shadow Fae.

"I did. The practice was common when I ruled."

"Not so common now." His father was among one of the only remaining rulers in Isila who kept a harem. "I'm unsure if I'll keep it. Of course, it could be fun, but . . . other things excite me more than females just waiting to be laid on their backs."

Intelligent conversation and a partner with wit.

True domination.

The two sides of Rhistel warred. Always.

"Have you put other thought into what kind of king you'll be?"

It was not often that Rhistel was taken aback, but the Shadow Fae's question made his spine straighten.

"Of course I have. I've been training and learning how to be the king of Winter's Realm since I was a youngling."

"Not in this world. Not how it is or will be in the future."

If and when Érebo brought his people back. Was it possible? The heir didn't know, but the Shadow Fae seemed confident he'd find a way. Or rather, a person capable of doing such things. What did he know that Rhistel didn't?

What a stupid question. Érebo had learned to use the Drassil network. A web that not only saw the trees' surroundings, but also heard the confessions and prayers of living fae and could give one access to the accumulated knowledge of the dead. Of course, Érebo knew far more than Rhistel. The fact annoyed the prince as much as it made him want to ask a million questions.

"I think your father hasn't considered how our realm will soon change," Érebo continued. "He will not welcome a return of my kind, no matter what he says to me while he needs me."

"He cannot lie."

"He can lie to himself and uncover the truth of how he feels later. When the war is over."

"What are you getting at?"

The king looked him over, assessed him, more like. "I allied myself with Winter's Realm. I mean to keep my promise, but the more I learn about the kingdom, the more I see how it could benefit from a new kind of king. Someone with more curiosity than innate prejudice."

Rhistel laughed at the dangerous line that Érebo walked. "I trust you as much as any other fae."

"I don't think that's true. In me you see yourself, a fae who has hidden for so long. One who wants to show their real face. Their real talents."

The heir studied the king. A part of him thrilled in not being able to anticipate anything about this male. So often Rhistel could simply take people at their word. And on the occasion that they twisted a truth or omitted information, he usually sensed it. Not so with the Shadow Fae. He had no idea what deeper thoughts Érebo had in his head.

The king pushed off the railing. "Just know, Rhistel, that I'm open to forming new relationships."

The king walked away, leaving Rhistel to stare after him.

CHAPTER 43
VALE

The ocean swells rocked the boat with rhythmic timing. Out the open porthole, water splashed against the edges of the ship, but I remained focused on the inside of the cabin. On Rhistel.

Since returning to the ship, Thantrel and I had been made to share a room with Rhistel, though my twin had only recently returned to the cabin. What he'd been doing, I did not know, but the look in his eyes was dangerous, and I wished he'd stayed above deck. Better yet, that he'd fallen overboard.

"We're skirting the coast of Winter's Realm." My twin leaned back against the wooden wall, arms crossed over his chest. "Just north of Stormy Bay, already."

Until he arrived, I'd watched the water flow by, smelled the salt and felt faint sprays of spindrift on my face. I'd seen the land approaching, and thought there was a large island in the middle of the ocean I knew naught of.

"Oh, you may speak." Rhistel waved a careless hand in the air.

"Impossible." It had taken us two days just to cross the channel to the island the mages called home.

"We've been sailing for less than a day," Thantrel added, his voice raspy from disuse.

"Sailing with mages has benefits. We'll be home in three days—perhaps four if the currents are against us. Then, you will be put to work, Vale."

My skin crawled. Under Rhistel's thrall, I'd killed a mage lord, and there'd been nothing I could do to stop myself. Since he'd loosened his hold on the ship, I'd felt great remorse. Despised myself for killing that mage.

"Aren't you at all curious what we're going to do with you two?" Rhistel asked.

Thantrel snorted. "Obviously, you want to lure our mates. Oh, and perhaps something else depraved and disgusting that I'm not curious about."

"Weren't you born in a whorehouse, Riis?" Rhistel's nose wrinkled. "And now you're mated to a dirty rebellion leader? You're not one to talk about being disgusting, now are you?"

Thantrel lunged, but Rhistel was ready and tightened his control. Thantrel reared back, a puppet once again.

"His mother was an elven noble," I said. "And our father owns dozens of brothels, so I don't—"

"My father is the King of Winter's Realm," Rhistel snapped. "You might have allied yourself with that spider, but not I. *Never me.* You'd do well to remember it."

My head exploded in pain as he bore down on me too. *Stand.*

I obeyed, hatred burning through me as my muscles complied.

"Thantrel, you'll be shoved away somewhere in Avaldenn. A place of unimportance." Rhistel began to pace. "However, I will devise a production to keep you occupied. Something —what did you call it?—*depraved.*"

Thantrel said nothing. Could not. Like I no longer controlled my own voice.

"Vale, you'll be leading your army. Voicing your disdain for the Falks." Rhistel smirked. "Perhaps we'll even promise them to the soldiers as a reward? If one lands a hit, they get to bed a princess. What a motivator that will be!"

The idea of Isolde and Thyra being abused brought tears to my eyes.

"That will be after Father and I have had our time, of course. We're both so curious about Isolde. And even Thyra has piqued my interest—after seeing her in your head, Thantrel. She's pretty enough and a strong female. I love bending those to my will."

A low growl was all Thantrel managed, though I didn't doubt he was fighting as hard as I was to break out of Rhistel's hold and pummel my twin.

But my brother's magic bore down harder, colder. Mental images of Isolde began to flash through my head. I blinked. What was going on?

"It's a skill I've developed after turns of research in the House of Wisdom," Rhistel answered my unspoken question with a smirk. "I'm not even sure our mother developed such talents. The idea is that a whisperer can supplant memories into another mind. We envision and then deposit. In time, the other person won't be able to tell if what they see is real or not. In time, we can change minds and hearts. I intend to do both."

I gasped as a sort of vision of Isolde slashing open Saga's throat filled my mind. Overtook it. Coldness washed through me. I smelled my sister's blood; it was so real. So visceral.

Not real.

"But does that matter?" Rhistel shoved another vision into my head. One of Isolde and Thyra freezing the cabal, killing them, and laughing as they did so. "All that matters is what you *think* is real. And I can change your entire perception in no time at all."

Even as the awful image stole the breath from my lungs, understanding dawned. Rhistel was wrong that he was the first to do this, though he had no way of knowing so.

I'd been under the impression that Mother had suggested things to the Cruel King, and that King Harald had merely done what she said. But this part of a whisperer's power, a facet I had not known existed before, made far more sense. Made things so much more real.

And I feared that, like the Cruel King, I would fall susceptible to such magic, and harm the ones I loved most in this world.

CHAPTER 44

ISOLDE

I sat in Lord Riis's brothel office in Myrr. Hoping. Calculating. Watching the portal of light on the far wall.

Night had fallen, and the brothel was busy. Feminine laughter sounded and perfumed air seeped under the crack of the door. Inside the office, however, was silent as the circle of light grew wider and brighter. Luccan pushed himself to his magical limits.

Watching the gatemaker was equally exciting and panic-inducing. Sweat poured down Luccan's neck, his chest heaved, and his face was ruddy with effort. Just like the last four attempts he'd made to force the gateway open for an extended period, he looked ready to pass out. Unlike before, however, no one stopped him. He became irate when we did.

Not to say precautions weren't being taken though. Clem, Arie, and Duran stood nearby to keep Luccan fed and hydrated after he emerged from each session.

His effort drove home the idea that nothing had come easy that day. Meeting the high lords had turned into a frustrating matter of question and answer. Of doubt. Of Thyra and me reassuring them the gateway could work.

My thumb rubbed my faded soulmate mark. No pain had come from it again, but I had a bad feeling about the coloring.

We're moving. As fast as we can, I tried to bring myself back from the brink of devastation that I had flirted with more often than not these past days. *Vale is strong. We'll save him in time.*

The Virtoris siblings, already gone from Myrr, were the first wave of our offense. From Grindavik, Sayyida would send a raven to Lady Virtoris to stop the king, or at least destroy a portion of his forces, before we got to Avaldenn.

The vast majority of our pronged plan, however, relied on Luccan's ability to widen a gateway and keep it open long enough for a sizable portion of the army to pass through.

So far, Luccan could force the gateway to the castle in Bitra to remain open for twenty minutes. An extension of about fifteen minutes over most gateways' limits if they were opened by blood. Thyra and I estimated ten people could run through at one time. Fewer when you added in the horses that many would ride. Too small, but considering the size of Lord Riis's office, where all the soldiers would have to funnel through, the gateway was as large as Luccan could make it.

Depending on how organized we were in the morning,

many soldiers would pass through while Luccan held on. And if Luccan opened the gateway many times—and took short breaks—maybe we had a real chance. That was, if the gateway didn't close on its own.

A knock came at the brothel door.

"Who is it?" Thyra asked as Clemencia got to her feet to answer.

"Qildor," a familiar voice called out.

I nodded to Clem, and she opened the door. The knight veered our way, and Clem returned to her love's side, ready to assist whenever Luccan let up on his power.

"What's going on?" I asked Qildor.

"Two updates. The most important being that the last armies from the small banner houses have arrived. We have a count."

"How many?"

"Five thousand."

I sucked in a breath.

"Lord Riis has a force of about three thousand in Bitra," Qildor added. "And the Virtoris ships will be of great use too." He tried to assure us, but I'd heard the reports from Avaldenn as well as him. It was estimated that twenty-five thousand fae had gathered outside the city walls. We were greatly outnumbered.

"We'll have to find a sneaky way to approach Avaldenn. What was the second bit of news?"

Qildor cleared his throat. "Queen Inga has been successfully placed in a magical stasis. For later."

Thyra had suggested the practice, and I'd demanded it so that Vale could say a proper goodbye to his mother. Both my twin and I knew how important closure was.

According to the fae who had preserved the queen's body it would not decompose for weeks.

I was determined to find Vale long before then.

"Thank you, Qildor." I turned to the trio hovering around Luccan, who was lost to his magic. "Ease him out."

Clem laid a soft hand on Luccan's shoulder as Arie made to catch his brother, should he fall upon releasing his power. Duran poured a goblet of water.

"Love," Clem's soft voice soothed. "Our princesses need a word. Come back to us."

The portal of light dimmed, the first indication that Luccan was backing off. It shrank with control until Luccan let out a gasp and released.

His knees buckled, as they had a few times before. Arie caught him.

"Easy, brother. Easy. Here's a seat." Arie settled his older brother into a plush velvet chair.

Luccan's body went limp, his arms hanging over the edge as his breathing began to slow. Clemencia took his hand, rubbed her thumb over it, and sat in silence, a soft smile on her lips. We waited, and when he was ready, he sat up. Duran offered him the goblet of water, which Luccan took and drank all the way down. Then, he twisted to face my sister, Qildor, and me.

"What?" Again irritation clouded his face. Luccan, usually so good-natured, didn't like being interrupted when he was undertaking a task.

"Will you be ready to make a true attempt at daybreak?" Thyra did not mince words.

"I think so." Luccan drank again. "But for now I need more practice."

"I think sleep would be more advisable." Much rested on Luccan's shoulders. My mate's fate. The fate of the kingdom, if we could make this the one and only battle in the war.

"I'm attempting something few can do," Luccan snapped. "I need the practice."

"You'll be no good to anyone tomorrow if you're exhausted," I shot back. "You're barely able to sit up on your own. Rest, Luccan."

"Just twice more. Then I'll sleep."

"Very well." Thyra stood. "We'll leave you to it then. You three, make sure he does what he says." My sister said to our friends. "Isolde?"

I rose, playing along, despite having no clue what Thyra was up to, and we left the office. The door shut behind us, and still, Thyra said nothing. Tonna, Sigri, and Halladora, who had waited for us outside fell in line as our guard.

The upper floors of the tavern were where the brothel was located, and we maneuvered our way through females and males in various states of undress and a few males being led to private quarters. It wasn't until we had made our way through the tavern portion of the brothel and on to the streets of Myrr that my sister turned to me.

Her eyes were shining with tears.

"What's wrong?" I asked, taken aback. My twin and I had grown close, but she kept her emotions close to her chest. "Why did we leave?"

"At the end, it all hit me. We're moving forward with

the war and saving them and . . . Luccan reminds me a little of Thantrel." A few fae on the street said our names. The Valkyrja took up their positions, and my sister wiped the tears from her eyes before they fell.

"What about it?" I pressed.

She got as close to me as possible. No longer did snow line the streets. Nor did frost cling to the buildings. A coolness lingered in the air today, but not enough to wear a cloak, and I felt our closeness as our shoulders touched.

"I want the mating bond," she whispered after a sleigh rolled by on new wheels that were more appropriate to a place without snow. "I feel like such a fool for denying myself. Denying him. *Us*."

"This is excellent news." I smiled at her, not wanting to state the obvious.

"It will be once we get them back."

"What changed your mind?"

"Since Eygin, I've been slowly coming around." She exhaled sharply, her edge still there. Still covering up a person who cared deeply for people. "Even if he is insufferable sometimes."

I shook my head.

"Then we got here, and I couldn't help but seek him out. Want to kiss him." She allowed herself a small smile. "Together we felt so right, and the more I got to know him, the more I realized he was perfect for me."

"He's a great person."

"Not bad on the eyes either." A smug expression took over her features. "We look amazing together."

I laughed, and the sound startled me. Since Vale and Thantrel had been taken, I'd felt so little joy.

"We'll get them back soon," Thyra added. "We have to. I have to tell Thantrel that I accept him."

My throat tightened at that image. "Stars, Thyra, I can't wait for them to be back with us."

"For us to make our enemies pay," she murmured, her voice full of fire.

CHAPTER 45

ISOLDE

The sun was breaking on the horizon when we entered the castle in Bitra.

Once our mother's ancestral house, imagery of the aura owls struck me the moment I stepped foot in the castle. My lips parted as I took in so much more that was out of place given the current owner.

The House Skau colors of blue and copper provided the sitting room with a pleasant ambience. Bookshelves lined each wall, and meticulously curated tapestries and paintings hung between each shelf. A single polished white statue of a female faerie stood by the windows, an aura owl perched on her raised hand. I knew little of the dead gods, but even I knew she represented a fae version of the goddess Mimeil. She had been the goddess that House Skau, also called the house of scholars, worshipped above all others.

"I think his guilt got the better of him," Thyra said after she caught me staring at the stony owls above the hearth. "I didn't understand that when I was here before."

Indeed. Not only had Queen Inga demolished House Falk by toying with our father's mind, but her actions had brought about the downfall of our mother's house too. They'd all died for their loyalty to Harald Falk. I inhaled, as if trying to breathe in that lost family, but got only the faintest hints of brewed tea and charred wood in the fireplace.

"Move along," Arie spoke with a soft command in his tone.

Lord Riis, Luccan, Arie, Clem, and Anna had arrived an hour ago to prepare the castle. Now Arie was in charge of keeping order.

For his part, Luccan sat in a chair, his entire focus on the gateway. I took heart that he was not already sweating and hoped he could continue to work his magic long enough for the entire army to pass through.

My sister and I moved out of the way, making room for those who would join us. As leaders of this war, we had walked through together. Just the two of us, a symbol of our unity. Thousands of soldiers and horses, gryphons, and our pegasi waited behind us, the line so long it extended from the brothel in the heart of Myrr to Ramshold Castle where masses of soldiers waited.

Bac, Aleksander, Livia, and our Valkyrja came next, the pegasi and a few gryphons at their side. Twenty seconds, the allotted time between waves of people, went by and more arrived. Some on gryphons, some on horses, some on foot. All armed to the teeth.

"Princesses?" a voice I did not recognize spoke.

I turned to find an ancient fae standing at the door, a tea tray in his shaking hands. At the sight of me and

Thyra, he let out a soft breath. "You look so much like them. Your parents."

"Thank you," I replied as we crossed the room to the servant. "You met them?"

"My daughter attended your mother before she left for the White Tower." The male gave a sad smile, maybe thinking that our mother's journey to become a healer had been interrupted by meeting our father. "I didn't know the old king, but there are many paintings of him. Though they're not on display here."

"Of course not." Thyra took a cup and poured herself some tea. I did the same. Sleep had not come easily the night before, and I'd likely need many more cups by the end of the day. "Lord Riis has informed the household of what's happening?"

The servant nodded. "I'm in full support."

"Well, that's good." Thyra grinned. "I'd hate to think what he'd say or do if you weren't."

Unease flickered across his face. "Dissenters would be locked up, but Lord Riis is not cruel, so they'd not be mistreated." The servant added as his gaze drifted over us, back to those owls. "That being said, my loyalty will always be to House Skau. Which means I am loyal to you two."

Thyra peered at him with interest. She'd been here before, during the heist at the Bitra coinary. Had she seen the servant then? Something told me no—that they'd done their best to be seen by as few as possible.

"What's your name?" I asked.

"Hátlu, Master of Household. For House Skau, and now House Riis."

"Isolde," I said, in case he didn't know which of us was which, which seemed all too likely considering few had seen us and known us by our birth names since we were toddlers.

"And so you're Princess Thyra," Hátlu said. "It's my pleasure to meet you both."

"Can you show us where the command is?" Thyra asked. "And send others to move the soldiers, gryphons, and horses into quarters where they may wait and rest until we're ready to move on?"

It was dawn, but about a third of the force had been up for hours already. They needed to get sleep when possible.

"Servants are already in the grand hall waiting. Food and drink are prepared, as are cots and bedrolls. As for command, I'll take you there."

After instructing Livia to take our pegasi to the stables, we followed Hátlu with our Valkyrja in our wake. I could not help but notice that the rest of the household did not all seem as happy to see us. Most watched us with interest —though some showed blatant distrust in their eyes. Did they see us and think we were more like our father than our mother? Mad and cruel?

I wasn't sure, but as we continued through the castle, the variety of looks we received were impossible to ignore. So much so that I felt great relief when we entered the study where Lord Riis waited. That was until I saw the expression of distress on his face.

"What happened?" I asked as Hátlu shut us inside the room of gleaming wood and shelves of books lining the wall. Bottles of liquor littered the small table behind the lord's desk. One I recognized as Dragon Fire.

Lord Riis held up a piece of paper, his hand trembling.

I still could not help but feel revulsion towards him, though it had lessened somewhat since Inga's death.

"News came," Lord Riis said. "All the way from Avaldenn, and I fear it's spreading quite fast. By design, of course."

"What is it?" Thyra cut across the room in five long steps. She took the page from Lord Riis and sucked in a breath. "So, it has begun."

I joined my sister, and when I peered down at the page, my heart dropped. A royal decree. One claiming Thyra and I as dangerous shadow wielders. Of course, there was no mention at all of the Shadow King. I had no idea how Magnus and Rhistel were going to present that tidbit to the kingdom, but the tone would be different from the article in front of me.

"There's no reason to wait any longer," Thyra said. "We have to release what we know of Rhistel. It will only help our cause. Might even make it easier to get into the city and take control."

Now that Inga was dead, there was no reason to withhold that information because it would not harm her. Some might even question if Vale was being controlled and try to help him.

"We'll do that now." I turned to go to the door. To send someone to find a scribe who could draft an official notice. Many notices. And then send those off from the aviary.

Before I took two steps, Lord Riis spoke again. "There's more. Something worse."

My spine straightened at his tone, solemn. Fearful.

I twisted, arched an eyebrow. "Worse?"

The high lord let out a long breath. "My sources in Avaldenn sent word. And if what they tell me is true, we may well lose much of the Virtoris Armada by tomorrow."

CHAPTER 46

ISOLDE

I stared at the map stretched across the circular table, so new the vellum still smelled strongly of the tanning solution.

"The Royal Nava is sailing along the coast." Bac's finger trailed along the northern coast of the kingdom. "And you think they'll hide within these islands?"

"It seems the perfect location to sit and wait." Qildor examined the map with an eye for combat strategy. "To hatch a trap."

"The Shivering Sea is not so big in this area." Lord Riis drew a line from Virtoris Island to the coast.

"King Magnus's ship is making excellent time," Aleksander added on the back of a yawn. At my insistence, the skin-changer had slept through the previous night, but he still looked exhausted. Even for a fylgjarn it wasn't natural to be in another creature's head so persistently. "It's been a couple of hours since I slipped behind Arla's eyes, but they could be north of us as early as tomorrow night."

"How?!" Thyra asked. "The journey from the mage court to Avaldenn should take four or five days."

"Mages travel with him," Aleksander replied. "Arla can't get too close, but I'd bet anything that they're using enchantments to move the boats faster."

Lord Riis nodded. "Mage merchant sailors are renowned for working such enchantments."

The Virtoris Armada could face not one fleet, but two. That wasn't even considering the threat of the mages on board the ships. We might lose most of our sea power. A great house. Those Sayyida and Vidar loved, and possibly even my friends themselves.

Across the table, Saga stood, silent and stoic, though I saw the fear in the taut lines of her body. I suspected she too was thinking of losing Sayyida.

"We can't let this happen," I breathed.

"I have a few larger ships at the coastal towns that sail under my banner." Lord Riis pointed out the areas where the ships would be. "Not many, but we could use the merchant ships to assist House Virtoris."

"Is it possible to get there in time?" I asked, trying to determine the distance from Bitra to the coast.

"We'll have to fly."

Which meant no army. Just fae who could fly, whether by their own steam or on the backs of gryphons and Rynni. We'd brought some of House Balik's gryphons in addition to our own and the few that Lord Riis still had on hand for his soldiers. That meant we had about fifty. Not enough.

"Can soldiers fly that far on wing?" I asked.

No way I could, but I'd been flying a very short time. Perhaps soldiers trained for this?

"With breaks, many can. But not all, of course. Some fae races do not have wings at all," Caelo said. "We're lucky that the weather is warm enough to fly for extended periods now. Perhaps to prevent fatigue and save their wings for battle, they should rotate their breaks on the gryphon's or Rynni's back?"

"And how many soldiers have come through the gateway as of now?" Thyra asked.

"Over seven hundred at last count. That was nearly an hour ago," Lord Balik said. "Luccan is holding strong."

"And if we don't go?" Thyra asked. "Will the Virtoris fleet truly be destroyed? Can't we send a raven to tell them to retreat?"

"We can." Lord Riis cleared his throat, "however, there's no guarantee the king won't send ships to their island to fight. That would keep them away from Avaldenn during the actual battle for the capital."

When we'd need them again to pummel the king's forces from the sea. No matter which direction we chose, we gave up a slight advantage or put our allies in great danger.

Thyra pressed her hands onto the table. "Isolde and I need to speak. The rest of you discuss every contingency. Every pitfall we may encounter, as well as every way we can succeed. Saga, join us?"

The princess cocked her head but recovered quickly and nodded.

I, however, continued to stare at my sister. She had experience with actual battles, small though they may be compared to what was to come. I had almost none. Around this table stood a group of lords, knights, and soldiers who knew better. What was she doing?

"I don't think—"

"Come," Thyra pulled me by the arm. "We'll convene in two hours' time."

We left the room and found Hátlu waiting, ready to fulfill our needs. Saga joined us, and our Valkyrja, all five, fell into a circle around us.

"Hátlu, is there a potions workshop?" Thyra asked.

"Of course."

"Take us there."

"What in the nine kingdoms are we doing?" I asked Thyra as we began walking.

"We're going to use the Frør Crown."

"The Crown?" I blinked, understanding where she was going but not how she believed we'd get there. "You mean the one that hasn't worked for me since the day I found it? And only works for you when you're sleeping?"

"Yes."

"*Stunning* idea."

Thyra arched her eyebrows. "Sarcasm is really more my thing."

By the dead gods, she was killing me.

"*How*?" I pressed.

"Saga told us that seers sometimes use a potion to ease themselves into visions. Isn't that right, Saga?"

"Yes," the princess answered.

"*She* hasn't even used that yet!" I added. "And she said it's very dangerous."

"So is losing the most powerful fleet in Winter's

Realm. Or giving up our only advantage and not marching west." Thyra cut me a glance. "We have to choose, and I'm going to use every instrument at our disposal." She patted the bag laid across her hip. As it so often had, the Frør Crown rested inside. "It must have worked for our family in the past, even if we, to my knowledge, have no seers after the one rumored to have created the Hallow."

She wasn't wrong there. After Saga had told us of her vision, we'd had the Scholars research our family tree. According to the records, there had been one renown seer many thousands of turns ago. He'd been the first to wear the Frør Crown, so we assumed that he'd also created it. Perhaps with the intent for his descendants to use the Hallow. Why else would a family better known for elemental magic keep such a thing? Revere it even?

I loosed a breath thick with frustration. "Let's hope they have that potion in stock."

The workshop was near the healing sanctuary. Healers often needed potions, even those that had little to nothing to do with their profession. As we strode by the sanctuary, I prayed that we wouldn't find ourselves inside it after what we planned to do.

Thyra approached the potion maker on duty, a very young dryad who looked shocked to see us. She told him what we needed, and he disappeared into the back rooms.

"Are we sure this is the best way?" I looked to Saga instead of my stubborn twin.

"Not at all," Saga muttered. "It's completely mad but, given the circumstances, it might also make sense."

"We'll be careful," Thyra assured me. "Take a half dose each."

I arched my eyebrows at her.

"Why doesn't Saga take it?" I asked. "She's a real seer."

"The powers of the Frør Crown are closely tied to the Falk line," Saga answered. "And yes, while I have some Falk blood, you two have more. I don't mind trying, but I think it will work better for you."

"Wonderful," I muttered.

Thyra blew out a humorless laugh. "If the Crown is going to do anything, we need it to be now. We need to know how to proceed. Our mates' lives may depend on it —not to mention the outcome of this war. Lives lost."

Of course I wanted to do what would bring Vale to my side, but in that moment, an image of Sayyida and Vidar emerged most clearly. Their mother, their other siblings, and countless sailors loyal to their house, waited across the sea to slow down the king. To fight for us.

On the other side of the coin, fae gathered in Bitra, prepared to march west and fight to take Avaldenn before the king arrived with more soldiers. For my sister and me to secure the throne.

No matter what we did, fae would die.

Thyra pulled the Frør Crown from her bag. The amethysts glittered in the flickering torchlight of the workshop, distracting me.

"I've spent so much time cursing that crown," I said, "that I almost forgot how beautiful it is."

"A piece of art." Thyra's eyes shone with equal reverence and distrust as she studied the Hallow. "And perhaps today it will give us useful information."

The potion maker emerged from the back, a vial of shimmering white liquid in his hand. He came to stand before us and bowed.

"Have you seen anyone use this before?" Saga asked the dryad.

"Once."

"And?"

"I don't know what you mean."

"Should they sit down to use it? Is it a violent potion? Did it *work*?"

Her basic questions reinforced just how little Saga knew about the potion. A rock formed in my belly.

"The seer sat before she took it and sank into a vision. The ordeal looked as natural to her as breathing, but she was a well-known seer."

My spine straightened. "We should find her, to see how it felt."

"She went to the afterworld three moons ago."

"Oh," I trailed off. "Apologies."

"I didn't know her well. Only met her once."

Thyra and I exchanged looks, and she cleared her throat. "Very well then. You're dismissed."

He returned to the back of the workshop.

"Well, that was awkward," I muttered.

"We should stagger drinking it." Thyra held up the vial. "Do you want me to go first? Or you?"

"Me."

Thyra's lips flattened.

"Not because I think it won't work for you," I said.

"After that one night, I'm sure it will. It was a protective instinct. But if the potion harms me, you shouldn't drink it. After all, we're about to march, or fly, into battle, and we all know you're the better fighter. We need you more."

Her face softened. "You don't have to protect me all the time."

"I haven't. But in this instance, I want to."

"Even if this is my idea that you don't agree with?"

"And Thyra is more apt to be able to have a vision?" Saga added, eyebrows pinched together.

"Yes." Crazy, but it was true. She was my sister, and I'd do anything for her.

Thyra held out the vial. "Bottoms up."

I took the potion, uncorked it, and drank half, tasting the salty, herby liquid as it went down my throat. "Not bad."

Thyra chuckled. "Here."

She'd extracted the Frør Crown from the bag and held it out to me. I took the Hallow, the metal cold against my fingers, and placed it on my head.

"Just ask, right?" I settled into a spindly wooden chair that creaked beneath my weight.

Saga nodded. "Ask the Crown to show you a possible future. We'll see if anything happens."

I closed my eyes and took a deep breath, allowing the potion a bit longer to weave through my veins.

Show me what will happen if we choose to go to Avaldenn. If we march as we planned and leave House Virtoris to fight on their own.

My stomach twisted at the words. I hated them but thought it was better to be exact. A second passed. Two.

Three. I was beginning to think this was all going to turn out to be nothing when the darkness behind my eyes vanished.

Water sprayed across my face, cold and hard as pebbles. Wind whipped; the sound of the air screaming punctuated only by cries of pain. Pleas. Sounds of the dying.

My heart hammered. I stood on the ship's deck, dozens of other vessels around me. As the boat lunged and swayed, I slid and caught myself by slamming my belly into the railing.

I groaned, but the sound came out as a whisper compared to the bellow that rang through the night air. Spinning, I saw Vale emerge from behind a mast and piled up supplies on the far side of the deck. My heart leapt, and I yelled out his name, but he didn't turn.

Because I wasn't on the ship. I was seeing how things would unfold, like when Thyra had viewed the past as an observer. Nothing I could do or say would change what I saw, and as Vale fought five sailors wearing Virtoris colors, I hated that limitation. Hated that I knew Vale was fighting against our side because he had no free will. That he was slicing and stabbing at those sailors on Rhistel's orders.

I hated it even more when a swell rushed up, unseen by any of those on the far deck, and tried to sweep us overboard.

"No!" I screamed right before the water collided with me, shoving me back against the railing. I grabbed on, the force of the water working against me, trying to drag me to the deep. Water filled my mouth, went down my throat, and then air saved me as the wave abated.

I couldn't die here, but stars, it had felt like I might. And as I ran across the ship, to where Vale and the others had vanished, I felt as though I was still fighting for my life.

I gripped the opposite rail and peered overboard. The Shivering Sea thrashed and churned, the water a dangerous gray. The clouds above hung dark and ominous. Three ships carrying the banner of the sea serpent were actively sinking and many more had caught flame. Torches on the sea. Fates, what had we done by asking House Virtoris to hold off the king?

Another massive swell rose up before I found Vale clinging to the railing, and I braced, fighting against the water once more. Once it was gone, I wiped the salty water from my eyes and looked for him again. But Vale was gone.

I leapt. Wind caught in my wings, but I pushed forward, searching, seeking.

Hundreds of bodies dotted the water, none of them Vale. Many were already dead. Cold dread gripped me at that thought. Vale could swim, but he had a terrible fear of water. Would he still with Rhistel controlling his mind?

I lowered and circled, trying to keep out of the reach of the water that undulated. Another ship approached, and I rose again.

I wished I had not. From higher up I spotted my friends on a different ship. Vidar and Sayyida had made it north in time to fight, and the pair stood back-to-back, twelve shadow figures closing in on them.

"No!" I tugged at my shadow magic.

But I wasn't there. I was in a chair in Bitra. Safe and warm and not on the ship! Not present when those same shadows speared through my friend's bodies and they slumped to the deck. Dead in an instant.

My wings failed me, and I plummeted into the sea. Into a tangle of bodies. Flailing, I pushed off the bodies. Blood pounding in my ears, I heaved myself up onto a barrel that had washed off the deck of a ship. I'd situated myself over the wet wood, and was stretching my wings, feeling for an injury, when I spotted him.

Vale's hair spread out around his head, his dark wings wide as *though he was stretching them. He was face down in the water. Unmoving. And as another massive wave crashed over him.*

When the wave was gone, so was he.

A scream tore out of me, so powerful it hurt my throat. I flung myself off the barrel and swam. Swam for my mate. Swam—a stinging sensation radiated across my face.

I was back in the workshop. Thyra stood before me, hand out, terror bulging in her eyes.

"You're here! You're safe!" She threw her arm around me and held me tight. "I'm sorry I slapped you, but we took the Crown off, and you didn't come out, and I panicked. I—by the stars, you're soaked."

I was, but not from water. From sweat.

My spine straightened, and I caught sight of the Crown on the floor. Thank the stars.

Unlike the only other vision I'd been given, I did not think I would have been able to rip myself out of that one. It had felt far more real, more visceral, than the first. Was it? Or was that just the Crown manipulating me?

"I saw Vale drown. Saw the sea take him." I swallowed. I could almost smell the sea water still, and I'd never forget the vision of Vale slipping beneath the waves. Manipulation or not, I couldn't take the chance that the events I'd seen would come true. "And House Virtoris wasn't winning either. They were sinking. Dying."

Saga clapped both hands over her mouth, and my sister's breath caught.

"We're not going to Avaldenn." I pushed Thyra away and stood. "We're going north."

INTERLUDE

LORD ROAR LISIKA, WARDEN OF THE WEST, HOUSE OF THE SNOW LEOPARD

The sun set over the horizon as Lord Roar Lisika looked out over the bow of the warship. His scouting ships had already reported that in the distance vessels flew the grayish-blue sails of House Virtoris and blocked much of the eastern entrance to the Shivering Sea.

Soon they'd meet those vessels, and destroy them. Without support from the Virtoris Armada, Roar doubted that whatever forces Isolde and her sister had amassed would be capable of breaking through the army surrounding the capital.

"Remain hugging the coast, Lord Lisika?" asked the captain of the vessel Roar had claimed as his own.

Fifty vessels sailed with Lord Lisika from Avaldenn. According to the king's letter, which had arrived in the small hours of the morning, he was bringing another fifty ships weighed down with mage fighters. The rest of the Nava remained near Avaldenn, ready to take on the Falks whenever they came.

"Until we see a fight begin, we stay close to the land.

In fact, go behind the islands when we reach them." He knew there were some not far to the east, in Lord Riis's territory. They would provide cover and protect them but were also not far from where the action would take place.

"And when we anchor, set up a night watch."

"One is already lined up, my lord."

"Very good. Dismissed." Roar didn't think the entire Virtoris fleet would come their way, not when they had likely been instructed to wait. But that didn't mean a ship or two wouldn't venture west and try to pick off some of his fleet. Or sabotage them. Best not to give the Lady of Ships the chance.

So tonight they would remain vigilant. And tomorrow, when two fleets converged, they would require every vessel to sink the House of the Sea Serpent to the frigid gray depths.

CHAPTER 47
ISOLDE

My thighs ached from flying on Arava through the afternoon and night and deep into the following day. When I finally got off her back, I would not be surprised if my fighting leathers and armor kept their riding form.

In the distance, the sun was slowly arching its way toward the horizon, and the gray blue of the Shivering Sea spread out before us. Seemingly never-ending. Dark clouds blanketed the most distant waters, in a way I did not like. A way that reminded me too much of the vision the Frør Crown had oh so kindly blessed me with.

If I never put that bleeding crown on again, it will be too soon.

An astonishing two thousand soldiers had passed through Luccan's gateway before it closed abruptly, all on its own. Luccan collapsed from the effort, and Arie, with the help of soldiers, rushed his brother to the healer's sanctuary. Anna, Clem, and Duran had remained at Ramshold to aid in Luccan's recovery.

After informing the high lords of what I'd seen and

announcing that we were going north, things moved quickly. We'd gathered our allies and soldiers and taken to the winds.

Five hundred flew with us. Among them were a mix of rebels, soldiers from House Balik and House Riis, and even a few dwarves from Dergia.

Those who had no wings had to ride on gryphons or dragonback the entire time, which greatly limited their numbers. If one didn't have wings to transport oneself, they had to be *exceptional* in magic or combat.

But even having wings didn't mean a fae would join us. Only those who could fly for hours on end were chosen. In this way we limited the number of rotations on and off the gryphons and dragon, all of which had to be completed in the air.

Thus far, we'd allowed only three stops to eat and sleep just long enough so we would not be useless when we reached the coast. Some would call the journey under such conditions horrific.

They'd be right.

The one glaring question that had plagued me during the journey north was: What happened to Thantrel? He'd not been featured in my vision, something Thyra had fixated on. Did she expect the worst? That he was dead and that was why he had not been fighting?

I cast a glance to my right, where Thyra flew on Lasvin. That steely glint haunted my twin's eyes. That promise of vengeance.

"We should descend," I shouted into the wind.

Caelo had spoken with a few ravens as we flew. They told him many large boats were hiding behind the islands off the coast. According to the ravens, the vessels were out of place—not fishing or merchant boats.

Just as we'd predicted. They had to be the Royal Nava, waiting for the king's ships to arrive. Then, and only then, when the armada had moved to take on the king's vessels would the Nava ships add their weight to the fight.

"I estimate we're about an hour's ride on foot to the coast," Thyra replied. "Aleksander? Where's Arla and the mage fleet now?"

Prince Thordur flew with Aleksander. The dwarf gripped my brother tightly as he joined with his hawk again. A safety precaution. In the moments that Aleksander took on Arla's eyes, he wasn't always in complete control of his body.

Aleksander returned to us and locked stares with me. "Judging by the landmarks Arla can see, they'll be here in three or four hours. They seem to have put on more speed. Whether by current or magic, I don't know."

"What if the hidden ships leave before we can get to them?" Thyra asked me.

"I can't say, but we don't have a choice but to eventually descend and get closer on foot."

Sian and ten other limiters were doing their best to create an illusion at the front of our forces, making us look like a storm cloud. However, Sian had clarified that with five hundred moving beings, it was impossible to create a perfect illusion and the closer we got to the Nava ships, the more likely it was they'd spot the chinks in our armor.

"And we need food and a little rest," I added because a quick glance at the fliers and riders revealed bloodshot eyes and sagging bodies. The moment we touched down, we'd drink and eat. If they could sleep for an hour, that was as much rest as they'd get, and by the looks of many, it wasn't enough. Then, we'd be on the move again.

Thyra jerked a nod, and together we raised our hands. Our aerial army slowly descended, doing our best to remain behind the illusion.

The woods came at us fast, the tall trees reaching for the setting sun. Pine limbs brushed my legs, clad in leather and segmented armor, and when Arava touched down, it was with a satisfied snort.

I patted her neck. "I suggest sleeping. We'll find water nearby, and I'll have someone bring it to you."

Arava knelt and then lay on the ground. Lasvin joined her sister, the black and white pair cuddling together. A soldier from Lord Riis's house approached to care for the pegasi, but I waved him off. It was irresponsible, but they needed sleep more than a good brush down.

"Princess Isolde! Princess Thyra!" a voice called out. I twisted to find Lord Riis waving us over, a map in hand.

These were his lands, and he knew them well, but not perfectly. I knew them not at all, so I joined Lord Riis, Lord Balik, his sons, and many of my friends.

"We're about right here." Lord Riis pointed to a spot within the woods. "A stream is close by, and I suggest filling skins and letting the animals drink before we leave because we'll be walking away from the water, not with it."

"That town closest to the islands. Do you think it's safe?" Arie asked, studying the map of his father's lands.

"I doubt the members of the Royal Nava will have left their ships at all. They need to be ready at a moment's notice. So it's likely the town is safe, and merely curious as to what's happening. However, we can't be sure they're loyal, even if they are my people. We go the wide way around."

Just because the high lord in the area was loyal to my sister and me, did not mean that every person in the area was. This part of the kingdom was not so far from Avaldenn. Surely by now the town had received word we were shadow wielders. As we released the news of Rhistel being a whisperer right before we flew north, we hadn't had time to equally damage our opponent's reputation among the masses.

The briefing ended, but before I left the huddle, Thyra gripped my wrist.

"I want to use the Crown."

I blinked. "You brought it?"

"In Lasvin's saddlebag. Couldn't risk having it on my person while fighting, but it'll be fine in there."

She'd said that she'd keep it in one of Lord Riis's safes because how would *any* crown be useful in a battle? When in all the nine kingdoms had she changed her mind?

"Why risk it?"

She swallowed. "I didn't get to because after your vision we went right into preparing to leave. But you didn't see Thantrel, and I couldn't get that out of my head . . ."

I felt like the worst sister in all the nine kingdoms.

"Of course, you want to see if you can find him. I do too. You have your potion?"

"Also in the saddlebag. I'll get it."

"And I'll have Astril fill our skins and retrieve water for Arava and Lasvin. But do you need to eat first?" Many of the soldiers were already sitting down and inhaling their food. Thyra and I had not eaten in hours, and as much as I wanted her to find some reassurance about Thantrel, we also needed to keep our energy up.

"I can eat as I walk."

While Thyra went to get the Crown and her potion, I sought Saga. Not because she could do anything once the vision took over, if it did, but because Saga gave me a sense of peace when it came to seer magic. Spotting her in the crowd wasn't difficult, and when I called out her name, she turned. I waved her over.

"What's going on?" Saga asked.

Usually poised and well dressed, my friend appeared disheveled, and even if she made her fighting leathers and armor look good, they still did not look *right* on her. She was no warrior, but had insisted on coming, anyway.

"Thyra wants to use the Crown to see if she can find Thantrel. Stay with us?"

"Of course."

I made quick arrangements. Once done, our other Valkyrja created a circle around Thyra, Saga, and me, cutting us off from the others.

"Bottoms up," Thyra sat on a large rock, drank her potion and then reached for the Crown, which she'd set next to her. "Hope for the best."

I took my sister's hand, and with the other, she placed the Crown on her head and closed her eyes. My fingers tightened around hers, and while I couldn't know what was happening in Thyra's head, I was certain I felt the vision take her.

She gripped me so tightly her knuckles whitened. I

cast a glance at Saga. That had been fast. Even faster than the Crown had worked for me.

"Because she's a dreamer," Saga said.

"No," Thyra hissed. "Get out! Get out!"

"Do I say something?" I whispered.

"Wait," Saga replied. "You'll know if it gets *really* bad."

I thanked the stars that I wasn't a natural-born seer. My winter magic might have been volatile to start, but it seemed far more straightforward than Saga's powers.

"By the gods, get out!" Thyra shrieked loudly enough for others to turn our way. "I will not let my mate die!"

"She's found him," I said. "I think it's enough. That's what she wanted."

"Agreed. She'll need time to calm down. Get her out."

I removed the Crown from Thyra's head, passing it to Saga before grabbing both of my sister's hands. I wanted her to know someone was there when she emerged from the vision.

Her ice-blue eyes found mine. "He was in a cabin, and it was flooding, but he wouldn't move. He was going to let the sea take him, and I had to watch!"

"Rhistel," I put the pieces we'd seen together. "He must send Vale out to fight but kept Thantrel tucked away. It's brilliant because it splits us up."

"Rhistel *is* brilliant." Saga looked at her boots, spattered with mud that the melted snow had left behind. "He's many other things too, most of them awful, but don't underestimate his intelligence. Did you see anything else? Guards? Traps?"

"I was in the room right away. It worked so quickly. I didn't think to look outside."

"On the same ship as Magnus and Rhistel, if I had to guess," I said. "I doubt they'll be difficult to find."

My sister stood, determination mixed with the faintest glint of murder in expression. "Well, once we find Thantrel and rip him out of the trouble he's in, the king and prince had better watch their backs because I'm coming for them."

CHAPTER 48

ISOLDE

The tang of salt teased my nostrils, quickening my pulse. On foot we would hit the coast within a half hour. Far less time if we flew. Which meant, our march under the cover of spruce trees was over. It was time to rise. I held up a hand.

Movement ceased, and when I turned, I found five hundred pairs of eyes watching me.

Exhaling, I removed my white fur cloak, a luxurious item that indicated my station. Thyra did the same and together we lay the furs on the ground. They'd kept us warm and protected from the wind while flying, but a heavy cloak would only help drag us to the depths if we were tossed in the sea. If we survived, we'd return for them.

I mounted Arava as Thyra got on Lasvin's back. Together we rose in the air, still covered by the thick trees and the illusion, but high enough so those in the back could see me.

"From here we fly," I said loud and clear as the pegasi

made circles above the small army. My voice carried on the sea breeze, and my silver wings unfolded behind me. Thyra flew at my side. "This may be the only battle we face against House Aaberg and their mage allies."

Stars, I prayed it was.

"This day may keep your families safe. Keep battles from your doorstep. Keep your pantries plentiful. All we need to do is win—and we have the advantage." I pointed in the direction of the ships. "They don't know we're coming."

"They believe Isolde and I will march to Avaldenn," Thyra's voice joined mine. "They think we'll play by *their* rules." She snorted. "Don't they realize we've been making our own all our lives?"

Rebel fists filled the air.

"Don't they know that when King Magnus killed our families and took the throne of Winter's Realm, he damned so many? For decades he did not control winter, and thousands suffered. All for his pride. His egotistical desire." Thyra's chin lifted. "Don't let the melted snow fool you. If King Magnus thought bringing it back would suit his purposes, he would. But we, my sister and I and all our people, will suffer no longer. We'll take down the White Bear and bring justice back to this land. Together we'll *all* make Winter's Realm a place of dreams. A land that thrives alongside its people."

Fists raised, and my heart lifted. While Thyra and I had the support of many lords, it wasn't like we'd spoken to each and every person. That was an impossible feat.

Now, however, we could see the support on so many faces. See the disdain for the current monarch. In the rebel's faces, I also saw a love for Thyra. And while I didn't think they loved me yet, they respected me. I caught the same respect in the eyes of many others and marveled.

Maybe the fact we wielded shadows was not such a horrible thing? The news had been released and these people didn't seem to care. Others like Geiravor and Yrsa had not either. But were they the rare ones? Or the many?

"The moment we leave this soil, we change the course of history. We will grasp the stars' attention!" I shouted. "We'll make them listen. Make their wills bend to ours!"

"Down with the king!" Qildor shouted, and a ripple of agreement rang out.

"And we'll bring Prince Vale and Thantrel home!" added Filip, sitting astride a gryphon not far away. "They've believed in many of you. Fought for your families. Forget not that we fight for a better kingdom, but also for those who have fallen into hardships. Fallen into enemy hands!"

"For Prince Vale!" a weathered Balik soldier agreed. "The fair and just Warrior Bear!"

"For Thantrel Riis." A faerie soldier clad in the black and red of House Riis raised a fist. "Never has a kinder— if a bit rascally—male lived."

More agreement. *Many* grins from those wearing House Riis colors.

"To making the stars listen!" Palms up, I lifted my hands in the air.

The army joined, flying up to our level, preparing to attack. Behind the crowd, Rynni transformed into a dragon. She wasn't a trained soldier, but she'd helped carry many through the journey here. Now, she'd follow, attack when possible, and when necessary, use her single blow of fire to devastating effect.

"For Winter's Realm!" Thyra called, and Lasvin shot to the sky.

I ascended with her and the moment we burst from the cover of the trees, my attention locked on the ships. Fifty huge vessels hiding behind a handful of islands, waiting for King Magnus to appear. Waiting to annihilate the Virtoris fleet from both the west and east. We soared to meet them, far faster in the air than on land. The distance halved in minutes.

"Incoming!" I screamed when the first blast of fire came rushing our way.

The army forked, seconds before the long stream of fire flew so close that I felt the sizzle of the flame as we adjusted course.

"Are we sure they weren't anticipating us?" Freyia yelled. As ever, the Valkyrja flew closest to my twin and me, our protectors. Our most trusted.

"Can't see how!" Thyra shouted back.

I couldn't either. We knew from how information had made its way north that King Magnus had eyes on us in Myrr. It was plausible that messages had winged their way to the loyalists, telling them that we had forces on the move. That we did not seem to be marching but trying another tactic. After all, it was difficult to contain all the ravens going out of homes and aviaries. So difficult that no one in Myrr had bothered to try.

But the general population of Myrr hadn't known where we'd been heading. They had only seen a line of soldiers coming out of a brothel, but each male and female in arms had been told to stay quiet about our destination.

Had someone told? Or was this spray of fire magic simply the Nava being prepared for an attack on any and all fronts?

Really, it did not matter. All that mattered was that we closed the gap. That we avoided the many streams of fire coming at us and seized those ships.

"Fly like the wind, Arava." I leaned over her midnight mane.

Her wings beat the air as if the wind had insulted her, and we picked up speed. My mare wove through the assaults, and I felt the glint of delight inside her at showing what she could do. How well she flew. Her power and might on display for all to witness.

We neared the ships, and I scanned below, searching for the lead vessel. It was easy enough to spot, as the largest ship with Aaberg blue sails and the house banner flew from atop the crow's nest, whipping in the wind.

"That one. Drop down a bit. I'll jump, and then you stay safe." I pointed, and Arava descended. She came in hot, and most of the sailors scattered, but a few remained. Those who must have thought they had magic strong enough to take on a pegasus.

Each one of them was mistaken.

Like dragons and ice giants and other wild creatures born of magic, a pegasi's hide was protective in more ways than one. Only the most powerful could penetrate my mare's skin.

The two attacks that landed bounced off Arava, and I retaliated in kind to those who tried to harm her, blasting them with icicles. By the time the sailors realized what was happening—that they stood no chance against us—it was too late.

I leapt from Arava's back, pulled Sassa's Blade from the scabbard, and fell upon my enemies with a frigid wind. They screamed and scattered as the gusts burned their skin, but not before I cut one down, my sword's sharp edge biting into his leg. A female whirled back, a metal throwing snowflake in her hand, but with a flick of my wrist she was frozen in place.

"I'm Isolde Falk," I declared, "and I claim this ship."

"To the afterworld with you, monster!" someone shouted back, and an arrow whizzed by.

Winged archers balanced on the horizontal poles above and two others in the crow's nest. Their distance would have kept them safe from me, but others in my army had spotted them too. My forces fell upon the archers and a few fae who had leapt into the air to fight, cutting them down, disarming them.

Bodies dropped to the deck with hard thuds, spattering the dark wood with blood. The smell of metal mixed with salt.

My throat tightened at the death, at knowing these males and females had probably done nothing wrong. Nothing but choosing to remain loyal to the king. I allowed my unease to pass through me, even as my blade arched and my magic blasted at one opponent, then the next. Another, another, another.

I spun and thrust and feinted and parried with strength that would make Vale proud. With every advance, I pictured his face. Pictured finding him and rescuing him, very much alive. Having his arms around me again.

Above, a few of my army still flew. Mostly gryphons and the pegasi and our archers. The winged creatures might be instrumental in a fast getaway, or in transporting the injured, and the archers would always be more effective from above.

On the decks, blood slicked the wood. I turned on my heel, taking the ship in a complete circle. That was when I saw a faerie I despised to the end of Isila and back.

Roar Lisika, his copper hair catching on the last rays of the sun, shot at opponents from the upper deck. He'd lost a leg, but that didn't negate his skill with a bow, and when five Riis soldiers ran at him, he did not hesitate. He shot. Hitting one. The other four swerved out of danger, only to come at him again, faster. However, seconds before they would have engaged the Warden of the West in swords, Roar shifted.

The leg he'd lost grew again, and I stiffened at the realization that his magic could render him whole in new forms. If I wasn't terrified for the soldiers, I'd have been in awe over the power.

But I *was* terrified. My blood pounded in my ears as Roar leapt at his enemies. Two claws met two soldiers, slicing them open. The other two darted away, but not fast enough.

His sharp teeth ripped one in half as he swiped at the other and punctured the fae in many places. Blood sprayed as both Riis soldiers collapsed.

I leapt into the air, determined that no one else should fall to him. Wind and the faintest sprinkle of rain began to beat against me as I soared for Roar. But before I got there, a white hawk dove from the sky and attacked the snow leopard's right eye.

I froze as a snarl erupted from the beast. Roar batted at his face. Arla was agile and fast, though, and she flew away, then back, attacking again. Drawing blood above Roar's eye.

I twisted and found Aleksander standing off to the side, watching with glee on his face. His expression told me there was history there. Something so poignant that he'd risk his hawk.

Not that Arla seemed to mind. After days of following a ship, she appeared to relish being on the attack.

Wait. Why is Arla here? She was following the king's ship, and they should not be here yet.

I lifted into the air, high enough to gaze out beyond the islands, towards the open sea. My stomach sank as a fleet of ships, at least a hundred strong, entered the Shivering Sea. We would not have time to meet with our allies and prepare for King Magnus had returned early.

CHAPTER 49
ISOLDE

We weren't ready.

Even worse, some of the Royal Nava's fleet had escaped our attack. At least twenty ships were sailing into the sea, towards the king's vessel—going to his aid.

House Virtoris's Armada was making its approach too, but between the mage ships escorting King Magnus and the Royal Nava's vessels, they were outnumbered.

We have to take the rest of these ships as fast as possible.

As a lord of the Sacred Eight, Roar was of the highest status aboard these ships, which meant he was in command. The sooner we took him out, the faster the sailors fighting for him would fold.

Aleksander had become distracted with two Nava sailors targeting him, but Arla continued her attack on Roar. As I soared to help, the hawk managed to hit the warden's eye, and the snow leopard let out a horrible sound. His paw shot up, batting dangerously close to the hawk. She swooped up and out of range.

The air around Roar shimmered. He was shifting again, and when Roar took his fae form, he lunged for his bow. Thanks to shifting magic, his quiver filled with arrows was already on his back. He nocked and loosed five arrows in rapid succession at the hawk. One came close to Arla. Too close. The hawk let out a screech and flew away.

Unfortunately for Roar, I had closed in, and he didn't see me coming. Sassa's Blade slashed, but Roar ducked just in time to avoid losing his head.

A smirk curled his lips as he rose, as blood poured from around his eye. The lid was mangled but it seemed that the eye was intact.

"My flying lessons paid off."

I sneered, and the shadows inside me shifted, yearning to break free. Perhaps I was a fool for not letting them, but using shadows, no matter the form, still drained me. This early in a fight, it was not wise to use up so much energy.

More than that, I couldn't deny that my ego wanted to defeat Roar and Magnus without this dark magic. I would save that pleasure for Érebo. Nothing would feel more right than killing him with the magic he'd forced to life within me.

"You have nothing to do with how strong I am," I retorted.

Roar laughed, the sound out of harmony with the chorus of battle on the decks of multiple ships. "I'm the *only* reason you are who you are." He tossed his bow to the side and pulled his sword. "Without me, you'd have died in the mountains trying to flee south. You would have been bled dry by a vampire or you might have just frozen to death. Maybe orcs would have been your end. The possibilities were endless for someone so weak."

"I suppose you did have your uses," I conceded. "Before you betrayed me, and I learned how snake-like you are."

"By the dead gods, Isolde, you're so ungrateful. The least you could have done was rise *with me*. Instead, look at what you've done. You've torn a kingdom in two. You and your idiot husband."

"My *mate*." I thrust the sword at him.

He had only one good leg and his eye was injured, but Roar's arms remained strong, and his grace and agility were impressive as always. Turns and turns of training among the strongest fae in the kingdom meant he was still a worthy opponent, and Roar deflected my attack with ease.

His lips curled into a snarl as he held out his own sword. "I should have known, shouldn't I? To fall for a lug like that when I was right in front of you. Offering you the world." He shook his head. "The stars truly can pair them."

"Get over it—with what little time you have left."

I thrust a wave of winter magic at him, and he retaliated in kind. I gauged his strength against mine. He hadn't been modest about his winter magic. Compared to the raging storm inside me, Roar possessed a light snowfall. A revelation I was sure that he was having too, as my magic rushed over him.

The vibration on the deck changed as he worked to negate the freeze I'd sent his way. He managed, but barely, judging by his blue lips and the way his hands trembled.

"You could try and run like you did before." I released the surge with a gasp. "Perhaps you can shift into something fishy and save your rotten skin?"

Taking the bait, he snarled and rushed me, sword arching high. I accepted the challenge, and our steel met in a dance. I spun out of an attack and rushed around a pole reaching skyward from the deck. Roar's sword bit into the wood as he chased me. I twisted to strike back, and in doing so I didn't see the pile of rope on the floor.

I tripped, and Sassa's Blade flew from my hands as I landed hard. Roar was there in an instant, bloodthirsty metal descending so fast all I could do was roll out of the way.

Not fast enough. His sword sliced off the tip of my left wing, and pain rushed through me like a tidal wave. Roar laughed at my shriek.

"I'll give it to Vale; he trained you well, but you're no warrior yet, Isolde." He kicked me in the stomach, and tears stung in my eyes as I tried to control the nausea rolling through me. Tried to go on. To get up and fight.

With one palm splayed on the ground, I pushed myself up, only for another kick to strike my lower back. I gasped and doubled over.

"This reminds me of the day we met." *Zuprian* steel met my neck and pressed into my skin. "You were on the ground looking so pathetic I could barely dare to believe my hunch about you might be right. And of course there was me standing there. Above you. As I should be." The blade dug harder into my skin. Blood welled and trickled. "I won't be saving you this time. I—"

Droplets sprayed against my face, Roar's blood, and

the sword's pressure on my neck vanished. I rolled again and jumped to my feet.

In the air, Thyra and Caelo fought sailors. My sister held her bow, and while she was engaged in fighting, she cast a glance over her shoulder, her face wild with fear. When she spotted me standing, I caught the barest flicker of relief.

A moan hit my ear, and I spun to find Roar on the deck, gripping his shoulder. Thyra had made a shot to save me. While in the middle of her own fight.

Heart racing, I searched for Sassa's Blade. The sunlight was nearly gone and with the crush of the night, ominous clouds were rolling in from the north where they already blanketed the sea and limited visibility.

Finally, I spotted the glint of my sword behind Roar. I lunged forward, but the bastard seemed to have expected my move and his own sword appeared, the blade arching.

My wings caught me, pulled me back, and I hissed through my teeth at the strain that single movement put on the injured wing.

With a chilled gust, Roar shoved me back into the mast. My head slammed into the wood, and I slid down. Stars filled my vision.

"I'll kill you!" a male voice cut through the haze, and the surrounding air moved as someone ran by me.

Roar laughed, and metal struck metal. Once. Twice. So many times.

I blinked, trying to regain my vision, and when the stars dissipated, leaving me able to see once more, I found Aleksander and Roar engaged in combat.

Arla circled above, but the hawk did not dare dive and

help Aleksander. Perhaps because they moved too fast for her to be sure where her talons would strike.

I groaned. I'd been so sure before. So cocky, but Roar had gotten me on my arse twice in short order. Embarrassment welled inside me, but I didn't allow it to thrive because what good would that do?

I may not be the best soldier in the army, or even on this ship, but I was still here. Still fighting. And I would not stop until I found Vale and Thantrel. Until Magnus and Rhistel floated at the bottom of the Shivering Sea and Érebo left this world one way or another.

I pushed to my feet. Swayed.

Shadow magic roiled inside me. Around blood, the shadows were even more active. More excited. The shadows had been waiting to be released since the start of the battle.

Now's your time, I thought as Roar's blade met Aleksander's belly.

INTERLUDE
KING MAGNUS AABERG, THE WHITE
BEAR, PROTECTOR OF WINTER'S REALM

The King of Winter's Realm stood on the upper deck, watching a ship bearing the sea serpent sail of House Virtoris shake with the force of a mage strike. A hole formed in the hull and the vessel sunk with a rapidity that made him smile.

A low laugh left his throat. "Fayeth's hubris seems misplaced. Is that all they've got?"

At his side, the King of Shadows let out a long hum. "They did not expect mages." He tilted his chin toward the sky.

The stars peeked through the fresh darkness, as if the dead gods were attempting to witness the events below. Well, they'd have little time to do so. Rain lashed at the decks, the beginning of the storm they'd seen on the horizon. "That being said, I have to disagree with your assessment. They're doing well. Two mage ships have gone to the depths"

The Winter King sneered. "Three of theirs compared

to two of ours. And I'm certain they have already sustained many more casualties."

Only a couple of the ships sailing with them had been overrun by enemies, and one of the sunken ships on the other side had been the lead vessel. The king would relish the memory of Lady Fayeth Virtoris soaring from the ship, her children at her back. They'd taken refuge on another vessel, slithering and hiding like the serpents they claimed as their own. But his forces would fish them out, and when they did, Magnus would make sure the traitors met their end at the bottom of the sea they loved so well.

"We could do more," Érebo stated. "*I* could do more."

"You should let him, Father," Rhistel added from his place a few paces away.

Magnus gave a noncommittal sound. The Shadow King and his heir had bonded these past days, and Magnus was certain Rhistel wished to see the might of shadows, just as Érebo relished watching Rhistel work. A mutual admiration that Magnus would keep a close eye on in the coming days.

That relationship aside, the king knew that all magic had limits. Fae tired, as any other creature did when they exerted their power. If Magnus and Érebo were to use shadows, the King of Winter wanted them to be used for the grand finale.

He would not have it said he won this battle only because of one ally.

"Not yet." The king tasted the salt of the sea in the air. Mixed with it was the undeniable tang of blood. "However, I do agree we need a change. A stunning moment in which to sow fear into their hearts." He made a show of thinking it over, though he already knew what the next step should be. "It's time to unleash another weapon."

Magnus locked eyes with Rhistel, Vale behind him, waiting to be commanded like a dog.

The Riis bastard was not there but locked and warded in a cabin. Currently, his mind was his own, for Rhistel could only control so many people at once, and only one fae to the degree they required during a battle.

"Send Vale in. Have him find the Lady of Ships and her children," Magnus said. "Kill them."

Rhistel nodded, and when Vale's hand fell upon the hilt of his borrowed sword, the king knew the command had been given. Would be followed without question, for Rhistel had done stunning work these past days. Terrifying to anyone with half a brain, but stunning nonetheless.

"And if the Falk sisters arrive?" Rhistel asked.

The moment only half of the Nava vessels had joined them in the battle, they'd known something was wrong. According to one sailor, the other half of the Nava ships were being commandeered behind the islands off the mainland. Lord Roar's vessel among them. The sailor claimed that the Warden of the West was engaged in battle. That a silver-haired female sought him out.

Who else could it be but Isolde Falk?

An unforeseen development, but truth be told, the king hoped Isolde finished off the high lord. Magnus was no idiot. He knew Roar wanted more than what he claimed to desire. He probably wanted the Crown of Winter, just like Isolde, making Roar a dangerous ally. Still, the king had not been able to deny Lord Roar, for his large army was too loyal to the High Lord of the West.

Had Magnus killed him, that army would no longer submit.

If someone on the other side of the war killed Roar, well, that was a different matter. And if it was Isolde Falk, all the better. Magnus could use that hatred to bind Roar's army to him and be free of the Warden of the West and every promise he'd made.

"If they survive the mage attacks. Have Vale find Isolde. He will take her life publicly." A deviation from their previous plan, but Magnus was willing to roll with the punches. He did not need to be the one to kill Isolde. Not when a spectacle would be far more impactful.

"The sister?" Rhistel asked, his face emotionless. He may not be of the king's blood, but Magnus had to admit Rhistel's ability to bury his emotions in times such as these made him an ideal heir. As did his ability to manipulate and control others.

"If she lives, bring her to me. If I'm giving up Isolde, I'd like to have that pleasure."

CHAPTER 50

ISOLDE

Arla's screech sounded through the din of combat as Aleksander fell to the deck, his eyes staring up at the bird.

Blood pounded in my ears. The sprinkle we'd been fighting in had transformed into fat drops of rain that clouded my vision. All around fae fought, screamed, groaned.

I seemed unable to move. Unable to breathe. To do anything but stand there in sheer horror as my brother's innards peeked out of his torso.

Roar's boot landed on Aleksander's chest. "You're so concerned and I cannot help but notice that his wings are like yours, Isolde." A smirk rippled across his face, so aware that I watched. How what he'd done affected me. "If I had to guess, that means I get to take down two white hawks today."

Roar leaned his weight into my brother's chest, and Aleksander let out a pained scream that was quickly swallowed by a gale of wind. The storm had well and truly arrived, in more ways than one.

Arla dove, her talons extended, but this time, Roar was ready. He sent a wave of winter magic upward to meet the bird. Arla froze on impact and plummeted.

Rage boiled through my veins, and a shadow figure burst out of me, so ready and willing to commit violence. But no. I would finish Roar myself, and I'd be sure the job was done this time.

"Get the bird," I commanded. "Take her to land. Get her warm."

The shadow flew as fast as the wind, catching the symbol of my house before she hit the ground, and flying Arla over the water, to land.

"Abomination." Roar stumbled back. Rain dripped off his face, illuminated by fire attacks blooming in the sky—trying to take down our flying archers and Rynni who swooped and used her enormous claws to pluck enemy sailors from the ships and crush them. "I didn't think it was true. Thought he was lying, like all his kind."

"Érebo can lie." I intended to take advantage of Roar's fear. "But he didn't lie about this."

Palm to the darkened clouds above, I called another shadow, felt the tether tighten as it appeared. "Go to Aleksander. Keep him alive."

Aleksander was not as small as Arla. To have a shadow fly away with him would greatly strain me. But there was no other choice.

The shadow soared to Aleksander and did as I commanded, holding his belly together while I prowled forward.

"The fae of Winter's Realm will never accept you. A

shadow wielder." Roar had backed farther away from my brother. He spat on the expanse of deck between us.

"Some already have," I replied. "And maybe others won't, but the truth is, they will have me and my sister, or a king who is willing to ally with King Érebo. The very Shadow Fae who once warred against their ancestors. And let's not forget the whisperer in line for the Crown of Winter."

Shock flitted across Roar's face. Then revelation. "Rhistel."

"I think my odds are better than you say."

Roar snorted. "Magnus is an idiot for his alliance. For keeping his son alive too."

"At least we can agree on something." I called another shadow, but this time it was more difficult. Two were already doing my bidding, one of them keeping someone alive, and while I'd practiced often with this magic, it wasn't second nature yet. Particularly not making shadow people. And yet, the dark figure materialized next to me, not in the concise form of a person like the other two, but good enough.

The Warden of the West stumbled away, plunging his sword into the scabbard before scooping up his bow and nocking the arrow.

"Shield me," I said as the arrow flew for my heart.

The shadow expanded, and when the arrow sank, it disappeared into the dark void. Harmless. Shock flitted through me, and that shadow vanished as I momentarily lost control over the figure.

A string of curse words left Roar's lips and he nocked another arrow, aimed, and loosed.

I did not call a shadow in time but spun out of the way. "You're out of arrows."

His hand shot back to the quiver, and he grasped at air. Discovering I was right, Roar pivoted on his heel.

"Running again?" I called out, calling my dark magic another time. "This is becoming quite a habit of yours, Roar."

Sweat joined the water on my brow as another vague shadow form appeared at my behest. "Bring him to me."

The shadow surged forward and seized Roar. The high lord began to shift, but with a breath-stealing push from me, the shadow grew too, able to accommodate whatever size Roar became as long I was strong enough to keep hold of the shadow. The warden growled and stopped shifting. He remained fae, though he didn't stop fighting. Kicking and thrashing in the air, Roar fought and fought, even as the shadow came to hover before me.

My control over the darkness strained, but I didn't let the exertion show on my face as I moved to stand before the male I'd once trusted. A male who had kissed me, sought to manipulate me, and then used me for his own means. I looked him up and down.

"I don't know how I didn't see how very small you were from the very start. Always using others. Me. Those human slaves. Magnus too—though I can't say I feel bad for him." I laughed. "He'll meet his end too. Hopefully at my hands, but if my sister wants him, that will work just as well."

Roar stilled. The shadow had him under the arms, and he hung there. Useless. Pathetic. Alone.

I scooped up my sword, turned it over in my hands. "Did you know this is Sassa's Blade? I wonder how long it's been since a Lisika has seen it up close?" My gaze drifted upward to meet his, and I took great pleasure in the fear I found there. "Maybe since Sassa's own husband?"

"We can make a deal. I'll swear to you. I have the largest army in Winter's Realm. Spare me, and—"

"*Spare you*? After all you've done to me? To those I love? After seeing how you use humans and sell them to *vampires*?" I shook my head. "I would never ally with a slaver."

"I have gold!"

"I don't give a damn about gold!" I lifted Sassa's Blade so that the edge graced that tender, throbbing vein in his neck. "You have nothing I could want. *Are* nothing I could ever want."

Roar sucked in a breath.

"Any last words, Warden?"

He lifted his chin, said nothing.

"Pray the Fates have mercy on you then."

One cut with so little pressure applied, and his neck opened. Blood poured, and I watched the life drain from Roar Lisika's emerald eyes.

"Release him," I said to the shadow when not a spark remained in the warden, "and then go."

The inky form vanished, and the absence of a tether to the being loosened my chest. I turned to Aleksander. My hold on my second shadow was still there, though beginning to fray with the effort of keeping it sustained—and thus, Aleksander alive.

I knelt, assessed the wound. There was so much blood. Too much. I was out of my depths.

Where was Rynni? I cast a glance across the ship but didn't find her. In fact, few fae remained on this ship. Only a half dozen or so were still fighting. Mostly I stood on the deck with corpses or sailors tied to masts.

I took over holding the wound together and nodded to the shadow. "Go find the dragon-fae, Rynni. I need her."

I wasn't sure that Rynni could heal this wound, but at the very least she might fly to the mainland and help get Aleksander proper care.

The shadow left, the effort of another large task draining me more. It was not as bad as when I used the shadows within Sassa's Blade, but noticeable all the same. Terrifying too, in a time when I needed every drop of energy I could spare.

I exhaled a long breath when I spotted the dragon rise from another ship and fly to mine. She shifted back in the air and fell into a squat as her knees absorbed the impact of landing mere paces from me.

"By Eirial's mercy." The dragon-fae came to kneel beside me. "How long has it been since he was struck?"

"Ten or fifteen minutes?"

She swallowed. "I can do a temporary bind, but he needs to be stitched up. And the wound cleaned before that."

My arms trembled. "I fear he can't stay on your back, but I can send a shadow to carry him to the town. That poses another problem."

"The fae there might be fearful of shadows, and not help him," Rynni said. "I'll go with and once we're on land, I'll carry him. Make sure there's a competent healer. You're fine if I go?"

My stomach tightened. No, I was not fine with that because though Rynni had only one good fire breath a day, that counted for a lot. As did her teeth and talons. Who knew when we'd need her?

Aleksander might be my brother, but he was only one fae in this army, and we brought precious few healers with us. Her strength aside, it was likely that we'd need Rynni again for what she did best.

"Come back quickly," I said finally. "Before you go though, how many others are injured? Fallen?"

"I've been called to close a dozen wounds. Fallen? I can't say, but we'll soon have a count. We're winning—have almost won entirely." She was already working magic, temporarily binding the wound. As magic poured from Rynni, I took the time to take in the ships around us.

Yes, the sounds of fighting on the other ships were dwindling. Almost gone.

The dragon-fae finished and sat back on her heels. She turned those keen healer's eyes on me and spotted the missing piece of my wing. "I can help with that too."

"Again, quickly." It might hurt, but my injured wing was still capable of flight.

"It will be superficial, but the pain will be lessened." Rynni made a motion for me to turn around, and when I did, Thyra landed right in front of me.

"Is Aleksander alive?"

"Clinging to life," I said as a tingling sensation began in my wing. The pain lessened somewhat. "Rynni is taking him to land. Should anyone else go?"

"A handful." Thyra placed two fingers in her mouth. A shrill whistle sounded and caught Bac's attention. He began flying our way, only to have Caelo join him.

The pair landed, and after a quick examination, I deemed them unharmed. Bloodied, particularly Caelo, but not injured.

"Bac, I need you to gather enough people to fly the most grievously injured back to that village with Rynni. Then come back." Thyra studied the area. "We'll be sailing to battle, but unless the storm worsens, you should make it in time."

"I'll come with you to get the injured situated on the gryphons." Caelo joined, and as fast as the pair had arrived, they were gone.

"I should go too," Rynni said. "Tell your shadow to trail me and disappear when we reach the town. Have it set Aleksander on the ground gently."

The moment Rynni was gone, the shadow followed with our brother.

"Fifteen dead on last count," Thyra said. "Those who aren't going to land may have sustained small injuries but can still fight. And we've taken all the ships that remain."

I marveled at how good she was at gathering information quickly and parsing what were the most important bits.

"Ideas on what to do with the living Nava sailors?" Thyra asked, ending her report.

"Congregate them on one ship and lock them up," I said.

The sailors might fight for the king, but they'd likely had no other option, and now that they were unarmed I would not kill them. If my sister and I lived through the night, and we still required soldiers, we'd do our best to give them a choice of who they fought for.

Thyra nodded. "We have twenty-five ships left."

That many had slipped into the sea before we took them? My stomach sank. We were so outnumbered, but we had to move on and come to the aid of our allies.

"Then we'd better start preparing to sail," I replied with more confidence than I felt.

CHAPTER 51

ISOLDE

Our fleet cleared the islands and sailed north toward the battle already raging in the churning sea. In the distance lightning cracked. Thunder boomed.

At the best of times, the Shivering Sea was a hostile environment, and this was not the best of times. Precious few of the soldiers on our side were sailors, and the storm added another dangerous layer. That was to say nothing about the actual fighting.

Magnus had been successful in recruiting mages, and he was using them to devastating effect. Their power lit up the darkening sky, and the fire and light it emitted reflected off the black clouds. Mage magic appeared best suited for long-distance attacks, and once we were close enough, we would be targeted.

"Adding an aerial surge would be advisable." Lord Balik came to stand with Thyra and me. Lord Riis was with him, his hands clenching the railing as we studied the events on the water. "It will divert some of the mage magic, so our ships can close in with greater ease."

"I hope you don't mean by our own wings," Thyra said. "The winds are too high for long distances and fae wings."

"Use the gryphons. Double up if possible so attacks can rain down the entire time."

"Timing matters even more than numbers here, I think," Lord Riis added his opinion.

Unlike the few times he'd spoken after Inga's death, his voice raged with fire. I fought for Vale and for Winter's Realm, but I had no doubt that Leyv Riis was fighting for the memory of his lost love.

"I'd wait until we're within range of the fire assaults," Lord Riis said. "They'll have less time to consider how to alter their attack to be useful on two fronts, by air and by sea. No doubt they'll go for the closest enemies first."

I swallowed. "Thyra?"

"I think it's a good idea. We're going in, right?"

"Of course."

"Spread the word," I said to Lord Riis. "Anyone who has ridden a gryphon in battle comes along. If there are extras, choose the best flier and pair them with archers and fae who have range in their magic."

"Thyra and I will join you with our pegasi." I was always grateful to Arava, but never more than now. Flying under my own steam would undoubtedly come, but after my injury, I wasn't sure how agile I'd be on wing.

Lord Riis left to give the command.

"You remain with the ships, Lord Balik," I said. "They need your guidance."

He exhaled. "Remember your vow."

I understood exactly what he meant. Sian and Filip were elite gryphon riders. They'd be among the fliers.

"They'll each ride with one of our Valkyrja," I promised. "Close to us at all times."

"That does not reassure me." Lord Balik spoke flatly. "You're prime targets."

"But the Valkyrja are highly skilled warriors and riders," Thyra countered. "There are none stronger for them to ride with."

I did not add that I wished for Sian to be with us because the Shadow King would likely target my sister and me too. Of course, we could fight shadows with shadows, but according to the history books, a limiter was truly the best defense and offense against shadows. If Sian could keep King Érebo's prodigious powers limited, we might have a better chance.

Thanks to the bond my sister and I were developing with the pegasi, finding our mares was easy. They lay on a cleared portion of the lower deck, resting alongside a group of gryphons.

My hand landed on Arava's strong neck. I felt guilty that I had to ask this of her after she'd flown for so long to get me here. "I need you again, beauty."

She stood and tossed her mane as if to say that she was always prepared. Always strong and capable.

I kissed her wet cheek, inhaling her musty scent, and mounted.

As we waited for our ships to close in, the images I'd seen of my mate in the vision continued to haunt me. I was certain that Thyra, too, had been thinking of what she'd seen. Likely, she had regrets over how she'd treated her mate. If we saved Thantrel, I suspected things between them would change.

Others arrived, readied their gryphons, and saddled up. Gryphons from other ships began appearing in the airspace above us, waiting for our word to move forward.

My knees squeezed Arava, and she lifted into the air to join the others. "We fly for the battle when we're in range of the mage attacks. No sooner. Try to deflect as much magic as you can to give our ships a clearer approach."

Not only were the ships weapons in their own rights, but they were also safe spaces and areas where the few healers we'd brought with us could work.

The riders gave the signal that they'd heard. As we waited to close in on the mages, I took careful stock of my force.

The Valkyrja were all accounted for, riding with cabal members as their partners. Livia and Bavirra had paired up, and the dwarven princess had her bow and a full quiver of arrows at the ready. Saga rode with Lord Riis, and Bac with Prince Thordur. All good matches.

This will work, I told myself as the sounds of battle, of falling rain, and churning waves grew louder.

Rain pelted us, and in the distance, natural lightning cleaved through the storm, sending shivers down my spine. As if tonight weren't dangerous enough.

Not that the danger mattered. We were here, in it, and on the attack.

Soon enough I'd save Vale. We'd defeat King Magnus

and the Shadow Fae who had wronged us. I told myself those things as if they'd already come true. For me, there was no other option.

The attacks from the mages, and some fae who had longer-reaching magic, continued to plow through the Virtoris fleet. With each blast of wood and each plume of smoke that arose in the air or sails that lit on fire, I thought of Sayyida. Of Vidar. Where were they in that fleet? Were they still alive?

"Get ready to fly!" Lord Riis called out, and I snapped back to the moment to find a mage strike fall into the sea close to the bow of our lead ship. My ship. "Princesses?"

"Go!" Thyra screamed. "Divert and engage whenever possible!"

With my sister's command, the fliers rose to meet the storm. Thyra and I got into position, spearheading the attack, our thick braids of silver-white and raven-wing black streaming at our backs. Behind us were the Valkyrja, each paired with one of our friends. Seen from below, we would be in the shape of an arrow with soldiers from both Riis and Balik camps and a handful of rebels rounding out our retinue.

"Incoming!" I shouted as a stream of fire blazed right for me.

The arrow split, one half going right, the other half left, and the fire burst right where my sister and I would have been. Inside me, shadows roiled, begging to be released, to go after the mage that had sent the attack and make them pay.

You will do your part later.

Though I no longer sensed my tether to the shadows I'd sent to land, I'd already expended too much energy using that dark magic. Even with the rest I'd had while we sailed, to use more so soon would be folly. I needed to utilize what came easiest to me first.

"That one came from the ship with the tear down the center of the sail." Thyra pointed.

My assessment was brief, the solution obvious. "A unit needs to take that mage, or mages, out. They have the best range."

Thyra gave the hand signal, and a team of four broke off from the back, diving for the very ship Thyra had noted.

Stars be with them.

Arava wove and dove through wave after wave of mage magic. Though the battle with the frost giants was my first taste of true combat, this battle felt so different. More real, somehow. The stakes impossibly high.

With each second that we survived, with each attack hurled our way, our ships surged closer. And as the fliers neared the enemy fleet, I shifted the plan toward our next phase of our attack.

I scanned the decks below for King Magnus, Rhistel, and Érebo. Whichever I spotted first, I'd target, though I hoped it was the king. The one who had started all this and had allowed my mate to hurt so.

Instead, I found not my enemies, but Vale. He battled so very far away, but his form was as recognizable to me as the back of my own hands.

The person Vale fought neared a flickering torch and

came into focus too. A fae whom I was not close with, but someone with great power. Someone I trusted and who was beloved by those I loved. And my heart lurched as Vale raised his sword and brought it down upon that very great ally.

CHAPTER 52
VALE

My enemy spun out of my blade's path, her movements fluid, like the serpent her house claimed as their own—boneless and slippery.

"I thought you were on our side," Lady Fayeth Virtoris hissed through clenched teeth. So much blood spattered her brown face that even the pounding rain did not wash the red away completely. Just like the blood of sailors that clung to every part of me.

"I stand with my father," the last word stuck in my throat before pushing through, "and my brother. With the true rulers of Winter's Realm."

She held out her sword, a thin, short blade. "Something happened to you."

"Isolde Falk tricked me." My blood burned hotter just thinking of that conniving female. The need to kill Isolde beat through me like a song sung repeatedly. She'd performed so many wrongs. All of them burned into the insides of my eyelids, inescapable even during sleep. After

I fulfilled my father's wishes here, I'd get the revenge I craved.

"Sayyida told me that she's your mate." The boat rolled against a wave, and the Lady of Ships took three surefooted steps back. "Trust me, Prince Vale, mates are not so common, but *I* know of that bond. My mate left his home court for me, and I would go to the ends of the realm for him. If Isolde Falk is your mate, she would not trick you."

A common belief, but Sassa Falk tricked her mate, and Isolde had fallen in her ancestor's footsteps. It was all so clear to me.

"You know nothing of what she is capable of." I closed in and thrust.

Again, the serpent dodged, but this time, I anticipated how she'd slink away. My second swipe struck true, gliding across the Lady of Ship's abdomen, parting the flesh.

She stilled, sucked in a breath. Her gaze lifted to meet mine as blood poured and the tang of metal perfumed the air heavy with salt and rain.

"If you're ever yourself again, tell my family I love them." She fell to her knees. "Tell them I have no regrets in the side we chose. And to lead well and follow their hearts for they're steadfast and honest." She fell forward, right into a pool of her blood.

A guttural scream sounded above, and I turned to find that in the time I'd been doing my duty, our enemies had sent an aerial unit. I scanned the sky, searching for the black pegasus belonging to Isolde. Before I could locate the creature, a heavy blow landed across my face.

I stumbled, caught myself on the ship's railing.

"How could you!" shouted a voice.

I straightened to find Vidar Virtoris standing in front of me, trembling with rage as he looked down on his dead mother.

"She's my enemy." My hand tightened on the hilt of my sword. "As are you."

"You're out of your mind, aren't you?"

I snarled.

"Vale, I'm your *brother*!"

"I already have a brother." I charged, ready to continue fulfilling my father's wishes, but Vidar turned and ran. I gave chase, but like his mother, he was fast and slippery. The Virtoris heir made it across the deck. Leapt over the rail.

I leapt too, my wings catching the wind as I prepared to soar into the sky and join those fighting amongst the starbursts of mage firepower. However, instead of flying up, Vidar dove into the sea. My breath caught, and I stopped in midair. The churning waves, made even more violent by the storm and the battling ships, looked menacing.

He'll come up sometime. He has to, I told myself as I sheathed my weapon. All I had to do was wait.

I was so engrossed in scanning the volatile waters I didn't see or sense the incoming fire attack until it was too late. Like half of the ship behind me, I went flying forward and was tossed like a limp fish into the waves.

CHAPTER 53
ISOLDE

My heart lodged itself in my throat as Vale disappeared beneath the towering waves.

"It's not him," Caelo yelled from where he flew close by. Sigri and Qildor were with me too, but the rest of the fliers had spread out some, to attack and avoid harm. "Vale would never harm Vidar."

I stared down at the water, now black under the stormy sky. Our forces were now aware of Rhistel's true magic, but Vidar likely did not know. He'd been on the sea when we'd spread the news.

"Circle, Arava! We have to find him. *Both* of them!"

Arava lowered and flew as slowly as she dared, all the while keeping alert for threats. Knowing she'd fly away at any threat to us allowed me to focus on the water.

Debris from the blast blanketed the water, making it impossible to see beneath. Seconds passed, and my belly tightened. What if they didn't surface? What if something had hit them over the head or impaled their bellies? Vale was not the best swimmer, and while Vidar, being from the

House of the Sea Serpent, had grown up on the water, the sea took easily.

Was I seeing the vision the Crown had given me? Altered by my presence, my attempt to change fate, and yet still so similar?

"We need to dive!" Caelo called out. "Before they sink too deep!"

I dug my heels into Arava's side, fearing the water. I could swim, but the sea thrashed, and I wasn't sure I'd survive such power. "Get closer."

She followed my command. Spindrift sprayed our faces, and Caelo removed his weapon, preparing to jump.

"Qildor! Caelo!" a voice shouted, not far away.

A waving hand caught my attention, and I exhaled. Vidar treaded water not too far away.

"To him!" Arava veered in Vidar's direction and hovered just beside my friend. We were positioned between two destroyed ships, both deserted or filled with corpses if the lack of attacks was any indication. One of the ships lolled our way, making my skin tighten. The ships moved with the water. What if Vale was under one?

"Are you injured?" I asked, trying to push aside my deluge of fears. If anyone was going to be able to swim and find Vale, it was the lord in the water.

"No." A wave bobbed him closer to me. "But Vale—"

"I saw what he did," I cut him off. Time was of the essence. "I'm so sorry, Vidar, but Rhistel is a whisperer and he's controlling Vale."

Judging by the look of shock on Vidar's face, I'd been right to assume that the news had not reached them out here.

"And Vale was tossed into the water right after you dove. Did you see him in the water?" *Can you get him?* My unspoken question hovered in the air. Vale had tried to kill Vidar, and I couldn't make myself say the words, but Vidar heard my unspoken plea, and he didn't falter.

"Bleeding skies." Vidar's attention snapped to the dark water. "Do you have your faelights on you? If so, give me one."

From the pocket of my leather pants, I fished out one of the faelights I carried and tossed it to him. Vidar caught it one handed, and without saying another word, he dove.

Caelo jumped into the sea after his friend. The rest of us continued to search from above, but it was too difficult to see far. The darkness was too all-encompassing, and the surface of the water was too littered with items and bodies.

My shadow magic bubbled within, promising aid. Sense told me not to, but sense had no place here. Nothing was more important than saving my mate.

I steeled myself to call that dark power just as Vidar's head popped above the surface. Caelo followed in quick order and Vidar helped him drag something up from the depths. Not something. Someone. My mate.

"He's not breathing. Get him on a ship!" Vidar shouted against the vicious wind and waves as Vale's head lolled to the side, his mouth open and eyes closed. "Someone take him!"

Qildor maneuvered his gryphon at their side, and the knight pulled Vale up and laid him across his lap. Once he was situated, the other two used their wings and rose out of the water.

"That's one of our ships." Vidar pointed to a vessel not too far away, but not so close enough that it was perfectly visible thanks to the rain and smoke dominating the air. "Take him there."

We flew to the ship, me in the lead, prepared to defend. Two smaller attacks came at us from a ship we soared over. I formed a wall of ice, stopping the attack, and creating a spray of shards when a mage struck it. One chunk of ice landed on an enemy's head, but the offending mage ran off to avoid injury, leaving our way clear. From what I could tell, the larger assaults were still focusing on the aerial force, not the incoming fleet, which would be here in minutes. The plan had worked, though I felt no joy from that fact. Wouldn't feel anything but fear until Vale awoke.

Arava landed on the deck of a Virtoris ship, and I jumped off her back. The scent of spilled blood and emptied bowels, less noticeable over the open water, hung heavy here. Sailors bearing the crest of the sea serpent on their breasts approached, fear on their faces, and not a drop of recognition.

"That's Princess Isolde." A flash of lightning illuminated Saga, her pink hair half burnt off as she ran up to me. I half wondered where her flying partner, Lord Riis, was, but when Sayyida appeared behind her, I understood. Saga had likely leapt from her gryphon to be with Sayyida. "Don't touch her!"

The sailors lowered their weapons, their faces relaxing further when the gryphon bearing Caelo, Halladora, and

Vidar landed. They didn't recognize me, but Vidar was their lord and the next leader of the house they'd sworn allegiance to. They knew him well and on sight.

The others, with Vidar in the lead, rushed a limp-bodied Vale into an interior room, and shut the door behind them.

"Was that *Vale*?" Saga asked, her voice high. Terrified.

"Yes, he was drowning," I replied, fighting the urge to follow and just not answer. Saga deserved to know. "We're trying to save him."

"We'll stand watch at the door." The protectiveness in Sayyida's voice hinted that she hadn't seen Vale kill her mother. My throat tightened at all he'd done, and knowing I'd have to tell my friend that news. Later.

"Someone watch and protect Arava. The gryphons too." I rushed into the cabin.

Vale laid on a bed in a captain's room judging by the nice furnishings and full bar on the far wall. Some of the liquor bottles had toppled and broken during the battle, and the smell of spirits filled the air, a shock to my nose after so much seawater and blood.

Qildor, Caelo, and Vidar were on one side of the bed, while Sigri and Halladora loomed on the other. Halladora was administering chest compressions, and I arrived just in time to see what looked like an entire ocean full of water spew from Vale's lips. He coughed violently.

"Thank the stars." I rushed to be near him. "Vale! I'm right here. Just breathe!"

As I reached the end of the bed, his eyes snapped open and locked in on Sigri, who stood closest to him. In an instant, the confusion lining his face hardened, and his hands, those large hands that had held me, caressed me, protected me and countless others shot up and wrapped around Sigri's neck.

"*Stop!*" But my voice was swallowed up by a snap. Sigri's body went limp, and before he'd released her, Vale's stare shifted to me.

His eyes weren't right. Not warm and deep and loving, but hard and soulless.

Vale pushed to get up. "You've seen your last day, Falk spawn. You—"

Caelo struck my mate on the side of the head with a pommel. Vale collapsed back onto the bed with a groan. I pressed my palms into the soft feather mattress, desperate for any kind of support.

"Sigri, she's . . ." I couldn't get another word out. Couldn't breathe.

"Dead," Halladora croaked in confirmation. She'd knelt to the level of her fallen sister in arms and held the dwarf's body to her own.

The truth pounded through me. The near-death experience hadn't brought my mate back to himself. Vale was not safe. Not to me. Not to anyone.

Originally part of the rebellion, Sigri been one of the first fae to swear to my sister and me, and even if her allegiance began with Thyra, I still valued her as a fae. I'd hoped that maybe one day, a friend too. That would no longer happen, and her death came at Vale's hands.

"He wanted to do the same to me and to you, Isolde," Vidar whispered, horror dripping in his tone.

My father had been called the Cruel King for the many atrocities he'd committed during the end of his reign. He had acted much like Vale was now. I allowed my gaze to drift over my husband, searching for the male I loved. When I got to his hand, I gasped.

One of his fingers was gone. The one bearing our soulmate mark. I gripped my left hand with my right. The removal of Vale's finger had to have been the pain I felt that day.

Pain crashed through me at all that he'd endured in just a few days' time.

How would we reverse Rhistel's hold on my mate's mind? And when we did, how would Vale cope both with what had been done to him and what he'd done? He was a warrior, but he longed for peace. To be only a shield and not a sword.

An earth-shattering sound came from outside. Fae on our ship screamed and shouted, and wood cracked and snapped.

"What was that?" I asked, though I was afraid to know the answer. Afraid of so much.

Qildor crossed to the window, pulled back the curtain. His mouth fell open. "You're going to want to see this."

CHAPTER 54

ISOLDE

I couldn't see the king, though I knew he had to be responsible for what I was witnessing. *How* exactly Magnus had managed to create such a thing, however, I could not fathom. The great ice wall in the middle of the sea was a marvel.

And a great peril.

By the light of the ships and fire attacks, I sized up the wall that had devastated nearly half of our incoming ships. Those at the back of the fleet were changing course, but ships didn't turn so easily in the best conditions. And if they managed to bend the sea to their will tonight there were still enemy vessels waiting to deal them damage.

Fae flew from the sinking vessels and soared around the wall only to land and immediately be engaged in combat. Others soared for the water and pulled our soldiers from the waves.

My stomach heaved, and the thunder booming in the night sky echoed my despair. I'd seen Magnus's magic before. I'd been the recipient of one attack and witnessed others. None of the times he'd worked magic around me had been like this. None of his threats and attacks had been so powerful.

"We have to shatter it." It was the only way I could see to give the rest of our fleet a path forward. Or at the very least, allow their magic to attack at a distance.

But I couldn't leave Vale unattended in this cabin, and only someone stronger than him could truly keep him in check. By the same token, we needed every available fighter we could get. There was only one thing to do.

My shadows came to the surface more slowly and with greater effort than before. I had far better control than a week prior, but my endurance was lacking.

*You **will** listen. Out with you. As many as will come.*

Only two emerged. They'd have to do.

"Remain here and guard the male in that bed. If he awakes, knock him out, but using as little force as possible. If the ship begins to sink, save him and take him to a ship with fae loyal to me on it. Make sure he's locked away there too. Do not harm him in any other way." I paused, trying to determine if I should add another command. With shadow figures it was best to be explicit. "Only those fighting for my side may enter."

The shadows, created in only the faintest image of a person, nodded what I presumed were their heads. I looked around them, prepared to give the order to move out, but the others were already standing at attention, their weapons drawn. I took them in, my gaze lingering on Sigri's fallen body last. Stars, how I'd failed her.

We exited the cabin to find Saga and Sayyida still at the door, weapons drawn and the hum of magic in the surrounding air. A mage lay dead on the deck, mere paces away.

"Saga, Vale is safe and being guarded by shadows, and I know you probably want to see him, but I need you." I gestured to the ice wall. "Think you can help Thyra and me collapse that thing?"

She swallowed. "Maybe."

I turned to Vidar and Sayyida. "You two stay with the ships. Try to attack vessels on the edges of the wall so the rest of our fleet can get through."

The Virtoris siblings dashed off to give their crews orders.

"This way." Saga led us to where the gryphons and pegasi waited, protected by a trio of sailors. Arava pushed the sailors out of her way and trotted towards me.

"I'm fine, girl." I patted her muzzle before I mounted. "See that ice wall? We're going to shatter it."

"Saga, you should ride with me." Qildor waved for her to take Sigri's spot.

I saw the question of what happened to the dwarf in the princess's eyes, but she didn't speak it as she joined Qildor.

My pegasus beat her wings. "Caelo and Halladora, find Thyra. Saga and Qildor, with me."

We soared for the wall, and my tether to the shadows watching over Vale stretched tight, a link to me, and an energy sink. Wherever Thyra was, I hoped Caelo and Halladora would locate her quickly because the closer I got to the wall, the more certain I became that Saga and I would need assistance. Up close, the black wall was thicker and more menacing than it appeared from a distance.

That wasn't the only thing I found. Illuminated by torches and faelights, Magnus's white hair stood out as we neared the wall. He had positioned his ship just off to the side of the ice, lest the structure shatter or fall, no doubt. And he wasn't working alone. A handful of mages were using magic to keep the unnaturally shaped frozen water afloat. King Magnus stood with them, his shaking hands above his head as he held the ice in its shape.

The king seemed not to have noticed when we stopped near the center of the wall. Perhaps his creation took that much concentration, but I thought it equally likely that we were simply very high up and the sky so dark and rainy. Most likely, Magnus would sense us attacking his creation before he spotted us.

I gripped Arava's reins and wound the rough leather around my left hand as I thrust my right at the wall of ice. Winter magic met winter magic. One formative, one destructive. My power penetrated deep into the ice, and I pushed for a deeper cold, a temperature that would shatter the wall from within.

The wall shuddered and dipped in the water, but a wave of foreign magic came over my power and forced the wall back up. The crack of ships against the ice reverberated from the other side. Not new ships, but the ones that had already hit. Ones that would continue to thrash against the wall until King Magnus released his wall.

Or until I break through.

Saga's power joined mine, pummeling the ice in the form of frigid wind. She'd sensed what I was doing and sought to amplify my power.

Saga kept up with the winds, striking the wall again

and again and again. Through the din of battle and storm and magical wind, King Magnus bellowed his daughter's name.

A grim smile stretched my lips, and sweat mixed with rainwater landed on my tongue. King Magnus treated others as toys. As rubbish. Vale had been loyal to the king for so long, had loved him, and yet Magnus permitted Rhistel to brainwash my mate. Let Magnus watch his daughter, his only trueborn child, work against him.

And let me end his reign. I forced more magic into the wall of seawater, and was rewarded with a crack appearing in the middle. The line grew vertically, stopping when it was as tall as me.

I gasped and released my magic, needing air. The wall was so very thick. To shatter it, I'd need to do that many more times.

"I'm here!" Thyra's voice hit my ear as she soared next to me. Just in time too, as a blast of pure magic surged at us from below. We split and veered, and the mage attack missed us, but not by much.

Astril and Freyia had arrived with Thyra, the Balik brothers riding with the vampires. Caelo and Halladora took up the rear. The latter with a haunted look in her eyes from seeing her friend die in front of her. Sweeping in from the right was Tonna, the last Valkyrja, and her rider, Arie.

"Send winter magic into the ice. As cold as you can make it. We can shatter it from within, and Saga is pummeling it with wind."

"Got it." Thyra nodded. "Qildor, ward us. Everyone else, attack the mages below!"

They got into formation, and Qildor's ward vibrated to life below us. It wouldn't keep out every attack—the knight hadn't had enough time to construct a ward of that quality—but at least it would dull the worst of them.

Thyra maneuvered Lasvin to Saga's other side. Together we blasted the wall of ice. It shuddered, and the crack inside grew, but as hard as we worked, King Magnus held strong.

"Dig deeper!" Thyra growled as Lasvin swerved to avoid another attack, this one fire-based, flung at us from a ship at our other side. Our Valkyrja and their riders retaliated, raining down arrows and magic.

More cracks formed, the sound muffled by the battle. We hit the ice together. A web of lines spread out from the center, reaching to the edges, the boundary where the ice tapered off.

"Again!" I screamed.

Our magic soared out of us, and this time, I felt the break in the king's powers. The fault in the wall gave way.

The ice cracked, split in half, and wavered, then began to fall. The first three large chunks rained down into the water and created waves. Smaller ones followed, and I hoped that some of them landed on the deck of the king's ship. Or better yet, on Magnus himself.

"No more wind!" I screamed, and Saga backed off.

Breathing seemed nonexistent as we waited for the ice to choose a direction. And when the wall fell towards us, away from the ships we'd stolen to join the battle, I cheered.

The ships in the front line were rapidly taking on water. Five had already submerged to the point of no return. I prayed no one remained on board as the wall crashed to the water, churning the waves more viscously.

Beyond, the last few ships were closing in, turning sharply to avoid the wall and the debris of vessels. With the wall gone, their range attacks could hit enemy marks, and they wasted no time in sending those assaults at mage ships.

"Yes!" I shouted, but my glee was swallowed by a monstrous roar from above as a spray of fire lit up the night sky. Arava darted back, her eyes wide and rolling. Fear rushed through me too. At least until I caught sight of where the fire had come from. My heart soared.

Rynni had returned, and she'd used her fire strike to take down four enemy ships.

CHAPTER 55

ISOLDE

Thyra's eyes gleamed with excitement. "We have a chance."

"We have to make the most of it." I pointed to the king's ship. "We have to defeat him *tonight*."

Thyra nodded. "But first, what happened to Vale?"

My heart swelled at her concern. "He's knocked out, but alive. I have shadows guarding him. Saga, maybe you should join him? Make sure he's well?"

Her father could die, and though she understood that fact and didn't support him, it wasn't fair to have my friend be present for such violence.

"I'll fly us there," Qildor said, and Saga gave a nod of agreement, her gaze dipping down only briefly before the pair soared off into the night.

When I turned to my sister again, it was to find that she wasn't alone. Two shadows floated alongside Lasvin.

"Find Thantrel. Bring him to the same place Isolde has kept Vale safe and help guard over both of them. Do not harm Vale or his sister. Attack only mages and those in Aaberg colors."

"If the ship sinks, save them," I added.

"Yes, if that ship sinks, save them. Take them to one of our ships and lock them up to protect others."

"That should be good."

The shadows disappeared, and Thyra exhaled. "I couldn't resist doing the same as you."

"How much more of that power can you use?" As much as I wanted to dive and kill Magnus right away, regrouping was far more intelligent.

"Not much. One or two more figures probably. If I switch to tendrils, I can last longer."

"I think I'm at my limit," I admitted, tugging at the magic again. Usually the darkness inside me was eager to come forth, but no more emerged from me. I'd drained myself at the worst possible time.

I did what I had to do. Aleksander would never have survived on the ship. And Vale . . . an image of him breaking Sigri's neck made my breath catch. He needed to be where he was. Guarded.

"We don't need them," Thyra assured me. "We're powerful enough with our winter magic, and if Érebo is there, we have Sian. He can signal the other limiters."

I glanced at Sian, and he nodded back. Despite his bravery, I couldn't help but feel a tinge of apprehension. We'd promised Lord Balik that we'd do our best to keep his family safe, but we were bringing both Filip and Sian into a fight with King Magnus and potentially the Shadow Fae King too?

"We won't leave." Filip's jaw tightened, and suddenly he looked far older than he really was.

"Half of us took vows to protect you against whatever may come, and we intend to honor them." Astril said.

I leaned over Arava's neck and peered at the ship below only to find that King Magnus was no longer there. Only chunks of ice littered the upper deck. Was he hiding in a cabin?

"Let's find him," I said.

We flew lower, the four gryphons and their riders behind Lasvin and Arava. A more thorough investigation revealed that no one was on the exterior portion of the Aaberg ship. I was debating having a vampire do a search of the interior when Thyra barked out a cold laugh.

"There he is!" She pointed ahead of us, to the west, at a ship that was separating itself from the battle. *Fleeing.* King Magnus stood on the upper deck, his telltale hair gleaming in the ship's faelights as he gesticulated at the dragon not too far away.

I snorted. "I think Rynni might have scared him."

He would have been stupid not to fear a dragon. And luckily for us he didn't know Rynni, unlike most pure-blooded dragon shifters, could only breathe fire once or twice before she needed a day to recover. Her flames were no longer a threat. However, the healer still had teeth and a wicked tail that she would use to great effect.

"He has more than a dragon to worry about!" Thyra cut west.

We dodged a coordinated assault of mage magic, and I peered down at the ships on water. Thanks to Rynni, many mages had been forced to jump ship and swim to other vessels. Those that weren't on fire. Some, however, seemed to be staying in the water—no matter how tumultuous the waves were. To them, the threat of being on another ship that a dragon might attack was too great.

The dragon rounded back, readying to target another ship with her claws, when suddenly, Rynni's maw opened. A roar blasted through the night, and the dragon began to thrash in the air.

"What's going on?!" I could see nothing attacking Rynni. No mage magic, which from what I'd seen, generally gave off light or looked like fire. But Rynni looked as if she was fighting an invisible force.

Not invisible. The answer suddenly became clear. "Shadows are attacking her."

Thyra scowled. "Sian, signal the limiters to help her!"

"And Érebo?"

"Take a shot if you have one." Thyra's mouth tightened as Rynni dipped closer to the water and two mages on a ship blasted her with fire. Not that flames would damage dragon scales, but who knew what other types of magic users were on that ship? "Freyia, watch his back."

Freyia and Sian soared off, the latter sending a beam of light into the sky. Signaling other limiters to join him.

I watched as we flew for the king's ship, torn and agonized while Rynni fought an invisible force. But Freyia and Sian closed in quickly and Sian blasted light magic at the dragon. A glow encompassed her, and the dragon became a beacon in the darkness.

Eerie screams filled the night and my shadow magic, useless as it was after so many uses, shuddered. Retracted to a place deep inside me.

Chills erupted on my damp skin. "That was the shadows!"

"I felt it," Thyra replied. "Look!"

Other limiters had already joined Sian and the light washing over the dragon was allowing us to see that at least a hundred shadow figures had been attacking Rynni. They were more detailed than the ones Thyra and I made, and far larger too, but in the face of the light magic, the shadow forms screamed. Some diminished in size. Some even disappeared.

"They have her," I reassured myself. "They have—"

My words died on my lips as Rynni plummeted towards the water. The dragon continued to fight as if she weren't dropping through the air and being attacked.

She'd hit the water in seconds, and then what? Could Rynni swim? If not, how would we get her out of the water? And would the shadows that remained continue harming her? Light could not penetrate so deep in the ocean . . .

"Change course?" Caelo yelled.

"I think—wait! She's shifting!" Thyra shouted back.

Rynni seemed to have struck upon the issue of rescue. Her massive body shrank and by the time she hit the water, she looked fae in body. But was she still in trouble?

"Filip and Astril! Go to her!" I yelled. The limiters were still fighting shadows, now flying free in the air and illuminated by flashes of light.

Astril gave me a look that clearly said she should be sticking with us, but Rynni might have used her last seconds of consciousness to shift. I had to be sure she would not drown.

"We have two more Valkyrja, Caelo, and Arie to back us up," Thyra said. "Go!"

Astril veered the gryphon to where Rynni had disappeared and flew away.

"Filip and Astril will find her." Thyra sounded as if she were trying to convince herself.

I hoped so, but really, there was no time to dwell on other matters. We were still targeting the king's ship. My hand grazed the grip of Sassa's Blade as I prepared to enter battle again.

"Bleeding skies! Did anyone else see that?" Halladora shouted.

"I did!" Arie confirmed. "Three ships disappeared. They were there one moment and gone the next."

My stomach sank. I had not seen that, but I knew what had happened. Érebo, wherever he was, had cloaked those ships in darkness. Were they retreating? Or preparing for stealth attacks?

"The Shadow King is hiding them," Thyra said, having come to the same conclusion. "Be prepared for anything."

"We stay the course," I added. Magnus was still our number one target.

The king had busied himself by targeting enemies who had fallen into the water. Killing them off one by one. He'd hit another mark when a swarm of gryphons and riders dropped from the gray clouds and chaos broke out on the upper deck.

Thyra shouted in disbelief. "It's an ambush!"

Yes, but who had gone after Magnus before we could? Why would they dare?

I urged Arava to go faster, to find the answer to those questions and when the king's challenger came into view, I understood.

Lord Riis and King Magnus were engaged in swords.

"Why isn't the king using his magic?" Thyra asked.

"Lord Riis's power is to negate," I reminded her, excitement building in my chest. "He must have nullified the king's power."

"Ha!" Thyra grinned. "How long does it last?"

"Arie?" I asked the Riis male riding with Tonna.

"Varies," Arie replied. Droplets of blood trailed across the bridge of his nose and down his neck, emphasizing that while I thought of Arie more as a Scholar, he'd grown up with Luccan and Thantrel and Lord Riis had insisted that they all train. Arie could fight well. "Who my father is up against, and their power level, has to be taken into consideration."

Once, Lord Riis had said that he could not negate more than three opponents during a fight. Considering Magnus was very powerful, I assumed Lord Riis could only focus on him—and likely not for too long.

"You ruined her!" Lord Riis's words hit my ear as we closed in.

"She was a deceitful whore!" King Magnus yelled back.

Lord Riis rushed the king, swinging his sword with fury and skill, but the king was ready. The two powerfully built fae struggled against one another, locked in an impasse, blade to blade.

"Might as well help him out, no?" The cold built around my twin. I recognized that sensation as her readying to send an icy projectile. I was about to warn her off in case she hit Lord Riis, when the spymaster let out a roar.

He fell to his knees. Struck. King Magnus kicked him in the shoulder, and the blade Lord Riis held fell, skittered across the rain and blood-slicked deck.

"No!" A scream ravaged my throat as Magnus brought his sword down. The metal glinted in a flash of lightning, and Lord Riis's head went flying.

Behind me, still on gryphonback, Arie roared. A struggle ensued, presumably Tonna keeping Arie on the gryphon. My wings snapped out, and I soared off Arava's back.

I landed behind the king, my boots striking the wood hard. Thyra hit only a second after, and other boots joined. When King Magnus turned to take us in, he smiled, as if he'd expected nothing less.

"Isolde. And Thyra." He pointed a pale finger at my sister. "The rebel archer." King Magnus wiped Lord Riis's blood off on his pant leg. "An orc and a faerie, presumably rebels, a Riis—unsurprising. And an oath breaker." His eyes lingered on Caelo the longest. Once a Clawsguard, King Magnus would take Caelo's desertion personally.

"You're outnumbered," I said.

"It's a pity Vale didn't find you, Isolde."

I fumed, which, I suspected, was what he wanted when he added, "And if only I'd killed you at the theater, Thyra, none of this would have happened."

"This was always going to happen." My chin lifted in defiance. "You've reaped your own end, Magnus."

"How presumptuous of you to deal out endings."

A pulse of magic erupted from the king, and I reached for my power, only to find he had not directed the attack at me or Thyra. No, we were unaffected, but everyone around us—our friends, those soldiers who had ambushed the king with Lord Riis, the king's own soldiers—were frozen in place. No help would come from this ship. It was only us and Magnus.

"I propose that we play by the rules of old," the king said. "The strongest wins the Crown of Winter."

I'd barely processed this turn of events when Thyra rushed forward. Steel bit steel, magic flew, and I dodged two wayward magical blows as I debated what to do. They were moving rapidly, both sure of their prowess and power. If I struck, I was just as likely to hit my twin as the king. So I held back and waited for an opening.

That moment came with the slash of enemy metal across my sister's shoulder. Thyra screamed and doubled over, and I sent a stake of ice right for the king's heart.

CHAPTER 56

ISOLDE

My stake was a hands breadth away from his chest, when the king deflected my attack. Thyra stumbled a few paces away, out of his reach, but the king was a quick thinker and sent a jagged shard of ice at my sister. The ice cut her upper thigh, and she fell face-first to the rain-slicked deck.

"That's not very noble of you, Isolde." Magnus side-stepped so that his back was not to me or Thyra. "Attacking before Thyra and I have finished is against the rules."

I laughed, and the cold inside me rose, chilling the air far more than the storm ever could. Another barrage of icicles materialized, and I sent them at him all at once, just like he'd done that one day to those poor actors.

"*Rules?*"

Magnus fought off my attack, but I hurled a second one at him. The exhaustion of before was no longer a factor when faced with the likes of him.

Frost and ice and storm and fury seemed to rage

within me. "You've killed so many. Made life awful for most. You *destroyed* my family."

I stalked closer as he fended off attack after attack. "Don't mistake my earlier hesitation to try and end your life as anything other than care for my sister. Because I do not give a gryphon's shit about combat etiquette, Magnus."

Winter magic pulsed from me, so deep and frigid that I thought he would not be able to fend it off. The king went still, and victory sang inside me before he broke my hold and retaliated in kind. Not before a dagger left my hand though.

Ice covered my skin, threatening to shred through to my deeper tissues. I struggled against his delving power as my dagger hit its mark, sinking into Magnus's shoulder.

He bellowed, and I fought frantically to break through the ice coating me. Burning my skin.

I failed once. Twice. Three times. Blood pounded in my ears as panic rose. I might have more raw winter magic than the king, but he had many turns on me. He'd experimented and used his power in ways that I could only dream of. He was better used to fighting through pain.

He yanked the dagger from his shoulder. Blood gushed from the wound with each step he took towards me, the weapon raised.

He sneered. "If you can't break my hold, you don't deserve the throne." The dagger pressed against my throat. "And why have I not seen your shadows?"

I did my best to snarl, but it came out as little more than a whimper.

Magnus chuckled softly. "You have the magic, but can't use it? Is that the issue? Well, Érebo will not be so disappointed that he missed out on watching you die then. If you're that weak, why would he waste his time?"

Seriously though, where was the Shadow King? And Rhistel?

"Worried about them, are you?" King Magnus dropped his voice to imitate concern. As if he was capable of such an emotion. "They're safe. As are a good number of our allies. Not that you'll ever see them again." The metal pressed harder into my throat, cracking the ice covering me.

"I would ask if you had any last words, Isolde, but the truth is, I've heard enough from you—" the king sucked in a breath and suddenly, his magical grip on me loosened.

"Get away from my sister, you bastard," Thyra growled, suspended in the air, wings fluttering to keep her in place as blood poured from her leg and shoulder. With her non-dominant hand, she palmed her dagger and struck, sinking the blade into the king's chest and pulling it out viciously.

He stumbled back, but instead of his hand going to his chest, it circled his throat. He wheezed.

I broke through his hold and though I felt as though a troll had nearly crushed me, I wasted no time in reaching for my sword. "What's going on?"

"Frozen windpipe. Like when you froze that one thug's arm." Thyra shrugged. "I could only muster so much power. Figured I'd better make it count."

I laughed. "Together?"

"Together."

We closed in as Magnus's gasps became louder, more urgent, and when we came to a stop before him, I couldn't help but smile coldly at the fae I despised.

"Perhaps we'll see you in the afterlife, but I think not." Thyra pressed her sword to his chest, and I added mine, right next to hers. "Just know, you deserve this end."

"He deserves worse," I repeated the words he'd spoken to me. "I would ask if you had any last words, Magnus, but the truth is, I've heard enough from you."

We thrust our swords into the king's chest, and I knew when Thyra released her grip on his throat because he gave two more shuddering breaths, the last he'd ever have, before slumping over our swords.

I planted my foot on his stomach and kicked his body off Sassa's Blade.

CHAPTER 57
ISOLDE

Word of the king's death spread like an uncontrollable wildfire, and the mages and Aaberg loyalists who remained surrendered in quick order. In truth, there were very few left to wave the flag of surrender, anyway.

A large number were gone to the afterworld, and the smell of death seemed to cling to every wooden deck.

Other sailors also reported seeing the three ships Arie and Halladora saw vanish into the night. Other ships had fled too, but as a ship normally would.

The consensus regarding the disappearing ship was as Thyra and I had suspected: King Érebo had been on one of those vessels, and he'd cloaked them in darkness to escape. Rhistel had most likely gone with Érebo—though I continued to hold out hope that he'd simply drowned.

I didn't know what would happen when the mages arrived in the capital, but that wasn't my problem at the moment. No, the first thing I thought of after unfreezing my friends, all of whom had burns coating their bodies, and leaving a grieving Arie in Caelo's care was Vale. The ship we'd left him on remained afloat, and my sister and I made our way there.

When we landed, it was to find the sailors abuzz. A sodden Rynni had been brought to this ship and though I could only glimpse her though the crowd of sailors, I saw she was awake, wrapped in a blanket, and being showered in thanks. We would check on her next. First, I had to see Vale.

Saga stood in front of the cabin door, a cage of ice shielding her. Upon catching sight of us, the seer waved a hand. Her cage of ice shattered and fell to the deck in shards.

Her face was bloodless. She'd heard the news then.

"Saga, I—"

She held up her hands, as if to ward my words away. "Don't apologize. I knew it would happen. He wasn't a good king, not even a good person, really, but I'd still like to be alone for a bit."

My friend left to come to terms with her father's death. Hate the male though I did, I understood.

After I'd learned who my father was, and of his horrible reputation, I'd still felt grief. Of course, my father's crimes were not his fault, but I didn't think it mattered. Saga had lost both parents in a few days' time and deserved to grieve in whatever manner she saw fit.

And soon I'd have to tell Vale that he'd also lost his parents. Lord Riis, his mother, and the male Vale had once called Father. My stomach tightened in anguish.

Knowing that Lord Riis had died fighting, and I'd never forgiven him for past actions, prompted a new level of guilt. I was certain that I'd carry it until my own death.

But there would be time to examine all the things I should have done and said later, so I pushed down the avalanche of emotions and entered the cabin where Vale was being kept. Thyra's shadows had found her mate and brought him here, just as she'd instructed. Thantrel sat by the porthole, unharmed save for a few bruises. He stared into the night, his shoulders tight and strained, but at our entrance, utter relief swept his face.

Thyra went to him, and they embraced.

"You dare return here?" Vale sat up in the bed. He eyed the shadows that I'd set to guard and protect him with the same fury that he directed towards me.

I tried to look happy and encouraging but managed only some weak semblance of my usual smile. "Vale, Rhistel used his magic on you. Deep down, you know I'd never harm you. That I love you, and do not lie to you."

He laughed. The derision struck my soul. Vale sounded nothing like himself.

"You've lied since the day I met you, Isolde," Vale hissed. "And the stars may have paired us, but others have helped me see I can't trust you. That the realm can't trust you or your sister."

My throat tightened. I turned my back to him and found Thantrel and Thyra watching. My sister appeared ready to lash out at Vale, probably to tell him what we'd gone through to save him. How many had died?

Thantrel released my sister's hand and came closer, his face filled with utter pity. "Rhistel didn't just use his magic on him, Isolde. He *tortured* Vale with visions of you, and he made every vision so visceral that it felt real. That's how it sounded, anyway."

I inhaled, trying to calm the way my heart rate kicked up at that idea. The concept was so diabolical—so *Rhistel.* "You're saying he's brainwashed against me."

"Very much so," Thantrel swallowed. "He didn't do the same to me because I'm not as recognizable as Vale. Also, I think Rhistel only had the energy to inflict that much damage on one of us. Once he began stealing Vale's mind, Rhistel's control on me loosened considerably."

"Yes, you seem normal." That, at least, gave me hope.

"The moment the Virtoris Armada came into view, I was told only to stay in a cabin, but otherwise, I had my own mind for the first time in days." Thantrel exhaled. "As terrified as I was when the shadows stole me from that cabin, I was also grateful to be free."

"You can't feel Rhistel any longer?" Thyra asked.

Thantrel shook his head. "I don't think so, but Vale clearly can."

"How long before he returns to himself?"

"I can't say." Thantrel cleared his throat. "All I know for certain is that he was able to work on Vale for two days."

Two days seemed like a long time to play with someone's mind. To inflict bouts of fear and torture one's own brother.

My chest tightened. What if Rhistel had caused irreparable damage?

"If you're here, I take it my father is dead?" Vale's question drew my attention back to him.

I turned, hating to deliver the news like this, but it

would have to happen at some point. Thantrel deserved to know too. Behind me, I heard Thyra approach Thantrel, and imagined her pulling him close.

"Lord Riis is dead." Thantrel gave a sound of shock, making my lungs tighten, but I had more to say. More to admit. "And so is Queen Inga. I'm so sorry, Vale. We—"

Vale shot to his feet. "You killed my mother?"

"She was poisoned by Rhistel, King Magnus, and those of House Ithamai. We didn't know when we took her from that cell in Grindavik that she'd need the antidote."

"My father wouldn't do that to her."

I stiffened. *His father.*

Gods, Rhistel brainwashed Vale so thoroughly he didn't consider Lord Riis his father any longer. Anger rose inside me.

"Magnus would do so, and he did." My chin lifted. "And when you come to your senses, you'll agree."

"You killed him too, didn't you?" Vale spoke through gritted teeth.

"We both did. Together," Thyra spoke loud and clear, as though trying to divert Vale's anger to her.

"I'll return the favor. To the both of you." The shadow figures I'd conjured swarmed angrily at his threat, but Vale didn't seem to notice as he laid back on the bed and stared at the ceiling.

I couldn't stand here and speak with my mate any longer. Couldn't hear him speak to me and my sister like this.

"Shadows, keep watch." Though the effort of maintaining their existence was more draining by the second; it was safer than having a fae watch my mate when he was like this. "Don't let him leave this cabin."

I exited the stateroom and made it three steps before I doubled over. Tears streamed down my face. I'd kept them in while speaking with Vale, but stars, I felt physically ill. Knowing that the love of my life wanted me dead was the worst kind of punishment.

Thyra came up beside me and placed a hand on my shoulder. "There've been many losses today, but he's not gone, just in a place we cannot go. Not yet anyway."

So much loss. We'd lost Sigri. The Virtoris siblings lost their mother. And Vale, Luccan, Thantrel, and Arie had lost their father. Oh, gods, the sisters in Grindavik too. I had so much to answer for.

I straightened and found Thantrel standing behind Thyra. The whites of his eyes were red.

"I'm so sorry, Thantrel. I can't believe I'm acting like this when you lost your father."

"Your pain is as valid as mine," Thantrel said.

I hugged him, and when he pulled away, he looked into the distance.

"The enemy sailors are contained?"

"Our forces were finishing the job when we came here," Thyra said.

"I'm going to find Arie." His wings spread out behind him, brilliant red and orange and yellow in the dark of night.

"Do you want me to come?" Thyra asked.

"No, but thank you. I want time with my brother and our father."

"I understand." Thyra kissed her mate's cheek before

he flew off to find his brother. To mourn with someone who loved his father like he did.

I exhaled. "We need to return to land. To Bitra."

"And plan our next move," Thyra added. "Érebo is still out there. And until I hear otherwise, I assume Rhistel is too."

If she was right—which I had to admit she probably was for it would be all too lucky to get rid of the heir and the king on the same day—Rhistel was likely already plotting how to end our lives. In the meantime, he'd spread the tales far and wide of the dangerous Falk twins.

We might have won this battle, but I had a feeling the war for Winter's Realm had only just begun.

Finish the series with A War of Winter and Wrath!

OF SHIPS AND SAGAS
THE WINTER COURT
SERIES, A PREQUEL STORY

This bonus story is alluded to in A Crown of Ice and Fury. It details an adventure taken by Saga and Sayyida long before the events of A Kingdom of Frost and Malice. This is the first sighting of beings with shadow powers in Isila in many turns.

CHAPTER 1
PRINCESS SAGA

I leaned far over the edge of the good ship *Trana*, reveling in the sea spray as the early morning mists swallowed Avaldenn. I exhaled.

With Frostveil Palace and all the gossip and fanfare that came with my home finally behind me, I had time to breathe. It might only be for two days, and I *was* here in a royal capacity, but none of that mattered. I savored every moment I was not under my father's thumb.

"Should we go to your cabin, Princess Saga?" asked Sir Yagril, my favorite Clawsguard. He stood a respectful distance away, brown hands clasped in front of him. He was always careful to give me space and allowed me to daydream and think, my favorite pastimes.

"I'd like to stay out here." I gazed out at the Shivering Sea, undulating beneath the eerie mist. "Maybe all day."

"Your father insisted you get your reading done."

Of course he would. Father hadn't picked up a book in many turns, but he expected his children to study. Only Vale, who favored the sword, received leniency, and that was because he was often on patrol or leading the army to battle orc tribes. Vale's twin and the heir to the crown, Rhistel, and I had no such excuse.

"Feeling seasick yet?" a voice called out, saving me from pushing back on Father's wishes.

My heart fluttered as I caught a whiff of golden apple on the salty wind. I turned, already knowing I'd find my oldest and best friend, Lady Sayyida Virtoris—or rather, *Captain* Sayyida—swaggering my way.

"You're going to lose that bet," I retorted with a playful smirk.

"We'll see. The sea has a mind of its own. Especially as we near Lord Armenil's lands."

A thrill ran through me. I'd left the capital of Winter's Realm before. I'd traveled all the way to the Warden of the South's black and gold palace, as well as to the lands of the Warden of the East. But I'd never been north.

The territory that Lord Armenil oversaw was said to be even more rugged than the mountains of the south, which I found difficult to believe. I was itching to see such land for myself. In the pocket of my trousers, my diary sat heavy, begging me to pull it out and document my thoughts on the journey.

"No writing. It will only increase your chances of becoming ill." Sayyida joined me in gazing out into the gray-blue waters of the sea. We hadn't gone too far from land, but the fog already seemed thinner, and we could see farther than when we'd lifted anchor in the port.

"How'd you know I was considering writing?"

"You always get this far off look in your eyes when

you're about to write. What do you put in that thing, anyway?"

Everything. Tales of court. What I could see of Avaldenn out the palace windows and the lives I devised for the fae of the city. My thoughts. My dreams. Sometimes, I even wrote of epic romances I wished to experience one day.

"Silly stories." I shrugged.

"With a name like Saga, no story you wrote could be silly."

"Most would beg to differ."

"Most people at *court*," she corrected, "and many of them are fools."

Though Sayyida did not spend as much time as me at the Winter Court, as a daughter of the indomitable Lady of Ships, she could not avoid the court entirely. I suspected my peer had joined the Royal Nava to get out of as many feasts, balls, and celebrations as possible. Though I wasn't in love with the water like her, sometimes I wished to follow in her footsteps. Out here, atop the lolling waves and standing in the riotous wind, one felt so free. Anything could be real, even the most ludicrous dreams of one's soul.

"I can't deny that most at court are not my cup of tea." I shot her a grin.

Sayyida returned the smile. How her black curls blew in the wind and her shoulders rolled back drew me in. She'd been confident all her life. Each and every one of the Virtoris children had an air of self-assuredness, but somehow, the sea made Sayyida even more charismatic.

Heat flushed my chest. Since I'd been old enough to

recognize such a thing, I'd known that there was a spark between Sayyida and me. However, as we were the daughters of a highborn family and a princess respectively, nothing could come of it. Common fae, even those of lesser noble houses, could, and often did, embrace same-sex unions for their children. Alas, among the Sacred Eight families of Winter's Realm and the Royal House of Aaberg—*my house*—that would never happen. I was not destined to be queen, but as far as my father was concerned I was a powerful pawn in the game of influence and might.

"I'm surprised your father allowed you to wear that." My friend gestured down at my royal blue trousers over which an asymmetrical half-skirt of gold flowed, exposing the front of my hips and legs. The dress was unique in that it allowed my legs to be shown and provided enhanced mobility. And yet, the back half flowed to my ankles and the entire skirt was attached to a bodice, so it was still, technically, a dress.

"He wouldn't have if Mother hadn't approved it first." I shrugged. "Truth be told, she didn't like the style much, but humored me. She thinks that all young ladies must make their own choices and mistakes," I raised an eyebrow the same way my mother had when taking in the dress, "at least, when it comes to personal style."

"Who made it?"

"Are you *actually* interested?" Normally, Sayyida cared little about dresses.

"It's pretty and not constraining like normal dresses. I might try it. Perhaps I'll wear it to one of those balls that Mother is insisting I attend."

"How the courtiers will talk! Lady Sayyida, wearing half a dress to formal events!" I replied, my tone playful. "I'm sorry to say that you'll have to wait. I had six others custom made. They take a half-moon each to create."

My friend snorted. "Such a pampered princess."

I swatted her shoulder, only for her to catch my hand and squeeze. As she did so, she turned to me and the light shone on her necklace, a locket displaying a gold dragon. It was lovely, and if I wasn't mistaken, new.

"When did you get that?" I gestured to the necklace but didn't let go of her, relishing the warmth of her skin against mine.

Her thumb rubbed over my hand. "When I last sailed to the Kingdom of Flame."

She'd only returned from that southern court a few days ago. "It's unusual."

She nodded to my legs. "When you're done with the seamstress, tell me her name before anyone else, will you?"

"Consider it done." I winked at her as I reclaimed my hand and brushed a wind-tossed lock of pink hair from my face. In the action, I didn't miss when Sayyida's eyes dipped and landed on my lips. My heart fluttered and, for a moment, the salty sea air electrified.

"Captain Virtoris! A moment?" a sailor called from behind, breaking the current pulsing between Sayyida and me.

I blinked as my friend pivoted and waved at the male.

"I'll be right there." Sayyida turned back to me and shrugged. "Duty calls, but I meant to ask earlier, do you need something special to perform your royal function? This is my first time in charge of a blessing."

While only eighteen like me, she'd already captained many ships in the Virtoris fleet. The *Trana*, however, was a brand-new royal vessel on its symbolic maiden voyage. During such voyages, a member of the royal house or a member of the religious community was always on board to bless the ship. Usually a Staret or Staretess sailed with the new ships, but most often my mother's brother, army Captain Vagle, did so. My mother even sailed once.

After much begging, I was finally blessing a ship.

"My mere presence is enough." I twirled my hand in the air. "Isn't that obvious?"

She rolled her eyes. "Pardon me, Princess, I should have known." A smirk grew on her lips. "I'll see you soon. Stay away from the edges, and remember, *no writing*. If word gets back to your mother that you became ill, you'll never be allowed on my ship again."

CHAPTER 2
PRINCESS SAGA

Beneath my feet, the ship rolled and swayed. Hours had passed since we'd sailed out of Avaldenn's port, and in that time, I had found my sea legs.

Sir Yagril, on the other hand, had decidedly not taken to sea life. The deeper the water got, the greener he turned. Despite the remedies the sailors had given him, nothing seemed to help. The poor faerie appeared as though he might be ill at any moment.

"Truly, Yagril. We're in the middle of the sea with my people. Nothing will happen to me."

"I cannot leave your side, Princess Saga."

"I don't think you'll be much help, not in your current state, anyway."

He scowled but did not reply.

Trying to be kind to the knight who had been by my side for many turns, I veered back toward the ship's railing. At least there, Yagril could vomit in peace if he needed to.

We reached the railing, and though the fog from the

morning had burned off, something else caught my eye. In the distance, a black cloud crawled over the waves, as if following a ship.

"Sir Yagril, do you see that?" I pointed east.

"I do, Princess."

"What is that blackness? It looks like—"

Before my eyes, the cloud picked up speed as it rolled our way. Within the darkness, light sparked, and a horn blared above. Shouts filled the *Trana* and suddenly fae were running about the deck.

I looked at Yagril. "What's going on?"

My guard shook his head and stared out at the sea. "I'm not sure, but I believe it would be wise if we—*blazing moon!*"

"Has to be mages!" a sailor called out. "They're closing in too fast to be anything else!"

But they were just . . . I blinked. The ship had somehow jumped over waves. It was so close I could make out the whites of the eyes of those on board.

One burly male grinned and something behind him fluttered. The sailor who suggested mages was wrong, at least in part. Perhaps there were mages on the ship, but these ones weren't mages. They were fae, which became all too apparent as a dozen sailors launched themselves into the air straight for us.

My stomach pitted. They had to be rogue bands of fae. Most lived in kingdoms with milder climates, but it was rumored that some had stolen ships from the Autumn Court and taken to the seas. They now acted as pirates, raping, razing, and pillaging along the coastlines of Isila, some even daring to strike the Mage Court.

"Princess!" Yagril tried to shove me behind him, but his cries caught the attention of one of the fae who changed direction and soared my way.

Thank the stars, my guard was ready, his long sword out and wind magic in his hand. He pummeled the attacker, sending him into the sea with a vicious splash.

Yagril did not, however, see the other two attackers coming. Nor did I. Not until it was too late.

A dagger soared through the air, plunging into my sworn shield's chest at the same moment an arrow came from the ship and caught him in the leg. Yagril fell, blood welling from beneath his fighting leathers, and thin gasps filled my ears.

"No! Yag—!"

"Come 'ere, little princess," a brute who looked to be half troll dropped out of the sky and grabbed me by the shoulders. "Ye must be from the Winter Court. Princess Saga, is it?"

"Get off me!" I fought to break free of his grip, unable to take my eyes off my guard bleeding out before me. Because I had two older brothers and wasn't a complete weakling, I actually managed to slip out of his hands. Free, I lunged for Yagril and pressed a hand to his pulse.

He was alive, his pulse still thundering, but for how long? "Yagril, I—"

"Get back 'ere!" This time when the male grabbed me, his grip was ironclad. "A princess will bring us a lotta coin. You—"

A gurgling sound ripped from his lips and wetness splattered the back of my neck. I twisted and found

Sayyida standing there, her dagger lodged in the ugly fae's throat.

"Are you harmed?"

"No!" I took in the blood splattered across her face with horror, but she moved as though she were uninjured. That had to be from someone else. "But Yagril needs a healer. Help me with him!"

"Let's hurry then."

I grabbed my guard's arms while Sayyida took his legs. Her gaze was raking the ship's decks. Suddenly aware of the shouts and growls, I took in the area too. Already, pirates overran the ship.

How had they reached us so fast? And was that an ogre?! Fear rushed through me at the sight of a fae-eating creature so close by.

"How many?" I asked. My guard's injury had blinded me, but this was Sayyida's ship, her fae to lead and protect. She would not miss a thing.

"Thirty. More quickly followed the first dozen. They must have heard your guard naming you as a princess and doubled down." She shook her head. "He needs to learn to hold his tongue."

"You can tell him when we save him."

"I will." She grunted and ducked as a steel star flew overhead, nearly stopping my heart. Unlike me, Sayyida took it as a matter of course and gestured with her shoulder. "Get to the lower decks."

Metal clanged, and magic spun through the sea air. The crew protected us, and they did so remarkably as we wove through brawls. We'd made it to the door that led below decks when one attacker slipped through the melee and came straight for us.

"Sayyida!" I shrieked because her back was to him. Not missing a beat, she dropped Yagril's feet, spun, drew her sword, and impaled the fae seconds before his blade would have run her through.

"Go." The captain picked up a groaning Yagril's feet once more.

Making sure I had a good grip on my guard, I released one hand and opened the door, steadying him again before he fell. The stairs down were ludicrously steep, considering we were on a ship.

"Slow," Sayyida said. "I'll lock the door behind us."

We shuffled in, and I was even more thankful for my half-dress and trousers. Had I been in a regular dress, I would have tripped. Once Sayyida maneuvered through the door, she locked it with one hand.

"That won't hold back anyone who *really* wants to get down here, but my crew will do their best to keep this area safe."

I swallowed as we descended. My brother Vale was a renowned warrior and had wanted to make sure I knew how to defend myself, even if Father didn't see the point. However, despite my brother's training attempts, I wasn't the best with blades. Could I hold my own against a troop of savage pirates? Especially ones wielding some sort of smoke magic that could skip their ship over a league of water in an instant? Unlikely.

When we reached the bottom, Sayyida jerked her chin to the left. From there, it wasn't difficult to find the healer as he popped his head out the door and gasped.

"Sassa's Blade! Get him on my table!"

We did so, shuffling through the cramped quarters made even smaller thanks to the herbs and potions that lined and hung from every available space and gave off the most unusual and pungent herbaceous aromas. When Yagril was settled, I studied him. He was passed out and his dusky brown skin had paled.

"It isn't fatal, right?" I asked the healer as he leaned over the knight.

"He has a pulse, and I think the dagger missed his heart. I won't know for certain until I extract it, though."

That did not invite confidence, but as the healer and Sayyida began working, I wanted to be useful too. "What can I do?"

"What magic do you possess?"

"Winter magic." When the healer circled a hand in the air as if to say 'yes, yes, but we need something *useful*', I blushed.

Normally, fae prized winter magic, the power that steadied our kingdom, but not here. Not now.

"I also have the gift of foresight. Occasionally. Not on demand."

The healer let out a puff of air, and Sayyida shot me an apologetic glance.

Foresight, too, was apparently supremely useless.

"Get that elixir." He pointed to the shelf. "Blue one at the top with the black cork."

I squeezed around the table and tried to pluck the bottle from the shelf. It didn't come loose easily, likely because of a sticking charm which was sensible on a ship. I pulled harder, and finally, the bottle came free. I rushed

back and handed it to the healer, who held up his bloodied, wet hands.

"Uncork it."

He might as well have added, *idiot*, and I wouldn't
have blamed him. I wasn't performing too well under
these pressures.

A *pop* filled the room as I pulled the cork. The healer
took the bottle and poured it into Yagril's mouth.

"What does it do?"

"Regenerates blood."

"But won't he bleed more when you take the dagger
out?"

"I thought you were a seer?"

My lips clamped together. A princess could take a hint.
I waited for another direction as the healer and Sayyida
worked. They'd liberated the blade from my guard's chest
when a horn from above blasted.

That had not sounded the same as before, and judging
by how Sayyida lost all the color in her face, it meant
something bad.

"I need to go up," she said. "Saga, stay here. Help
Healer H—"

The door to the chamber burst open to reveal three
brawny fae.

CHAPTER 3

PRINCESS SAGA

"That's the princess!" In the back of the trio, a faerie with antlers, cloven hooves, and a squished face pointed at me.

The room was small and crowded and with Yagril bleeding on the table, I couldn't risk erratic movements. Unfortunately, I was also closest to the door, and the male in the front seized the advantage, grabbing me and shoving me back to their friend in the doorway. The fae with the antlers lifted me over his shoulder and ran.

"Release her!" Sayyida screamed.

Blade hit blade and the terrified screams of the healer cut through me as my captor whisked down the hallway. Kicking and thrashing only succeeded in hurting my legs against the fae's hard body and the stairwell's railings.

"Let me go!" I shouted.

"Shut yer mouth." The fae threw open the door to the main level.

Sayyida and I had left the deck in chaos and in our

short time below decks, nothing had changed. Blood ran with seawater, fae fought fae, and there was no clear winner yet.

But if I left this ship, the pirates would have gained a valuable hostage. Who was I dealing with here?

Again, I cast a glance around. Save for giants, full trolls, and orcs, it appeared every order of fae was present, and despite their many differences, they all shared a commonality. A mark of three concentric circles was branded on each of their forearms.

Mentally, I ran through the house crests in my kingdom, and the most influential noble houses of the other eight kingdoms. I could not place such a mark, and as the fae carrying me launched into the air, I ceased trying to recall it. I shrieked as we landed heavily and the fae lifted me from his shoulders.

"Look what I got lads!"

Cheers rang in my ears as the oaf presented me to the pirate crew, a host of rugged and scruffy fae. I jerked, trying to fight out of my captor's grasp, but this time, his grip was strong and unyielding. And as one of his colleagues appeared from the crowd with a metal net in his gloved hands, my mouth dried up.

"Iron," the incomer hissed.

From the scarred markings on his neck and the broken way in which he walked; I assumed this male was some sort of water fae. Merman, perhaps? They could transform for short periods of time, though they did not walk smoothly, and the area where their gills should be resembled scars. "Stay still, girl."

"No!" I screamed. "You can't! I—" a painful cry tore up my throat as the iron weave net landed on my black wings, sizzling the flesh there.

"If ye stay still, it won't hurt as much," the fae that had taken me spoke. "Less places for da iron to hurt."

I swallowed, trying to control the pain rooting me in place, and failing. Few races of fae could handle touching iron, and faeries were not among them.

So I fell in line. I stayed still, because moving felt like my wings were being simultaneously stabbed and lit on fire.

"Good pretty princess," my captor growled. "Now, let's get ye below decks. The captain will want to see ye. Prepare to leave."

The crew dispersed, some rushing to the rigging, others to the bow, and elsewhere. My heart lodged in my throat as the antlered fae gripped me by the arm and guided me. Iron cut deeper into my wings with each step, and I whimpered.

"Soon ye'll be locked up."

"Great. Locked up and with iron draped over me. Can't wait."

He looked affronted. "We won't leave those on. We're not barbarians, we ain't."

I did not have the strength to argue. Under the stinging weight of the metal net, it took everything I had to walk across the deck to my prison.

"Prepare to retreat!" someone called out in warning, and my captor swore.

"Not yet!" he screamed back, stopping me. "We needs more time!"

I exhaled a shaky breath. I needed to get my head on straight and try to escape. Eyeing my captor sidelong, I took a chance.

"Take me back," I wheezed the words, hating that they sounded so much like begging. "I can convince my father to pay you. *Only you.* But you have to take me back."

The fae stiffened. "You think I'd mutiny against my captain? My queen?"

His queen? My lips parted. Pirates did not ally themselves to kingdoms, but this fae did. Where did they come from? Where—?

My thoughts stopped as my attention caught on the smoke crawling across the deck, swirling viciously. Others gave it space, as if they feared it, though to me it looked the same as the smoke the ship had been riding when it was transported from one place to another. The mage wielding it had to be near, though I couldn't see them.

"We gotta move! Ye can't be out here!" the fae rumbled and shoved me.

I cried out in pain and fell to my knees.

"Get up! Get up, Princess. I—"

"Stay away from her!" a voice I recognized yelled and suddenly the fae shepherding me below decks was on the ground, blood spurting from a wound in his forehead.

Shockingly, he rolled to his knees as if nothing had happened and sprang to his feet. "Harpy!"

"You're going to wish I was a harpy," Sayyida growled, and I smelled the fresh apple of her soap a moment before the veil of iron lifted from my back. I was free.

I gasped and spun, my wings still aching, but at least

now I could move more freely without fear of burning them more.

Blade in hand, Sayyida slashed at the larger fae, the blows cutting into his chest, shoulder, and cheek in rapid fashion. Her long, dark hair flew around her, a windstorm of black tresses.

"Fly Saga!" she screamed. "Go back!"

"I-I can't!" I replied. Merely stretching my wings to their full span was too much.

"And she won't!" Another voice bellowed from behind.

I spun in time to find that Sayyida's appearance had not gone unnoticed. Three male fae lumbered my way.

"Sassa's bloody Blade!" Sayyida barked. "Enough is enough!" She pulled back and let her dagger fly. Before her opponent dodged, the weapon sank into his face. He fell, and my friend pointed at me. "Come here."

I shot to her side, eyes wide. Was she going to fight off all three? Carry me back to the ship? That was a sizable risk with the others on her heels.

Instead, she did none of those things, and rather reached for the dragon necklace. "You owe me, Saga."

She opened the locket and flames erupted. I shielded my eyes as a roar burst through the air.

"By the Faetia!" I whispered when I caught sight of a beast made of flame, a dragon, soaring in the direction of the fae who were coming after us. The monster opened its mouth and spewed fire so fast the opponents could not beat it. They went up in a blaze. The dragon pivoted and surged upwards, launching into a sail and then shifting to catch the ropes afire.

"Come on." Sayyida hitched her arm around my

waist. I cringed as she brushed the back of a wing. She caught the motion and gave me a regretful look. "Sorry, but we have to get out of here. The others are doing their best to regain the ship, and I have three in the air covering us. We have to seize the moment."

I nodded, determined not to put us in more danger, and my friend gripped me tighter and lifted us into the air. Her wings strained under our combined weight, but turns of buffeting against wicked sea winds had made her a strong flier. Once we reached two of the fae she'd brought to cover her, both busy fending off more opponents, another sailor joined us.

"'Scuse me, Princess Saga," he murmured, as he helped Sayyida bear my weight.

I said nothing, too mesmerized by the pirate ship below. The fire dragon was one thing, but the smoke was also astonishing. Thick black coils of smoke that resembled snakes swirled over the ship and into the ocean, churning the waters.

"Is that helping them sail?" I asked as, despite its burning sails, the other ship moved to retreat.

"Who knows?! All I care about is getting you back to the *Trana*!" my friend replied as we descended.

Swift heartbeats later, we touched down on our deck. A quick sweep of the ship told me that the battle was over. We'd won, though not without sustaining injuries on both sides.

Hostages were present as well, bound with chains around their hands and feet, and seeing as they were all massive, they were giving our sailors a hard time of keeping them under control. Sayyida shouted a few commands to quell the unrest, and the sailors took to fulfilling them.

Feeling useless and achy and like nothing but a problem, I faced the sea in time to watch the flaming pirate ship disappear into a cloud of smoke, exactly the way it had arrived.

CHAPTER 4
PRINCESS SAGA

"Saga, come with me." Sayyida snapped me out of the daze of watching the flaming pirate ship vanish as she took my hand. Her palm was warm and sticky. I looked down to find blood covering her fingers.

"Are you hurt?" I asked, guilty that I hadn't asked sooner.

"None of the blood is mine." She smirked. The expression was so familiar it made my heart clench. "It will take more than that to spill Virtoris blood."

Cocky as ever, that was Lady Sayyida Virtoris. I snorted as she pulled me below decks. I thought we were going to the healer, but when we turned the opposite direction, my eyebrows lifted. Moments later, Sayyida slipped into her own cabin, the captain's cabin. She shut the door behind us.

"On the settee."

"You're incredibly bossy."

"I'm responsible for the Princess of Winter's Realm's

wellbeing, so yes, I am bossy and will not apologize for it. Now, *sit*."

Slowly, because my wings still ached, I shuffled to the couch and lowered, careful to keep my back from touching the velvet, bluish-gray cushions.

Sayyida strode to the side of the room and opened a cabinet to extract a bottle. "This potion will help your wings. It has to be applied topically."

I tilted my head. "Why do you have it in here?"

"A leader sometimes needs to lick their wounds in private. If I sustained a non-fatal injury, I'd want time to think over what happened without others around, so I stocked up."

She took after her mother in that way—proud, not wanting others to see her pain. Well, most others. As younglings, I'd seen Sayyida cry numerous times. It came with the territory of growing up together.

"Lean forward," she murmured as she joined me on the settee. "I can get the healer, but he's probably still working on your guard. Or my sailors. A few were injured. You don't mind me doing it, do you?"

I swallowed. Parts of a faerie's wings were sensitive, and others did not usually touch them. Exceptions existed, of course. As a royal, people often bathed and dressed me. And then there were intimate moments, none of which I had experienced yet at eighteen sheltered turns.

My cheeks flushed as I imagined Sayyida running her hands along my dark wings where they met my back.

"Not at all," I choked out.

Her touch flitted over me, soft and gentle, and my marred flesh tingled beneath her ministrations.

"Breathe," Sayyida whispered, and only then did I realize that I'd been holding my breath.

I exhaled as she gently rubbed the potion into my membranous right wing. Once she was done, she moved to the left. Where her hands touched, my wings tingled and tightened at the base. I hoped she didn't notice.

"That was a lot," I said when the silence and the sensation became too much.

"Being overtaken by a pirate ship? That's every other day at sea."

I snorted. "Sure it is."

"We took care of it, didn't we? No fatalities on our side, either."

"A near miss." Guilt that my guard had nearly died swept through me. He was hurting because of me.

Fingers wrapped around my shoulder, turned me back so that I faced her. "Sir Yagril wasn't your fault. It's his job to be there to protect you. He knows the risk. Everyone on my ship understood there was a risk in having you aboard."

A sharp inhale sank into my lungs. "Are you saying that pirate ship attacked because of me?"

"That came out wrong." Sayyida set the bottle of potion down and wiped the excess that coated her fingers onto her bloodied trousers. "They didn't know you were here. They seemed surprised by it, but once they learned, their aim changed from looting to faenapping. And no matter which royal is aboard a ship, that's always a risk. Even other members of the Sacred Eight are a liability—even me." She trailed off, her lips pursed in a way that told me she despised that her noble blood was more valuable to a pirate than who she had become through her own sweat and tears: the captain of a royal ship.

"Vale would have been fine."

"Your brother is a great warrior, but he's no natural on the sea."

That was true. Water was one of my older brother's failings, a fact that his twin reminded Vale of at every opportunity.

"The attack was too fast," Sayyida said. "You did your best. My crew doesn't fault you for being taken."

I nodded, still not feeling great about it, but willing to move on. "What do you make of the smoke?"

"Smoke? Looked more like shadows to me."

Ice crept through my veins because, on second thought, she was right. Smoke would have smelled and been hazy, it would have thinned with the wind, but shadows lived by neither rule. These had been more a bending of light. Of space too, maybe, seeing as the boat had crossed a large distance in a second. I didn't understand what I'd seen.

"How do they make them? There hasn't been a Shadow Fae in so long." And there shouldn't be any at all . . .

"At least four thousand turns," Sayyida agreed. "Perhaps they have a couple of mages aboard though. That's not outside a mage's skill set."

Mage magic varied more than that of other orders. There could be many mages capable of making shadows. Sometimes I envied their magical order, and their ability to continue to learn new types of magic as they aged. However, the downfall to most mages was that they did not heal quickly, and they were not as agile as fae, vampires, elves, wolvea, or dragons. They relied heavily on power to keep them safe, and magic always came at a cost.

"I thought so too, actually, but I didn't see a mage on the ship." Amidst the fae they'd be noticeable. Most mages could easily pass for human, but no fae could.

"Seems more likely. Mage magic can move ships quickly like theirs did too." Sayyida shifted in the seat and the gold glint of her dragon locket caught a beam coming in through the port window.

I motioned to it. "You never told me your locket did that."

"This?" She fingered the necklace as though it were nothing and not the exact thing that had helped us escape. Her gaze dipped to pause on my lips. "Not anymore. It's only supposed to work once. The dragon lord I got it from said to use it wisely. On a loved one." She stiffened and looked at the ground, but there was no going back, no taking away what she'd said.

The words rang between us and the very air in the room warmed, became electrified. Though she could have meant as a friendly sort of love, her actions spoke differently. And so did the pounding of my heart.

Could it be?

Did I dare?

"Sayyida?" I whispered.

"I—that . . . I meant—"

Stammering. Confident, bold Sayyida Virtoris was *stammering*. I wanted to laugh and cry at the same time because it became crystal clear she'd meant what she said, what she'd done.

She just hadn't realized it.

Slowly, I cupped her cheek. "Thank you for using the locket to save me."

Gray-blue eyes met my own, and the cabin's temperature seemed to rise even higher. I leaned forward, closer to her.

Sayyida leaned in too and slowly our lips met, soft and exploring. Goosebumps erupted along my arms. I was kissing her—the girl I'd secretly fancied for many turns.

And it felt so right. So perfect. I wanted more.

I wanted it all.

Had anyone been around, I doubt we'd have noticed. The world became Sayyida and me, and unsaid words and unexplored moments come to life in a kiss.

But like all good things, the kiss came to an end too soon. Sayyida pulled away and we stared at one another, chests heaving, hearts pounding.

"Saga," she whispered. "What are we doing?"

"I—I don't know," I replied, taken aback.

"You're betrothed to my brother."

The heady excitement crashed down to the depths of the Shivering Sea. The worst thing was, I could say nothing against her claim. It was true. The entire kingdom knew it. Though my brothers were older, I, alone of the Aaberg children, was betrothed because Father thought females were best for creating alliances and bearing heirs to tighten those alliances. My throat tightened.

"That's arranged," I whispered through the pain.

"Does that matter?" Sayyida rose, her eyes dashing to the window, the cabinet, anywhere but to me. She was

694

looking for an excuse, and luckily for her, it came in the form of a rap on the door.

"Captain?"

"Yes?" Sayyida replied, tone too high to be natural.

"There's been a problem."

She straightened her hair and shirt and, sparing me a glance, strode to the door and opened it. "What's that?"

"The captives." His voice dropped, "they're dead."

"Bleeding stars! How?"

"They had poisonous crystals on them. Ate 'em when their guard turned his back."

"Did we get information from them before that?"

"Not enough to know who they are, where they came from, or why they attacked."

Sayyida swore and turned to face me. "I have to go. Stay here as long as you wish. And use as much potion as you want."

I studied her and the mask she'd been able to put on while I sat in place, frozen and exposed. And broken.

"Sure."

For a moment, my friend paused, but then she exited the cabin.

I stared at the door, brokenhearted, knowing the only person I'd ever wanted had shut me out.

Finish the series with A War of Winter and Wrath!

THE NINE
KINGDOMS OF ISILA

The Blood Kingdom - vampire
The Elven Kingdom - elves
The Winter Kingdom - fae of various races
The Autumn Kingdom - fae of various races
The Spring Kingdom - fae of various races
The Summer Kingdom - fae of various races
The Wolvea Kingdom - wolvea shifters
The Dragon Kingdom - dragon shifters

Each kingdom is colloquially described as a court, though technically, the court is a specific place or places in the larger kingdom.

Some kingdoms have additional names, such as the Winter Kingdom being called Winter's Realm or the Dragon Kingdom being called the Kingdom of Flame.

THE HIGH NOBILITY OF THE KINGDOM OF WINTER

HOUSE AABERG - ROYAL HOUSE
King Magnus Aaberg
Queen Inga Aaberg née Vagle

Children
Prince Rhistel Aaberg
Prince Vale Aaberg
Princess Saga Aaberg

The royal house is not a part of the Sacred Eight.[1] They do rely heavily on the families of the Sacred Eight but the royal house is distinct from all others.

Before the White Bear's Rebellion, House Aaberg was a member of the Sacred Eight. Since the rebellion House Riis took their place as a reward for loyalty to House Aaberg.

The Sacred Eight Families of Winter's Realm

*** Lord Sten Armenil - Warden of the North - Head of House**
*** Lady Orla Armenil née Balik**
Children
* Marit Armenil - female
* Connan Armenil - male
* Rune Armenil - male
* Tiril Armenil - female
* Jorunn Armenil - female
* Raemar Armenil - male

*** Lady Vaeri Ithamai - Warden of the East - Head of House**
*** Lord Tiarsus Itamai née Skau - deceased**
Children
* Hadia Ithamai - female
* Adila Ithamai - female

*** Lord Tadgh Balik - Warden of the South - Head of House**
*** Lady Kilyn Balik née Armenil**
Children
* Sian Balik - male
* Baenna Balik - female
* Eireann Balik - female
* Saoirse Balik - female
* Fionn Balik - male
* Garbhan Balik - male - deceased
* Carai Balik - female

700

* Filip Balik - squire to Prince Vale of House Aaberg - male
* Colm Balik - male

*** Lord Roar Lisika - Warden of the West - Head of House**
Unmarried
No children

*** Lord Leyv Riis - Head of House**
Unmarried
Children (only the children at court are included)
* Luccan Riis - male
* Arie Riis - male
* Thantrel Riis - non-binary

*** Lord Airen Vagle - Lord of Coin - Head of House**
*** Lady Eliana Vagle - deceased**
Children
* Queen Inga - married to King Magnus Aaberg
* Captain of the Royal Guard Eirwen Vagle - Father to Lady Calpurnia Vagle - his wife has passed to the afterworld
* Fival Vagle - acting lord in their family seat in the midlands - male
* Selah Vagle - married to a wealthy Jarl in the midlands - female

*** Lady Nalaea Qiren - Lady of Silks - Head of House**

*** Lord Virion Qiren née Ithamai - deceased**
Children
* Aenesa Qiren - female
* Thalia Qiren - female
* Iro Qiren - female

*** Lady Fayeth Virtoris - Lady of Ships - Head of House**
*** Lord Kailu Virtoris née Oridan, from the Summer Court**
Children
* Vidar Virtoris - betrothed to Princess Saga of House Aaberg - male
* Sayyida Virtoris - female
* Njal Virtoris - male
* Amine Virtoris - female

EXTINCT GREATER HOUSES - ALL MEMBERS OF THESE NOBLE HOUSES WERE KILLED DURING THE WHITE BEAR'S REBELLION

House Falk
King Harald's royal house
House Skau
Queen Revna's birth house. She married into House Falk and had six children with King Harald.

Beneath the Sacred Eight there are hundreds of lesser houses. These are led by jarls of various territories.

---

1. Prior to the White Bear's Rebellion, the Sacred Eight were actually the Sacred Nine, with House Skau being the ninth member, and House Falk being the royal house.

Acknowledgments

This book, like all of the books in this series, was such a joy to write (I hope I can say the same for A War of Winter and Wrath too). I can't wait to continue the story of Neve and Vale and Winter's Realm. Huge things are coming for the world of Isila, and I hope readers enjoy it.

Thank you to my husband, my biggest cheerleader and best friend. I still can't believe I get to do this life with you and that we continue to learn and grow together. We really are a lucky pair and I love you.

This book would not have been as much fun to write if I did not have my weekly neighborhood writers meet up. My writer's salon as I've recently started calling it. Our little coffee shop group is constantly growing and fluctuating and I'm thankful for every member who listened to me worry about how to move armies across vast snow-covered lands and not slow down the pacing of this novel. The anxiety was real.

Another shout out to my fellow romantasy authors, many of whom I've had the pleasure of meeting in the last year. This community is special and all of you make it so much fun.

Last but definitely not least, a huge thank you to my ARC team and especially the following members for typo-hunting for me: Bobbie Jo Schultze, Tash Langton, Shirley Bostok, Mortisha Johnson, Saundra Wright, Kaylie Willis, Fran Fox, Liz Ford, Sadie Nickles, and Katy Cross.

All the magic,
Ashley McLeo

ALSO BY ASHLEY MCLEO

<u>The Winter Court (Crowns of Magic Universe)</u>

A Kingdom of Frost and Malice

A Lord of Snow and Greed

A Hallow of Storm and Ruin

A Tower of Gold and Goblins - companion novella

A Crown of Ice and Fury

A War of Winter and Wrath

<u>Coven of Shadows and Secrets (Crowns of Magic Universe)</u>

Seeker of Secrets

Hunted by Darkness

History of Witches

Marked by Fate

Kingdoms of Sin

Bound by Destiny

<u>Standalone Novels</u>

Curse of the Fae Prince (The Spring Court: Crowns of Magic Universe)

<u>Spellcasters Spy Academy Series (Magic of Arcana Universe)</u>

A Legacy Witch: Year One

A Marked Witch: Internship

A Rebel Witch: Year Two

A Crucible Witch: Year Three

The Spellcasters Spy Academy Boxset

The Wonderland Court Series (Magic of Arcana Universe)

Alice the Dagger

Alice the Torch

The Bonegate Series - A Fanged Fae sister series

Hawk Witch

Assassin Witch

Traitor Witch

Illuminator Witch

The Bonegates Series Boxset

The Royal Quest Series

Dragon Prince

Dragon Magic

Dragon Mate

Dragon Betrayal

Dragon Crown

Dragon War

ABOUT THE AUTHOR

Ashley lives in the lush and green Pacific Northwest with her husband, their dog, and the house ghost that sometimes makes appearances in her charming, old home.

When she's not writing fantasy novels she enjoys traveling the world, reading, kicking butt at board games, and frequenting taquerias.

For all the latest releases and updates, subscribe to Ashley's newsletter, The Coven. You can also find her Facebook group, Ashley's Reader Coven.

9 781966 080169